YESTERDAY
—— WAS ——
LONG AGO
part two

ISBN-13: 978-0-578-60992-8

**The Yesterday Was Long Ago
Part Two**

Cover Design by Kerry Prater.

Interior Design by Katharine E. Hamilton

Editing by Lauren Hanson

1914

1

"Extra! Extra! Extra!" was shouted and heard at every street corner, with many young men in their Sunday best holding bundles of papers to lessen the workload of a nearby over-crowded newsstand. Usually, it was attended by only one old man who could be, on any given afternoon, caught napping. The masses of worshippers got the "Daily News" right after leaving church in order to spend the rest of the day with their families. But this was no ordinary Sunday afternoon. Even the leisurely strollers came from the nearby parks and were anxious to find out more about the latest arriving bulletins. The printing shops even called their work force back to supply the demand. Once again, it involved an assassination which brought excitement to the habitually lazy Viennese, who prided themselves on just muddling through life.

Many of the passersby could still vividly remember the hideous crime which befell their lovely Empress Elisabeth by being stabbed to death. This was only sixteen years ago and followed a long string of warning signs which were, as everything else at the high court, nonchalantly disregarded. One was not about to get involved and change an undeservedly good lifestyle, and cared little about the

James ~ Yesterday Was Long Ago

struggling masses, "as the poor will always be among us." By now, the closely watching, concerned crowd knew it involved the assassination of Franz-Ferdinand and his wife Sophie. He was the heir to the throne despite his morganatic marriage to a Bohemian Countess, for which the Emperor never forgave him. Both were shot to death while on one of their state visits to Sarajevo.

"They rode in an open car!" cried one in disbelief. "They should have known better."

"The murderer's name is Gavrilo Princip!" screamed another, as if the name of any Slav was of importance. "I'll bet my last Kreuzer that he belongs to a terrorist group!"

Though it was no secret that the Emperor disliked his nephew, due to his views on politics among many other things, it was quite another matter for a dirty Serb to kill any Austrian. "They all should be thrown in front of hungry wolves," spat one bystander, causing a chain reaction of outburst, each one fully agreeing with his statement. It prompted the ever-present police to disperse the roaring crowd in a hurry, as experience taught all of them never to take a chance involving politics.

"Now what?" was the question heard most frequently, fearing the worst already. And all that on an exceptionally beautiful Sunday, June 28, 1914, when just hours before, only the blue sky and the warm weather mattered. Now the blue skies were turning to deep, dark clouds again and all the pleasantry switched rapidly to a call for some kind of retaliation. Many suggested an immediate occupation as there was no love lost between Austria and the forever restless Balkan, whose many little states had only hatred towards Austria in common.

The newly printed leaflets stated that the Emperor and his entourage had left Ischl to arrange a proper funeral. Insiders knew that the former 'lady in waiting', Sophie Shotek, would have her proper social standing even after her death. However, the slain heir to the throne, well aware of their special royal plans, had secretly secured a burial place so both could rest in peace without any Habsburgers nearby to haunt them even in their graves. After a short, unprecedented funeral in a small town called Artstetten, south of Vienna, the Emperor and his staff continued as if nothing of significance had happened, including the shots in Sarajevo, and returned, undisturbed, to their yearly vacation spot the following day. He enjoyed far too much the daily walks with Katharina Schratt, whose villa, *Felicita*, was his sanctuary for the last twenty-seven years, though their deep friendship was believed by most to be purely platonic.

After reading that no other head of state, including Germany's Kaiser Wilhelm, had any intention of interrupting their present leisure time and no further demonstrations were taking place, one just continued to enjoy the warm summertime to the fullest, as good times are in a habit of ending much too soon anyway. At present, life just went on, nobody noticing the enormous challenge looming on the horizon.

Philip Reinhardt, too, bought some of those many offered newspapers and discussed the news at the dinner table. He broke all previous sets of rules declaring that any sort of debates involving politics or religion were never permitted at the table. One had to enjoy a meal, and to discuss either subject was not enjoyable. To Philip's total amazement, no one showed any reaction or gave the impression they even cared. Their vacation plans were made well ahead of time and an assassination of a Habsburger was not about to spoil anything. School vacation started the following week and each one of their children relished the time with one or the other parent. Most of their enjoyment was repetitious, but all involved traveling and being two months away from Vienna.

Victoria, upon hearing the sad news, felt she had sleep-walked through the last fourteen years, while watching and enjoying her four children grow up, like any other family. Philip was the best father any boy or girl could have asked for. Along the way, he also became his wife's closest friend. Their platonic arrangement seemed to suit each other, as neither quarrels nor accusations ever existed. Each one managed their life like other countless families did and made the best of it for the sake of their children. Any other alternative would have had a devastating affect without gaining anything.

~

A few of their dearest relatives were already buried or suffered illnesses that old age had in store for them. Verena, a widow who had also become Victoria's close friend, was extremely devoted to her grandchildren, and Anette seemed to thrive on growing old. Grandmother Lotte von Wintersberg, to both old women's great relief, purchased a small villa in Berlin with money left from her late brother Frederick. It was very near the Kronthalers', who were, by now, retired and still the most reliable friends anyone could ask for. The Reinhardts also made sure that Lotte was still very much a part of their family life, seeing each other at every opportunity. Although Peter and Paul loved both grandmothers and Anette equally, mountain climbing with their father for the last few years took priority by cutting their visits to Berlin somewhat short. But no one minded their new plans, as Elisabeth and Gisela loved Berlin more than Vienna, and found her small villa more charming than their palace and castle put together.

However, the main get-together always took place in Salzburg, Ischl, or Vienna. Lotte was still in the dark over Victoria's and Philip's arrangement. If Verena was ever suspicious in any way, she never uttered a word. Anette, on the other hand, was well-informed years ago, but Victoria knew she would take the secret to her grave.

Presently, her brother Kurt was in a wheelchair and it was only natural that Anette took care of him. Lillian, his beloved wife, died four years earlier of diabetes, only a few months before Hannes, which caused the family immeasurable grief once more. The once proud and upstanding officer, whose age never showed except for his white hair, became a brittle old man in no time, unable to walk, and had only one wish— to die as soon as possible so he could be with his Lillian again in a better world. Verena, who fared only physically better, grieved daily for Hannes, insistent that Kurt was given three rooms at her mansion, personally spoon-fed him, and went, weather permitting, to each other's spouse's gravesite. Kurt Essler's other, much younger relatives came only through a long line of marriages and cared little for him, calling him, in his present state, an oddball, among many other unflattering names. This was one of the main reasons Verena moved him to her own place, leaving his estate strictly to his few reliable caretakers, until things changed for him mentally. But there was also another reason, and doubtless the main one— their neglect towards him. They all were extremely angry and hurt that Kurt and Lillian had started to give many of their treasures away while still alive. Both were informed by many of their close friends that almost everything would end up at the auction block and, as usual, sold to the highest bidder. Money was the only thing they ever wanted, as each came from a noble family and brought their own valuables as dowry. They felt absolutely nothing towards any item that had held sentimental value to either of the Esslers.

Lillian, being considered a Reinhardt regardless of her adoption, had received at her marriage to Kurt many items of great value from Stephany and Karl, which had belonged for generations in their family. And there were those many pieces of priceless jewelry that had also made their way through many generations of Reinhardts. Now Victoria was the owner of each one, not only from Lillian's side, but Verena's and Anette's too. It prompted her to state continuously that she owned more of those precious stones than most jewelers in Vienna, including the House of Lamberts, still famous for being the jewelers to the court.

Upon Lillian's death in 1910, a new will was drawn up immediately by none other than one of the Wilands.

"Thank God," Verena uttered in sadness about the loss of Lillian, but nevertheless very glad that Wiland's children and grandchildren turned out to be the best lawyers the City of Vienna had to offer. The Reinhardts broke their chain of architects right after Karl's death, with Hannes being a Doctor of Medicine and, in Philip's case, an engineer turned industrialist. It was a fitting combination of his interests, and he was in awe at the new progress in machinery, combined with talent and the opportunity to visit the best universities with great encouragement from Robert, whom he admired more than anyone else. Ironically, Robert Eckhardt died two years before Karl. Not only were both eighty years of age, but each one of them had worked until their last day.

~

Ever since Victoria's and Philip's children became of 'traveling age', their visits to Grandmother Lotte and the nearby living Kronthaler, who took an early retirement after his wealthy parents died in order to take care of all their property, became very frequent. Aside from a sizable estate in the country, they also bought a villa near Lotte so she would never feel alone. Both of their sons entered, to their utter surprise, the best military academy in Potsdam and seemed to enjoy the rigorous discipline. Manfred von Wintersberg must be tossing and turning in his grave! It became a standing joke by everyone who had known him.

Both of the Esslers, of course, were frequent visitors at Lotte's and the Kronthalers', who took them to their estate to enjoy life in the countryside of Prussia... or as everyone insisted, Germany. It was, therefore, by mutual consent that Ernst Kronthaler received Kurt's collection of miniature ships and Irma got several exquisite pieces of Maria-Antoinette's collection, with the Reinhardts given the first choice at every item. They not only declined, but added some of their own items to be shipped in six huge crates to Berlin in time for Christmas, though both families had to miss that year. Each box was carefully placed in a crate that read "In gratitude of our long and sincere friendship." Ernst and Irma nearly fainted, and their first Christmas without their sons was, without a doubt, so much merrier trying to place all their beloved gifts in a very special place. The following year, the Kronthalers reciprocated with two beautiful Orlov Trotters from their own estate, with a note that read, "For people who have everything, but never enough horses!"

~

Since Hannes' death, everyone knew that he had been a victim of his own research. He had become obsessed with finding a cure for diabetes mellitus, knowing by now that it was an inherited metabolic disorder, and fearing that he could be the next victim. His lifeless body was found early one morning in Dr. Billroth's famous clinic where he spent many nights during the last years of his life, trying to find cures for many ailments… among them diabetes.

"It was his favorite place," a sadddened young doctor mumbled to the entering astonished doctor who shared his passion for research. "But he was not the first and won't be the last," he stated. "Some of us just feel a certain calling for it, and Hannes was one of many."

"Greatness is always born out of much pain," Philip choked at the family-only funeral. It was widely known to be Hannes' fervent wish and Verena made sure that his will was done. Franz-Xavier couldn't come as he was crippled with arthritis and stayed presently in a home for aging priests, refusing the Reinhardts' offer of a more comfortable place like their own hospital. Despite their difference in religion, their love for each other was never affected, as both men served the poor.

Once again, the Reinhardts lost two of their most beloved people and were left with the task of looking after Kurt and comforting him, though they needed lots of comfort themselves. *"It all seemed like yesterday and yet it was quite a few years ago,"* Philip thought, looking at his beautiful wife and children, who right after the death of Hannes moved into Verena's mansion quite happily, as the once beloved 'dream house' on the square became rather uncomfortable as far as the children were concerned. Verena was now surrounded by all her loved ones, including Kurt. This time, even Anette became a blessing as she doted on Kurt like on Alex previously, and still made time for helping Philip's children with homework whenever they were in need.

Elisabeth, the first born, was now eighteen and an excellent student, taking up the field of medicine along with biology, and showed great interest in science but never talked much about it. Secretly, she hoped to become the second Madame Curie, the only woman she had ever idolized. Gisela was another story. Nothing she started was ever finished, besides being a rather poor student at school. Her many tutors were perpetually frustrated at her lack of diligence. Aside from that vice, she had from time to time a new, fanciful dream, like becoming an actress or singer, but her parents and all other members of the family knew that in time she would outgrow it and let it go at that. Peter and Paul were only ten when the move to Verena's mansion took place and were, like their sisters, rather glad about it, as their rooms were larger and somehow had less stairs to climb. Victoria and Philip were pleased that both boys were very studious, though Peter, like his sister Gisela, had so many plans for his future that it caused now and then quite a few laughs.

The dream house was rented out once more, but this time all agreed wholeheartedly on the choice, as the new tenants were the Wilands. Both brothers, Arthur and Victor, would use the first two floors for their ever-expanding office and the upstairs as their living quarters, each one now having a wife and two children. They were assured that after Verena's death it would be theirs to buy, so any changes within their house were alright with the Reinhardts.

Since Hannes never wrote a will, feeling he never owned anything to begin with, it was of great importance for Verena to write a will with the new tenants as her lawyers. Their father, who was in their circle of friends, died several years previously of cancer, leaving both sons his prosperous office as their inheritance. However, by choosing them, she had not the faintest notion that Anette Essler was one of their clients too. Anette inherited upon her mother's death quite a sizable amount of gold coins, knowing Kurt and Lillian would get everything from his father. The coins were her own dowry by marrying an Essler and came with a tear-stained letter that her marriage was a big mistake and she felt so very guilty by making Anette pay for it. Arthur and Victor Wiland were told about it from their late father and kept the box in a safe, among many others of their wealthy clients, as Anette was at that time still caring for Alex. Robert, Jr. had also left her all his money, seeing in her the most selfless and unappreciated human being he ever encountered. Having abandoned his relatives on his last visit to America in 1876, he left Philip his two factories and his fully furnished elegant villa in a prestigious neighborhood. He never could foresee what a blessing it would become.

So 'poor Anette' was now a very wealthy spinster, planning to leave everything to Victoria. And 'poor Victoria' became, a few days after Hannes' death, the sole heir of all the Reinhardts' possessions. After noticing both Wilands' surprised expressions, Verena lost no time in answering the few obvious questions. "Stephan has chosen the monastery as his so-called home. After his death, everything could possibly end up in the Vatican. We still give a lot to our church, Franz-Xavier being the main reason, though we are not even allowed to see him."

Both lawyers agreed. "He seems to be the one who loves to suffer."

Verena gave a sad nod. "And as far as Philip is concerned," she continued. "he is the sole owner of two prosperous factories and in the process of opening a third one. He also inherited not only Robert's villa, among other things, but my late Papa left him the dream house, which both of you are renting. As you can see, my son is not short-changed in any way. However, in case of Victoria's death…

God forbid!" she stammered. "You will take care of the inheritance until the grandchildren become of proper age."

"You know we will," both said in unison, though still astonished.

"Then let's have a glass of wine together."

"We feel very honored, Mrs. Reinhardt."

They all gave their signature and signed the date of December 3, 1910. It was exactly a week after her husband's funeral. Nothing was left to fate; this was business. Doubtless, her Papa had taught her that too.

"Something is not right. In all our experience, and that includes our late father's many cases, no one ever left their first born out on everything they own," Arthur related to his brother on their way home.

"You've taken the words right out of my mouth. Either she still feels guilty about her behavior towards Mrs. Victoria Reinhardt until her return from her self-imposed exile in Salzburg, or she has by now found out about Philip's philandering and is afraid that one of these days he will find a mistress who would end up with all their immense fortune." Victor sighed, still amazed.

"Be that as it may, Verena always knew what she was doing when it comes to business," Arthur replied. "And I cannot think of another lady than Victoria who will be more worthy of everything."

Both brothers were in full agreement before entering their home, which one of these days would be their own dream house.

~

The shrill ring of the telephone awoke the dozing servant, Konrad, who wished, like the rest of the staff, that the Reinhardts never had installed one to begin with. All hated the loudness of it, as there was, so far, no way to dampen that noisy box which still was placed, almost hidden, in a corner in order not to degrade the beauty of all the other furniture. But it was one of the necessary and modern conveniences any servant had to get used to and endure.

"Reinhardts' residence. Konrad speaking," he answered politely, suspecting Verena to be the caller, as she had left two months earlier for Ischl and Salzburg to make some changes before the arrival of her family and friends.

"This is Mrs. Reinhardt, Konrad. Are any of my children there?" She almost pleaded.

"Sorry, Madame… but they should be here shortly."

"Don't tell me they went for their usual ride like nothing happened," she replied, slightly irritated.

"No, Madame. Excuse me as I am not quite certain of the details, Madame, but they went to the train station to meet Countess von Wintersberg. I was never told when the train is arriving. Maybe there is some lateness after all, as they should be here by now.

"I'll say! Everything is upside down. I imagine you heard the heir to the throne and his wife got shot."

"Yes, Madame."

"Any idea how Vienna is reacting?"

"No, Madame. I am on duty, and the rest of the servants have the afternoon off. So far, no one has returned."

"Well, Konrad, have one of my children call the moment they arrive."

Before he was able to give her assurance that he would relay the message, she had already hung up. He had noticed her quivering voice. It was so very unlike her, as well as the abrupt hang-up without wishing him a good day. He felt, therefore, relieved when the family arrived barely an hour later. They all appeared happy and undisturbed, including Lotte, with the exception of carrying lots of newspapers. Anette was the first one to embrace her close friend Lotte, while Philip went to the phone the moment he got Konrad's message.

"I would have called you right away, Mother, but we left shortly after our meal to hear more about it. No, the train was on time… but why are you sounding so upset? None of us is. The people here have not been permitted to assemble anywhere since the first bulletin reached Vienna. Undercover policemen are all over the place. I recognized so many of them."

"You may not realize it, Philip, but it could mean war. It's not just the latest incident… it has been brewing for a long time and not only in Austria. The Emperor left for Vienna in a hurry. You should have seen the confusion at the station. He and his entourage are something else!"

"He had to leave hastily since he has to be there for the arrangement of the funeral, and to make sure that Countess Sophie will never enter their own burial ground. After all, the crypt of the Capuchin's church is only meant for royalty."

"Of course, you are right, though Empress Maria-Theresa made one exception."

"But Franz-Josef will not. You'll see!"

"You are right again, Philip. We just talked about the same thing as soon as we heard about it. But the way I see it, she may not even want to be among those Habsburgers. That poor dear had to live with so much humility, ordered by the 'all highest' and executed by his feeble court. Thank God their marriage was a happy one, if not the happiest among all those… well, at the moment I cannot think of a name low enough. Look how Franz-Josef treated his son! Never gave him one day of joy! We just saw him again with his lady-love, Katharina, this morning. He gave us his little nod, permitting Helena Nordman and me to greet him. As if we care, or anyone else other than his own clique."

"As a pair of 'poor commoners'," he jested. "he may feel like he was doing you a big favor."

"Oh, I am sure he does. Ischl is too small of a place to avoid them and Helena and I are not about to change our morning walks. Aside from the fact that we love his route, it has the best smelling flowers."

"Mother, dear, calm down," he encouraged softly before she had a chance to itemize each flower. "Nothing much will come of it, so just relax." But like many Austrians, he was not sure how much more the country was willing to take.

"Well then, give the Countess my warmest regards, and I am looking forward to seeing you in ten days. All of you!"

"Wait a minute, Mother. The Countess would like to say a few words to you. Bye-bye."

"And a good day to you too, Verena Reinhardt. I am so happy to be here again! It's getting quite lovely."

"Then stay longer," she answered in honesty. "What is in Berlin that you cannot have here? We'll talk about it when I see you. Did you hear about the assassination while the train stopped? Were they selling newspapers there too?

"Only after we reached Linz. According to the papers, he was shot around noon."

"How silly of me not to take the time in to consideration. I am very uneasy about the whole thing. I don't know why, but everyone in Ischl is too."

"I am not in the least. Austria and Germany are friends!" she emphasized in her strong Prussian accent with great pride. "The Balkan states give everyone lots of trouble and our Emperor always calls them a 'bunch of contemptible scum, not worthy of a single German bullet',," she said with assurance.

"Thank you, dear Countess. Friends are always a comfort in time of need, and I am looking forward to seeing you.

"And so are we. My daughter wants to say something too," she finalized, handing Victoria the phone, who asked in all sincerity if she or Philip should take the next train to Ischl and bring her back.

Philip was happy to hear that she declined Victoria's offer, as time was very important with the possibility of even his own scheduled vacation being cut short. Verena had calmed down somewhat, and felt happy at how much Victoria cared, knowing she was not capable of lying and would have taken the next train to Ischl.

She walked on the arm of Marlene, who in many ways replaced Elsa, only the times were quite different. Every evening they walked the beautifully manicured lawns, arched hedges, admiring their special imported trees along with the great variety of flowers, which kept her fifteen gardeners fully employed at her places in Salzburg and Ischl. The statues came from decaying castles in Italy, as did some of the splashing fountains, giving a multitude of noisy birds a first-class sanctuary. It was in no way different from any other Reinhardt place, except for its size. They lived and loved beauty and made sure not one meter was ever neglected anywhere. Verena, like her ancestors, made sure the 'R's on every entrance meant 'Royalty'.

"You know, Marlene," she said, taking a seat on an old stone bench. "Victoria is my greatest treasure. Her kindness towards me is overwhelming."

"I agree wholeheartedly, Madame," she replied sincerely.

"It seems whoever meets her, loves her." But Marlene also recalled the time when Verena Reinhardt's life had come virtually to a standstill. Curtains were drawn, no visits were made, and none were accepted, and that included her husband. Only very slowly had she resumed her routine, looked at the 'Villa Karl' with great joy, and visited the one Doctor Reinhardt referred to as a quack. And it was not just because her Papa had died, but her son was marrying a Prussian.

Marlene was glad that at least her husband had lived long enough to enjoy their togetherness with Victoria and grandchildren, though Philip took his time to forgive, but she also wished her Aunt Elsa could have one day experienced the enormous change in her lifelong mistress… or by miracle lived long enough to call two fine ladies 'Mrs. Reinhardt' like the present staff and servants did. Marlene hoped secretly that one day she would be called to serve Victoria, as she was doubtless everyone's favorite.

~

In all those years past, Victoria had a lot of chances to meet so many different types of Viennese and thought frequently of her father's warning and observation. There were even times when she would have liked to tell him how right he was. Coming from his own daughter, he may have liked it. It was mostly in regards to their undeservedly famous, polite and friendly reputation, which was for a man like him nothing more than 'oily courtesy', with deeply hidden aggression underneath, be it a smug shopkeeper, a sly servant, pompous official, or greedy speculator. They all fell in the same category. Their exploited workers and servants were treated as less than animals, though the employers only profited by their hard labor under the most deplorable conditions. But she also had the great fortune to meet a multitude of the best Viennese, who would have surpassed any of his beloved Berliners, for whom he had the highest regards, with Kronthaler being the exception, of course. No Austrian was ever noble or brave like a Prussian. For him, his love and compassion belonged only to his country!

And there was Philip. The man who drove his father-in-law to an asylum and a sudden death due to a massive heart attack, which no one mourned, but some of his foes possibly applauded. Except for Philip's regular visit to his so-called 'cafe houses', with a reserved room upstairs to bed a girl from time to time, he inherited all other good traits, giving his parents all credit by citing them as the best example. As he was raising a family now on his own, he came to realize more and more what it took to be a good parent; a much harder task than he expected, as they were now four teenagers.

Though a very authoritative man when it came to business, he was better known and admired for his excellent working conditions, when most factories were called 'sweat shops'. Fainting for lack of air, food, and exhaustion were the order of the day. One just kept on working as rarely anything better presented itself. Philip was also known to treat the highest paid engineer to the lowest paid apprentice with the same respect, knowing he was in need of each one. Once again, and not unlike the household servants, they were proud to be called a Reinhardter.

Though immensely rich, he never wasted a day with idleness, let alone live like nobility, yet never cared if he would be snubbed by calling himself a hard-working man. His was old money, and a new upstart, no matter how wealthy, would never gain entrance to any of the many clubs he turned down, using time as the main excuse. 'New money' had a dubious and vulgar ring to it. It would take quite a few generations to prove they were worthy of it. Then theirs would be 'old money', carefully molded by their past. And the past was what still counted, though a new century started fourteen years ago and a great turmoil awaited many empires. As Stephany and Otto Reinhardt would have said many years ago, "We shall see!"

~

Presently Philip sat in his usual reserved seat at Cafe Pracher, glancing through some of the many newspapers, their oversized headlines predicting Emperor Franz Josef would perform a miracle again. 'Peace at all cost' he heard being debated at the next table, as a war would mean the end for many. Dozens of voices gave their opinions while he searched through his briefcase for a list, which was carefully prepared weeks ago to surprise his daughter Elisabeth, who would graduate in two days with high honors. She told her parents a year ago that she planned to attend an excellent university to get three years of pre-med education, as her mind was made up to be a Doctor of Medicine. "More and more women nowadays take that step once considered odd or eccentric," she emphasized strongly.

The family was very proud of her and his gift had to be very special. She was, after all, the first Reinhardt woman to enter a university, though each one was highly educated and well-read. Although Philip had everything a man's heart could desire, his own personal life was never quite fulfilled. It was a situation he hated himself for. To make things worse, Madame Lydia, whom he considered his own female Sigmund Freud, had a stroke two years ago and was unable to speak. One of her nieces took over, but he never entered the place again, as for a man like him, it had lost its meaning. Afterwards he made his rounds and visited different cafes, only to encounter some of his acquaintances, who he never suspected, let alone some of his regular party guests.

He never feared any indiscretion as they, like himself, had a wife and children. But it changed his mood afterwards, adding some embarrassment. After all, he was the man most envied by everyone else. Only a trip to Vienna's most expensive gift shop, Rodeck, eased somewhat his feeling of shame and guilt. He would buy something very special for each member of his family, including Anette, knowing how happy Victoria was to see in him a good son, father, husband, and friend. But he wondered frequently if she realized that she, as a wife, was the main reason for his present state… or if she had by now forgiven him for his extra marital affairs each time before a child was born. Would the bedroom door have ever opened if any of her many operations made her a whole woman again? Now, after almost nineteen years of marriage, their love for each other was still shared, but he had the distinct feeling that even her desire for an encounter in the bedroom was a long time gone. Everything was too late.

As he drove himself home with the back seat full of neatly wrapped Rodeck gifts, he felt like he had been sleepwalking through all these many years. He had time to think back to when all the turmoil of her operations began, barely six months after the birth of Peter and Paul. By then, she had one of the parlors made into a sickroom as Hannes and Verena wanted the family together so no one would be deprived of seeing Victoria as much as possible.

"You gave life to four adorable and healthy children," Verena stated one day with Hannes' agreement. "This is a first for all of us, and that entire calamity brought the family only closer together."

The children sat at their mother's huge bed, listening to one of her stories when Philip entered, very elated. "Don't anybody move. I'll get my camera set up. It will be a picture we all will treasure for years to come."

"A permanently sick mother? It's almost two years," she said, astounded. "Wait until I am up and well again," she pleaded sincerely.

"No, darling. This photo is very special, and it shows how loved you are. Love is really all that matters."

"The only thing," Hannes voiced with a wink towards Verena.

"I think Philip is very wise," Verena said, and all kept their smiles while Philip set his camera in place, having captured his family in one of their happiest moments.

"As I was saying before our photo session," Verena continued after the family left for some games in the park. "I was tortured for years by having only one healthy son, and yet I should have felt overjoyed to have at least one. Poor Stephan! He was so pitiful! He needed special shoes to keep his balance; otherwise there was no chance of improvement ever. Even Philip loved him very much, though Stephan took right from the beginning to Father Christopher. It was like an omen of things to come. We all were devastated when he left for the monastery, which is cut off from the outside world," she sighed deeply. "And yet, I was born somewhat deformed but thanks to our connection to the best surgeons, I could be helped. As a matter of fact, my Papa never noticed until my brother called me 'an ugly cripple'," she shivered. "Of course, to a little handsome boy I must have been, as it was in a moment when I pulled my loose tooth."

"Children can be quite cruel. I hope was severely punished. I know I would have made sure of it!" Victoria replied bitterly.

"Yes and no, my dear. Papa never forgave himself for leaving his family. When he lost his wife, he lost his mind. He suffered from her loss until the day he died."

Before she started to blame herself for being born, Victoria reached for her hand and interrupted politely. "Thank God he was blessed with a daughter like you. Not many are so fortunate."

Though she had heard those remarks from different friends before, coming from Victoria it felt like an ointment on a forever open wound. "You are such a precious thing. I know Papa would have loved you as much as I... we all do!" For a woman like Verena Reinhardt, there was no higher compliment to give away. It even surpassed Maria-Theresia's special medal . . . the only Habsburger she had ever admired.

~

Philip had, for almost two years, endured and mentally suffered with Victoria's many operations, hospital stays, and recuperations at home, that along with his self-imposed abstinence, he prided himself in being a good and faithful husband and father, who had a lot of making up to do. He also went through a stage of enjoying family life only. The growing up of his twins to normalcy may have been another reason, as they were constantly on his mind. The first three months, they looked nothing like Elisabeth or Gisela and, being aware that his mother and brother were crippled at birth, he begged his father to look his sons over on a daily basis, a task Hannes enjoyed enormously, as his grandsons started to giggle and were well on the way to catching up to normal size and weight.

At two years of age, they were happy, healthy and spoiled. Hannes called their two wet nurses 'saviors', and they were paid handsomely by each Reinhardt personally. They came running towards anyone they recognized with the same speed both girls did, though Elisabeth and Gisela confided they let them win, as they were, after all, the 'grown ups' in the family.

In the meantime, Victoria and Philip became the closest friends and confidantes, embracing and caressing each other more than many other couples possibly did who had very little in common aside from their sexual routines imposed by the Catholic Church to enlarge their family.

The young Reinhardts, consisting of Victoria and Philip as well as the older like Verena, Hannes, Lillian, and Kurt, were always seen arm in arm, be it at the opera, theater, or any other social gathering. After each of those occasions, providing Victoria felt well enough, Cafe Pracher became a tradition, and all were happy to hear that the following spring, a new Pracher would open at the Ringstraße, serving outdoors as well.

They encountered so many friends who assured Victoria how hard they prayed for her recovery, and a speedy one at that, but were thinking in all likelihood about their many parties and gala evenings including their famous New Year's ball. After all, the year was 1902!

Victoria looked beautiful and Philip gave every indication of being still as much in love with her as when they first met. Family life seemed best, regardless of Victoria's slow recovery. But by year's end, her bleeding resumed, stronger than previously, and Doctor Reinhardt had another specialist examine her thoroughly. A new date for an operation was set, and this time she was forced to spend Christmas at the Reinhardts' hospital, where she came to a conclusion that the way life presented itself couldn't go on forever.

"Philip," she uttered at the first given opportunity, having spent a sleepless night praying for courage. "Your father just told me that this operation may not be the solution either. I see no reason to go into more details than we have already, but I cannot expect a man like you to wait forever." She sighed, reaching for his hands. He understood her meaning at once and how much it must have hurt her to release him. "I only beg of you not to have any affairs with any of our or your parents' servants, as it would be a humiliation I would never be able to take."

"I don't believe what you are saying, Victoria! How can you?"

"Let it be our secret, Philip," she interrupted. "and you continue to be a good father. Also, no half-brothers or half-sisters will be tolerated; that much you owe me for giving you your total freedom," she finalized with the same determination she did on that fateful New Years' eve when she locked her bedroom door for good.

He still didn't know why he had never answered her. He only kissed both hands and she knew it was a promise he would keep. Twelve years later, their marriage was still strong, if not better, as no questions were ever asked and no lies had to be given.

Now Philip was forty-eight and a very dashing man, whose hair started to turn gray at his sideburns, adding even more to his good looks. He smiled at his wife who, despite only four years of age difference, could almost pass as his daughter. She was still exceptionally beautiful, with barely a few tiny wrinkles around her eyes. Next to her stood a strait-laced Elisabeth who, unlike her mother and sister, had no interest in fashion and rarely smiled. By now, the family called her "Madame Curie", and she never objected. Her future plans were only known to Grandmother Lotte, who like the rest of the family, stood at the train station, waiting to start their vacation in Salzburg.

Gisela, who was everybody's favorite because of her ever-present high spirits and good-hearted behavior, had only the dark curly hair and green eyes in common with her sister. Otherwise, she was in every way the opposite. At seventeen she became also quite flirtatious whenever a splendid looking officer in a light blue uniform smiled in her direction. "Austria made in 1900 the first prize for the most stunning uniforms," she told them as the train arrived, causing even Elisabeth to smile in reply. "Don't tell me you read it in a book."

Peter and Paul, at fourteen, were just as different from each other as their sisters. However, in looks they both got their father's deep, brown eyes, which Verena claimed came from her side of the family, the Rombergs, with her mother Louise being the most beautiful one, of course. The boys were tall for their age and gave the appearance of great strength. If they had little else in common, every type of sport appealed to them, as presently the trip to Salzburg meant mountain climbing. Philip was elated that Paul showed a great interest in mechanics; how things work and could be improved. Once finished with his schooling in Vienna, he would be sent to Germany to one of the more advanced universities than Vienna had to offer. Peter, though highly intelligent, remained still undecided. Since his school grades were excellent, no one was ever concerned or worried about his future.

Since the express came directly from Budapest and all first-class seats were reserved, the Reinhardts heard only Hungarian spoken, never understanding one word. They were glad not to be forced to give their opinion of an impending war. After all, their vacation had just begun. The next stop in Liuz proved to be perfect as the chatty Hungarians left and two Bishops took their seats without uttering a word. One had to assume they prayed for peace. But the following stop in a town called Wels made up for it. The remaining two hours promised not only to be lively, but a full account of the present situation down to the last detail as to why there had to be a war, which the Emperor's son had long ago foreseen, but no one had believed him.

"I cannot wait to be in Ischl and watch the faces of the few privileged aristocrats surrounding Franz-Josef," one said, and the Reinhardts were glad to arrive in Salzburg with Verena and two carriages waiting anxiously. The new taxis were not to her liking, calling them a piece of metal with an engine. Horses were alive and breathing; motors were puffing. Therein lies the difference.

After a sumptuous dinner and a pleasant chat, avoiding any hint of the present situation, let alone rumors of war, they retired early, deciding on Ischl for the following day. Philip and his sons had to prepare at least two days for mountain climbing, and this time they would pitch a tent at the 'Loser Mountain' feeling they were ready, though under the strictest guidance of their father, to learn about ropes and spikes the safest way. Also, two weeks away from women's chatter along with their regular boring visits was considered a nice vacation. The women were in total agreement with the early departure of their men. In fact, they welcomed it.

The week of Franz Lehar's operettas started; a wonderful treat in the beautiful theater that no one was about to miss. Europe's colorful and extravagant elite was, at such events, greatly represented. The Reinhardts were used to it and recognized the same faces with their same monologues year after year. It was always where they have been, where they are going, and with whom they have dined or spent a lovely time, be it at the fountain while sipping warm healing water, attending outdoor concerts, or walking the beautiful esplanade where Franz Lehar had a small but gorgeous villa.

The town's inhabitants were a world apart from Austria's high society. They wore during daytime the traditional "Dirndls" and were at most gala evenings simultaneously underdressed. However, many owned little mountain chalets, taking great pride that their country was considered so very beautiful.

After Philip and his sons returned from their mountain, a stack of letters and telegrams were awaiting him, stating his immediate return to Vienna was urgently necessary. The first thing he was told was that the Emperor was leaving Ischl the following day, causing Philip to remark, smiling, "Well, at last we have something in common, as I plan to leave at about the same time."

The newspapers claimed that Austria's court gave the Serbs an ultimatum, overlooking Franz-Josef's opinion. His present ally, Kaiser Wilhelm, saw an opportunity to add to his country's greatness and prestige by declaring, "It's now or never," affirming a war on Serbia on the first of August, 1914. Austria and the British had done the same already by the end of July, with Russia also mobilizing with borrowed money from France. Many young men started to march with great 'hurrahs', let alone their enthusiasm at the promise to be home again by Christmas, after having beaten the Balkans once and for all. It was, supposedly, the beginning of a war to end all wars!

The Reinhardts stayed in Salzburg without Philip, considering themselves very safe, as the last fifty years had instilled a lot of confidence. Then the time came for them to depart for Berlin, never changing their well-planned schedule, while staying at Lotte's villa or with the Kronthalers, who presently said that their two sons would consider it a great honor to serve their Kaiser. After all, it was their profession and they trained long enough for it.

"So did Alex," Verena thought, who reluctantly went with her family to Berlin.

2

While three of the Reinhardt children played cards after a long, vigorous day of playing tennis, with the older group of ladies crocheting, the door flew open with Elisabeth shouting, "I did it! I did it!" Then adding to a visibly astonished family, "I am accepted at the Robert Koch University, entering this September; actually in a few weeks!" she said, throwing her book satchel to the nearest chair. The looks went from shock to bewilderment, with Verena's face turning colorless, while Victoria's crocheting needles dropped and Gisela stopped her card game, annoying both brothers.

"Can you explain yourself better?" asked her mother.

"Yes, Mother, after I catch my breath! I am entering in the Robert Koch University for a three-year course of study in pre-med. How about *that*!"

"We have the best medical schools in Vienna! What in the world made you think of Robert Koch in Berlin?" came from Verena, showing her strong disapproval.

"Grandma is right," Victoria replied, though she was less astonished.

Elisabeth turned red and put herself in a kneeling position. She had expected to hear high praise and great pride, not frustration and disillusionment. "Don't you understand my position, for God's sake?" she said, growing irritated. "If I had passed my test easily in Vienna, everyone would assume it was our name and connections, including Reinhardt Hospital! I doubted, also, impartiality on all my tests. Let's assume, on the other hand, that I failed. I would have been too ashamed to face any one of you or walk the streets of Vienna. Aside from the fact that our city always recognizes good experiences in a foreign country and Robert Koch is the best."

"True," replied Paul to everyone's amazement. "Papa will send me either to Zurich or to Germany."

Verena, after slowly regaining her color and composure, looked toward Elisabeth with a certain pride. "Well... if you see it that way dear child, I have to agree. My Papa's four-year stay and study at the best university in Paris came in very handy on many occasions."

Victoria and Lotte exchanged glances with a small wink only understood by the two of them. Lotte had at least one grandchild with her, while Verena was always surrounded by four, wasting very little time about the other grandmother's desire to share at least one or two children, as Berlin, too, had a lot to offer as far as elite schools were concerned.

"I hope you will stay with my mother," Victoria replied, being certain both had planned this all along. Also, the Kronthalers may have had an influence, as Ernst's nephew is a well-known doctor at the hospital.

"Of course, Mother," was her short reply. "I only return to Vienna to pick up a few of my personal belongings. I plan to buy new clothes right here in Berlin, with Irma Kronthaler as my guide. I truly admire her taste."

Now it was Gisela's turn to speak. "I don't believe what I am hearing!" But she got only a smile in return.

"I hope you and Countess Lotte will spend the usual holidays with us," Verena almost pleaded.

"Nothing will change, Grandmother. Where else would we be? And three years will just fly."

"How well I know!" she quipped. "You are talking to a seventy-year old expert."

Lotte, too, smiled. "I agree. So, let's open a bottle of fine wine and have a toast to our future doctor!"

"Let's not forget a toast for peace," Paul interjected, with the full agreement of everyone present.

~

Upon their return from Berlin, Vienna appeared no different from the city they had left. The Reinhardts stood at their balcony, waving and throwing fresh-picked flowers at the long line of soldiers, with some young wives or sweethearts running at their side until they reached the train station, followed by a tearful farewell. "Until Christmas." Philip had invited a few of his top engineers for a small dinner and a long discussion.

"Some Germans are dismissed already. The French seem to be in retreat. The war is almost over!" Gregory Newmann confirmed in confidence during their meeting in great secrecy, being very pleased about it.

"Almost," Philip answered, still concerned. "What worries me is that we have huge orders, ball bearings being only one example, aside from a request to transform our peace-time production to war. So far, my young workers are still getting drafted, leaving the place day by day. We are quite in a bind. I am open for all kinds of suggestions, including calling my former retirees back."

"Men who plow the fields are out of the question, not only for their lack of training, but food production is equally important for our troops," stated one engineer, whose son had left a week earlier.

"France's retreat may be exaggerated. There are also other countries who have decided to join the war. However, it's against Germany and us," another commented.

"I agree with Mr. Reinhardt's statement that *almost* will never do it for the Kaiser in Berlin."

"Right," Gregory Newmann added. "Kaiser Wilhelm is ready for a big showdown. All those Prussian Hohenzollerns suffering from megalomania! Their greatly admired Krupp factory has, for a long time, worked feverishly on all sorts of new weapons. Their intent is not to store them and collect dust."

"I agree, Gregory," Philip concurred. "Just watch our eighty-four-year old Emperor follow the orders from Berlin. So far, no one else is on our side. What else can he do? And just to think that some families expect their loved ones back by Christmas is downright heart-breaking. And my two sons are only fourteen. God, oh God… if one of them would have to go, I wouldn't know how to handle it," he said finally, before he arose and told them to get a good night's rest.

The Reinhardt household was again in an uproar. Once more, it involved one of the despised von Waldens. This time it began with a small accident at Vienna's newest skating rink, involving Gaby von Walden, a child of ten years. But as far as Verena was concerned, it was a continuation of their ongoing feud. Her grandson, Paul, was a casualty, with a sprained ankle. Since her son, Philip, couldn't be bothered with trifling matters, and considered the unfortunate incident settled, Verena took it on herself to get to the bottom of it and pay a visit to the von Waldens; a first in many generations, but to her, well worth it. "That ugly von Walden brat has to apologize and the sooner the better!"

The troubles began a week before Christmas when Philip brought Paul home on crutches, saying, "I am sure the boy will tell you all about it," and left in a hurry to go back to his factory. Verena listened attentively and had Paul repeat the story over and over again. Though he told the truth the way he saw it, that 'von Walden brat' should have refrained from calling him a name. But the friendly handshake and conversation between Philip and a von Walden officer got really the best of her! She was resentful and livid to say the least. How could her own son do that to Paul, even after the little girl of no more than ten years of age gave a very sassy answer. An apology, she felt fully convinced, was owed to Paul. Not only would he miss his very first hockey tournament, but he was fearful his school would lose the game without him. This accident was, in her opinion, inflicted on purpose by a von Walden, who didn't belong on this newly erected ice rink to begin with. They still were, as they always had been, the only impoverished family in Lindenfels, with their rundown estate caving in, though still considered a castle, and acting like high nobility.

The disrespectful answer according to Paul was a most serious matter. That girl blamed the accident on the 'wild boys' and spoke up for all the others, with a lot of nearby guests hearing it.

"Did you, yourself, push any of the roped poles?"

"Yes, Grandmother, we all did. There were eight little show-offs trying to impress us boys with their boring figures and little jumps until their two coaches arrived. We, on the other hand, had needed more space. You know… for hockey."

Paul slept lightly on a chair, his leg propped up, while Verena waited, angrily, until Philip returned a few hours later.

"Did you know the boys' school would rope off part of the ice rink?"

"Sure. It was only for two days and they even had the bigger part. It was either no practice or obey the set rules. I didn't think it would be such a big deal."

"Well, to your son it is a very big deal. He was their goalie and is doubtless eliminated," Verena snapped, loud enough for Paul to wake up. "Aside from that, a *von Walden* called him an idiot who cannot skate. I won't stand for it . . . even if you will!"

"She did not, Mother. Paul is lying," Philip protested, giving a stern look in his son's direction, who was wide awake by now.

"She called him a nincompoop, which means the same thing!"

"It does not," he retorted sharply. "When the Major and I asked what it meant, the girls answered that it was a new name around their school. Those girls were just as serious about their practice because the winner competes against Vienna's best. It takes quite a lot of talent and discipline considering their ages. I, for one, wish them good luck," Philip finalized, looking once more at his son sternly.

~

Philip Reinhardt and Major von Walden were, via mail, fully informed of the two days of inconvenience, as the boys' skating rink needed a bit of repair, aside from their fences covered with blankets to avoid any distraction. There were too many hecklers from deprived families who would have the time of their life staring and screaming at the privileged hockey players from the most expensive Rudolfiner-Elite school. Their headmaster made sure that his boys' privacy was guarded at all costs.

Major von Walden was presently on two weeks furlough, with his departure date set for his return to France on December 20. He took great delight in watching his little tomboy, Gaby, skating for her upcoming event, while his eleven-year-old son Andreas, Jr., was at home helping with some chores for an early Christmas. His German-born wife, Astrid, had only one servant during this hectic time with every young man by now in uniform. Being the daughter of an officer herself, she accepted any challenge without a word of complaint. Their marriage was very happy, only at times dampened by the Major's difficult son, Bertram, from his first marriage, whose mother had died while giving birth to a stillborn girl in 1900. Bertram, who had just turned eighteen, had lived a life well beyond anyone twice his age. The many different reform schools were of little or no help, as he was still a compulsive liar, having everyone around him convinced that he was the most sincere and honest human being that walked on this earth. While officially enrolled in one of the many existing art schools, he spent most of his time in a well-known hotel, whose other specialty was known to only a chosen few. The owners never revealed Bertram von Walden's name, for numerous and obvious reasons, with the result being that his parents were left completely in the dark.

He was staying at his best friend's house whose mother—a widow for many years—was a former art teacher which was of great help for his own development in drawing, aside from enjoying the company of both young students in her own lonely retired life. Also, his two little step-siblings, Andreas and Gaby, would interrupt continuously with their piano and violin lessons, he assured his parents, who were, if anything, very relieved, having never missed his presence in any way. His visits were sporadic, with his friend always in attendance, both behaving in the most pleasant manner, their drop-ins never exceeding one hour. The military had already called on him and he would leave one week after his father's furlough. Therefore, he decided to spend a few days at home, as Christmas was the slowest season for his regular and married clients who had, on such rare occasions, an obligation towards their families and had no other choice but to give the impression that all was well.

Victoria Reinhardt, too, was on this unusual and fateful day extremely busy and involved with Gisela's rehearsal, where she had the honor of playing the part of Virgin Mary. It had to be perfect or someone else would take her place. In any case, Victoria would see her son's practice in the weeks to come, but her daughter's rehearsal was a one-time event.

Philip sat two tables apart from Major von Walden, completely unaware of anyone's attendance, discussing with a group of engineers the newly received orders pertaining to the war, while trying to keep an eye on his son. Peter was chosen for left defense and took the matter for what it was… only a game. For Paul, it was a personal matter. The outcome of the hockey game depended on him alone. Just then, Philip's internal debate was promptly interrupted. "Excuse me, Mr. Reinhardt, but I think this hobbling young man is one of your sons."

"It certainly is my Paul," he acknowledged, noticing his limping son being helped by his brother and a teammate, followed by a loud chatting group of girls mimicking the occurrence quite excitedly.

"That little girl tripped me!" Paul moaned in agony, pointing towards Gaby, while trying at his brother's suggestion to put his foot down.

The Major, like several other parents of the assembled girls, stood up, very curious about any of their own daughters' involvement, knowing it implicated a Reinhardt and a von Walden. However, Gaby lost no time, whenever she felt wronged, in speaking up.

Being the youngest and smallest of her private school, she was also the proudest in being chosen as a skater of excellence, and courageously confronted Paul's father. "Sir, we did nothing wrong. Those wild boys pushed our separating poles closer and closer towards our space, giving us barely any room for our own practice."

"What practice?" Paul retorted with a sarcastic grin.

"For our own championship," she retorted hastily. "You boys are not the only ones competing."

Major von Walden and Philip rose from their chairs, realizing that this dispute involved mostly their own offspring, while the rest of the parents remained quiet, anticipating a Reinhardt-von Walden confrontation. Both men had crossed paths on Vienna's Ringstraße, always waiting for the other to say something first. Now they had no choice but to speak.

"I am Philip Reinhardt, the boy's father." He smiled pleasantly, stretching his hand.

"Andreas von Walden, the girl's father," he replied rather humbly, having observed his daughter's candid behavior. "I think we have a problem. Your son is hurt," he said, very apologetically.

"Only if we make it one," Philip replied congenially, with Paul watching and resenting his father's courtesy. *"Doesn't he know about the von Waldens?"* he thought furiously.

"She," Paul pointed in ire. "called me a clumsy nincompoop, who doesn't know how to skate!"

"Only after you called me an ugly brat and pushed the pole towards me," Gaby retaliated with her head up high, as all the girls nodded in agreement.

Both their fathers looked at each other and laughed.

"I am so sorry, Mr. Reinhardt. I am leaving in a couple of days and it is very hard for me to punish my daughter." The Major sighed. "But I am more than happy to pay the hospital bill."

Philip dismissed the offer with a wave and smiled. The Major turned to Paul and said in all honesty, "I have watched you and consider you one of the best players. It's such an honor to be a goalie. Those little girls don't know the first thing about this rough sport, which is only played by disciplined and hardy young men like yourself." Paul was extremely pleased as all the girls stood around to hear it.

"Ha!" Gaby retorted with all the sarcasm she could muster.

"As you can see, Mr. Reinhardt, she is a handful; my very own tomboy and quite the opposite of her brother," he replied, looking apologetically from Paul to Philip, who rather enjoyed her courage. His Gisela may have acted the same way, he thought to himself as the Major continued. "Why don't you girls leave now and let us men settle it?" They all left wordlessly as told, with Gaby giving Paul the most defiant look.

Philip and the Major felt themselves being watched and both men were only too happy to disappoint the curious onlookers. "I assume you are leaving for the western front?"

"Yes, four days before Christmas. As if my presence couldn't wait. But then again, it is my profession so I shouldn't complain."

"Good luck and a safe return," Philip replied, shaking his hand very firmly. "I'd better take care of my son who seems to be quite upset."

"Many thanks again, Mr. Reinhardt." And turning to Paul he added, "My sincerest apologies on behalf of my daughter, as I know she will never apologize."

While Paul gave him a friendly nod of acceptance, Philip said with a wave of good-bye, "We haven't heard both stories yet, Major Walden." His attention was now directed fully towards his son. "Now listen, Paul, there is always another game next year. But for many of our brave soldiers who fight and sleep in frozen trenches, there may never be another one. And if there is, he may be missing a limb or two, or even be blind. Just take a minute to think about it. I won't listen to another word of complaint until we reach the hospital," he said, rather annoyed, for all his engineers to hear. "Excuse me, gentlemen, for this unexpected interruption, but after I bring my son home I will have to return to the factory. If anyone of you feels up to it, and it's not too late, I would appreciate your presence in helping me out." They all assured him that they would return within the next few minutes, knowing the urgency of their newly arisen situation.

"That's a Reinhardt all over again. His late father was the same, and from what I gather, so was his grandfather," one on the engineers said proudly, with each of the rest in agreement. Two of them had their sons at the front, and all were only too happy to be part of a team who tried very hard in helping to shorten this ever-spreading war.

~

By midnight, Philip was still up in his own converted home office and was buried behind a load of paperwork when Verena, too upset to sleep, entered. "What is it now Mother? How can I ever convince you that I am a very busy man and lost much too much time, no thanks to Paul," he growled. "I may have to work through the whole night again."

"Paul is in severe pain! He is crying... well, almost," she corrected herself. "I told a servant to bring his bed in my room. Victoria and Gisela came home very late and tired, so I didn't bother them with anything in order to give them a good night's rest."

"Thank God for that. Poor thing has so much on her mind the way it is. Her mother's broken hip and Elisabeth's cold; wonder what will be next," he sighed. "Don't think for a moment I don't know a sprained ankle hurts more than a broken one. I had my share of them. You can vouch for that, Mother. I will talk to him more about it when Victoria is present. He has to learn to accept injury in every sport, but especially ice hockey and mountain climbing. He is also quite daring on the ski slopes."

"Oh, Philip… it's not only that. His spirit is broken and his confidence is crushed because that little von Walden brat questioned his skating ability," she responded bitterly. "And Paul is also very upset by your friendly and outgoing behavior towards her father," she sighed. "You seem to have conveniently forgotten that it was a Major von Walden who killed my Aunt Christina and caused my grandfather's death because of it. Never mind all the suffering of my grandmother."

"So that's why you cannot sleep and came to see me. I won't be involved in any kind of story that happened over sixty years ago. Neither Major von Walden nor I were born then or even knew that devil. This poor officer is leaving for the western front the day after tomorrow, but if you want to ruin his nice Christmas, go right ahead. Just leave me out of it, as I got a very good impression of him."

"YOU WHAT?" she shrieked and continued so loudly, not hearing the frantic knock on the door with an excited Anette finally making her entrance.

"Be quiet for a moment," she shivered, looking scornfully at Verena, who replied resentfully. "Who are you to burst in and—"

"Kurt is dead. He gave a loud moan, which woke me up, and when I rushed to feel his pulse, he was gone!"

Philip did not let her finish the sentence as he ran towards his room, knowing she kept an eye on him the last few weeks.

"I am so sorry Anette," Verena cried, clutching her hand. "I didn't mean the way it sounded. You know that. The whole thing was strictly between Philip and me, involving Paul's sprained ankle and the way it happened."

"I know," Anette mumbled in sympathy.

"And all that because of a good for nothing von Walden brat! I am so angry and bitter that I will pay them a visit they will never forget... of course after Kurt is buried," she added, fuming.

"He is dead!" Philip said, visibly shaken, as he loved Kurt and Lillian like a second pair of parents. At times even more. "I will make all the necessary arrangements," he uttered, putting his arm around Anette. "Now he is with Lillian," he assured her as an afterthought.

"And I cannot wait to be with Hannes," Verena mocked, leaving no doubt about the present circumstances. "Go on with your work, Philip . . . if you can, that is."

Anette sighed. "I will handle my brother's affairs as instructed by him after Lillian's death. He wants only us and Franz-Xavier at the gravesite, just like Hannes."

"That's wonderful," Verena replied, relieved. "Both were so much alike."

"I, myself, will try my utmost to get Franz-Xaver to come, even if someone has to carry him. After all, he should be permitted as Kurt willed all of the Essler estate to his home of disabled priests. Not one iota to his greedy relatives!" Anette smiled, extremely satisfied.

Verena and Philip looked at each other aghast. "When was that decided?" Verena asked, still in a state of delight.

"Right after he got special permission to visit him, giving the Bishop a strong hint concerning his will. After taking one look at that God-forsaken place, he made up his mind right then and there. Of course, the Bishop never expected to get the Esslers' castle too! It will be auctioned off and his relatives may have to bid against each other. That will be a sight and I will be there watching. You can bet on it!"

"Count me in Anette. I am so relieved about his gracious decision," Verena sighed. "Now we have something exciting to look forward to."

"If I have time… well, I'd better not," Philip stated. "It was just a thought to watch their faces, if nothing else. And Anette, before I go back and bury myself in work, I'd like to tell you that Kurt was waiting for this moment a long time."

"I know, Philip. Thanks for all your kindness towards him."

He didn't answer, holding back his tears when he returned. *"Work is a salvation,"* he thought, closing the door.

Both women cried in each other's arms before calling the hospital.

3

The small funeral was over, which had included a very distraught Franz-Xavier, whose difficult transportation was provided by the Bishop himself. The doorbell rang constantly, and it was always for Anette from one or the other far reaching relatives who paid their respects and wished her 'happy holidays' simultaneously.

"Nice try," she told Verena. "They are convinced I am the executor of his will. Just wait until they find out they have to fight not only the home for priests but the Church as well. Quite a task!"

Verena was only too glad to hug Franz-Xaver for the last time, but otherwise had no intention of overlooking the von Walden affair. Paul's mental condition grew worse after Uncle Kurt's death, but she knew her grandson well enough, and felt this was only one more thing at his lowest point in his life, and she would personally see to it that he would be his old self again, though he was the most quiet of the four grandchildren, even under the most happy circumstances.

Marlene was sent with a note to the von Waldens, knowing that she was trustworthy in every way. Baroness Astrid von Walden returned a cordial letter stating her surprise, and that anytime at Mrs. Reinhardt's convenience would be all right with her. The Major never informed his wife about the incident on the ice rink and, like Philip, considered the matter closed, and Gaby was instructed never to utter a word.

After a long walk at as fast a pace as possible, a nervous Verena stood waiting to face a von Walden. A young, spritely maid in proper uniform took her, very respectfully, to the main parlor, while directing Marlene to a plain room with a table and three chairs strictly reserved for waiting servants. She asked, in the kindest way, if a cup of hot tea would do. Marlene gladly accepted, while Verena surveyed the tastefully furnished room and thought it didn't match the outside at all. Just then, in came a young, graceful, and charming Baroness.

"So very glad to meet you, Madame. After all, we are neighbors." Verena was slightly taken aback at her frank statement, not knowing how to interpret it. "Please take a seat," she added, noticing her discomfort. In no time, it became quite obvious that the Baroness had no idea about the incident.

"I am truly sorry to intrude on such short notice, but I consider the matter of my grandson's sprained ankle quite important, aside from it having a worst effect on his mental condition."

Astrid von Walden looked very puzzled and replied hurriedly, "So would I, Madame! But where do I fit in?" she asked, perplexed, her thoughts racing towards Bertram, who had decided to spend his last few days before leaving for the service in her place.

"Oh no, not you... but your little girl. She tripped my grandson purposely at the skating rink, causing him to fall and sprain his ankle, which in turn eliminated him from his hockey team, possibly for the rest of the year. I strongly feel she owes him an apology," she sighed, relieved at having gotten that much off her chest.

"I am so sorry to hear about it, Madame, and will see to it that he gets an apology in a hurry," she replied while ringing the servant's bell. "Hermine, interrupt Gaby's lessons whatever they may be and have her come at once."

"Yes, Baroness." She bowed slightly, not unlike the servants at Verena's place, Marlene being the only exception.

"My husband left a few days ago and I give you my word I never was aware of this unfortunate incident. But may I ask why you waited this long to see me, Madame? We should have cleared this matter right away with my husband present, as he was with my daughter. That much I do know," she stated rather firmly.

"We buried my brother-in-law, Kurt Essler, two days ago. There was simply no time."

"Oh, yes, I read about that," she said, unmoved, thinking of his age, status, and military record. He, who always was considered to have a plum job in any combat, as the joke was he couldn't stand the sight of blood.

"So you can understand why I couldn't see you sooner. And my own son considers the matter settled, refusing to take any part of it." She continued to explain that she had come to set the record straight, before confronting the headmaster at the school, when a lovely and dainty little Gaby entered, bowing very courteously with a smile.

"I know you from some pictures in our school, Madame."

"Gaby, how often do I have to tell you not to speak unless spoken to?" Astrid admonished.

"So sorry, Madame. So sorry, Mama." While Astrid's face took the expression of severity, Verena compared Gaby to a china doll and began to question Paul's sanity in calling her an 'ugly brat'.

"What exactly happened at the skating rink and why was I never informed about it?"

"Because Papa told me not to, as he and Mr. Reinhardt had already taken care of it. You know how he is, Mama. He didn't want to upset you before leaving."

Both women looked at each other in silence, knowing she told the truth. "Did you know the Lady's grandson has a sprained ankle because of you?"

"Not because of me, Mama," she retorted, feeling hurt. "He was the leader in teasing us girls about our silly jumps, pushing the separating poles towards us so we had no space to skate. Those wild boys were twice our size and twice as many. You can ask each girl yourself."

"Then where on earth were your coaches? Or whoever was in charge?" Verena inquired, upset, seeing the situation in front of her.

"I have no idea, Madame, but when they returned the harm was done. Your grandson was the only one hurt and we girls followed him to his father's table and told our side of the story."

"And then what?" Astrid asked.

Gaby stated the story matter-of-factly, not the least bit sorry for his sprained ankle, let alone ready to apologize.

"How old are you, Gaby?" Verena inquired kindly, smiling, feeling her grown-up manner didn't match her size.

"Next month I will be ten," she answered proudly.

"What school are you attending?"

"Maria-Theresia's. And I am the youngest on our sports team and the best in my piano class."

"Humility is not one of her virtues," Astrid apologized, ready to dismiss her.

"My two granddaughters went there too. A very fine school, Gaby. You should be very proud." She shook her hand and patted it.

"Thank you, Madame," she replied with her head erect, returning to her room. But Verena's stunned expression left no doubt that she was wondering where all the money came from.

"Then may we drink a cup of tea to our children's school?"

"If it's not too much trouble. I am glad to take a cup."

"Rather a pleasure," she said courtly and ringing for Hermine again, ordering some baked goods with it.

"I have a childless sister and brother-in-law living in Lausanne, Switzerland. We are extremely close and visit each other frequently."

"Beautiful place," Verena remarked in a murmur.

"They arrive tomorrow late afternoon for two weeks. Usually they are a few days earlier but with him being a dentist, he had a few patients to take care of. In any case, *they* are paying for my children's education. They give them knowledge and we give them love and discipline."

"Consider yourself very lucky," Verena replied sincerely.

"I do, Madame. Very much so."

Hermine arrived with a tray containing Limoges' finest china, and Verena's plan to give von Walden a piece of her mind ended as she was distracted with the most pleasant conversation until she was ready to leave.

"Well, today is the twenty-third and with the school vacation until the 7th of January, there is nothing we can do about it."

"Unfortunately not. And I am very sorry about your grandson's condition, truly I am."

"And I am equally sorry about my intrusion. On the other hand, however," she sighed with a smile. "I am very glad that we met. As you stated so rightfully, we are, after all, neighbors."

Astrid called for Gaby to tell her good-bye. Andreas came along, his arm around his sister, protecting her, and again Verena had no choice but to admire their looks and behavior.

When Philip had said he liked their father, she had shrieked. Now she would have to tell him how much she likes his family as well.

"Good-bye Gaby. I am glad to have met you Andreas." She smiled at both. "You know, Gaby, that I believe every word you said. No apology needed. I will make both coaches responsible."

"I am glad you feel that way, as my children know the consequences of lying to anyone," Astrid voiced sternly, and Verena never doubted her statement for a moment.

Marlene was already in the hall, engrossed with von Walden's servant in discussion about the war. Hermine told her that two of her brothers are in the service with one of them already wounded. They wished each other a 'Merry Christmas' anyway, knowing there is not one merry thing about it.

"May I ask you if all went well, Madame?"

"Of course, you may. It went so much better than I ever would have dreamed. The Baroness von Walden is a most congenial lady, and her little well-behaved daughter's face reminded me of a beautiful doll I still own. Aside from that, she is extremely mature and unafraid to speak her mind. Quite a surprise if one considers her strict mother. Once the holidays are behind us, I will have to confront Paul again. The way I understand it, *he* was the main instigator. And this time, I put Peter and his visiting friends next to him. So far, his brother pretends not to have seen anything at all. Of course, be that as it may, I blame the coaches who left boys and girls without supervision, relying on the parents to watch. If Victoria would have been there, nothing would have happened... which reminds me that I am glad I told her not to worry, as our daily walk would take longer. This snowless Christmas-time is the first I can ever remember," she sighed, linking her arm in Marlene's. "Can't you just see Philip's reaction when I tell him where I went and what a great time I had?" Marlene nodded in amusement.

"I feel very bad about the way I treated them. Of course, it was their long-buried relatives who gave us trouble about 'their piece of land', and we had to prove over and over again that it was never theirs. But the young ones are a different breed. Now they will get some because I say so. I admit to being stubborn about the poor street lighting between our places, never realizing how dark it is."

"Madame, it is the first time we have walked in the dark. We are never back later than four unless in a car or carriage."

"Right, Marlene. Nevertheless, there will be plenty of changes."

They reached the huge, ornamented but dimly lit iron gate, enclosed with tall boxwood hedges, along with a great variety of shrubs and spruce trees, and Marlene, too, thought about this snowless and spiritless Christmas, with every young servant in the war and the sons of many of their employees too, leaving them little choices but to attend the traditional midnight Mass.

No sooner had Marlene tried to open the gate, then from out of nowhere, came a short and skinny man whose face was barely recognizable, standing in front of them, blocking the entrance. "Can you not see the big 'NO TRESPASSING' sign?" Verena asked, highly annoyed.

He only responded scornfully. "I am Bertram von Walden." He grinned, satisfied, from ear to ear, enjoying the startled look of both, while waving his small lantern in front of him. "This place could use more lights… but then again one could then see the von Walden shack. You!" he added scornfully, directing his carefully planned accusation at Verena. "You, old bag, went to our rotten place to squeal on my little half-sister so she would get punishment for Christmas instead of a little gift. That would suit a heartless tyrant like you just fine!"

Verena overlooked his statement and replied. "How on earth did you get here and why don't you go away?"

"By taking a shortcut no one else knows." He grinned, getting a small bottle from his back pocket.

"Mrs. Reinhardt just wanted to get to the bottom of the incident on the skating rink. We were just talking about how sweet and beautiful the little girl is and she believed her and—"

He quickly brushed her off. "I am not talking to an old maid. You are nothing but a slave in good clothes." Then he turned again to Verena. "I want to get you off, once and for all, from your high horse, which all of you Reinhardts have ridden at our expense much too long," he sputtered, taking a fast swig from his rum bottle. "I am leaving tomorrow, or I wouldn't have been at the house overhearing in the adjoining room your carefully laid out accusation. People like you don't fool me a bit. Aside from that, we poor von Waldens possess a diary too!"

"We have nothing to hide." Verena said calmly, though her heart was pounding.

"Oh, no?"

"Not at all. I haven't said one unkind word which could have upset anybody, least of all you! Neither you nor your brother was ever mentioned."

"Half-brother," he corrected. "but you were poking around enough to find something, or you wouldn't have paid a visit to 'trash' like us, who live in a place not fit for your horses. And all that one day before Christmas, as it couldn't have waited. It must have cost you quite a few sleepless nights, let alone the pain and humiliation. Well, never mind all that. One pays sooner or later for his shortcomings."

"Your mother is a very fine lady and I plan to make some drastic changes."

Before Marlene had a chance to vouch for her statement he interjected. "Stepmother, if you please! However, she is a very good one if I say so myself, but gullible like my father… or let's say easily deceived!" He laughed thinking of all the lies he had fed them since he left school at fourteen. "But it's because of you Reinhardts that we are condemned to live in poverty and shunned as social outcasts, better known as the 'poor paupers of Lindenfels'. I waited for this heaven-sent opportunity to pay you back for a long time, as I have nothing to lose, but give you the same merry Christmas that you set out to give us… without any success, I may add." He laughed again and took his last sip of rum. "You may just as well know that I am your son, Philip's, very own pimp. Only he has no idea who I am! How is that for a surprise as a Christmas gift? A low-down von Walden a step ahead of Vienna's high society! HAHAHA!" he roared in pleasure, holding his little lantern closer to her face to watch her devastated reaction in utter delight. Verena had read such words occasionally in novels, which were considered French classics, but had never heard them spoken.

"You have had too much to drink young man. And your imminent departure for the front may also be contributing to your behavior," Verena replied in a conciliatory tone of great understanding, while her heart was pounding and her shaking becoming quite obvious, with Marlene putting her arm around her waist.

"Please, Baron von Walden!" she pleaded kindly. "Can you not see how upset Mrs. Reinhardt is getting by all your lies just to get even?"

Now he was really getting livid, as nothing is worse than calling a liar by his name, especially when on rare occasions he spoke the truth. "Lies? Lies?" he repeated, gratified, as it enabled him to take the truth even further. "I have been supplying the famous and dapper Philip Reinhardt for quite a few years with young virgins so he wouldn't catch syphilis! And that almost on a daily basis, as he has an addiction to what you would call 'a sinful lifestyle'. Of course, he pays top price and I have him a highly secretive replacement already," he said triumphantly as Verena started to swoon, holding on tightly to Marlene. "Now you have a very nice Christmas and never set foot in our glorified stable again or all of Vienna will know about it! So far, it's only between you and me, as your old maid will never utter a word, providing she knows what is good for her!" he threatened, disappearing into the dark just as fast and unexpectedly as he had arrived. One could only hear the rustle and cracking of some trees and bushes, leaving no doubt that he knew his way around. He would never reveal his whereabouts to anyone, but buy a new bottle and get a restful night of sleep. After all, this was a man without a conscience and this encounter was just one more episode in his wretched life.

"Please, dear Mrs. Reinhardt, calm yourself or you will spend the holidays in bed. Don't believe a word from this drunken outcast. He is widely known as a blackmailer, among other things, and I am surprised he didn't ask you for money. I've never met this little monster before, but one cannot help but hear from the servants that he gives his family a lot of troubles. They don't even know or care where he lives. Well, I'd better not say anything more; enough was said already. We should have taken our regular entrance with all the lights burning. Then nothing would have happened. And all those lies!" Marlene babbled as fast as Verena's heart was beating.

"No, Marlene," she stammered, almost out of breath, and motioned for her to sit down on one of the stone benches leading to the side entrance of the castle. Ironically, it was their first shortcut too as they came from the von Walden place, and it was mostly used by servants who had their own little houses as their families grew, since the Reinhardts had only single rooms meant for their live-in staff. "No, Marlene," she repeated having taken the seat. "For years, I tried to fool myself about their marriage. Even my dear, late husband expressed, from time to time, his doubts, but left them in the end unspoken, knowing we couldn't change a thing." She opened her chinchilla coat, starting to perspire, while at the same time feeling cold.

"Better close your coat, Mrs. Reinhardt. It is very chilly. Better yet, you stay put and I'll run to the castle for help. It's only a few minutes, after all, we walked more than an hour without a pause.

Verena agreed gladly. "Marlene?"

"Yes?" she turned around, already on the run.

"Not a word to anybody. I'll take care of it myself. It's between Philip and myself."

"You know me better than that. I swear to it." And with that promise, she raced as fast as she could until she reached the door, pounding with all her strength as it had no pull.

"I think Mrs. Reinhardt is about to faint!" she shouted, puzzling even the doorman.

"Where did you come from? Why this road? We sent some servants through the park as we were getting worried."

"She is sitting on the fourth or fifth stone bench. Better get more help, as we may have to carry her!"

Victoria descended the stairs, having consoled herself for the last hour that Verena could be on a last-minute Christmas shopping trip as she had done a few times previously. And as Marlene was with her and there was no snow or slippery weather, there was nothing to be worried about, but she had still ordered some servants to be on the lookout. Now she ran equal to Marlene's pace after overhearing her plea for help.

"Good Lord! Where have you two been to take this dimly lit road?"

"Mrs. Reinhardt decided this morning to visit the von Waldens."

"No!"

"Yes, and you can believe me when I tell you they had the best time together; drank tea, had cake and promised to see each other again."

Once more a long, drawn out "no" followed from Victoria in great amazement.

"That's the reason why we are so late, and Mrs. Reinhardt insisted we take this shortcut." It gave her goosebumps to think of Bertram's explanation for his sudden appearance. "Remind me to get the gas lights in better condition; but then again the servants use lanterns."

They arrived, out of breath, with a few servants following one by one, as the young, spry ones were in the military service. "I got a wheelchair!" one screamed and both looked at each other in relief, noticing Verena's fur coat on the ground and she in an awkward position slumped on the bench.

"Can you get up Mrs. Reinhardt?" Victoria asked kindly. "Let's put your coat on. We are all here to carry you home."

It became obvious that she would have to be lifted and carried on the wheelchair, with more of the blankets put around her.

"Marlene, please, I know you are exhausted but now that I have enough help, get a head start and call the ambulance."

"Never mind my condition," she answered and was on the run again.

Though not able to speak one word or show any kind of reaction, Verena held Victoria's hand so tightly. Maybe she felt sorry that she was the wife of her unfaithful son.

Anette and Marlene stood by the wide opened door, awaiting their arrival. "The ambulance is on the way. It may arrive any minute," Anette stated, holding her arm around Marlene. "Poor thing is out of breath."

"I always said you have more than two eyes and the instinct of a wildcat," Victoria joked, while directing the servants to put Verena on the nearest couch. They were still in the process of taking her coat off when the ambulance arrived. After all, it was a Reinhardt who needed help from their own hospital! The doctors who belonged to the Reinhardts' social circle and two medical orderlies a bit further in the background had the stretcher already in place.

"Who was with or spoke last with Mrs. Reinhardt?"

"I was," Marlene said shaken, taking a look at her mistress who was on the couch with two doctors taking her pulse and checking her heartbeat.

"Miss Marlene is my mother-in-law's companion for almost fifteen years now," Victoria interrupted kindly, knowing a doctor's attitude towards a servant.

"Then please come with us in the ambulance for a few more questions as there is no time to lose."

Victoria followed without being asked; but then she was a Reinhardt and poor Marlene would need moral support. Now both sat facing the two doctors who had notepads on their laps, while scribbling and asking Marlene questions.

"Were you walking at an unusually fast speed?"

"Yes. Very fast. I was surprised that my mistress was even capable of going that fast without pausing at all until now."

"And the reason for it?"

"She didn't want to worry her family, as time just slipped up on her and it was getting dark."

"Were you shopping?"

"Oh, no. Mrs. Reinhardt decided to pay the von Waldens a visit."

"Oh, God! No wonder her heart beats at this rapid pace," one doctor uttered, being aware of their long family feud.

"From what Marlene told me, they had a most pleasant visit, with tea and cake and a promise to see each other again," Victoria interceded.

"Now that would be a miracle." The attending doctor smiled, with all present agreeing wholeheartedly.

"My mistress even said to me that she will make some drastic changes to better their impoverished lifestyle. She felt very guilty," Marlene added, causing another surprised stir, when the ambulance halted as they reached the hospital. The doctor ordered both ladies to take a seat, while planning to get a hold of the Baroness as he was sure her companion was not present when the conversation took place.

"I imagine Mrs. Reinhardt told you about her guilty feelings on the way home."

"Yes, sir."

"And we thank you for the information as it gives us something to go on," he finalized, following the arriving stretcher to the Emergency Room in a hurry.

"Mrs. Reinhardt," Marlene said, still shaking. "I am so grateful you came with me. Otherwise I would have been even more nervous. I don't like to talk to doctors."

"You haven't done one thing wrong, Marlene. I will stay here until we all drive home together, as I am sure they called my husband, too."

Marlene's face reddened. A few minutes later, the head physician approached Victoria in a very professional manner, though he was a family friend of long standing. "My dear Mrs. Reinhardt... what a surprise for all of us at the hospital. And hearing about the out-of-the-ordinary visit your mother-in-law took. So far, we detected a slight stroke, but that is not our only diagnosis. We put her in complete isolation as all her other symptoms point to pleurisy. Her extremely high fever and difficulty in breathing are two reasons. We put her on oxygen but hope it won't develop into pneumonia. As I stated, the stroke was slight; let's hope there are not more following. It's still a puzzle to all of us, as her heartbeat, too, is unbelievably fast," he sighed, somewhat worried. "My colleagues tell me she went to see the von Waldens. Why on earth would she do that?"

"Oh, I can answer that question," Victoria said hurriedly. "Her favorite grandson, Paul, sprained his ankle at the new skating rink. Unfortunately, the little von Walden girl was strongly suspected to be the reason for his fall. I imagine she went there to settle a score. Isn't that right, Marlene?" The doctor shook his head wordlessly.

"Well, it started out that way," Marlene replied. "but then she liked the Baroness, had tea with her, and believed the little girl."

"Thank you," replied the doctor with a fixed smile. He left again, but not before turning around and verifying that the Baroness and Philip were already on their way.

"And all that commotion before Christmas Eve," Victoria mumbled.

"Mrs. Reinhardt said that this year would be a very different Christmas anyway. Nothing much to celebrate with every young man gone and many of the servants grieving," Marlene remarked as Astrid von Walden appeared, almost out of breath, walking straight towards Marlene and Victoria.

"And again, a good evening," the Baroness addressed Marlene before she introduced herself to Victoria. "What a terrible shock that we should meet under these circumstances. Mrs. Reinhardt and I had a surprisingly good time together, considering the circumstances of why she paid me a visit to begin with."

Now they noticed a small group of doctors talking, as a visibly upset Philip came rushing through the emergency door. The phone call came just as he was about to leave his factory after wishing each and every one a happy holiday, looking eagerly forward to a few relaxing days himself.

"I drove as fast as I could thanks to the clear weather. What happened to Mother?" he asked while shaking each doctor's hand, addressing each other on a first name basis.

"You may want to give your wife a deserving wave, or better yet bring her along to the office." He gave a slight nod to Baroness von Walden, though he was puzzled as to why she and Marlene would be in an intense discussion. Upon entering the office, the head physician spoke first. "Philip, I hate to tell you, but your mother undertook a so-called visit to the von Waldens." Philip looked stunned, unable to give an answer. "But from what we hear, both women seemed to have had a very pleasant time together; at least that's what we were told by her companion. Of course, we haven't had a chance to speak to the Baroness, as she too just arrived."

"We'd better call her in, in your presence," said Dr. Breuner.

"As you wish," Philip answered.

The Baroness explained in few sentences the reason for her unexpected visit, pertaining to her grandson's sprained ankle and who should be made responsible, and ending by agreeing that they would meet each other the day the school resumed. Philip only shook his head, knowing the skating rink story only too well. His first thought was that she had wanted to give them a miserable Christmas, and it had backfired.

"That trip could have waited until school began, providing there was any reason to begin with," Philip replied, until he suddenly thought of Kurt's death. "Good Lord, we just buried Kurt Essler. I will never understand her obsession with that little incident, which my son Paul and myself explained to her all over again."

The doctors bowed their heads in sorrow, knowing how much his uncle was loved by anyone who had the privilege of knowing him. With an "excuse me doctors, I know you will do your best," he was ready to leave.

"Philip, don't be too upset. Maybe some good will come out in the long run. Maybe it's the end of this long running feud," Dr. Breuner mumbled while the two women tried to get better acquainted.

"That will be the day," Philip whispered, still furious when he left, followed by Victoria and Astrid, who ventured to ask the Baroness' hometown before moving to Lindenfels.

"Baden-Baden," she replied, and Victoria and Philip exclaimed in delight. "Baden-Baden? We are frequently there during the school vacation with our children!" It sounded like it was rehearsed in unison.

"You are?" she replied, equally enthusiastic. "Then we will have to talk about it, as I am very homesick."

Philip offered her a ride home, both apologized for the inconvenience, and promised each other visits as soon as their households settle down, as Astrid expected her sister and brother-in-law for a two-week visit. Though Marlene in the back seat felt very relieved, all the questioning coming at least temporarily to a halt, she forged a plan to leave the Reinhardt household as soon as possible. For one reason, the unpredictable 'Bertie the pimp' might show up again, but the main one was if her mistress in her delirious condition revealed his name! Then what? Since she mentioned several times that her sister was expecting her first baby shortly, and with her husband in the war, it would be a great comfort to her sister if someone was there to help out. Philip agreed wholeheartedly, knowing she would be back as soon as her mistress improved and was in need of her. As far as Marlene was concerned, Tyrol was far away and the perfect solution. She would write the Baroness von Walden about how guilty Mrs. Reinhardt had felt, knowing it would make her feel much better. The Reinhardts were, however, very surprised at her fast departure but, since their household was in an extremely gloomy state, they felt she would be happier with her sister and let it go at that, expecting her prompt return.

It was New Year's Eve of 1914, and there were no joyful gatherings anywhere, let alone a New Year's party. However, when the bells started their usual ringing, Philip entered with three glasses and a bottle of champagne. "I don't know if you two even heard the bells," he said, noticing Victoria and Anette very engrossed in conversation pertaining to Paul, who was in an extreme state of depression.

"It may sound crazy, but let's drink to a happy New Year anyway. Maybe the war will come to an end and all our boys will be home." He omitted that his mother was still in complete isolation and had not spoken a word. She had suffered a second stroke and the doctors expected more to come.

Bertram von Walden was already in uniform and on the train to an unknown destination; Astrid and children were deep asleep.

1916

4

Ever since the unfortunate accident
on Christmas Eve of 1914, Victoria had had to take over the
chore of keeping up with their diaries, a tradition dating back
to 1509. She, however, had her own idea of entering the daily
boring accounts, and so far as she was concerned, barely
anything noteworthy happened. For most people around her,
it became a struggle with many a husband, a father, or a son
at the front-line. And today, while half of Vienna was
watching their more-or-less beloved Emperor's funeral, she
took the opportunity to read those few pages of 1915 and to
catch up with 1916, as she had numerous notes locked in a
small leather box, a gift from Anette, who took over the reins
with Philip's and Victoria's full consent to run the
Reinhardts' large household by keeping everything as it was
and as it should be.

Looking back at her scribbled pages since Christmas
of 1914, it showed that Verena suffered several more strokes
which left her soon afterwards paralyzed. Then she fell in a
coma, and so far, had never recovered. Victoria was very
sympathetic towards her condition, paying her a daily visit

and stroking her face when leaving. But Philip and Anette showed very little compassion and added after each inquiry that, after all, she was seventy-two, 'while our young soldiers are living and dying in their mudholes'. Verena was laying in her mansion in Vienna with three nurses taking their shifts just watching her, and then changed the rather embarrassing subject, knowing the war was still going on.

Lindenfels castle was not being occupied, as all the firewood and coal was used for every purpose involving the war. With all young male servants gone, it was not hard to find a place for any woman servant, as men's work had to be done by them. No one seemed to mind as long as they were employed at the Reinhardts. Philip, too, worked many late hours. He was still more angry than sorry about his mother's condition, feeling that it all could have been avoided.

Elisabeth's letters from Berlin sounded more and more like medical reports, and she also had a nice boyfriend from Holland. Both vowed not to take any trips until the war was over. Gisela graduated on July 3, 1915, and entered a school to become a kindergarten teacher. "It will take three years of hard studying," she would answer harshly whenever one of her brothers teased her about it. Both claimed she needed only mediocre qualifications.

Peter, the most happy-go-lucky of all the Reinhardts, was very much like his father in younger years, but promised to follow in Elisabeth's footsteps in becoming a doctor. So far, no one believed him! Paul was absorbed with technology, visiting his father's factory and foundry whenever time permitted. Very much on the serious side, he was the only one who cared about Verena's well-being and came to see her on a daily basis, mostly trying to lessen his own guilt. After all, she went to the von Waldens for his sake, and he still considered that 'ugly brat' responsible for his grandmother's condition.

As for Victoria herself, she became close friends with Astrid von Walden, both spending a great deal of time at

Vienna's military hospital, helping not only with rolling the freshly washed bandages, but also writing letters for any wounded soldier who was incapable of doing it himself. Letters to or from home were as important as their daily food rations.

All parties came to a complete standstill. With many of their husbands or sons at the western front, only an occasional after-hours tea was taken. The Linden trees of Lindenfels took great pride in supplying its inhabitants with their tasty leaves, which needed only hot water. After all, the town was named in the trees' honor.

That was all Victoria had put on the pages of her next diary for the year of 1915, as anything else mattered to her very little. However, arriving at the Spring of 1916, it would become quite a different story.

～

By now, every newspaper had finally refrained from referring to the heavy battles on the western front as 'skirmishes' with no victories or defeats. Also, the phrase 'trench warfare' was eliminated. Millions of lives were lost already with the Russians taking the heaviest toll. Though their army and cavalry fought to their utmost, they were poorly equipped to counter the well-prepared Germans and Austrians, as Russia fought on Serbia's side. At present, Verdun was the main battleground between the German-Austrian army and the French, with each side equally determined to win at all costs, though it had consumed the lives of hundreds of thousands already, and all that only for the sake of gaining a few miles. Parisians once more began to barricade themselves, just in case.

Victoria received a letter from Irma Kronthaler, proudly stating that both of her sons were looking forward to marching in the streets of Paris; it was just a matter of time. Victoria was too upset to answer and asked Philip how her friend could even entertain such a cruel thought! Didn't she realize how many lives were already wasted just to satisfy a few stupid and heartless emperors?

"No, Victoria, both of her sons were trained for war and they are in the middle of it. She doesn't even permit herself to think of defeat or that it will affect either of her two sons," he sighed. "Let's hope... well, never mind." He left without finishing his thoughts.

Astrid, too, kept Victoria up to date on all arriving letters, be it from her husband or stepson Bertram. She was especially pleased about his beautiful drawing and poetry. "Maybe the war will make him a better young man," she stressed after each letter. "But then again, why would it have to take a war?"

"Let's hope for the best in any case," Anette replied, though she was doubtful.

The greatest surprise came the following day when Lt. Colonel von Walden sat at home, hidden with Andreas, Jr., and tomboy Gaby, with Hermine opening the door, not giving to Astrid the slightest indication of her husband's sudden arrival. Hermine had put one more plate at the supper table, but it had escaped Astrid's attention, as the von Waldens had changed their lifestyle by taking all meals in the kitchen.

"You are fifteen minutes late for supper, Madame. Where have you been?"

With a most astonished look and loud shriek of "Andreas!" she flew into his outstretched arms. "For how long?" were her first words, still in awe.

"Four weeks, dear Astrid, including a few days of travel time, of course. They couldn't spare any of us during the holidays, though nothing of importance was going on. So, you see the first of April turned out to be 'April Fool's Day'. Our two children who played on their seesaw, and Hermine behind the plow were equally startled. Only our ox showed indifference. I imagine they already took all of our horses?"

"Except mine," answered Gaby in delight. "The Wertheims keep him hidden until the war is over, but I can ride whenever I want to."

"How very generous."

"Mrs. Wertheim said they never came to them, never expecting Jews to have a horse with no grounds to plow." Somehow it made sense, as their well-manicured garden and riding path was well hidden behind tall trees and shrubbery.

Though Astrid kept her husband well informed, there was still so much unsaid. After hours of discussion, she fell asleep in his arms and he carried her to bed. It was almost dawn. He, however, was still wide awake noticing all the many changes with many more to come. Hermine behind the plow was one sight he was not likely to forget, though many poor families had farmed this way for years. But how will they harvest with no male help around? What was left was either too young or too old. This war may continue until the last man has died, he himself included, and then what? A young widow with two children, and an unpredictable stepson who will continue to be evil should he ever make it home. There was also the small pension to consider, which will be almost worthless with the usual inflation after every war.

He decided right then and there to sell this troublesome place, as his relatives were paid off when they left a long time ago. Astrid and the children had always loved the city of Vienna, its good schools, and nice parks. Lindenfels and its wealthy inhabitants always snubbed them anyhow. And with this prolonged war going on, it was as good a time as any to leave. He would present his idea over breakfast before his children left for school. He was not even able to finish the sentence before Astrid and the children roared a loud and joyful "YES"! Only Hermine asked, "What about a food shortage? Berlin is already having one."

"We will have an agreement with the new owner and make sure to have a garden." Hermine was glad to hear. "After my bath, I am paying Isaak Wertheim a visit." He related his plan to his overjoyed wife, who had already written a note to Victoria, giving her a reason for a visit, which seemed to be important enough as far as she and the Reinhardts were concerned. By the time Andreas was dressed and ready to go, Hermine had returned from her mission, claiming to have been lucky enough to catch the oncoming trolley within seconds.

Victoria, in turn, suggested a luncheon the following day at the Reinhardt place with both husbands present. Andreas was amazed at their swiftness and remarked that if they had generals who acted that quickly, the war might be over.

"I was terribly afraid you would change your mind," Astrid replied with a hug and a kiss.

Isaak Wertheim was extremely surprised about the visit and request, but regretfully declined to accept any commitment until he spoke to the Reinhardts first. *"After all,"* he thought to himself. *"the long-standing feud was always about those few meager acres."*

"As a matter of fact, we see them tomorrow for lunch and I will be glad to discuss the matter," Andreas replied, promising to return as soon as possible.

"I have only a very limited time to settle my personal affairs. And it is my fervent desire to do so now."

Isaak Wertheim agreed and added in parting that Lindenfels is a most desired location and no one ever sold anything as far as he could remember. Shaking his finger like a school teacher reprimanding his pupil, he advised not to settle for a crown below 5,000.00 per acre.

Aside from Isaak's concern about not getting cheated, Andreas was very surprised at the high value of his place, as he knew there were about six acres left many years ago when his father took care of his departing sisters.

Victoria related to Philip this unexpected offer. He arrived somewhat earlier than usual, looking very exhausted after being at work since four a.m. As always, they had their customary glass of wine with Anette, who ordered Philip to have a day of rest after taking a look at him.

He only laughed. "In my place no one looks any better."

However, he perked up considerably and was extremely astonished when Victoria repeated that the von Walden's place was for sale. "I am buying it at the first given chance. Even my late father wanted to enlarge our hospital. And now with the war on, Vienna will need more infirmaries and since von Walden's and our properties join, it is the perfect solution. I will use the extra space for a rehab center. Many wounded soldiers will have to learn to walk again. And some with wooden legs! I saw it first-hand when visiting some of my former employees," he sighed, shaking his head sadly.

"I see them every day, Philip, and I am more than happy about your noble idea."

He smiled, taking her hand in his. Just as Victoria was about to continue, Anette jumped up like she had been stung by a hornet.

"I am buying the von Walden's place," she choked with emotion. "for the very same reason you just suggested. By God, you Reinhardts own 40 acres in Lindenfels alone, and I don't even own a half. My father gave everything to Kurt!"

"And he in turn left everything to those poor, worn-out priests. Just think about it Anette," Philip interrupted. "with your fortune you could have bought much acreage a long time ago."

"Ha! Not in Lindenfels; don't think I was not at the lookout."

"Well, that's true, but you can buy von Walden's property tomorrow if it benefits the hospital. That was the only reason I would have bought it. Not because we need more land."

With Anette visibly calming down, she began to apologize, claiming her late fiancé, Alex, never got any recognition and that everything would be done not only for his sake but for all soldiers.

"Well, the von Waldens come tomorrow for lunch. It's between you and them," Victoria concluded.

"If you give me permission, Anette, I'd like to shake hands with Major von Walden again." Philip smiled with a wink.

"He is a Lieutenant Colonel now," Victoria replied.

"That's even better," he joked, still watching Anette's embarrassment.

"It's such a grand idea, Philip, and it will still be in the Reinhardt name. After all, Alex was your uncle."

"I don't care for whom you name it, Anette. I hope you believe me." She gave an assuring nod.

"But speaking of ideas? Name it 'Philip'! With all the old stones from von Walden's place, we can build a monument right in the middle of the town's square, surrounded by a well-kept circle of flowers, and beautiful iron work. How about that girls?" he smiled, very pleased with himself about the momentary idea. "It will be for all of our fallen heroes since the existence of Lindenfels." Now Victoria started to weep. "Our registrar office will be only too glad and proud to supply all the names of every soldier who fought and died for Austria," Philip concluded, suddenly ceasing to be tired.

~

The following day, the Reinhardts and von Waldens welcomed each other. Though they were aware it was for business reasons, the main topic was the ongoing war, especially Verdun. Over refreshments and hors d'oeuvres, the von Waldens were told that both Wilands were expected, too.

"Strictly at my request," said Anette curtly. Andreas also hinted politely about Verena's reaction in case of a recovery, while Anette pursed her lips, showing a most satisfying grin like someone who had beat a Reinhardt at their own game.

Victoria answered sincerely that her mother-in-law would be delighted and happy. Philip retold his short encounter with Isaak Wertheim, including his honest advice, and added with a smirk, "I imagine he knows my mother's reputation quite well,"

But Astrid stated matter-of-factly that Isaak's brother Martin and his wife Ida were not only the most kind family in Lindenfels, but the only ones extending social invitations to the von Waldens.

"That is before you met us," Victoria said sincerely, with Philip adding quickly, "Amen to that!"

"Of course, I have to find a suitable place for my family first."

"Indeed, you do. On my part there is no time limit," Anette replied.

"Unfortunately for me there is. I have about three weeks left," he said when Arthur Wiland arrived, not only a bit late but without his brother, who had a severe migraine.

"Poor fellow; seems to have them quite frequently. However, never underestimate the brain of a single Wiland!" Philip jested, asking everyone to enter the dining room.

After Andreas' short explanation of the reason for selling and Anette's desire to buy it, Arthur, too, was stunned and very pleased. He agreed also on Isaak Wertheim's choice for a good deal as he knows every available house.

"Any idea how much the Baron can get for his place?" asked Philip.

"It depends on the acreage. I suggest a surveyor through Wertheim's connection. He will make sure there is no mistake. One acre should sell easily for 5,000.00 crowns, though no one is selling."

It was Anette's turn again. "Well, according to Verena's estimate, we're talking about six-and-a-half acres."

"Forget the surveyor," Arthur laughed aloud, joining in with the rest.

"I will pay with gold coins," she said self-assuredly. "Isaak will get a much better bargain in a good district. If anyone deserves a break in life, the von Waldens do," she smiled sincerely.

"Thank you ever so much," both said in unison, too startled to say anything else. Their hearts were racing as it seemed to be a done deal, with gold coins on top of it.

"You can, of course, pay the seller in Austrian crowns," Arthur said in departing, forgetting that the von Waldens were in possession of very little money no matter what the currency. "People are nowadays hoarding gold coins, as they are harder to come by."

"There is plenty to go around. You ought to know that," Anette replied with a wink, reminding him he was her lawyer, too.

The von Waldens departed just as they had arrived—elated and relieved about the swift business deal. Anette lost no time and went in rapid strides to the phone, hoping to find Isaak still at his office.

"Mr. Isaak Wertheim?"

"That's me, alright," he laughed.

"This is Anette von Essler," Victoria heard her say in a very dignified manner. "The Baron and Baroness von Walden just left the Reinhardts' place, with Lawyer Wiland present, of course, who suggested that you may be the only one familiar with all of Vienna's available houses to buy."

"Glad to hear that. Let's say I try to stay current. By the way, we do know each other from my brother's house. Am I correct?"

"Of course, you are. Your family was the only one who also showed kindness toward the von Waldens. Now that we have established that much, I am asking you to find them a nice place to live in Vienna. They may come to see you later today or tomorrow. The Baron has only three weeks to settle his affairs. And just in case you are wondering why I am calling you on this, I am buying von Walden's property as is." Isaak was stunned to say the least. "At Philip Reinhardt's suggestion, it will be used as a rehab center for our soldiers. It's the ideal setting with their path joining the hospital."

"Speaking of good luck and a noble thought!" he replied, still in awe.

"Philip, of course, would have bought it also, but I want the place in memory of my late fiancé, Alex, who was a Reinhardt as you know. Von Walden's structure will be torn down and the stones saved for a monument in the middle of Lindenfels for all our war heroes, dating back to God knows when.

"I am deeply moved," he sighed.

"But there is another reason I am calling on you. Not only do I expect you to find the von Waldens a very nice place but also to get them a good bargain, as they may pay the seller with good monetary currency… at least a great part of it."

"Like what?" he replied quickly and with great interest.

"Gold coins. I thought you might like to think about it."

"Indeed, I would!" he said excitedly. "I shall do my very best."

"I thought so, Mr. Wertheim, as such an opportunity doesn't come often."

Victoria, who couldn't help but overhear the conversation, walked towards her in shock. "I didn't know this business side of you!"

"My late mother and Robert Eckhardt taught me a lot, knowing I would end up with only what she would give me. As for Robert, he and I developed a very close friendship. He admired my devotion to Alex. He left me all his American coins and plenty of it. So, you see, now I am able to put all of it to good use," she concluded, very content and proud.

~

By now, the Wilands were in touch with Isaak Wertheim and he knew exactly how much the von Waldens were willing to spend, as Anette had offered the price of 35,000 crowns but paid all of it in American gold coins. Though he had his distant relatives on his seller's list, he would show their place as a last resort for fear the von Waldens might think it was prearranged between Jews. So far, he showed them every available villa, but the von Waldens looked at the place from outside and never bothered even to go in. It was either the location, size, or condition from outside, never mind all the small gardens. They claimed repeatedly to have only the welfare of their two children in mind, which meant good schools and parks nearby.

Isaak still had the luxury to drive a car, though his business was at a very low point. Now he had little choice but to take a chance with his relatives he barely associated with and drove to the fifth district called Margareten, where he parked on an elegant side street. "Please get out, as I have to give you some background on this oversized villa." It was a huge villa built in perfect baroque style and von Walden thought him crazy but was willing to listen. "This place was completely redone and made into two large apartments. It has more space and larger rooms than most villas, if I say so myself. The previous owner was a banker who died about three years ago, leaving his estate to his only daughter and her husband. There is a very large garden, which used to be a small manicured park, but they had to use some of the flower beds for vegetables. I am telling you this just in case you worry about getting hungry. Half of the garden is yours of course." The von Waldens were immensely relieved. "Now to the main point: only the first floor is for sale as the owner won't be bothered with renting. He is a professor at the nearby academy and his wife had a little girl just a few months ago. So far, they have turned quite a few families away... but also the opposite is true when they hear the name of the late Aaron Bernstein. It is the only Jewish villa on Mayerhofstraße." The von Waldens looked at each other, perplexed, as Vienna was known for its tolerance of Jews.

"That is the last thing on our mind as we are good friends with your brother and his family," Astrid replied, with Andreas in agreement.

"But aside from the Reinhardts, you are the only ones in Lindenfels," Isaak replied truthfully.

"We are so-called nobility and are shunned too," came from Andreas. "I say let's take a look."

"I am quite anxious to see inside," Astrid ventured, as she loved everything else she had seen so far.

All loved the place at first glance. They admired the large, multi-colored glass door with intricate ironwork up front to prevent breakage. Once entering the oversized oak paneled hall, they observed built-in closets, a library, small and large dining rooms, and a silk-covered main parlor leading to the outdoors. Isaak pointed to the large kitchen with pantry and mentioned the toilet and a bathroom with tub. On the large patio were weather-beaten cast iron furniture and quite a few stone sculptures to enhance the well-kept garden. The von Waldens were overcome, not knowing where to look first.

"It's made for us," Astrid whispered happily.

"We'll take it… providing the price is right."

Isaak watched while Andreas, Jr. put his arm around his mother and Gaby jumped for joy. "I'll make it right, Baron von Walden. That is, after all, my job," he replied, adding that the owner will be just as pleased to get a fine family.

The von Waldens heard a few steps when a young, sophisticated lady descended the stairs from her apartment above. "I am Gertrude Silverman," she said with a friendly kind of arrogance. "I couldn't help but overhear your complimentary reaction and just had to meet you." The von Waldens introduced themselves while both children bowed slightly but without a word. "I myself had that monster of a house completely redone. My late Papa left everything as it was for over twenty years after Mama died. Memories, I suppose." Gertrude Silverman walked with them again through the apartment, outlining a few more details, pointing to a smaller side door next to the main entrance. "It could be used as a guest room. The servant rooms are on the third floor. There is only one married couple from Croatia living upstairs, our two male servants are also in the military and as for a nanny, I plan to raise my little daughter myself."

"So did my wife," Andreas said, and Astrid couldn't possibly tell her there were, for a time, three children, including his son 'Bertram the terrible,' but instead answered to Mrs. Silverman that at present, she had only one woman with four of her other servants on the western front. Her stepson was never mentioned; that story could wait until the proper time.

The price of 15,000.00 crowns was astonishingly low as it included all maintenance and heating. "We are more than happy to take this apartment. Mr. Wertheim will take care of the rest," said the Baron.

Gertrude observed Astrid and her children embracing each other with the happiest expression they were able to give.

~

"The apartment is finally sold!" Gertrude told her husband, Martin, the moment he entered the nursery to take a gleeful look at his daughter, Anna. She erased all his stress from his long hours at the Academy, where a shortage of teachers was taking its toll.

"Glad to hear it. One less thing on your mind. I know you chose the right people," he replied, showing only interest in his sleeping child. Anna was now five months old and all his attention was directed at her, a very disappointing fact to his wife.

"Jews?" he asked, leaving the nursery with her on tiptoe.

"Believe it or not, impoverished former nobility from Lindenfels who sold their land and run-down estate to Anette von Essler, who has lived for several decades with the Reinhardts."

The Reinhardt name, of course, rang a bell. "What's their name?" he inquired, his interest changing.

"Baron von Walden. At present, he is a Lt. Colonel in the Cavalry and on leave. He has a very beautiful and cultured wife from Germany and two well-behaved children attending private schools in Vienna; one of the main reasons for their move. At least that's what I was told.

"Age of the children?"

"Oh, about ten and twelve. The boy is named Andreas and the girl, Gaby, even curtsied slightly while the boy bowed gallantly, never uttering a word."

"Well, I never heard of a von Walden, though I am forced to teach quite a few of those spoiled brats from Lindenfels. I am also aware by meeting with their parents that they are quite anti-Semitic."

"The von Waldens are not! Rest assured," Gertrude emphasized strongly. "They have been close friends with the Wertheims, according to Isaak, who showed them the apartment. He and the Wilands will handle everything else."

"Then I have to apologize." For Martin Silverman the matter was closed, as the money, like everything else, was his wife's to begin with. She, in turn, would never discuss anything of monetary value, considering it a very private matter, never to be shared.

While for the Silvermans the subject was closed, it was wide open in Lindenfels, making its usual rounds, and the inhabitants considered it the best news in years. Anette supplied just enough information to keep those curious bunch of social climbers guessing. She simply wallowed in her achievement. She was, for the first time in her life, to be in a position to throw all the incoming invitations away.

"I had to be seventy-six to do what I always wished I could do someday. Thank God I lived long enough!" was her frequent reply to both of the Reinhardts, who shared her well-deserved joy.

The von Waldens planned to move the first week in July, with the children safely in Switzerland. Astrid's sister was so happy with Andreas' decision to sell, she planned to bring Andreas, Jr., and Gaby back herself in September, as she couldn't wait until Christmas to see their new place.

"Ingrid writes that before we do anything, we should have these uncomfortable chairs re-done," Astrid read to Andreas with a smile.

"Throw away whatever you like, Astrid. There are only a few vases and photos worth keeping. The rest of the valuables were taken from me a long time ago. I have no sentimental feeling for anything else in this place. We buy antiques to our own taste so our children can be proud to have their friends over. I can imagine how they sometimes felt," he uttered in dismay.

As for Astrid's wealthy and noble parents, Kurt and Ilse von Donat, who still resided on a sumptuous estate near the spa of Baden-Baden, there had come only a stern warning that an impoverished Austrian officer just would not do. That was their only contribution to her marriage, as the widowed Andreas von Walden and Astrid von Donat eloped. His son Bertram was in care of a distant relative who was only too glad to return him to his father and his eighteen-year-old wife. Her sister Ingrid, who married a well-to-do dentist from Lausanne, got a very generous dowry. Dr. Henry Lebrun suited the Donats just fine, though he was twenty years older.

Both sisters' marriages were very happy. Ingrid shared, without her family's knowledge but with her husband's full approval, some of her inheritance to pay for the von Walden children's best private schools and any other lessons Andreas and Gaby showed interest in, which were many. Before his departure, he asked Astrid to return every crown, as he considered all the money only a loan to be repaid at the first opportunity. Ingrid and Henry refused, but suggested putting the money in the Bank of Lausanne to further Andreas' education in becoming a surgeon, and Gaby... well, at least she had a well-deserved dowry should the occasion arise.

To Astrid's amazement, Anette proved herself immensely helpful. Not only with her many suggestions for the apartment alone, but she gave many of her own belongings to fill the von Waldens' new apartment, as they were stored in the Reinhardts' attic after her mother's death in case she would ever marry. She was neither too proud nor too embarrassed to take them, with Anette assuring her they collected only dust.

It was two days before Andreas' departure when the von Waldens finally had a chance to reciprocate with one of their own dinners at their place. The end of April was still very cold and windy, but Philip Reinhardt didn't mind, as he was anxious to see the inside of the place for the first time. Anette, of course, was included as always, knowing the place as well as Victoria.

After an exceptionally well-prepared dinner and equally good desert, both men decided to go to their smoking parlor with Andreas stating that absolutely nothing pertaining to their furniture would go in the new apartment, except a few of their paintings and a bit of silverware which none of his sisters wanted. With that assurance, he opened the door and a painting of Bertram von Walden, Philip's former pimp, stared in his face! It took a man of strong fortitude not to show any reaction, but to take, in all calmness, the offered seat.

"Those are my children whom you hear playing the piano upstairs!"

"I was wondering if you hired some musician!" Philip joked, surprised at his calmness.

"This one is my son from my first arranged marriage, for which I never forgave my parents. This boy gave us nothing but troubles; I would say from the moment he could walk. Bad seeds from both sides of our family is the only explanation I can come up with."

"Where is he now?" asked Philip very calmly.

"Somewhere in the west... or wherever. He only writes to my present wife, who still believes she can change this black sheep. Thank God he never comes around since he left two years ago, though I know he must have had two short leaves. But as a perpetual liar, among other things, I don't care where he is. Believe it or not, I have not the faintest idea how he made a living before the war. The only schools he knew were reform schools, as no one else would take him. Only God knows how hard we tried," he said in final tone, going upstairs and introducing Philip to his still playing Andreas, Jr., and Gaby, the tomboy.

"Remember me?" were Philip's first words to her.

"Yes, sir, from the skating rink. And you know what? Even your mother believed that your son was one of the instigators pushing us girls in a small corner!"

"You know, Gaby, that boys will be boys… if we like it or not." Andreas and she only smiled as their father, after a short introduction was ready to go downstairs.

"No telling what Gaby would come up with," he thought, having no idea what his son Bertram's painting did to Philip.

After all three left von Walden's place, Philip was the first to speak. "And just think how mother poisoned everyone's mind about the von Waldens! I don't know of anyone who is nicer or has suffered more." Both women agreed.

~

The same night became sheer torture to Philip, as he could not possibly confess to Victoria. This time he knew she would not forgive him, for more than one reason. Not only was Astrid a friend since their first encounter at the hospital, but how does a husband explain that he had his own pimp who supplied him with virgins! She would possibly accuse him of being after his daughter, Gisela, whom he favored because she was 'his sunny child', making everyone around her happy. But in the process to find a way out, he found the way to his ever-present puzzle about Verena's sudden condition. Doubtless, Bertram heard the conversation from a nearby room and saw a chance for revenge. A man like him never has anything to lose, regardless of the outcome.

The last look on his mother's face would always haunt him… regardless of how he felt about her at many times in his life. And then the sudden departure of Marlene, who left in such an unbelievable hurry, possibly afraid that Verena would wake up and confront her son after all. She was not one to lie or be dragged in the middle; nevermind her surprise to hear about her master's well-kept secret. No matter how much and how hard he thought about a solution, this time he had no choice but to sit it out and wait for a miracle, providing such a thing existed. The only consolation was that his own father called him a perpetual liar, and no one would believe him should the opportunity ever present itself. Thank God they were moving far enough away; but on the other hand, a sort of friendship had developed between the two families.

Exactly as planned, Astrid Walden and both of her children left for Lausanne, Switzerland. The only difference was their mother would only stay three days, catch up on the latest, and deposit a large amount of money in the Swiss bank. Then she was ready to decorate her new place with Anette's suggestions and Hermine's strong arms. The apartment was handed over in mint condition and any desired changes, including wallpaper, would still be paid by the Silvermans, with Gertrude extremely grateful to be paid with gold coins from America.

Von Walden's children were in the best of care, as their neighbors had a nineteen-year-old son, who was discussing medicine with the thirteen-year-old Andreas. He considered Lucas Rossatti his idol, knowing him all his life. 'Tomboy Gaby' used to ride on his broad shoulders until she was five and he watched her swing on the trees, calling her 'a little ape.' The Rossattis also had a small, mongoloid boy, Eugen, who had just turned five. He was Gaby's favorite to play with, as he had the biggest smile whenever she entered his playroom, even applauding with his little hands. Though he was barely able to walk or talk, she felt a sort of pride that he had chosen her as playmate over his nannies or his parents, who inwardly wished that he was never born.

While Lucas was above average at any subject of interest to him, poor Eugen only smiled whenever his brother took him on his shoulders. Aunt Ingrid played the piano with Gaby and gave her extra lessons in horseback riding, French, and Italian. Rossatti came from the Italian part of Switzerland and conversed with her only in their language in order to perfect hers.

The summer passed too quickly, and this time it was Aunt Ingrid who brought the children back, being extremely curious about their new apartment. She, along with the children, were in great awe upon entering the luxuriously decorated place. "It must have cost you a fortune!" were her first words after embracing her sister, Astrid.

"You wouldn't believe me if I told you," she replied, telling her of how much came from Anette and the generous Reinhardts. The children, already in the garden on a newly erected swing, screamed, "Mama! We now live in paradise!"

Gertrude Silverman, who was never told where all the furniture, curtains, or rugs came from, was extremely pleased to hear it. That evening, she told her husband about meeting Astrid's sister, the enthusiastic outburst of the children, and the kindness of being given some chocolate. Martin only answered in delight, "and there are still some stupid inhabitants in Lindenfels calling them paupers and were glad to get rid of them! It shows again, one should never believe what one hears," he said, very pleased.

5

It was one of those typical gloomy, dreary days in November when the eighty-six-year-old Emperor Franz-Josef was laid to rest. He had died in his sleep nine days previously but was laid in state for his subjects to pass and pay their last respects. After all, the dutiful monarch reigned for sixty-eight years like a brave soldier, and the time was considered by many to be too long. Now he was finally among his equals and peers, as the family tomb at the Capuchin Habsburg burial ground was carefully prepared.

The Viennese lined up early at their own beloved Ringstraße, which was only two generations ago viewed with the greatest skepticism. What was to be the greatest funeral of the century was, if anything, a rather eerie event. Aside from a few black flags, dark draped fashion stores, only the permanent sunken lamp posts, which were brightly lit, had some black crepe paper hanging down, possibly to give the long, grieving procession a more caring look. Only the black, highly decorated horses who pulled the catafalque, followed closely by his grandnephew, his wife Zita, and their large brood of children was worthy of watching. The new, twenty-nine-year-old Emperor, with barely any training, called himself 'Karl the First', but the satirical Viennese christened him instantly 'Karl the Last' of a country which was in the process of collapsing.

The Reinhardt family stayed at home, knowing that in the following days, if not weeks, they would hear everything in detail. One would only hear of the Emperor's many sorrows and brave posture while losing a brother in Mexico, a son through suicide, and his wife to an assassin; nevermind his mistress of long standing. Somehow the former stage actress was, for the poor, lonely ruler, always accepted.

~

Victoria and Gisela were packing their suitcases to make a short trip to Berlin, for more than one reason. Victoria's mother and daughter refused to travel while the war is still going on, feeling very strongly about taking a seat from a soldier who was lucky enough to get a furlough. Though Victoria felt the same, and had not seen her mother or daughter in two years, there was also another reason for this trip. Gisela's fiancé of two years had just broken their engagement a few days ago, claiming that he was not ready to make a commitment. But her father told her the truth a few days ago, that he had asked Philip if the marriage would make him a partner. After all, he was one of the main engineers, with Philip relying heavily on him to run the firm during his absence. Philip's answer was a straight no, expecting his daughter to be married for love only, though she would get a substantial dowry which included a spacious apartment in one of the Reinhardts' houses. Two days later, all pre-arranged marriage plans for the following spring were canceled. Gisela was heartbroken, and her parents somewhat embarrassed, both feeling pain for their daughter. A trip to Berlin might be a temporary solution for a needed change of scenery. With Victoria planning to stay only one week, but with the option of a longer stay during the Christmas vacation, all agreed heartily to the plan.

While packing to catch the night train, one of Verena's nurses rushed excitedly through the house looking for Victoria. "Madame, please come with me. I think Mrs. Reinhardt just drew her last breath! With a loud moan, she turned her head and there is neither pulse nor heartbeat to be felt."

The doctor was called instantly, and he confirmed her death. "She was in a coma for almost two years. This will be a relief to all of you," he uttered matter-of-factly, having just dealt with the passing of two severely wounded soldiers who were not even twenty years old.

Once more, Philip came within the hour, with the undertaker just leaving the mansion. Without saying a word, but looking at his wife and daughter, both knew their trip had to be postponed. Philip wished he felt more grief or remorse of any kind, but thought for a split second that she never lived to tell him what had happened that ominous night. Again, it was to be a family funeral only, including the trusted servants of long standing. But the Reinhardts and Anette felt that Astrid von Walden and her two children should be invited as they were the last ones Verena had spoken to. No one took much notice, but since that fateful day, the von Waldens and Reinhardts had visited each other on a regular basis. But Paul was furious watching 'that ugly brat' put a white rose on the closed casket. The rose stood out because the other flowers were chrysanthemums in various colors.

Due to the extremely cold weather, Gaby wore a black stocking cap with her navy blue school coat, and borrowed her mother's gray, woolen shawl which covered almost all of her face. The Reinhardts stood in line to receive condolences from their employees, with the von Waldens being at the end. But Gaby still was angry at Paul. She shook everyone's hand, expressing, slightly in tears, her sorrow, still remembering Verena's last words, "I believe you, Gaby," which made her feel better. However, when she recognized Paul, who had grown considerably taller over the last two years, she put her shawl back up covering her mouth, giving him a venomous look which no one else noticed as she was the last in line. Paul was now even more bitter towards her inexcusable behavior. His only thoughts were, *"One of these days, I'll get even!"*

~

The following day, Arthur and Victor Wiland came, this time rather curious to see Philip's reaction to not being mentioned in Verena's will, considering the Reinhardts' enormous wealth. Instead, they got a surprise by his indifference towards the whole matter. "I am so glad she made up finally with my wife. I never thought she felt *that* guilty. As a businesswoman, she doubtlessly felt that I have more than enough."

"She did, Philip," Arthur Wiland replied curtly. Victoria turned red and had to sit down, completely overcome by Verena's unexpectedly generous gesture.

Philip only smiled, but asked nevertheless, "When was the will written?"

"Two weeks after your father's death," Arthur replied, putting the paper in front of him.

"I will make a will right now giving all of my inheritance equally to my husband and children," Victoria stammered.

"As you wish, Madame," Victor said, with Philip's indifference. In 1916, life for the new Mrs. Reinhardt had just begun.

1918

6

An exhausted Philip entered his home and told his family to stay inside for the next few days, as the spreading unrest was coming closer to the inner city. "There are strikers carrying red flags all over the place. I have sent all my workers home as none had planned to participate."

"My goodness, today is only January 14 and the New Year has had already more uprisings than I can remember," Victoria replied, concerned.

"Well, as for myself, I don't blame anyone. If one thinks of the present situation with the ongoing war—death in the millions, let alone the wounded and missing, and still no end in sight, except the rumors about the peace treaties that end up being just that, rumors!" Philip finalized angrily while putting his arm around his wife and the ever-present Anette, who added, "Until the Kaiser in Berlin says otherwise, the war won't end!"

Though it was now an open secret that Austria's new Emperor had tried to make peace several times with one or the other country, Germany's headquarters let him know in a hurry who would have the last word.

Philip asked about his sons' whereabouts, only to be told that all schools were closed, and he would find the boys in the library. "Well, coal has become almost like gold," he answered, planning a card game with Peter and Paul, who he had not seen as often as he wished. Gisela was in her room either doing some needlepoint or reading a love story.

Until now, the war was only discussed as it pertained to some friends or acquaintances who lost a loved one, or that someone was missing only to be told later that he had died. The many wounded were a great concern to Philip, as the list was endless! So far, only the black markets were thriving, as almost all stores were now closed for lack of items to sell. The average Viennese was forced to exchange many of his valuables for food or coal just to stay alive. The Reinhardts, however, still belonged to the group of lucky ones. They turned all their landscaped flower gardens into a field and planted anything that could be used for food. They not only supplied their large household staff and children, but most of their friends in the city too, as Lindenfels had been only castles, manor houses, and plowed fields for the last several years. Many inhabitants also cut their trees down to keep warm, but the Reinhardts had coal from their factories. Anette brought food to the von Waldens and the Silvermans, as their converted garden was just not sufficient. In addition, Astrid's sister still made her trips from Switzerland and brought quite a lot of food and spices, which had become unobtainable. There was always some chocolate included so the family would have some sweets from time to time.

By now little Anna Silverman was almost two years old and the von Waldens spoiled her with cookies, while Gaby was always overjoyed whenever asked to babysit. The von Waldens and Silvermans had become quite friendly, though Martin still suspected every member of nobility to be 'anti-Semitic'.

Astrid and Victoria helped at the military hospital on a daily basis, always returning home and saying, "Let's hope the war will end soon." Victoria was amazed that Philip never mentioned his mother since the will had been read. She suspected that his mother knew about his infidelities all along, with the strong possibility of having had him watched by a private eye. There could be no other explanation, as all of the Reinhardt fortune was hers alone.

Most of the servants never uttered a word about Verena's death either. After all, she led a life of extreme luxury for seventy-two years and was pampered by her late Papa and Hannes beyond anyone's imagination. It was well understood that Victoria was in every way a better replacement, though Anette had the vigor of a woman half her age and ran the place as if it were her own.

Philip's sons, at eighteen, were already their father's height and were known to be not only handsome, but also kind and never showing off their wealth. Paul had still not forgiven Gaby von Walden, though he never uttered a word. With her mother and brother, however, he was extremely polite, but Gaby never came along on any of their visits. While the three men were having a good time playing cards, Victoria and Anette shared their usual cup of tea. From time to time, however, both couldn't resist walking to the window and watching many of the wounded and crippled waving their red flags. Doubtless, they had returned from the war extremely disillusioned, reading and hearing about the revolution in Russia, not knowing that so far, it had brought them only death and misery.

"When I think back to just one year ago—and it is possibly a very selfish thought—nothing really happened which was to me of great signifance. Scanning my diary, I encountered mostly empty pages, omitting of course the on-going war. But we took only a belated trip to Berlin, and yes, America entered the war and yes again, Russia had an uprising... but this was all so far away and foreign to me. And without a loved one involved— I am almost ashamed to say that helping in the hospital or giving food away seems not quite enough!" Victoria uttered.

"You've done more than your share," Anette replied.

"When Paul mentioned that England now has new weapons called tanks, which run on tracks instead of wheels, I never thought of the damage and lives it would cost until Paul gave me all the facts," she answered quietly.

Both women were glad when Gisela interrupted. "You know, I was just thinking while watching the unruly and noisy crowd below us. In 1914, we were rather happy and waving cheerfully, believing by Christmas it would all be over."

"We remember. If we only knew then what we know now," Victoria replied sadly with a long sigh.

~

Several days later all headlines stated that America's President Wilson suggested fourteen points to end the war! Austria was number ten, where it put forth that the people of Austria-Hungary should have the right of autonomous development.

"Nicely said," Philip answered sarcastically. "It shows he is poorly informed, or he would know that Hungary, like everyone else, wants their own independence from us. In the end, we will be carved into little pieces. I hate to think of the outcome, as we depend on all those little countries for one thing or another; especially Hungary, our main food supplier."

"Well, Father, it will be the black marketers who will be profiting from all the misery. Thank God we don't depend on them," said Peter rather proudly.

"But let's not forget the millions who don't have it," reminded Philip, with everyone else present agreeing wholeheartedly.

~

Spring had arrived, all schools re-opened, and the factories worked overtime, while the unrest continued in every country that was involved in the war. One looked to a bleak future and hoped that one of these days the rumors would become reality. Victoria arrived from her daily activity at the hospital and was glad to find a stack of letters, which had doubtlessly been mailed weeks before. "I can't believe it!" she shrieked, after opening her daughter's letter first. "Elisabeth married that Dutchman, the last day of February!"

"So what?" Anette replied. "Holland is a neutral country. She may have a better future there than here."

"You should have seen that snobbish doctor! Actually, he was her teacher in Biology; twenty-two years older, bald, and even shorter than she!" Victoria fumed. "My mother never said a word about him at our visit last year when we met him. Even Gisela didn't like him," she tried to justify.

"Elisabeth was always her own woman and Lotte may not have known about it either," Anette replied with indifference.

That prompted Victoria to open her mother's letter quite nervously. "Well, well. Just as you suspected, Anette. It was a surprise to her too! I imagine they told her one week before, as it was a small civil ceremony with only two of their own friends as witnesses."

"As long as they love each other," Anette said calmly.

"Mother writes further, they will take a train to Amsterdam the moment she finishes her studies. She plans to do her residency in his city's hospital. Needless to say, he teaches there too and for the time being, they will live with his parents. I just cannot believe it!" she lamented, still shaken. "Well I should be grateful she let us know his name. It's Adam van Dreesen and I don't like it either. It's not a 'von' like in our nobility, possibly from a town called Dreesen, a suburb of Amsterdam."

"Nevertheless, Elisabeth van Dreesen sounds good to me, especially if she puts the title of 'Doctor' before it," Anette replied, rather pleased. In her opinion, Victoria never liked any of Gisela's suitors either.

"Wait until Philip hears about it!" Victoria tried to console herself.

But she got another surprise. Philip reminded her gently but firmly of all the opposition both of them had encountered, not only from her father, but also from his mother, who left her family for four years! 'As long as they love each other' came like an echo from him and Anette, who had uttered the very same words just a few hours ago. Gisela, however, was on her mother's side agreeing, that the doctor had behaved like a first-class snob towards everyone. Peter and Paul heard about it hours later, and while Peter admired his teaching profession at the Robert Koch University, Paul only shrugged, reminding them that Elisabeth cared only for knowledge in the field of medicine to begin with and let it go at that.

Victoria felt defeated but had no choice then but to write a letter of congratulations with no offer of an invitation to Vienna. To her great amazement, she received an eleven-page letter in return from Adam, writing about his own upbringing in Holland. Being the only son after six girls, he was for his parents the greatest joy, though a lot was expected of him. Three pages were devoted to his great love for Elisabeth, which had developed gradually, and he assured her that he had proposed only after he was absolutely certain. She was quite pleased with his frankness, and there was nothing she or anyone could do about it unless she was willing to lose Elisabeth.

The Kronthalers' mail had arrived too. Since there were three letters from her, she didn't know which one to open first, as the dates on the stamps were unreadable. The first letter stated that Ernst was extremely sick with influenza at a hospital in deplorable condition, as the sickness spread as fast as the plague. Then her oldest son Wilhelm was in a hospital for the blind! She hoped that at least her other son Ernst, Jr. would make it home, as so far, no letters had arrived the last four months. Otherwise, not a word about Kaiser Wilhelm, or how he dictated to Austria's new Emperor and their worn-out army, which, like his own, was ready to collapse. Of course, those ugly Frenchmen were responsible for her son's blindness, which once more aroused Victoria's wrath with a long sobering letter in return. At the time of the arrival, and Irma by now agreeing with her, her husband of almost forty years was dead. One more dead among the many thousand civilians who didn't even have to fight on the battle front.

Peter blamed all the misery on Russia and the Bolsheviks, knowing very little else to say, and Paul lamented that Germany's flying ace, the Red Baron, was shot down. "Germany's planes bombarded Paris by moonlight," he added, as if the war was only about technology.

One could still read in the daily newspaper that Germany had a new cannon called 'Big Bertha,' which shelled Paris again, killing over eight hundred civilians. Or that the Allies captured 40,000 Germans on one of those many battles on the river Somme. Aside from that, the Berliners trampled on posters of their Kaiser Wilhelm.

"That should give that bastard something to think about," Anette mumbled with a high fever as Paul read all the latest to her. He was astonished at her language but didn't think much about it as all tempers were high.

"You know, Anette, for the first time I believe the war will come to an end, simply because there is nothing left to fight," he replied, tip-toeing out of her room and re-telling Philip about the incident. "Well, it's Germany who asked America's President Wilson if they could stop now, mind you. 'Peace with honor.' Of course, America refused.

Astrid von Walden arrived looking quite distraught, with a telegram in her hand which stated that Colonel von Walden is among many other brave men declared as missing. She could and would never know that her husband had drowned while fleeing across the Italian river Piave, where 45,000 barely alive and exhausted Austrians who made that gruesome journey fell prisoner to the waiting Italians.

"Of course, I am so relieved that I decided to leave my children in Lausanne. My sister and brother-in-law insisted on it as many neutral countries started to take those half-starved children into their safe homes. Switzerland has stopped giving visas to foreigners for the moment, or they would have half of Europe to accommodate. On the other hand, I will never leave until my husband comes back, whenever that may be."

"Prisoners of the so-called 'missing' arrive on a daily basis, dear Astrid," Victoria soothed with Philip adding, "In all the commotion, he will show up sooner than you think." He hoped this was true for her and Andreas' sake, whom he truly liked, but felt sweat running down his back, feeling that if anyone would return it would be 'Bertie the pimp'!

"If I may, I'd like to pay Anette a little visit, as I don't plan to leave my house frequently with all those many demonstrations."

"By all means, Astrid. You know she thinks the world of you." Entering her room, they found a shivering and feverish Anette not recognizing anyone. Both women shrieked simultaneously. "Oh, dear Lord! She needs a doctor fast," Victoria cried, running to find Philip, who had just talked to Paul. He was confiding to his father that something was wrong with Anette, not wanting to alarm his mother. He ran to her room, got her in his car, and went to the hospital, but it was too late

"All of you take a hot bath in sulfur and do this quickly. The sick started to arrive by the hundreds and, the way I see it, it's just the beginning of the Spanish flu!"

Philip started to shake and couldn't suppress his feelings, with tears flowing in front of the physician. It was so unlike him, as he never even showed any emotion at his mother's death. Arriving at home with the sad news, it was not much different. Victoria and Astrid were in each other's arms, with the children in shock and unable to believe it.

"I just talked to her!" Paul stuttered, almost in a trance. We all loved her so much."

Only the servants bowed their heads slightly, out of the usual respect for the dead, but each of them had, by now, lost someone much dearer to their heart than old Anette, who only made sure the Reinhardt household ran smoothly.

Despite all the ongoing tragedy, Vienna's cafehouses, theaters, and even the opera house kept their doors open as usual. That was what Vienna wanted and needed.

~

Within a few weeks, between October and November, all former countries that entered the 'war to end all wars' had collapsed. Kaiser Wilhelm, the man mostly responsible for all the misery with more to come, went quietly with his family to Holland, like nothing had happened. Austria's Emperor Karl I had gone, by the end of October, to a small town in Hungary. After his peace proposal was rebuked by America, Austria became a Republic. One could find leaflets that read 'Down with Habsburg.' After all, they were co-instigators of a long, drawn-out war, disregarding the lives of millions, and made, like Germany, peace offers only after their empires were ready to collapse completely. On November 11, an armistice with Germany was signed, with Austria preceding them on November 3!

THE WAR WAS FINALLY OVER!

~

In front of Vienna's still elegant and timeless Hotel Imperial stood a few English officers, smiling while reading through their own newspapers that the war had ended. "How about that?" expressed one, "Now we can go home!"

Right after Anette's death, and without telling anyone, Philip went to Berlin to bring Victoria's mother to Vienna. He knew both felt all alone and needed each other desperately; Lotte, who doubtlessly missed Elisabeth, and his own wife with the loss of Anette. It was the least he could do, he felt strongly, as Berlin had become a battleground for civilians. Many new political parties made their entrance and, along with the rampant spreading of influenza, this was no place for an old lonely woman who had her own family in Vienna living so much better. Though both encountered many difficulties by changing trains so many times, their determination finally won out, as he made his entrance on the arm of Victoria's mother.

"Our Christmas present to each other… though a bit early," Philip stated to an extremely surprised and happy family.

"How can we ever thank you?" Victoria mumbled still in disbelief.

"Why the gratefulness, my dear wife? It is I who will never be able to repay you."

"For what?"

"For everything!" he answered, with a wink only she understood.

"I must have a bath to get four days of soot off me," he replied in jest.

"And that goes for me too," Lotte replied. "And then we will talk and talk and talk."

"Also eat and eat and eat," she heard the grandchildren laughing in unison.

At the first opportunity, Astrid von Walden was introduced to Lotte von Wintersberg. Both felt they were long, lost relatives, as each had heard so much about the other. Of course, Lotte years ago had her first lessons about the 'dreadful von Waldens' from Verena, and had then little choice but to endure her lengthy stories. Then came Christmas of 1914. Verena was hospitalized, and Lotte broke her hip and never traveled anywhere until Philip came to take her to Vienna. Their many changes from one unheated train to another would always stay on their minds, as it took almost four days to make it back. Now she, daughter Victoria, Astrid, and Mrs. Ruth Wertheim, who just celebrated Hanukkah, sat together forging a plan.

By now, many returning soldiers, who had expected to be rehired by their once noble families in Lindenfels, found out that the nobility as they had known it as former servants had ceased to exist. Vienna, Lindenfels, and the rest of Austria began to suffer what was referred to in many circles as 'a severe reduction complex'. The country was now only a seventh the size of its former empire, which dominated for six hundred and forty years under the Habsburgs' rule. Also, the once fifty-four million different ethnic groups shrunk to barely seven million, with a third living in Vienna. Austria evolved from a former giant to a little dwarf.

So far, only eight of the Reinhardts' thirty-five young, male servants had made it back. But they knew that many more would come. After all, only five weeks had passed since the peace treaty was signed. By now, Victoria and Lotte's plan created with the help of her friends Astrid and Ruth Wertheim took shape. The Reinhardts would open their castle in Lindenfels for the first time during the winter since the war started. Somehow, Philip would come up with coal or firewood for one or two days. It would give every returning soldier a chance to get not only a hearty meal, but Ruth Wertheim suggested clothing for those poor fellows who were still in their ragged uniforms. "We have lots of pants and jackets in supply as everyone wore only a uniform," she said, pleased.

The fact that some food may be made from *'ersatz'* wouldn't matter a great deal, as the volunteers from Lindenfels still had lots of the real stuff. By now, most of the Viennese were lucky to find a butcher who sold them horse meat. Jelly or jam was, for years, made from beets; saccharin replaced sugar; coffee was boiled from chicory and beets. Never mind the many ingredients the cooking oil was made of. Unless one went to the black market, one just did without it and stayed hungry and cold. But Lindenfels was in the country, and so far, everyone had survived quite well.

Victoria was pleasantly surprised when her three children volunteered, forsaking their traditional skiing trip. And all other Lindenfelsers were enthusiastic too, many asking to be part of this generous undertaking. It proved again to be a Reinhardt village who lived by the motto, 'To be noble, courageous, and brave'. All able soldiers from Lindenfels hospital were invited, who could make it out of their beds, along with any sons of Victoria's friends, and Philip suggested driving to the train station, where many lonely and tired men would be waiting for a train to take them home. Every station was overcrowded and unheated. Something had to be done.

~

No one in the newly formed Republic of Austria looked forward to a Christmas Eve with no exchange of gifts or even a Christmas tree. The midnight Mass was the only reminder of the holiday, and some Lindenfelsers would make sure that their skeptical and condemning priest would be well-informed beforehand about their act of kindness by inviting every reachable soldier for a good meal and a nice chat to show them that not all was lost. He mentioned it right from the pulpit, also inviting himself, as many brave soldiers may have doubted God's existence.

Astrid refrained from attending the Mass, always hoping her husband might just surprise her again. It wouldn't be the first time either. But the first surprise came in the early evening, with both Silvermans paying her a visit along with a large basket of baked goods while explaining their own holiday. "We hope you don't mind, but the baked goods are left over from Hanukkah."

"Why on earth should there be any difference? After all, we are worshiping the same Creator," she answered in delight. Gertrude also mentioned that she, too, would be at the Reinhardts' castle doing her little part, as there would be a lot of clothing from Martin. He only smiled, never one to give any opinion to a Gentile, although he admitted to himself that he hated being called a Jew.

Just as Astrid was ready to call it a day, having all those fine delicacies put in the cupboard, there were three knocks on her window. She opened it abruptly, only to encounter two men right below with one on crutches saying cheerfully, "Merry Christmas, Mother! May we come in? I brought a friend along and we can only stay for two hours."

Astrid didn't know if she should laugh or cry, run or stay. But given no choice, she simply opened the door, noticing a tall husky young man behind her son. While Bertram's two arms were held up by crutches, his friend was loaded with packages. "Good Lord, Bertram! You always knew how to surprise people. Please come in!"

"This is my buddy and lifesaver, Rupert Foster."

"So happy to meet you. Make yourself comfortable," she stammered while slowly regaining her composure, when Bertram stated frankly, "Of course, you would have been happier if father had surprised you, but such is life. He may be here in no time at all… believe me."

"He was declared missing, Bertram."

"Same thing, Mother," he replied. "Missing men are usually the prisoners who arrive on a daily basis. You'll see." Personally, he cared nothing if he ever saw his father again; however, his stepmother was very gullible.

"Where do you live?"

"In the ninth district near the general hospital."

"But that is quite a long way from here. With Andreas and Gaby in Switzerland, I have plenty of space here... please," she pleaded, looking at Bertram and Rupert and both knew she meant every word of it.

"My father will pick us up around eleven, Mrs. von Walden. He is glad to forsake the midnight Mass," he smiled. "He brought us with a sled, waiting to see if there was still a light on."

"So you knew where I lived! When did you arrive in Vienna?"

"Beginning of September, Mother, but I looked so bad. I didn't want to shock you, or the family, for that matter. I got seven of my toes frozen in 1917 and would have been dead if Rupert, who was a medic, didn't carry me out of this muddy ice hole. He carried me on his back to the next field hospital, which was not much warmer but had a bed and blankets, aside from doctors who amputated my toes." Astrid cried openly now. "Then I ended up in an overcrowded infirmary in Linz and I didn't want to write my family for many reasons."

"For heaven's sake, why not?"

"Father, for the main one. I just can picture him telling me that I was not strong enough to withstand a cold winter."

"Oh, Bertram. He would never say that!"

"Oh, no?" You never knew what was going on between us, Mother," he smirked sarcastically. "If you don't mind,

Mother, I'd like to relax and catch up on all the news… like why you sold the place in Lindenfels, although I am elated you did."

For the next two hours they talked until Astrid came to the subject of the money he was owed from the sale in Lindenfels. "Bertram, we owe you money and among other things, I'd like to get the very best of civilian doctors so you can get your balance back."

"Mother!" He smiled at her naïve suggestions. "No one can put seven toes back. In time I hope to walk with a cane. Considering that most of our buddies died, or lost two legs, or arm and legs, and never mind the many blind guys, I am a very lucky fellow."

She didn't know what to answer and directed the questions at Rupert. "And you, Mr. Foster?"

"I was even luckier; just got brushed with a bullet while carrying the wounded on a stretcher."

"That horrible, senseless war. It could have been avoided," she cried. "And as always, the responsible ones fled to safety and live comfortably like nothing ever happened." Both nodded in agreement.

"Mother, don't you want to open the gifts Rupert and I brought you and the children?"

"Oh," she stammered. "I assumed those were your belongings and you came to stay."

"I always had a place away from home, except for the few days before I entered the service in 1914," he replied. "Most of it's from Rupert's parents' grocery store."

"Well, you are lucky indeed," she smiled in awe, with Rupert helping her unwrap.

"Don't worry Mrs. von Walden. My parents hoarded their goods for years, or sold for Swiss francs only. Now we are heavy into the black market," he smiled like it was the only thing to do.

Astrid came to a large carton and looked in awe at the contents. "A very warm coat for you, Mother; pure wool and fur-lined. How about it? It will keep you warm."

"Oh, my God!" she stammered, slowly looking from one to the other.

"I'll get clothes for Andreas and Gaby after their return, but here, have some chocolate! And as for the money, Mother, keep it until I need it. Right now, I can give you Czech crowns, which are going up in value... and Swiss francs."

"No, no, Bertram. I have your inheritance in a Swiss bank in Lausanne, plus some hidden here."

"Keep it and let me take care of you for a change," he smiled proudly.

"What a turnaround," Astrid thought to herself. *"Just as I predicted. If only his father could see him; but then again he might not approve of the black market."*

"And if you get caught and arrested?"

"You are looking at a policeman without his uniform, Mrs. von Walden," Rupert answered, pleased.

"We work hand in hand with those poor returning and crippled soldiers, who have no chance of working anywhere and no way to feed their families. We owe nothing to our former empire. Now we are a Republic with dozens of parties trying to get the upper hand. Believe me, the worst is yet to come. Sooner or later, there will be a revolution," he finalized while handing her real coffee, butter and many other items she forgot still existed in Austria. She thought of her family in Switzerland and wondered if she should get her children back. But Rupert and Bertram predicted a revolution; like in Berlin and other cities, it could easily happen in Vienna. When both recognized the snow bells of the oncoming sled, Astrid insisted, for more than one reason, on meeting Rupert's father. The resemblance was astonishing, and she felt good about it, as Bertram had told the truth. She tried her coat on, with Bertram looking quite happy.

"We got your coat for sugar, rice and flour," he laughed aloud.

She explained about the big day in Lindenfels tomorrow for anyone who served the country, while thanking and squeezing him for the perfect fitting coat.

Both promised that they would try to be there, providing Rupert's father could enter this famous castle.

"But of course," she replied happily. "There will be hundreds of people there. Why should one more matter?"

Bertram, however, couldn't wait to see Philip Reinhardt's reaction, though he, himself, would pretend to meet him for the first time. He had never said a word to Rupert about his former life, only that he hated his father and lived with a friend. Rupert would have never understood, as he was still waiting to meet a pure girl.

~

Christmas Day turned out to be beyond everyone's expectations. It was a combination of 'good will towards men', and then becoming a festive and happy party, where most of the soldiers and officers experienced their first joyful event since entering the war. All of Lindenfels was represented by each family, regardless of whether or not they had lost a loved one. Even their own wounded sons were brought along to intermingle with the rest of the newly arriving soldiers, who came via ambulance, horse sleds, or any other available means, providing they were not able to walk with the help of nurses, who volunteered for a chance to see a great and well-known castle. The inhabitants of Lindenfels sent some of their servants with food and men's clothing. The servants were told to help with any chores Lotte and Victoria Reinhardt were in need of. They were only too happy to oblige, as they were so curious to see the inside of the castle they had heard so much about from their employers. The table setting was done strictly by the Reinhardt servants, as well as their regular chores. Every possible comfort, including chairs brought down from the attic, was thought of under the direction of Victoria and her newly and carefully chosen head housemaid, Mrs. Gerber. Since Anette's sudden death, she was the most qualified and respected one to take over, and had always been considered Anette's right hand helper.

So far, the surprise was the early arrival of Isaak Wertheim and the rest of the Wertheim family, who owned several clothing stores in Vienna. They were followed by their servants with boxes and armfuls of clothing. Then came Martin and Gertrude Silverman. He came reluctantly at his wife's insistence, though he, too, went in his closet to give suits away he hadn't worn for years, which was in every way unusual.

By noon, all rooms were filled almost to capacity and the mood was extremely joyful. Everybody talked to everybody and the three Reinhardt children, Peter, Paul, and Gisela, had the time of their lives. So many new and grateful faces was to their own liking. And as always, Gisela and a nice young man, who never spent a day on the battle front but helped his father with his prosperous boot factory, were equally smitten with each other. After all, she was not only a Reinhardt, but was very pretty and charming.

Philip, having the luck to get unlimited rations of gasoline, went to every given address to get a wounded soldier to his castle with greatest pleasure. Lotte von Wintersberg, Astrid von Walden, and Victoria were doing their utmost by greeting every arriving soldier, then turning them over to any waiting Lindenfelser to supply him with a chair and food. The Silvermans and Wertheims were busy finding the right size clothing for everyone, and even the elusive Martin seemed to enjoy himself listening to war stories.

"I don't believe it!" exclaimed Astrid quite loudly to Victoria. "There is my Bertram, along with his friend and father. They came after all. As I told you before, I doubted they would show up."

"Dear Lord, this must be Bertram on his crutches, but those two other ones carry so many packages they look like Santa Claus!" said Victoria.

"I told you all about my gifts," she replied, striding towards the trio.

She embraced Bertram very heartily but clumsily because of his crutches. Then she greeted Rupert and his father with their many stacked up packages. One could only see their eyes. Lotte was right behind her, showing them the large table where still more gifts and clothes were expected, as Philip also invited many doctors from Reinhardt's hospital, who had their day off. Astrid was glowing with pride, not only about Bertram's perfect mannerisms, but his appearance in a good suit. She introduced him to Lotte and Victoria.

"I regret deeply that I had not the pleasure to meet Miss Anette Essler," he uttered in a tone as though he knew her personally. "Mother's letters were always full of praise for this fine woman who changed our lives completely, along with you, dear Mrs. Reinhardt. I can only express a heartfelt thank you, and hope to meet your husband too." Then the two Fosters were formally introduced, and Victoria took it upon herself to introduce them to the Wertheims and Silvermans. Both families had not had a chance to leave their chosen places, as so many wounded soldiers were still in their ragged uniforms and trying to get some of the clothes.

"Mother," whispered Bertram. "I will stay right here with the Wertheims and Silvermans and plan to snub the rest of those hypocritical Lindenfelsers, as they snubbed us for many generations… and then some!"

"As you will in time notice, I planned to do the same!"

"The Wertheims were our only visitors as far as I can remember," Bertram replied.

"But I'd like for you to be very nice to the Silvermans. They are the ones whose house we live in. I have the feeling you will get along with him as he teaches art and history." It took no time at all for Martin Silverman to captivate Bertram while discussing ancient Rome.

Rupert and his father lost no time in opening carton after carton to hand out cigarettes, chocolate, fine biscuits made in Switzerland, along with writing paper, pencils, and envelopes that already had stamps on them. Each soldier got this with a hearty handshake and thanks for fighting in the war. Even the Lindenfelsers gave both men a hearty ovation while every soldier stood up. It was quite a moving moment and Bertram lost no time in telling Martin Silverman the story of how he and Rupert met on the battlefield. After the boxes were almost empty, Victoria put a servant in charge so every newly arriving soldier would get his fair share. Victoria gave both Fosters the opportunity to see the castle and give a bit of its history, which both never expected but enjoyed immensely.

Peter and Paul also joined the group in their conversation, with a Reinhardt servant keeping their table supplied with food and refreshments. The Lindenfelsers had a great time among themselves, as each one made the many arriving soldiers comfortable and exchanged stories about their own sons, who were either dead or still missing. All others who returned were presently enjoying themselves, too. Gisela was next to her newfound love, Wolfgang Burgdorf. He was highly educated and one of four sons from the well-known leather goods firm, who had stores in many districts of Vienna, and were considered very prosperous even before the war. Three of his brothers entered the war with two known to be prisoners in Italy and were expected home soon. One was still recuperating in Tyrol. As in so many cases, including the Reinhardts, they had had to convert their factories to many items needed in the war and from shoes, handbags, and belts, they made boots and other parts for the soldiers to wear, and that included saddles and packs for horses, which made them enormously rich. Their isolation and tête-a-tête conversation was not long overlooked, and rumors began to spread that Gisela was in love again! Victoria, after hearing about it, answered smilingly that it would last only a short while, like all her previous flings. To herself she thought, *"She's her father's daughter."*

Rupert looked at his watch, reminding his father of the time and went to Bertram to do the same. Martin Silverman was clearly disappointed at his early departure, but Bertram replied with a big smile, "May I remind you that we live in your house, just a few stairs below you?"

Martin's expression showed that he had completely forgotten. "Serves me right. Each time I discuss history, I am not accountable for anything else."

With a laugh and a promise of a visit, Bertram and Rupert, along with his father, started to leave when Astrid intercepted them. "Wait a minute, Bertram. Mr. Reinhardt just arrived with two wounded soldiers and has given orders to do everything possible for them. It was his last trip." She moved to introduce the two men. "Mr. Reinhardt, my son and his friends are on their way home, but I want you to meet Bertram, his friend Rupert, and—" Astrid began as Victoria made her way towards them.

"You have no idea how happy those gentlemen made our soldiers with cigarettes, chocolates, and many other things," Victoria interjected. "Many, many thanks!"

Philip's legs were shaky when he looked at Bertram, who pretended to have met him for the first time.

"Glad to meet you, Mr. Reinhardt. We heard how busy you were in fetching our war buddies from every direction. We all are overwhelmed by your hospitality."

"It was a pleasure, Mr. von Walden," was all Philip could come up with and he thanked the Lord that all three were in a hurry to leave.

"Philip, please rest now. You look exhausted and the whole thing was a great success."

"I agree with your wife, Mr. Reinhardt. You need some rest."

"I couldn't agree with both of you ladies more," he replied, almost wobbling to a chair.

"Bring Mr. Reinhardt some tea with rum, please," Victoria said kindly to one of her servants, who worked extremely hard but very cheerfully.

"Good Lord! The way I see it, there must be at least five hundred guests here!" he muttered, elated but his thoughts were with 'Bertie the pimp,' who had made it back just as he feared.

"You have no idea how surprised I was last night, Mr. Reinhardt," Astrid commented, informing him in detail about everything. "He is a completely changed human being," she added proudly. "Although he never tells me why on earth he doesn't want to live with me with so much space."

"He may in time," Philip answered, somewhat calmer after taking her stories into consideration. Somehow, he didn't trust him, but there was nothing he could do about it. He had the same handsome features, though he was considerably shorter than his father, from whom he inherited the light blonde, wavy hair, and gray, piercing eyes with extra-long and heavy lashes. That, along with flawless skin, were his best assets. It was only natural to have chosen a friend like Rupert, to whom he looked up like a protecting big brother.

Especially after the loss of the main supporting toes, as his balance would be forever gone.

Astrid had told Philip about his condition in the presence of his wife, and now he wondered seriously if or when he should tell her about their encounter at Breuners? After some soul searching, he decided to wait, as it also involved Astrid, who had not the slightest idea and appeared to be quite happy about his supposed change for the better. With the pleasant day behind them, they arrived home in great spirits. Victoria suggested a long rest for Philip who looked quite tired. The boys were packing for the next day's skiing trip and Gisela mentioned happily that Wolfgang had invited himself, which caused the family only to smile, with Lotte's remark of what a nice young man she found in all the tumult.

"He is from Burgdorf's leather firm."

"So what?" retorted Peter.

"So, he is not after the Reinhardt money," Gisela replied curtly.

Victoria was also tired but very pleasantly so and, giving only a smile, said, "It turned out so much better than I thought. Many thanks to all of you. And I have never seen Astrid happier, with Bertram's return in the company of such nice and generous people." All agreed, including Philip who was still quite worried.

~

It was an entirely different Christmas in Switzerland. Their citizens were convinced that God loved their country very much, and therefore gave them neutrality. It was one way to see their luck.

Having been in Lausanne and entrusted to their caring relatives, Aunt Ingrid and Uncle Henry, since the beginning of July, Andreas and Gaby had escaped the downfall of the once proud Empire. According to all the newspapers and all the newly arriving children whose faces showed a combination of hunger and misery, the aftermath of the war was even worse, let alone the so-called spread of Spanish flu, which, in time, took the lives of millions.

When both children read about the sudden death of Anette, they had cried bitterly and hoped their own mother, along with the kind Reinhardts, would be spared. Neither Ingrid nor Henry showed any reaction, other than telling them the flu befell mostly the old ones. Aunt Ingrid's interests were always of a different nature. Shortly after their arrival, she enrolled Andreas and Gaby in one of the best private schools and, although they didn't start until the middle of September, there were tutors for every possible subject, considering that Austria's schools were, due to the war and closing many weeks due to the shortage of coal, far behind. There were also lessons in ballet and piano. Andreas played violin and needed gymnastic lessons, never mind all their household chores, so that their playtime was limited to two hours at the most.

Andreas walked to the nearby soccer field where the Swiss boys were glad to have an aggressive newcomer, and Gaby spent her playtime with the Rosattis' mongoloid boy, Eugen, who, after taking the first look at her, smiled happily. One reason was that she always thought of new little games he was able to participate in.

Alfredo and Isabella Rosatti owned a famous Italian restaurant in the main business district. She would spend the morning hours there, overseeing every detail, leaving nothing to chance. Her own household consisted of a maid and an old, but kind nurse for Eugen. The cooking was done by her. It was quite a different matter with the Lebruns. His dental practice was within walking distance from his residence and Ingrid, having the advantage of attending one year of finishing school in Lausanne, ran the household by herself like clockwork. Once a month, a couple would take care of the windows and rugs. The beautiful rose bushes surrounding both villas were her hobby and the Rosattis were glad she included theirs too.

Alfred Rosatti and Henry Lebrun's villas had, at their front view, very little space, but both families bought their places, although three years apart, for their oversized backyards, which were only separated by short hedges. They knew each other previously and developed over the years a very close friendship. Both houses had large French doors leading to identical patios, surrounded by Ingrid's roses. The rest of the yard was still a playground, but only Gaby and seven-year-old Eugen took advantage of it. It consisted of a large sandbox, a seesaw, and a swing set. Throwing balls was started quite frequently, but as Eugen never caught one, he brought her the jumping rope instead, as he was fascinated at her performance and applauded each time. It was no surprise that the Rosattis were overjoyed at Andreas and Gaby's one-year stay, regardless of whether their parents returned. It all depended on Austria's situation.

With several weeks of school behind them, the rhythm was not very different from their own private school in Vienna, with the exception that only French was spoken. Since they spoke it in all their years of visits, aside from learning it at their own school, there were not too many problems.

The Rosattis, who came from the south of Switzerland and spoke Italian among themselves only, were more than happy to help with their language, and being Austrian, their German was flawless, with many students asking for either Andreas' or Gaby's help. Their first report cards were outstanding, with a note adding that their behavior was excellent. Andreas was sure he wanted to be a Doctor of Medicine, and had, at fifteen, the great advantage to be tutored by Lucas Rosatti, who, at twenty-one, had three years of medical school behind him. And Uncle Henry, in whose profession he saw only a man who pulled or filled teeth, proved nevertheless to be very useful in answering every one of his many questions. But in Lucas Rosatti he saw a scientist, and his admiration for him knew no bounds.

Gaby still envisioned herself as a ballerina, but after seeing Swan Lake, Giselle, and Sleeping Beauty she changed her mind. She had dreamed of being the principal dancer but upon hearing of their serious training hours, she settled on becoming a piano teacher. During the winter months, swimming and tennis were replaced with Latin and endless hours on the skating rink to practice the required figures of a perfect three and eight. So far, skiing was considered only fun.

By the time Christmas arrived, Andreas and Gaby were greatly surprised to receive skis and all the necessary clothing with them. Lebrun and Rosatti were already informed about the children's missing father months previously, but were told not to breathe a word, knowing how upset they would be. Both families never met the officer, but after folding Astrid's note, they only replied to each other that he was, after all, a professional. But Astrid got a nice letter of hope in return. Lucas, after being told in secrecy, was very sorry. He, like the rest of the two families, loved Astrid, not only for being Ingrid's sister, but because she never complained or said a bad word about anyone and was only filled with good thoughts, despite the many hardships she had to endure by marrying a poor Baron.

Lucas went every year during Christmas vacation to ski in the Alps. Mountains relaxed him, be it climbing or skiing. But at present, he was asked by his parents if he could spare one day and take Andreas and Gaby on a smaller mountain to ski. It would be an exception, as Gaby was by far not as skilled as Andreas since he had started at a much earlier age. Their parents taught them like most Viennese at the nearby Vienna woods, but tomboy Gaby was unpredictable, always trying to out-do her brother. However, Lucas skied at difficult slopes, where Andreas could only fantasize about it. "Andreas," Lucas asked kindly. "My parents have suggested we three go skiing. They feel sorry for Gaby to be left out. Both of our families have older people over each year for dinner. Gaby and you have never met them and would only be bored."

Andreas was elated. "Why should I mind? I feel so honored to be asked after hearing you have skied for thirteen years. In comparison, my sister and I are pupils!"

Lucas smiled humbly, but was very, very happy. Gaby would be near him!

"I'll bet your parents feel sorry for us. We have everything a skier would need, but we wondered if we could ever use them while in Lausanne."

"Trust me," Lucas promised. "We will ski quite often if I can help it."

Andreas' face glowed with excitement. It was one thing to ski on hills, but quite another with a skilled man like Lucas in Switzerland. "I may sound like a sly fox, but if we tell my aunt that those trips will be lessons, she will give us permission. She is determined that Gaby and I excel in anything we do," Andreas concluded.

Lucas was overjoyed at his plan, knowing it would work with Ingrid and he could be near Gaby. Though he felt ashamed to admit it to himself, Lucas was hopelessly in love with Gaby, who just turned thirteen in July. However, he knew and had loved her since he saw her first at the age of three, when she was the cutest toddler he had ever encountered. She had almost demanded that the eleven-year-old Lucas carry her on his broad shoulders or push her on the swing set. The seesaw was shared between Andreas and herself. After the end of their summer vacation, he always felt sad and lonely. Now the tall, but very shy young man was neither handsome nor ugly. His strong physical appearance was his greatest asset, but his light tanned skin left much to be desired. His black hair was curly, and his dark brown eyes seemed to be far away. But as a future doctor, not too many girls would have turned him down, but then again, he had never even dated, let alone given any indication of contemplating marriage, whenever asked by his relatives in sunny Locarno, where the Italian-speaking Swiss marry very young.

When Astrid brought her two children for their vacation, she usually stayed a week with her sister. But this time she was told that her friend Isabella Rosatti had a new baby which was quite special. She also asked her never to give any indication that the little boy was a mongoloid. The year was 1911. Gaby had just turned six. And the eight-year-old Andreas, after having seen the child, declared again that he wanted to become a doctor, as he had seen several mongoloids in Vienna, each being led by a nun.

"How strange," his aunt said solemnly. "That is exactly what our neighbors' son, Lucas, said." Being fourteen, he had no sense of direction except to study the next few years, as he never wanted to work at his father's noisy restaurant with lots of people. Therefore, his preference was pathology, as it meant spending all his time in a laboratory.

After Gaby took the first look at him, she became very attached to Baby Eugen and by watching her caring for him, though still in a cradle, Lucas became even more smitten with her kindness. He wished his many thoughts would fade away and he would get her out of his mind. But with each yearly encounter, he loved her even more. As far as Lucas was concerned, he had never seen a more radiant, beautiful girl, with flawless skin, bright blue eyes and flaxen blond hair. She was truly a sight to behold. And now at thirteen she could have easily passed for fifteen, but was fully unaware of it. Her walk, too, was light and straight, on which even the forever critical Aunt Ingrid commented, but gave Gaby's twice a week ballet lessons the credit for, as she did with her great improvement in skating. And now Lucas had a chance to take her skiing, but more than that, be near her for a whole day. It was only a two-hour train ride and was considered *the* mountain for many skiers from Lausanne.

The following summer, Astrid made her yearly visit, but also to tell the children their father may be somewhere in prison and was the previous year declared missing.

"He will be back, Mama," consoled Andreas, but Gaby took the news very seriously, went into her room and wept. Ingrid asked if the poor children could stay another school year and Astrid was very glad to oblige after seeing both so very relaxed and happy. Astrid confessed that after being so alone with Hermine and having nothing else to do than wait for her husband's return, a depression had set in and the Wertheims suggested typing and some secretarial skills and they would be only too happy to hire her.

It was Bertram who brought her a typewriter so she could also practice at home. Six months later, she worked in Wertheim's bookkeeping department and started to enjoy life again. She felt wanted and needed. It took her barely twenty minutes with the trolley and should her husband make it back, Hermine would call the store. Now she had her first week of vacation and sat with her sister Ingrid, discussing the future of Andreas and Gaby.

She elaborated on those many political fights and demonstrations, which after a year in peaceful surroundings could have a very negative effect. Never mind all the risk on their way to and from school. So, one year longer was agreed upon, making everyone involved happy… especially Lucas who had already forged a plan. Astrid talked endlessly about Bertram's great change, how kind he was supplying her with anything she wished. She also mentioned Foster's kindness. "That lovable Bertram just gives and doesn't even take a franc from his inheritance." But Henry and Ingrid knew that one of these days he would collect.

1920

7

"*Lucas will be a* Doctor of Medicine in a year," the visiting Rosattis said with great pride, as he was the first one in their family to have something accomplished other than a Chef of Cuisine in France or Italy.

"I plan to take my residency in Vienna," he replied, matter-of-factly.

"Wonderful!" Astrid applauded.

"You can even stay with us. I have an unused guestroom as Bertram lives with the Fosters."

"I'll think about it," he said nonchalantly. "It will all depend on the travel distance, as I will send my resume to the Wilhelminer Hospital."

"Whatever is right for you, Lucas, but you are more than welcome."

The Rosattis thanked her, knowing he wouldn't be lonesome in a big city, despite those long hours of practice and study. Only Gaby somehow changed, feeling certain that her father was dead. From a happy tomboy, she had turned to a sad, young, but still beautiful girl.

The year of 1919-1920 went by much too quickly. Aunt Ingrid tried to give even more lessons while switching other ones. But by school's end in July, the Lebruns and Rosattis agreed on a month vacation together before bringing the children and Lucas to Vienna. The Rosattis insisted on showing Andreas and Gaby where they lived and went to school in Locarno, and the children fell in love with the little and large towns on Lake Maggiore. Andreas and Gaby considered those places, surrounded by palms and the great variety of southern shrubs and flowers in every possible color, more beautiful than Lausanne or Geneva.

They had to take little Eugen along, who had turned nine, but looked like five and was only interested in holding Gaby's hand. He spoke as much as expected, but many children, seeing for the first time a boy like him, kept on staring with a certain grin or smirk which didn't go unnoticed by the Rosattis, but made no difference to Gaby. At Alfredo's and Isabella's place, the boy would mostly stay inside, or if lucky, played in a small backyard. To take him to Vienna was out of the question and all arrangements to keep him in Locarno were made well beforehand.

~

The Rosattis had never seen Vienna, but were not particularly impressed until Astrid and the children took them sightseeing. The Lebruns went to the health spa of Baden but when they returned, they complained that Austria was falling apart and if it weren't for their Swiss francs, they would have starved, never mind getting a beautiful room in a first-class hotel. After one week, the Lebruns and Rosattis were ready to go home, and both families felt sorry for Andreas and Gaby but wouldn't dare to ask Astrid to take them back again.

The Reinhardts were in Salzburg and the Silvermans in Tyrol, so Astrid had no chance to introduce them to any of her friends except to show them the Wertheim store where she worked, but the owners were with the Silvermans in Tyrol, too. They did get to meet Bertram and his friend, but were not overly impressed, regardless of his friendly manner. Rupert was their favorite, despite Astrid's effusive praising of Bertram.

"Hello, Andreas. Gosh have you grown the last six years." Andreas smiled sweetly, but his reaction was only "Glad you noticed."

He could deceive anyone with his look at Gaby. "Isn't she beautiful?"

"Thank you, Bertram. I try not to let it go to my head," she replied.

"Well, every young man in Locarno and Lausanne was of the same opinion," Isabella Rosatti said.

The Lebruns and Astrid felt very flattered but kept quiet. Their mother was pleased that both of her children inherited the best features from their parents and Ingrid believed that without education and perfect mannerisms, beauty alone is a bore. All kept smiling except Lucas. He was seething with jealousy since he left Locarno, and now in Vienna it started to be the same all over again. Gaby was his and his alone. He disliked Bertram the moment he laid eyes on him, and Bertram told Rupert after their short visit, that he reminded him of an undertaker. But Bertram had long ago forged a plan after seeing the arriving photos from Lausanne. But like everything else in his life, he kept it to himself. He never trusted a single soul, and with Rupert, he only told him what he wanted him to know as it was the best way to handle him.

~

Andreas and Gaby were blessed with the talent of quick adjustment. Despite the big change in Vienna, they felt right at home and admired the many new items the late Anette left for Astrid in her will. Their former school friends made them very welcome, as they had grown taller but were otherwise the same. It was an open secret that if anyone wanted to survive, one went to the black market, providing one had foreign money, as the Austrian crown became less valuable by the day. Therefore, neither Astrid nor the children felt bad when Bertram and Rupert brought them any goods. Rupert was always in uniform and Gaby found him very handsome. Bertram developed the habit of calling Andreas 'brother' and Gaby 'sister', always adding how happy he was to have a family. His father was never mentioned, and Astrid asked her children to do the same.

By now, all the vacationing families had returned and resumed their daily routine. Four-year-old Anna Silverman seemed to remember Gaby as she gave her a big hug. The only change occurring since their departure was in the Wertheim household. Martin Wertheim's brother sent his son for two years to Vienna's Academy of Fine Arts to learn drawing. He also spent some time at the store to learn the quality of different kinds of silk, wool, and cotton, which came ironically from his father's department store in New York. Needless to say, it was never sold, but only bartered among their Jewish friends.

The boy's name was Samuel, but everyone called him Sam. When introduced to Bertram, they conversed about art but both knew immediately that Sam was also looking for girls. That was no problem, as never before were more women available to be easily had. There was a great shortage of men, as many were either dead or otherwise crippled. Bertram turned from time to time to 'Bertie the Pimp' and returned to his former place. Mr. Breuner was, therefore, very elated to be introduced to Sam, the American client, where a few dollars represented a fortune. He assured him that Sam would be in the best of hands.

Bertie also learned that Philip Reinhardt never returned, but was informed that he visited new places for his own pleasure. Presently Vienna's morals were at their lowest point, but for some reason the girls never looked prettier.

Sam mixed his art classes with Breuner's, knowing Wertheim would never suspect a thing. Bertram would comment from time to time that "some people are just plain gullible." Otherwise, Fosters suited his lifestyle, with Rupert being the best friend he ever had, and his work was a pleasure. But deep in his heart, he had a master plan, though it would take time and the right opportunity.

Astrid was, as usual, invited to the Reinhardts' and was told not only to bring her own two children but their friend from Lausanne too. Gaby accepted the invitation this time after hearing that Paul had studied in Zurich.

"Mrs. Reinhardt is quite a lonely woman now with three of her children gone."

"But the Reinhardts have so many friends," protested Gaby.

"I would call them rather 'acquaintances', but be that as it may, many died and for many, life has changed completely for the worse. As I said, Elisabeth, the oldest, is a Doctor of Medicine, married to one, and on the way to Nairobi, Africa."

"Wow!" said both, surprised.

"They will work as missionaries, as it was their plan as soon as they met in Berlin."

She sat thinking of Gisela. "Gisela, the second oldest, has nothing but bad luck with men. She decided to live with her grandmother and stay in Berlin."

"Berlin?" interrupted Andreas. "It is the worst place for a lady like her. That city has almost more fights and uprisings than all others in Europe combined. Every newspaper writes about it."

"Well, Andreas, they don't live in the middle of the city like the Reinhardts do. The outskirts and suburbs are quiet."

"But they all are starving and breaking benches to get firewood!" he said, almost out of breath.

"Not a Reinhardt! They always manage with foreign money quite well."

"Oh," he sighed, feeling relieved.

"Peter is in the second year of medical school and is doing quite well."

"Gosh, mother! In time we will only know doctors. Lucas is one already, and Peter Reinhardt and I are future ones," Andreas concluded, when the doorbell rang and there stood Lucas.

"We were just talking about doctors," Gaby exclaimed happily. "And there you are! The only real one we know." She chatted away while leading him to the parlor.

"Hello, Dr. Rosatti," Astrid greeted him with a slight embrace.

Andreas shook his hand heartily and came right to the point. "Gaby and I just wondered if we still can call you Lucas."

"And why not?"

"Mother just called you 'Dr. Rosatti'."

"I will change that in a hurry, as she knew me as a boy too."

"Never mind. There is a difference. We are older and it's only proper."

"We'll talk about it some other time, Baroness von Walden," he teased. I came here to tell you that I have four tickets for Saturday night at the opera."

As always Gaby jumped. "What is the title?" from Andreas, equally excited.

"Puccini's 'Madame Butterfly.'"

"Great!" all said in unison.

They all drank hot chocolate and were, as always, glad to see him. Bertram, however, gave him the impression of an actor on a stage. He was, in Lucas' opinion, a permanent performer. Once again, their dislike was mutual. Bertram would always refer to Lucas as 'the funeral director'.

Astrid told him they were invited to the Reinhardts' for the upcoming Sunday afternoon and mentioned how anxious their son Peter was to meet him, as he too was a student of medicine, hoping to be a surgeon like his grandfather, Hannes Reinhardt. He gladly agreed as, so far, he hadn't met anyone he liked in particular at Wilhelmina's hospital.

Philip and Victoria were elated to see the von Walden children again, telling them how much they had grown. Philip avoided saying how beautiful Gaby was for fear Victoria might take it wrong. And Peter, after having said his welcome back to Vienna, was very pleased to meet Dr. Lucas Rosatti, knowing how excellently the school in Lausanne taught its students. But Vienna, despite the aftermath of the war, was not far behind. Lucas thought of taking an extra year in the University for pathology. He knew his parents wouldn't oppose him, as most hospital administrators come from the line of pathology. Andreas was somehow proud to be with Lucas after noticing how impressed Peter was by his humbleness, and Lucas had never entered a palace previously with so much sincere friendliness.

Peter directed his first question to Andreas. "I heard you will soon join my school."

"Next year. I cannot wait, as I have wanted to be a surgeon ever since I was a little boy."

Lucas laughed. "He already has lots of training behind him. His uncle is a dentist but knows more about medicine than most family doctors."

"The best I got from you, Lucas. You are a born teacher and have the born patience to go with it."

Lucas only shook his head with a humble gesture. Philip, watching with pleasure how well those three fellows got along, suggested room service for the three of them, feeling they wanted to chat as much as possible among themselves.

Victoria was especially happy about Peter, who seemed to be, at times, very lonesome with Gisela now gone too. "Well then, I have the honor to dine with three beautiful ladies," Philip smiled, taking a seat among them.

Lucas was still more dumbfounded when he entered Peter's room, who had the door wide open to his study, with another one slightly ajar that was doubtless his bedroom. His so-called 'rooms' had more space than Rosatti or Lebrun's entire villas, he thought, and he was equally astonished about his easy-going manner. The study had a skeleton and an enormous amount of books, some of them dating back to when the study of medicine started. They could talk enough about it even while they ate, and Andreas was relieved to hear that he could spend extra time as long as Lucas brought him back.

"I am afraid for the boy all alone after dark. Those fellows with their red armbands even make me nervous during the day."

"Me too," Victoria agreed. "They call themselves the 'Reds', 'Communists', 'Social Democrats', you name it. As with the war, it all has to end one day."

"Mrs. von Walden?" Philip asked kindly just before leaving. "I hope you will give your son permission to visit with Peter, time permitting that is. Without Paul and Gisela, he feels very much alone. Somehow, he has not taken to many students to call them friends, but I observed that both of our boys like each other."

"I don't object if he gets a safe passage home. As I stated, we live in dangerous times."

"You may be assured of that," Victoria interjected, and asked why they have never seen Bertram again.

"Oh, he is still the same as far as timing is concerned; comes for one or two hours with this friend, brings us things he gets from the black market. I know it sounds horrible, but our money is almost worthless, so I give him Swiss francs," she smiled.

Philip was extremely relieved but still cautious.

1922

8

1922 was here and the time had come for quite a few changes. Lucas finished his extra studies and both von Walden children were to arrive for their usual vacation in Lausanne. Lucas hoped that during the summer he could tell Gaby how much he loved her.

He had talked the previous year with his father about it, but was advised to wait, as the girl was only sixteen. Also, there was no other indication than that she saw him only as a good friend with whom she had grown up. He suspected, however, that the plea for an extra year in Vienna to study was in one way connected to be near Gaby. Now Gaby would be seventeen, and with her exceptional beauty, she was not only stared at in Locarno the previous year, but he noticed, not without jealousy, that Vienna was now not much different. He was afraid that even Peter Reinhardt, with whom she had a lot of fun at every opportunity, might just sweep her off her feet. So, July was to be the month for him and the thought that she might turn him down caused him many sleepless nights.

July brought changes to some other families he had the fortune to get to know better. The Wertheims left for France to meet his brother in LeHavre, tour a bit of the country together, and spend some time in Vienna before he took his son Samuel home. He had graduated and they were very proud of him. The Reinhardts' son, Paul, was returning from Zurich's prestigious university, but would meet his family, as usual, in Salzburg. The Silvermans would spend this year's vacation in Italy. Little Anna was six by now and ready to travel. So, with everyone out of the way, Bertram saw that his long anticipated opportunity had come to pass.

The families would leave and the graduates celebrate; except Astrid of course, who considered Bertram more of a son than the reserved Andreas, who spent most of his free time with the Reinhardts and Lucas. Gaby developed a very nice friendship with a girl named Renate Steger, whose father was her piano teacher, and both girls dreamed of playing on the stage. The rumor in Vienna was that new money would make its entrance soon and the black market would be disappearing.

"Mother dearest," said Bertram in his most sweet and pleading voice. "Can Gaby come with me to Sam's graduation party? He invited lots of nice, young people. She may even meet someone interesting!"

"Well, the Wertheims are in France, but I am sure you and Sam can be trusted. But bring her home no later than eleven."

"*Eleven?*" he acted surprised. "I'll have my sister home no later than ten."

"Alright. That is even better, as I'll be back from my prayer meetings by then. Andreas is going to be at the Borgner's party. Their oldest son graduates from law school. I set no time limits on him at his age. Lucas is at a small dinner at his professor's house. He abhors a noisy crowd. Besides, in two days he will be leaving, taking Andreas and Gaby with him to Lausanne."

"Like I always said, Lucas should be an undertaker or funeral director," he smiled wickedly.

"Oh, it's not that bad! The kids have always had a great time with him."

He never gave any reply as his mind was occupied with other matters. Gaby was not the biggest hurdle, and his stepmother would by now believe anything. After all, it took three years of acting to convince her he could be trusted with everything. But it was Rupert he was mostly worried about until they arrived at their destination. They told Rupert's parents that both would attend a big weekend rally in the blue-collar worker town of Steyr. He never mentioned any of his other carefully laid out plans. And to make it appear very sincere, he would tell him his life story, which was just one more lie. Both belonged to the Communist Party and their former war buddies wrote to each other regularly, but mostly to Bertram who was always full of new ideas, which Rupert lacked. They planned to open their headquarters in Steyr, with Bertram as their leader because he had the will to do it, the money they needed for it, and the willingness to leave Vienna for good. Rupert's parents wondered why they would choose to leave on the late train, change in a small town called Grein, and wait until midnight for the next one.

That little non-descript village was known for its vortex, which was quite an awesome sight. This whirling mass of water and air could be admired from a bridge with a heavy, safe guardrail, still making quite a few onlookers dizzy. When Rupert was recovering from his wounds in the hospital in Grein, his parents had come for a visit, and called it a whirlpool, which could suck you in if you were not careful.

"Rupert is on duty and we will certainly see it on our return trip." The Fosters had been satisfied with Bertram's reply.

So far, everything was going according to plan and Sam, whose only wish before his return to New York was to go to bed with Gaby, would get his wish at his party. After all, among a big crowd of students, a few heavily spiked drinks, and six bedrooms upstairs, it should not be too much of a problem.

Bertram brought Gaby to Wertheim's villa at eight, with the promise to fetch a few more girls from her school. That suited her fine as, after the proper introduction, she felt lost and was almost ready to leave. But then drinks and all kinds of fine food were served by a hired waiter. Wertheim's servants left, as always, at seven, completely unaware of an impending party. More and more young people arrived but she looked in vain for Bertram with his promised friends of hers, as he claimed it would be a surprise.

Bertram was already on his way to the Fosters' to pack a few things for the weekend and arrived simultaneously with Rupert, still in uniform, but off duty for the next three days. Rupert was looking forward to the trip and had packed the previous day, knowing he would have to help Bertram. Although he used only a cane and had special shoes made, he had never acquired the balance to stay upright without anything to hold on to. Rupert got used to it, and as a friend, he didn't mind.

Bertram ordered a taxi to have plenty of time for the train station and as Rupert helped with the suitcases, he found Bertram's quite heavy. "What in the hell did you pack?"

"I'll tell you on the train." It was first-class of course, as they wanted privacy.

"Rupert," he began the moment the train began to move. "I have a lot to tell you and hope you will understand and still be my friend." He started with his gloomy childhood, which was caused by his father's hatred and physical abuse, his different reform schools, and his job as a pimp at Breuners. Rupert listened while giving from time to time a sorrowful nod, as he knew of many cases very similar in his line of work.

He was just about to compliment him on his turnaround and the love for his family he supported through all those meager years, when Bertram started to tell him the rest of the story, without the slightest sign of guilt or remorse on his grinning face.

"Let me tell you Rupert, for Gaby I collected from Sam three hundred dollars. He wanted her in the worst way, as he had never bedded a virgin. Herbert Blumenfeld gave me 500.00 Czech crowns and Abbe Koch was only too happy to give me 300 Swiss francs, as both don't care whom she had before. It's all in our suitcases, and we are going to live like kings in France each time you visit me, because of course, I can never go back to Vienna, and I mean never. Therefore, I decided to stay in Steyr under a different name that only you and your family will know, as I can trust all of you. I left mother a goodbye note under her pillow with some money, though she is still in the possession of my inheritance. But I don't need a damn thing from a von Walden. That name is, as of tomorrow, gone for good. I guess I was always generous to her because she gave birth to Gaby," he smirked.

With the dim light bulbs above them, Bertram couldn't notice how Rupert's face had turned white and his heart was pounding as never before in his life. How he wished he had a gun to shoot Bertram at the next station like an attacking mad dog. But now, his thoughts went even further. If he is capable of selling his lovely innocent sister, aside from leaving his trusting family along with Gaby to live in shame, sooner or later it will also spread from the district to their schools. And there was Lindenfels, who hated those von Waldens, according to Bertram. Wertheim will be the first one to know it, with Sam blaming everything on 'Bertie the Pimp'. Now his mother's anguish, Gaby's ruined reputation at school, and Andreas' name at the University! Once more the von Waldens are finished... and once more Bertram was the villain. He was a man without any conscience, which was, according to Rupert's training, the most dangerous kind. But he couldn't lose his temper yet; just question him calmly and set a trap.

"Bertram… after all you have told me—and it shows me a different kind of man than I have never known in all these years—" He paused, watching Bertram's uneasiness. "how do I know that once we arrive in Steyr, there is not a pack of low-down scum like yourself waiting to take both of the suitcases, give me a merciless beating, and let me fend for myself? You insisted that we not wear our red badges, though Vienna is referred to as the Red City and we go to a communist rally?"

"We travel first class," he interrupted uneasily. "You have gone crazy, Rupert. Your whole facial expression has changed. I am really hurt by your accusation."

"You? Hurt?" You have enjoyed that sort of life and I wonder how you got to know Sam so well."

"Mother works for the Wertheims' store."

"But you and I never went there, unless you were his pimp while I was on duty."

"Alright, so I introduced him to my former boss."

"For money, I assume?"

"Why not? Sam brought Herbert and Abbe—all very wealthy Jews. He made plenty of money. Hell, I am not a charitable organization. I take it from whomever I can get it."

"And don't give a damn who you hurt," Rupert finalized when the train arrived and he read the large sign, 'GREIN ON THE DANUBE'. Only Rupert and Bertram descended, as most people took a night train for a much longer way.

"Don't you feel sorry for Gaby?" Rupert asked, for his own personal reasons.

"Why should I? At seventeen, it's high time she knows what she got it for," he laughed aloud, while Rupert locked the two suitcases at the station's special department. "Like I told you," he continued. "I served so many so-called gentlemen virgins, and to tell you the truth, I enjoyed all their whining and at times crying. I knew they would be back the next evening for more."

"Not your sister, Bertram, and you know it!"

"Who cares? She was always the apple in Father's eye and could never do wrong; less so with Andreas. But what am I talking about it? I've got plenty of money and will never be found. If Austria gets too hot, I leave for France."

"Ah ha! And you think I'll follow you wherever you go?"

"Why wouldn't you?" he answered, feeling trapped. "We were in France during the war. That country is full of foreigners."

"Not Germans nor Austrians, Bertram. And I am sure you are only trying to get out of something. So why don't you start by giving me the keys to our suitcases. After all, it's always me who has to carry your loot."

"Here they are," he said after some hesitation, feeling he was on trial. But he had to go along, for once they arrived in Steyr, everything would change. He would have his keys and baggage back in no time.

With the noise of Grein's vortex coming nearer, Bertram said, "I hope you don't plan to show me your parents' stupid waterfall!"

"Hmmm, and I thought you liked God's miracles, like you said the other day in front of your mother."

"I did?"

"Yes, right after the prayer meeting."

"I told you why I did it. If it weren't for Gaby, I would have never even visited… just like during the war. I visited and lived in whorehouses." He talked louder now as the noise of the gushing water came nearer.

"As a peeping Tom? Or as they say in French, *voyeur*?"

"Don't get sarcastic. It's not my fault that I got shortchanged."

"No, it's not… but it's not anyone else's fault either. And after all I've heard tonight, you were born to hurt people. You played up to your mother to hurt her loved ones, and played up to my good-hearted parents to hurt their loved one. In their case, its *me*!" He pounded on his big chest. "But I won't let this happen to them." Bertram shook, unable to hold his cane still. "Just keep on walking until I tell you to stop," Rupert sneered. "Come on… just walk." Rupert knew that place quite well, and any mistake could take him down right along with Bertram, who went on his knees, begging Rupert not to harm him. Instead, he punched him all over his body. "This is for your poor sister! This for your poor family! And this one— is for me!" He held one arm on the iron railing and pushed the almost lifeless body he once saved many years ago towards the wild gush of water, throwing the cane after him, watching both as they disappeared within a split second. To him, it felt close to midnight, the white mass of water giving him plenty of light for this unforeseen tragedy, which a day previously was unimaginable.

He lit a cigarette, walked slowly back, fetched his baggage, and waited two hours on a bench under a small roof for the next train back to 'Red Vienna', as it was presently called. The city was also known for its high suicide rates, so this was not suspicious. If he had brought Bertram in front of a judge, he would have lied his way out of it and gone free. But in the process, he would have made sure that Rupert's police captain would have him resign or even fire him. Somehow, he felt the last of the bad von Waldens had disappeared. May the good ones have a long, happy life. He would tell his parents the whole truth, as he knew they would understand. Also, a promise to leave the Red party would be made, as both were very much against its violence. He would also see the von Waldens and tell them what they should know, but still had to concoct a story of how Bertram had disappeared. Suicide would be plausible since Astrid had received a good-bye note under her pillow.

~

While Lucas enjoyed dinner and a lengthy conversation with his professor, he felt it was not a very congenial surrounding. There were ten to twelve couples present, but it looked to him as if they were gathered on short notice and had very little in common. The food was served by two servants who were rather unsure, and the hostess had had too much to drink. He wondered if he had been spoiled between the von Waldens' and Reinhardts' get-togethers, which were always a delight. However, he was grateful about one thing. Since they had very little else in common other than how lucky Switzerland was to be spared the war, he also was constantly asked why he was still single, since so many beautiful girls in Vienna are just dying to find a husband like him. He replied, with one of his rare smiles, that he had had little time to look because he was studying for the last ten years.

"Well, now when you return to your lovely country, they will undoubtedly surround you with their mothers nearby."

"A doctor is always a good catch," interrupted the half-drunk hostess.

"Not necessarily," was his short answer, but he made up his mind to visit Astrid von Walden soon and tell her about his love for Gaby, which had lasted for as long as he could remember. Looking at his watch, he realized that it was ten and time for him time to go. He said his good-byes, thanked the inebriated hostess, and shook hands with his kind professor, understanding completely why the poor man spent all his time at the university, including weekends in the Research department.

Lucas knew that Andreas was at a graduation party and his mother would never go to sleep until he was safe at home. It was no different when he took her children to a concert, play, or opera. She was always up and waiting, glad that nothing had happened. He was sure all lights would be on and Gaby asleep by now. Astrid greeted him with a mixture of surprise and relief, as Bertram had promised to have her back no later than ten, but if one is having a good time, she shouldn't be too worried, she calmed herself.

"What brings you here at this hour, Lucas?"

"May I come in?"

"Of course. Has anything happened?"

"No, no. The party was a bore. I feel sorry for the Professor, as the guests didn't seem to know each other."

"You don't say! But I heard he has a sick wife."

That was a typical answer one expected from a woman like her. "Mrs. Walden," he stammered quietly as not to disturb her sleeping daughter. "I have something of great importance to ask you. As you know, in two days we will be leaving."

"And I will not go along until my sister apologizes!" she interrupted sharply.

"No, it's not that at all."

"Oh good."

"I think you should know that for quite a long time—I even hate to tell you for how long—I have been in love with Gaby and want to ask you... should she feel the same about me... of course I'll give her time... would you object to a marriage? I know she is seventeen tomorrow and I need your permission, just in case Gaby would be willing."

Looking at him rather pleased but still in shock, she said, "Why Dr. Rosatti, I should feel very happy about it."

He told her with a sigh of relief that his parents were informed about it a year ago and would love to welcome her like a daughter, having known her all her life.

"I feel the same way about you, Lucas," she replied, embracing him heartily.

"Of course, the wedding will be in Laussane as my many relatives have all the facilities for a big wedding."

"I'll be there," she promised, hoping Gaby would say yes. She looked at the clock again. "She should be here any moment now."

"Who?" he asked.

"Gaby. She went with Bertram to Wertheim's party, as Samuel and some of his friends are graduating. She never attended one before and Bertram felt she might enjoy being among young people.

"He did, did he!" he said furiously.

"Why do you look so upset Lucas? Bertram will be here shortly."

"Bertram?" he uttered in disgust. "Why would you trust him?"

"Why not? He is very reliable."

"I wish I could feel that way."

"You two really never cared for each other, which is a shame since you are both such nice young men."

As the clock struck eleven, he had had it. "I am going to get her back and I will tell the Wertheims politely why."

"They are not there. They are in France. It's Sam's own party."

"What?" he screamed and was on his way.

~

He could hear the noisy and singing crowd, after arriving via tram at Wertheim's spacious villa. On graduation night at all big universities, taxis were reserved well ahead. Before ringing the doorbell, the guests were still singing what seemed like a different tune in voices which left much to be desired. *"Well that is how a party is supposed to be,"* he thought. But his Gaby in a place like this? Who would she know? Bertram and Sam Wertheim were all he could think of.

A tipsy girl finally opened the door, hugging him with "Please, sir, come right in. We are in need of sober men; the rest are on the floor snoring or drunk." He only smiled to gain her confidence. The half sober ones had, at times, two girls on their laps or were in many cases on the floor in unsightly positions, when he asked the nearest ones, "I am looking for Gaby Walden. You know where I can find her?"

Whoever paid any attention and understood him, shook his head and slurred, "Never heard of her" and "Pour yourself some wine."

"Then tell me, where can I find Sam Wertheim?" he inquired further while seething inside.

"Oh, him… you can always find him upstairs in a bedroom. Better knock first a few times as he may be busy," he grinned coyly.

His heart pounded faster, fearing the worst. All bedroom doors were wide open, looking undisturbed, except for one. He didn't even bother to knock, entering a small sitting parlor, with an open entrance which was obviously the bedroom. There was Sam, whom he had encountered several times from the store previously while asking for Astrid. He was still in an elegant suit and tie on the floor, asleep or passed out. He didn't care, but noticed Gaby on the bed, with her head on the side, still lots of vomit on the pillow and floor. He checked her pulse and heartbeat, which was alright, but knew at once that one of the men got her drunk and had tried!

Doubtless her sick condition had discouraged them some. However, he suspected Bertram in the scheme right away; no telling what deal he had made. Or was Bertram trying to get her too? He lifted her dress and saw some bloody discharge and his first thought was rape! Running downstairs, he asked aloud for the location of the phone and dialed his former hospital to send an ambulance, as inconspicuously as possible, to Hirschenstraße 47, as he wanted to avoid a scene. He knew and liked the Wertheims, and the reputation of the von Waldens was at stake. It was, without a doubt, the carefully planned work of Bertram, who was nowhere to be found.

He waited for what seemed to be an eternity at the hallway until a small ambulance arrived.

"Dr. Rosatti, do we need a stretcher?"

"Absolutely!"

Hearing it, a few slightly intoxicated girls pulled their partners strongly by their sleeves, whispering rather in panic. "Let's get out of here. Someone is dying!"

"Where the hell is Sam?"

In no time, the place emptied itself. Many were staggering out and taking some deep breaths for fresh air, obviously wondering how they would make it home. Bertram had made a promise to many that a few taxis would arrive by midnight when the last trolleys were ending their routine fares. Lucas tipped each ambulance attendant in Swiss francs, asking them to forget the incident.

Arriving at his former working place, he summoned a colleague in the nearby emergency room to give Gaby a thorough checkup, just in case she was in any way molested. Two doctors returned from the examination telling him that she was alright, but had her menstrual cycle, and a nurse was in the process of cleaning her up and making all other arrangements. However, they suggested to put a tube down her throat to get the rest of food or alcohol out. "Although she is still asleep, she is from time to time moaning. I suspect something was put in her glass."

"No doubt about it," the nurse replied.

"Well then, that explains it. She may have been too weak or too sleepy to get all of it out." the entering doctor confirmed.

"Her unsuspecting mother gave her permission to attend a graduation party at the Wertheims'."

"You mean the Wertheims from the department store?"

"Yes and no. The Wertheims are in France vacationing, but trusted their nephew with a party. Absolutely no supervision. You should have seen that crowd."

The doctor smiled and sighed. "How well I remember!"

Lucas only gave an agreeing nod, having never known any of those days. He looked at his watch and was surprised to notice that the last tram had left already and thought of a worried Astrid. "May I use the phone and call the girl's mother? She must be sick with worry by now."

"Over here, Doctor Rosatti."

He explained the present situation, told her Gaby was in the best of care at the Wilhelminen hospital.

"Your former place?"

"Yes, Mrs. von Walden, and not a word will be said to anyone. Poor thing didn't know what she was drinking; otherwise she is alright. Did you by any chance see or hear from Bertram?"

"No... I am sorry."

"Good, because I would let him have it."

"I don't know what you mean. He only wanted to have his sister with his nice friends.

"I'll talk to you tomorrow."

With that statement, he hung up and directed a question to the waiting nurse. "Will there be anyone with her until Miss von Walden wakes up?"

"I will. And I have to get some of the usual information. By the way, we worked together for a few days, Dr. Rosatti."

"I thought I knew you, but couldn't quite place you. Where at the hospital?"

"The mortuary," she smiled. "And thank God they realized how useless I was."

"Not useless. It's not everyone's favorite place. But remember, the dead ones do us no harm," he recited, before a doctor took him by his arm.

"I was supposed to work until midnight before you came in," he said in jest. "And now you need a ride home!"

"Right! Now that would be very nice after my horrendous experience of a few hours ago."

"Glad to do it."

They only talked about his return trip to Lausanne, and this time for good, with very little chance of ever returning to Vienna. Gaby was never mentioned.

∼

The moment Andreas opened the door, Astrid told him that a good and a bad thing happened in the last few hours while he was gone.

"Just tell me the good first so I'll be able to take the bad one better," he smiled.

"Andreas," she sighed. "Lucas wants to marry Gaby!"

"I could have told you that!" She looked astonished. "Now the bad thing, mother?"

"Well, Bertram took Gaby to Wertheim's party, and she drank much too much for her own good," she said, searching for the right words. "Lucas came by, as I said, to ask for her hand in marriage and when I told him she was at Wertheim's party, he got very upset, went to them and found Gaby drunk and took her to the hospital. He just called a short time ago telling me she is all right but decided to let her rest overnight there."

"Now who does Gaby know in Wertheim's circle that Lucas and I don't know?"

"Well, Bertram took her over there and promised to have her back by ten."

"*Bertram!*" he yelled. "And you let her go with him?"

"I thought he was reliable, though now I am not so sure. But maybe he got drunk too? Who knows what goes on at a party?"

"Didn't you tell me that the Wertheims are in France?"

"Yes, it was Sam's party and everyone there graduated from his university."

"So, what does that mean, Mother? They wouldn't try with a girl like our Gaby?" he yelled again. "Why didn't you tell me about it? I would have gone with her! First thing in the morning I'll ride over there."

"Don't make a big thing out of it, Andreas. They all are so kind to us."

"Well let's hope for the best. Good night, Mother!" he said finally, seeing that he upset her terribly.

9

Grabbing her pillow to sleep, she felt some paper rattle, and turned her light back on, only to find four fifty Swiss francs notes and a piece of paper saying, 'Good-bye. Bertram.' She jumped out of bed and ran to Andreas' room.

"Andreas, I know you are tired," she pleaded almost in tears.

"I am not! I am thinking of poor Gaby and her experience at her first party."

"Well something isn't right… look at it!" She threw the money and enclosed good-bye note on his bed and started to shake.

"Does this surprise you? I never could imagine that scoundrel was so nice to us for nothing!"

"Don't say that, Andreas. We are talking now of more than three years. I was sure he had changed for the better."

"Then why has he never lived with us? Unless he lives a secret life we, or rather you, wouldn't approve of!"

"Rupert and his parents are very nice people."

"I agree, but both fellows live in an apartment at Rupert's parents."

"I will call him. Maybe he knows."

"Yes, why don't you?" Needless to say, no one answered. Rupert was on his way back to Vienna to see his parents and then to visit the von Waldens at once.

"I get no answer. Maybe I'll call his parents."

"No, mother. You'll just worry them in the middle of the night. Rupert may not have told his parents where he is going or he is on duty. Let's wait until tomorrow. But before we do anything, let's wait for Lucas and Gaby. She will tell us everything. Please calm down, Mother, and get some rest."

"How can I after the note and money? It has to mean something."

"He was always secretive, unpredictable, and like his father said, a compulsive liar."

"Not since he returned from the war. My God, Andreas... he was always so good to all of us," she lamented in tears, almost furious at Andreas for calling him a liar. She thought of her husband... where was he when she needed him most. But then again, Bertram would have never been around. Astrid never slept a wink and was brewing coffee when Lucas and Gaby arrived.

"Good morning. We were lucky to get a taxi cross-town," he said in an upbeat tone. Gaby looked straight at her mother's tired face, but nevertheless said firmly, "Don't ever send me with Bertram anywhere!"

"I won't, Gaby. I had no idea... I am so very sorry. Look at that," she said handing both the note.

"Ha!" Lucas replied. "That is probably the money." He didn't elaborate further, but gave Gaby a chance to tell her mother what she told the doctors in his presence.

"Now tell me exactly what happened the moment you left the house," she pleaded, stroking her hair, while Lucas served them the coffee.

"He brought me to Wertheim's and promised to bring more girls from my school so I would feel comfortable. Once in the living room, he introduced me to some students who didn't know who he was, as I overheard some people ask about it until someone answered that he was Sam's and Abbe Koch's friend. Sam came over and told the waiter to get me a glass of wine, and Bertram left, I thought, to get my friends. Then Sam came again, and had a friend with him by the name of Herbert something, and I asked for some raspberry soda, which he did bring me. It was so hot in the room I gulped it down and that is the last thing I remember until I woke up at the hospital."

"Oh, dear God!" Astrid cried, with her hands folded looking towards heaven.

"Don't worry Mrs. von Walden, no one touched her. I had her thoroughly examined."

"You did?" Gaby's face turned bright red. "When?"

"Around midnight… as soon as I got there. You were still deep asleep," he smiled. Thinking of her monthly period immediately, she moaned, covering her face instinctively. "Oh, dear God!"

"Gaby, those were specialists. That's all they do."

"How can I ever thank you, Lucas? You came at the right time."

"Never mind. Men have an instinct too. And while we are talking about it, I'll take a ride to the Wertheim's, hoping the pig is up by now!"

Astrid looked shocked at his outburst, but only replied, "Don't get too upset, Lucas. I'll settle it when the family is back."

"Right… with him denying everything and us in Lausanne," he replied and closed the door.

"Mother, I had my monthly, you know… so you see, I was safe; but I didn't want to tell Lucas or the doctors that I saw Bertram give Sam a wink and turned away from me when they whispered. After all, for you, Bertram meant family."

"No more Gaby. As a matter of fact, the moment you children leave, I have a warrant out for him, but first I'd like to call Rupert again." Gaby felt relieved. "I have a feeling everybody knows more than you and I do, Gaby."

"Indeed, we do," said Andreas upon entering the room, kissing first his mother, then Gaby on both cheeks. "I'll bet Mother didn't sleep at all, and me just a few hours. Gaby, I was so glad to hear your voice."

"You don't know how I felt when Lucas brought her back."

"I can imagine. Where is he now?"

"Going to see Sam Wertheim."

"That should be quite interesting. Lucas with his Swiss accent and Sam with his Jewish one, though both speak German well… but nevertheless—"

After ringing the doorbell several times, a male servant finally opened the door. "I am Dr. Rosatti, and would like to see Sam Wertheim," he said kindly to the surprised servant.

"Please come in. The place is in a big mess. As long as my wife and I have worked here, we never experienced anything like this at all. Mr. and Mrs. Wertheim are out of town."

"That's why I am here," he interrupted, knowing the rest of the story.

A chubby young man with a rather arrogant look on his face walked down the steps, tying his monogrammed silk house robe. He didn't even bother to say good morning or excuse himself for the messy place. "We celebrated our graduation," he said with an hauteur Lucas hated with a passion.

"I am Dr. Rosatti, Gaby von Walden's fiancé, and according to my sources, I know where all of you ... well, let's call it graduated."

Sam knew at once that he was not only a doctor's doctor, but also a man he couldn't talk down to, never mind pick an argument. That he was Gaby's fiancée was his biggest surprise. *That Bertie will get his,"* he thought to himself.

"So, what can I help you with?" he asked with a mixture of fear and sarcasm.

"I'd like to know how you were able to get Miss Gaby von Walden to come?"

"Very simple. Please take a seat. Her brother Bertram said she could attend my party and I agreed."

"A man like you has to do better than that," he said very curtly.

"Why don't we wait until Bertie von Walden is present. Somehow I'll feel better."

"To begin with, we both know he is her stepbrother, is called Bertie the Pimp, and according to the note he left his mother, he is not coming back."

"What makes you think that?" Sam asked very uneasily.

"The note said 'good-bye' and included some money he must have received from selling his stepsister," he said calmly as he watched Sam's face tighten. "Will you settle with me…or with the police? As I have the distinct feeling that rape was the intention, and I'll tell you why. Before midnight, I came to this God-forsaken bawdy house and was told by those drunken 'graduates'," he emphasized strongly. "that I would find Gaby and you in one of those upstairs bedrooms. You can imagine how happy I was to find my sick fiancée in the bed, unconscious and you on the floor nearby. Well, either asleep or unconscious." Lucas made sure the nearby servants heard every word, and Sam was too occupied to notice them. "I called the ambulance."

"You did?" he jumped up.

"Don't worry, it was from my former hospital. They were told by me to be discreet about it." Sam gave a sigh of relief. "Now it's your turn to tell me the truth, and I mean the *truth*!"

"I cannot because I am too embarrassed, afraid, or plain ashamed," he said, looking at the floor. "But I swear I did not touch her. Frankly, I don't know how I got upstairs either. Since I am never drunk, I suspect some foul play was involved, and I suspect none other than Bertie, and that's the reason he is not coming back, or Vienna would have one more prisoner in jail."

"Well, Mr. Wertheim, the reason I spared you more difficulty is because everyone I know thinks very highly of your relatives, and it is for their sake that I shall not pursue this matter any further. I know you are among many who have been had by Bertie the Pimp and I am sure you knew him under this name quite well."

Sam nodded. "I know, as a doctor, you must have seen plenty."

"I would say not quite a crowd like that from last night."

"But I assure you no one was raped."

"How would *you* know? Anyway, I am leaving for Switzerland; the chances are we will never see each other again as you will return to America."

"In a month. My parents and I want to see more of Austria. We were all born in Vienna and immigrated about twenty years ago," he said, feeling extremely relieved. "And I am sorry we had to see each other like that. But I will tell all my family, so they won't hear it from someone else. As you know, it's never repeated the same way."

"I know," Lucas said, though he was sure Sam would never tell them the whole truth. Both blamed, in parting, Bertie the Pimp, being sure he would not be around for a long time.

~

"How did it go?" was Astrid's first question.

"Well... in the beginning I did not like him at all. But as I cornered him and he knew he had no way out, he apologized sincerely. I imagine he thought he could try to put his charm on Gaby, possibly get her to submit, but a rapist he is not! He blamed everything on Bertram. God only knows where he is hiding."

"Lucas, I swear to you, the moment he comes back I'll have him arrested."

"I'd like to see that," he smiled.

"Rupert called and would like to talk to all of us. We all have to hear what he has to say. He possibly lied to him too, or Bertram would be with him. After all, they were friends," Astrid lamented.

"A man like him is a Judas!"

"And just to think how good his parents were to him. By the way, did you mention to Gaby what you told me last night?"

"Yes, I did, as the opportunity presented itself, otherwise it would have been the very wrong timing, considering those horrible circumstances. I was called by her nurse the moment she woke up and by six, I took the first tram to see her."

"Well, what did she answer you ... if I may be so frank?"

"You may be, Mrs. von Walden. I was more shocked when she took everything so calmly and only replied that she had expected it someday."

"How wonderful for both of you!"

"That's what I was thinking. You have not the slightest idea how I thought for years, why would a beautiful girl like her take on a guy like me?"

"Don't degrade yourself. There is not a girl that would turn you down."

"Strange you should say that. I heard the same words last night at the Professor's dinner party."

"You see?"

"Well, they didn't know how sweet and beautiful Gaby is... that's the difference."

Gaby heard some voices in her bedroom and assumed Lucas was back. "Hi, Lucas! Was he rude, conceited, or both?" Gaby smiled at him warmly. She felt exhilarated after Lucas' offer but was not about to show it.

"Everything considered, it went quite well. He promised to tell his family all about it."

"So what?" she stated ironically. "Knowing them as mother and I do, they will buy him a new suit or get him a new expensive watch for being so innocent and honest. He will twist everything around and throw it at Bertram."

"As it should be," Lucas replied.

"Speaking of a watch," Astrid said handing her a box. "I baked a cake for this evening too, waiting for the whole family to be together, never thinking it would turn out this way."

"It turned out quite well for me." Lucas smiled while Gaby opened the box. "How very beautiful, Mother!"

"Wertheim had it shipped from America, among many other items for themselves," she verified, fearing someone may think it came from Bertram.

"Mother, this is a gorgeous watch. Even the box is elegant! Maier & Berkele Jewelers since 1887." She took her old one off and put the new one on immediately, giving each one a look at it.

"Happy Birthday, Gaby," Andreas said, feeling a bit embarrassed, as all he could afford were small earrings. "Once I have money, you'll get nicer things."

"You are the best brother anyone could ask for. You are priceless!" He liked her opinion of him, as he felt the same way about her. Lucas came next with a nicely wrapped book.

"It's a love story," he smiled. "just right for a young lady like you."

"I heard about it," she raved, very pleased. "Renate is still reading it; she got it for her birthday too." It was Charlotte Bronte's *Jane Eyre*, one of the first translations in French.

"Thank you so much, Lucas. It's something I will always treasure," she said with a gleaming face.

"Your Aunt and Uncle will give a party for you upon our return. Then, I'll have another little gift, and hope you will like it just as much."

"I am sure I will," she said, when Hermine, still dressed up from her four-hour journey, entered. "Happy Birthday,

Gaby," she said, obviously relieved that the cake was still not cut.

"How was your vacation," Astrid asked.

"It was raining most of the time. I should have stayed here, as my parents and I didn't part on the best of terms."

"Oh, wait until you hear our story." Astrid grumbled, trying not to appear angry. "Later. Much, much later when our children are gone, and you and I are all alone."

"That bad, Baroness?"

"Worse," Astrid answered.

"Now with Rupert appearing any minute, the family will be complete, and we can sing 'Happy Birthday'. After all, he was, for the last few years, part of our family too." They all nodded in agreement, and Hermine gave Gaby a box and went to her room to change her travel clothes, but thought about her mistress' remark; and with no sign of Bertram, she knew something was wrong, but would never permit herself to ask any questions pertaining to von Walden family affairs, let alone the shameless Bertram.

Rupert came in fully unprepared for Gaby's birthday, and his face showed his frustration.

"Never mind, Rupert. I am surprised at myself for pulling a small party off. We were only waiting for you with our singing, since you have one of the best voices." He only gave a forced smile, and all present could see he had been through a big calamity too, never mind the real truth.

No sooner than the cake was finished, Gaby had showed Hermine and Rupert all her presents and tried Hermine's light blue hand crocheted sweater on, the phone rang. Astrid, standing nearby, picked it up and heard a thunderous voice demanding to speak to Bertram. "Bertram is not here!" she replied curtly, and everyone got quiet.

"That cannot be true, Mr. Blumenfeld, as he has plenty of money. But be that as it may, if your son is owed money, I will make sure you or he gets it back very soon."

"Good, and he borrowed from Abbe Koch too."

"Then he will get it back as well. As you doubtless know, Bertram is not my son and has not lived with his family for the last ten years."

"Is that so?" Then you better watch out for your little girl, too, because she is a drunk!"

"I'll make you pay dearly for that remark, Mr. Blumenfeld. My daughter went there invited, got a spiked drink, and ended up in a hospital to get her stomach pumped. The doctors immediately suspected foul play," she fumed. Gaby held Lucas' upper arm very tight and Andreas got up simultaneously with Rupert to show support. "What do you mean, you will investigate? I have a policeman already here to get to the bottom of this mess. Yes, you can talk to him." She handed the phone to a rather anxiously waiting Rupert, knowing how much better he was informed, while she took a seat next to Lucas, who put his arm around her and said, "Calm yourself. I will not leave here until the matter is settled. All I have to do is send a telegram." Gaby reached over and nodded in agreement.

"This is Sgt. Foster. What's your problem?" he asked firmly. Blumenfeld repeated his story, adding 'foreign money' scornfully, feeling well above a little Sergeant of the police force. After all, he owned four hat factories and hats were bought even if one could not afford a good dress to go with it.

"There is no problem in getting the money back as I am in possession of it. But Bertram did not—I repeat DID NOT—borrow it. Those three boys gave it to him."

"*What for?*" he screamed. "That's the dumbest thing I ever heard if you don't mind me saying so."

"I do mind, Mr. Blumenfeld. Not because I work for the police department, but because we are always investigating parties where certain girls are in high demand. Do I make myself clear?"

"Very clear, Sergeant, but neither of those boys are in need of buying a drunken von Walden girl, no matter what her mother thinks. I have known their family's reputation all my life from my patrons in Lindenfels. I imagine that's why you are there to investigate."

"I am, but not the way you'd like to believe. I will make damn sure that those two rotten boys, Herbert and Abbe, will never again get any entrance in any of the Wertheims' parties, and that includes you and your wife. The Wertheims will be informed as soon as they return from France."

"They were not there?" he asked, perplexed.

"No! Only their nephew Sam, who, like your boys, also 'borrowed money'. You can tell that bunch of liars they can pick it up at Breuner's or call my police station in the ninth district at 74 Hahngasse!"

"Who in the hell is Breuner?"

"Ask your son and he will tell you all about it. Good day, Mr. Blumenfeld. I am sure we will meet again."

"Thank you, Rupert. Now, finish your cake. God, when will this all end?" Astrid cried.

"Don't worry, Mrs. von Walden; and you, Gaby, look all upset too. I will get those Jews and I'll get them good!"

Again, there was silence as no one ever said anything negative about the Wertheims or Silvermans. However, they were the only Jews Astrid had ever met and Rupert had possibly more experience. Lucas felt grateful to Rupert and complimented him. Now, he felt Astrid was in good hands and they were ready to leave as planned. He took Rupert to the side and whispered, "Go easy on poor Mrs. von Walden. Don't tell her everything at once."

"Not only that," Rupert whispered in return. "I will only tell her what I feel she ought to know. There is not a thing she can do about it anyway."

"Thanks."

"We decided to leave tomorrow as scheduled," Lucas announced. "With Rupert and Hermine, you will be in very good hands."

Astrid smiled, relieved, as she wanted to spare Gaby anymore unpleasant accusations, knowing she was telling the truth. She was sure Rupert would be the best help possible.

"Here are the names of those two doctors who examined Gaby. There is also the document from the hospital in case you need it," Lucas stated matter-of-factly, and Rupert, taking the first glance at it replied, "That's all I need. And will that self-important Blumenfeld ever be sorry he gave us a call!"

"Rupert, how much did you have to give them? Or is it not any of my business?"

"Don't mind telling you, Mrs. von Walden. Sam gave him 300.00 dollars, Herbert Blumenfeld 500.00 Czech crowns, and Abbe Koch 300.00 Swiss francs."

"And you got the money?"

"All of it and then some."

"Wonder what the money was for?" she inquired, stunned, when Andreas blurted out, "FOR GABY, MOTHER! I am sure *he* had planned it all along!"

Gaby and Astrid held their hands in front of their faces with Hermine saying, "For the first time, I feel I am ahead of you, Baroness ... and it took me only twenty years!"

Lucas and Gaby were still holding hands tightly and Lucas said, tongue-in-cheek, "I don't mind a day like this at all. Happy Birthday again, Gaby! It will be a day we will always remember."

Astrid opened a bottle of wine and said in jest, very definitely, "For men only!"

Hermine laughed, preparing the glasses on a silver tray. "Just for a moment I'd like to be Hermann," she giggled, and everyone applauded wholeheartedly.

"Of course," Astrid agreed, thinking that no one would have ever offered one crown to get her to bed. As sweet as she was, no man ever had any desire to court her.

~

Blumenfeld's household was quite a different matter. Richard told his upset wife, Rosalia, to stay out of it, as it was an affair between gentlemen; providing one could call them that. They awaited the arrival of Sam Wertheim and Abbe Koch. Blumenfeld lost no time in calling both of them to set the record straight. Once more, it was a case of déjà vu involving Gaby Walden.

Sam was nervous, not knowing how much Herbert's strict and conceited father knew. Abbe Koch, Sr. was a problem. Those two boys had a lot to worry about. A trip to Paris was at stake, and all that for a blonde beauty no one even had gotten near. Sam spoke first. "What's this all about?" he asked, knowing that he had nothing to lose.

"How much does Bertram von Walden owe you?"

"Who wants to know?" he replied sharply, feeling it was none of his business.

"I do, because my son, Abbe, and you must get the money back."

"I don't care about the money. I have plenty more," he replied dismissively.

"Well, those two boys don't."

"That's not my problem. My party was free and what they do with their—"

Abbe's father entered nervously, interrupting the conversation. "Why did you call me to hurry over?"

"Your son and my son are owed money and the policeman at the von Waldens will give it back."

"You have to be a little more specific than that, as I haven't the faintest idea what you are talking about."

"Bertram von Walden borrowed their money for their Paris vacation, and I had to call the von Waldens who are being investigated by the police. Don't you get it now?"

"If Abbe is so stupid and loans some guy money who is unreliable, then he has to stay in Vienna! Period! I am not his bank."

It was Sam's turn again, seeing that Abbe's father, though a banker, had a simple solution. "I am leaving because your boys' money is not my problem. And if the police come to me, I'll tell them the same. Damn that party!" Without a good-bye, he left.

"That fellow goes back to America soon the way I see it, he fits in the 'roaring twenties.'"

"They swim in money." Herbert finally opened his mouth.

"I'd like to know from anyone of you two, who is Breuner?" The old Koch knew, but only shrugged his shoulders.

"We go there, at times, for breakfast and meet some of our school buddies," said Herbert.

"It's a café like many others," Abbe continued.

"And I guess that's where the von Walden boy hangs out. Someone quite reliable from Lindenfels told me that he is not only in the black market but also a pimp."

"We didn't know that," Abbe objected, and his father knew at once that he was lying.

"The von Waldens are friends with the Wertheims. Those two may have known each other from there," Herbert answered.

"No way. That von Walden woman said he hasn't lived with them for more than ten years."

"Sam invited everyone to his party."

"Then how come the policeman will have to investigate further because the von Walden girl had something in her drink, and passed out, ending up in the hospital?'"

"How would you know?"

"There were about 60 to 70 people there."

Both Abbe Kochs were ready to leave, as the situation got on the old man's nerves. After all, he visited Breuners from time to time, with his wife always claiming a health spa was the only thing she ever needed. It's a clean and secretive establishment and he was not the only one who went there. Also, the girls are regularly checked for any kind of venereal disease. It's not Blumenfeld's place to question him. But then again, money was all he ever cared about. "Next time you make me come that far, be sure it's important!" he said in a huff, and both left annoyed.

"Well, I tell you this much, Herbert. I am going to get to the bottom of all this. If it takes me a year or two, who the hell cares? I got time."

10

Lucas, with Gaby proudly on his arm, and Andreas left for Lausanne. Astrid and Hermine were waving, glad that at least her two children would be spared the next two months, as Rupert never told her anything until they were gone. He had promised to visit the first day after his off-duty hours, but although she loved Rupert, she was not looking forward to what he had to say.

"Sorry to be late," he uttered at this arrival. "but I met those three boys at Breuner's, gave them their money and hope never to see or hear anything about the whole affair again." He gave a short description of the trip, some carefully selected reasons why they took the trip to Steyr, and then the change of trains in Grein with Bertram's disappearance, who promised to be right back.

"God only knows how everything was planned down to the last detail," Astrid replied. "And to think he sold his sister to the highest bidder. Of course, Sam would have liked her as well as other fellows, but with this money there are lots of good-looking, blue-eyed blondes to be had. I'll bet it was Bertram who talked him into it." She paused for a moment and asked how to go about getting a warrant without half of Vienna knowing it.

"I will take care of that too, as he has to be reported missing," he said calmly, knowing it would be only a formality.

"How did your sweet and kind parents react?"

"Like you. Astonished and sad, as they treated him like my brother."

"Rupert, if there is money left, give it to them. I am sure he lived there almost rent-free, and if he owes them, I will pay. I am not poor. My money is in Switzerland and I am only too happy to repay."

"There is nothing to repay. I kept what was left. With that feisty Blumenfeld, we may even need a lawyer. Otherwise, I'll give some to my parents and I'll keep the rest."

"Great. Did you know Lucas asked me for Gaby's hand in marriage?"

"No, but I felt that he had her on his mind all along."

"How strange. No one was surprised but me. Even Andreas suspected it for a long time. Like my late husband used to say, I always have to be told things, as I never see them, let alone suspect them. Gaby and Bertram are the best examples, though I shouldn't use both names in the same sentence". All in all, Rupert said only the things he felt she ought to know so she could defend Gaby's honor. "Yes, Sam, Herbert, and Abbe gave Bertram money for Gaby. Each one wanted her, but Sam wanted her first, being convinced she was a virgin. While on the train, he confessed things that I was completely unaware of, like being a pimp at Breuners. He had never planned to return to Vienna, but changed his name just in case. He disappeared in Grein with lots of money in his jacket and pants."

"It was always a habit of his, even when he left for the war. I got it mailed back from the military, including his civilian clothes," she replied.

Rupert skipped the story with Verena Reinhardt, knowing how close she felt with the young ones.

"You know, Rupert, I shouldn't be too surprised if those few communists who planned to come to Grein for the rally gave him a good beating, took the money, and left him there. Most of them are gangsters and rogues. I wouldn't be shocked if they threw him in the Vortex." Rupert only gulped, thinking that perhaps she was not that naïve, after all. "Whatever they did, he had it coming. He possibly lied and cheated them like he did all of us."

"Hard to say," he replied somberly. "As long as our friendship doesn't suffer."

"Never on our part Rupert. You tried your best to make a decent human being out of him… aside from saving his life during the war. My late husband always knew he was a hopeless case."

Rupert embraced her and promised to bring his parents. She smiled and hoped he would keep his word.

~

When a telegram arrived with news that Gaby had become engaged and all the details would follow via mail, she felt very happy for more than one reason. Lucas loved her and would do anything to be a good husband, provider, and father, should, God willing, some children arrive.

And as for her future in-laws, they had loved Gaby as long as they had known her. Astrid would, when the time came, take a train to Lausanne and take a large amount of money out to give her daughter a proper dowry, especially now, when she had proved to be a very strong girl who could take life as it is, not as it should be. But right after the return from her prayer meeting, she would write to Ingrid and Henry a letter of apology. She left it up to Gaby and Lucas to tell them about Bertram. Mostly she wondered about Ingrid's reaction about the forthcoming marriage, as she paid for all her many, many lessons in every field available, seeing her as a pianist. But then again, Lucas Rosatti, with the exception of skating, did all those things too. Now they can do them together. Also, her Latin and many other subjects would come in handy, after all, she would be a doctor's wife with lots of friends to entertain. Lucas should not only be in love, but also proud of her and the way she saw it, they had a lot in common.

She was ashamed to admit it, but Bertram being out of their life was nothing but a blessing. One of the sisters at her prayer meeting set her straight once she told her the pathetic story.

The Wertheims returned from France and gave Astrid a call to see if she would like to meet her husband's family from New York as they planned to leave in a month. Naturally, she was happy to see them all again. "The Silvermans will be here too, so it should be a nice little party," Ida Wertheim added delightedly.

Not a word about Sam's party was mentioned, only the beauty of France, the many castles on the Loire, and their upcoming three weeks' travel to Austria, with a return to America via Le Havre. Sam was extremely nice to Astrid and all seemed to be very happy about Gaby's and Lucas' engagement.

"You have a very nice and beautiful daughter who is marrying a fine doctor," Sam declared, and all Astrid could think of was that he was not far off from his other lying friends, never mind Bertram who topped them all; and as strange as it seems, he was never mentioned.

Victoria and Philip Reinhardt and their family had also returned home. Astrid told Victoria all the latest gossip, and about Gaby's engagement and how happy she was about it. "At least I have one nice thing to look forward to. Also, Andreas will be back, and I hope Peter and he will stay friends, as Mr. Blumenfeld speaks very ill of Gaby to protect his own lying son."

"Just let him try with me. You know Philip's mother was one of his best patrons, and you know how much she had to say about the von Waldens. I heard it over and over again, despite Philip's strong opposition," Victoria confided.

"I miss Anette so very much," Astrid said, tears rolling down her cheek.

"No more than I do." Victoria replied. "The children have their own friends, and my husband and I are just not enough for each other." Astrid was told he had a mistress by no other than Ida Wertheim, who knew that girl, as she was no older than twenty-two. But she never let on and said only, "My work at the Wertheims' and my church in the evening are the only things I look forward to."

"At least you have something," Victoria answered before she departed.

She found Paul pacing up and down the large hallway— a habit he acquired from his father, Victoria thought— and asked him why he was so nervous. He had just returned from purchasing a hat at Blumenfeld's, and lo and behold Richard Blumenfeld himself was at the store taking inventory. It didn't take him long to talk about his poor, unjustly accused son who refused to be seduced by the drunken von Walden girl, who, by the way, asked several low moral guys for the money in advance, then got so drunk that someone had to call an ambulance, which took her out on a stretcher to the nearest hospital to have her stomach pumped. "I got this all first-hand from my son, who left the moment the party got out of hand. God, I am so proud of this boy. Of course, I called that von Walden woman to get for Herbert's friend the money back, so they could all start their vacation to Paris. Poor boys didn't know any better." He took a deep breath and continued. "Would you believe the police were already there to investigate?"

"I am not surprised at anything, though the lady and her son are very nice."

"The world is deceiving, Mr. Reinhardt, just like your late grandmother told me," he smiled. "Give my best to your family," he said by way of dismissal, glad to have gotten a new customer.

Paul repeated the story word for word to his astonished mother, but appeared worried when he promised to warn Peter about Andreas' friendship, as those messy rumors were all over town. "Like I always said, she was an ugly brat years ago, and now she is an ugly harlot who prefers to make her rounds at parties."

Victoria only listened, but would set the record straight at the dinner table. Blumenfeld was known to repeat anything, especially about people like the von Waldens. She knew Verena brought quite a few stories back, though she hated gossip. But he had the most fashionable hats in town, so people came back to him as he stayed mostly at his main store in the elegant first district. Paul felt elated and somehow vindicated, as he still had not forgiven her for his broken ankle, let alone missing the game.

"Well son, you have it all wrong. We'll discuss it at the dinner table, as I have all the facts."

He only gave her a cynical smile. "I imagine you went to see Mrs. Astrid von Walden and the lady told you that ugly brat's side of the story."

"No, Paul. She told the truth, because she doesn't have to protect anyone. That so-called ugly brat is one of the most beautiful girls in Vienna and has gotten engaged to Dr. Lucas Rosatti."

"She is getting married to a doctor? The poor man will be sorry, that's all I can say. Peter mentioned him frequently in his letters to me. He must be very nice, but will have to find it out the hard way."

At the dinner table, Victoria asked her son to repeat exactly what he had told her.

"It's a pleasure," he replied. Victoria had never heard him repeat a story, no matter who told him something, but this was a von Walden, and she saw all of Verena's teaching coming through. She noticed Peter tried to interrupt him, especially when he went on about her being ugly and her loose morals, but told him he would get his chance. Philip was the most uncomfortable, expecting Bertram's entrance any moment.

But then came Victoria's turn. All listened, including Paul, who knew his mother never tolerated any interruptions. Peter and Paul looked astonished when told that Astrid had a warrant for Bertram's arrest should he ever dare to return to Vienna.

"She is a very strict woman," said Philip, feeling very relieved. Peter was almost pale with fury, while listening to Paul's story, knowing Blumenfeld quite well.

"I think we should take the hat seller to court for slander. How about it mother?"

"Before we do, I'll pay him a visit and set him straight about his lying son."

"Make sure he and Abbe Koch are present."

"Yes, and I shall pay Mrs. Wertheim a visit. They are just as innocent as the von Waldens."

"And as for Gaby, my dear brother, she is not only the most beautiful girl I have ever laid eyes on, but was innocently talked into going to a party by her devious stepbrother, Bertram. I know her, Dr. Lucas Rosatti, and Andreas better than you do. And if I see or hear another derogatory look or remark about them, you'll find yourself in the hospital. And I mean it, brother! You are no better than Blumenfeld, who is known to be a gossip."

"Paul does not gossip." Philip jumped to his defense. "It just happens to be a von Walden, and my late mother did quite a good job on him."

"Ha! Grandmother didn't even know that Bertram von Walden was known as 'Bertie the pimp'."

"Quiet!" yelled Victoria. "I will not permit such language at the table."

"Sorry, Mother. I am only wondering why we end up in an upheaval each time the von Walden name is mentioned."

"Because Gaby got the best of you, and no one has ever since," Philip smiled, relieved.

As expected, Astrid and Ingrid made up again about their differences pertaining to her new religion, with a solemn promise on Astrid's part never to talk about it to strangers, or for that matter to any devoted Catholic again. Uncle Henry, who never interfered to begin with, only remarked that her poor sister had not much else to look forward to, and like so many other people, it was their only comfort, as her many prayer meetings replaced a much-needed social life.

The Rosattis and Lebruns were overjoyed at their son's wedding plans, as Lucas wouldn't be happy until Gaby became his wife. The date was November the 7th with an extended honeymoon in the Bernese Alps for skiing. A luxurious hotel in Gstaad, known for being *the* meeting place of the old and newly rich was chosen, in appreciation for having their wedding in Locarno among all the Rosattis' relatives, who proclaimed it their personal holiday. There was this fine young Dr. Rosatti, the very first in the family to carry not only a title, but walking down the red carpet with his most astonishingly beautiful wife on his arm, leaving most of them gasping and others envious. Many of the Rosattis' marriages were arranged by the forever meddling parents, thinking more of money and property than their love for each other. But as long as they were fruitful in bringing a large brood of children to this world, very little thought of happiness was given.

Astrid and Andreas were extremely elated, being convinced that theirs was a marriage of undying love. If Ingrid was somewhat disappointed that her beloved niece was now a wife instead of a pianist, bowing from the podium of any concert hall taking her applause, she never mentioned it. Also, those many lessons from tennis to horseback jumping, skiing, and Latin were not wasted, as Lucas participated in everything himself. Skating was another story. It was the sport she loved the most, but Ingrid knew, in time, she would get her way from a man who trusted her and loved her unconditionally. Henry, too, gave in reluctantly. It didn't matter as she always ended up on the ice rink anyway.

Lucas felt like the luckiest man on earth and while he was convinced that Gaby loved him in the kindest way and would be a loyal wife, his way of loving her would possibly never be reciprocated. Be that as it may, he was willing to wait. By observing many married couples, he knew that their children would bring them much closer.

1923

11

By March, she knew she was pregnant, and both were ecstatic and waiting anxiously for the month of September. They decided to stay in the temporary apartment overlooking a park with a large playground. Lucas knew how hard Gaby would work to make the place beautiful, and felt that in her condition, it would be too strenuous were they to move. After all, their present living quarters were only a short walking distance from their families who shared their newfound bliss.

Alfredo and Lucas went to Germany to purchase a Daimler, as the transportation to his hospital consisted of twice changing the tram, and the waiting time made him uneasy, as he could never be at Gaby's side quickly enough. The German car raised quite a few eyebrows. Many had not forgiven Germany's prolonged war quite yet, however, no one else produced a better car anywhere in Europe and they put all the criticism aside, feeling that a big part of jealousy played even a larger role. There were not too many cars, let alone a Daimler, in Lausanne.

Gaby's days were spent between the Rosattis, who taught her Italian cooking, and Aunt Ingrid, who gave her many tips she herself called, 'lessons of course', from the finishing school she attended. There was also the French cuisine to be taught, being completely unaware that Lucas enjoyed the von Waldens' and Reinhardts' meals the most, always asking his wife to make him something Austrian. Her newly acquired Italian and French recipes were strictly for their guests, including in-laws who were quite proud of how much they taught Gabriella.

The baby was due any day now, and on Lucas' advice, Gaby hired a nice young midwife who took daily walks with her and would stay as long as necessary. The many visits from the Lebruns and Rosattis helped to shorten her otherwise lonesome existence, as Lucas frequently worked overtime. Eugen was put in a home for mentally disturbed children, as he also developed epilepsy and showed many other signs of uncontrollable fits not even his parents were able to handle. It was done two months prior to the birth of the baby, as he greeted his beloved Gaby so exuberantly, the Rosattis were afraid he could possibly harm her or the baby. Isabella prayed every waking hour for a healthy, normal child, while Gaby herself never wasted a minute thinking about it. Presently, both families were trying to find the right names for a boy or girl, although Gaby and Lucas had chosen one the day her pregnancy was confirmed. For a boy, Alfredo Henry, to give both men a part; for a girl, Isabella Marie, as Gaby loved her mother-in-law's name. She was, therefore, hoping for a girl, expecting to have more grandchildren coming.

When the following day her first labor pain started, her midwife Susanne, a widow from France, was right at her side, preparing everything for the birth. By eight in the evening, Alfredo Rosatti's nerves got the best of him and he decided to take a taxi to Lucas' hospital. Lucas had decided to work a few evenings overtime to spend at least a week with his wife after the birth of their baby. After knocking at his laboratory's door, Lucas opened it as he was just in the process of leaving.

"Our Gabriella's labor pains are just a few minutes apart!"

Alfredo, having his taxi waiting, couldn't even finish his sentence when Lucas screamed, "Great! I'll get her some flowers!" and jumped in his car.

"My son brings his wife flowers at least two to three times a week," he told the driver proudly, who only replied, "How nice." When Alfredo arrived at the second floor, he heard the cry of a baby.

"Congratulations, Grandpapa!" his wife greeted Alfredo joyfully. "You have another Isabella Marie to cope with. I am so proud she chose my name."

"How is our Gabriella?" he asked instantly.

"Doing great. It was an easy, normal birth. She can have a dozen more!" she jested, thinking, 'God forbid!'

"Did you get a hold of Lucas?"

"Sure did. He was just leaving but screamed to get some flowers first."

"Well, one good thing is our florist never minds opening his back door for a good sale. I know it's going to be something very special," she replied, waiting for Lucas' gloating face. Alfredo was permitted to see his first granddaughter.

"Here. Take your new addition in your arms," Gaby said happily, seeing his face jovial as never before. "Next time, I promise you an Alfredo Henry," she proclaimed, while he whispered only, "As long as they are healthy, six girls will be fine with me," thinking doubtlessly of poor Eugen.

The midwife laughed out loud. "We were six girls and five boys."

"There you have it, Gabriella. What amazes me is her dark, curly hair," he emphasized.

"Just wait until she opens her eyes; the deepest and darkest brown you've ever seen."

"Lucas should be here any moment. He went for flowers first, as you can imagine."

"I hope he comes soon as I am very tired."

"Then why don't we let you sleep for a while." He smiled when Susanne knocked at the door and told him, "Someone is here to see you," took the baby, laid it in the crib, and told Madame Rosatti to take some well-deserved rest. She neglected to say they were two policemen, fearing the worst.

"Mr. Rosatti, we assume?"

"Yes," said an ashen-faced Alfredo, noticing his wife passed out on the floor.

"We're sorry, but Dr. Rosatti died instantly in a car crash. He hit a lamp post trying to miss hitting a woman crossing the street."

"Where?" he asked, as if it mattered.

"Rue de Soupirs. We need you to come along to identify him."

"Oh, my God!" he repeated several times. "I am not sure I am strong enough."

"Sorry, Mr. Rosatti. You will have to try."

Susanne whispered that Gabriella was now sleeping, and she would take care of her until the Lebruns arrived. Alfredo left in the police car minutes before Ingrid and Henry entered the house. The midwife left the door slightly ajar and recognized their happy voices at once. Their beaming faces changed immediately when a teary-eyed Susanne confronted them, putting her finger at her lips and whispering that Gabriella and the baby were asleep. It was an instant surprise after noticing the almost lifeless body of Isabella Rosatti, their faces turning instantly to stone.

"It's Dr. Rosatti," she continued to whisper. "He died hitting a lamp post," she stammered, still in tears. Ingrid held both her hands to her face and cried, "No… it cannot be!"

"That fellow always drove too fast and I warned Gaby more than once never to ride with him," Henry replied, more furious than shocked.

"Mr. Rosatti just left to identify his body, but mama and baby are asleep, not knowing what happened. Please, Dr. Lebrun, can you help that lady?" he asked, pointing towards Isabella.

"As a matter of fact, I always come prepared no matter whom I visit," he grumbled, reaching in his jacket, and took a small bottle and raised her head, waving it back and forth. She opened her eyes slowly and looked, if anything, forlorn. Henry put a finger in front of her mouth telling her quietly that Gabriella and the baby were asleep.

"But my son is dead, Henry! What are we going to do?"

"Go on living like the rest of the people who have lost someone they loved."

Her mouth was too dry to give him an answer. Susanne brought some water and, with the help of Henry and a still shaken Ingrid, put her on a comfortable couch. "Who will tell Gabriella?" asked Isabella.

"I will," said Ingrid sternly, without a moment of hesitation.

"I think it's best if we all are very near her," echoed Henry. "She will need all of us."

"That's how little you know about her strength! That girl has had to prove herself all her life."

"But never in a situation like this, Ingrid. I lost a son, she a husband and—"

It didn't take Alfredo very long to notice how unsympathetic the police were towards his son's death. *"Or is this all they deal with and, therefore, just another matter of routine?"* he thought to himself. Alfredo tried to be strong before they reached the destination of the accident, but his voice was full of emotion. "You know his wife gave birth to his firstborn child just an hour ago. I went to the hospital to tell him all about it. He told me he would stop at the florist to pick up some flowers and I imagine he hurried home."

Without any trace of feeling one way or another, one answered rather sarcastically. "Your son was always speeding, even if there was no reason for it. If he hadn't had the 'MD' next to his license plate— though he worked in a laboratory—" he remarked in a cynical tone. "we would have given him a ticket the first time he nearly ran over a woman with a child on each hand. He stopped abruptly within one meter or they would have been buried by now."

"I'll say!" his partner replied. "He had no regard for human life. I guess that's why he worked with the dead ones."

Alfredo was too weak and upset to give him any reply, as they had already reached the destination, with a few policemen and onlookers standing nearby. There was his son, his head on the steering wheel and a huge bouquet of red roses next to him, completely undisturbed. After signing a few documents, an ambulance was waiting to take him to a funeral home.

"Take those roses to your daughter-in-law and tell her how lucky she and the baby were, not to be in his car." Without saying goodbye or that they are in any way sorry, they dropped him off in front of his house.

"The heartless police dropped me off. Here are the flowers Lucas bought our Gabriella. Somehow, those two sergeants made me stronger, so I will be the one to tell her." His wife cried even louder as Alfredo told them the policeman's opinion of their son. It got very quiet and they all heard the baby crying with the midwife consoling her, doubtlessly taking her out of the crib.

"We all go in. She needs us," Henry whispered, not being sure if Gaby was awake too.

The midwife appeared saying, "Madame Rosatti is awake, but now I stay in the living room." They only nodded and went in, worried about who would speak first. Other than consoling her with 'it was God's will', nothing else was on their minds when they entered together, Alfredo still with the roses tight in his hands. It was Ingrid who went to her bedside, putting an arm around her.

"Gabriella... we all have to be very strong. Lucas went for those roses... and ended up dead on the lamp post on his regular shortcut through the Rue de Soupirs."

"Did he kill anyone else?" was her first stammering and concerned reply.

"Oh, no!" said Alfredo, a bit cheerful. "The policeman said he tried to avoid hitting a woman who crossed the street without looking."

Gaby looked from one downtrodden face to another who still awaited a loud outcry or some kind of weepy reaction, but instead she tried to sit up with everyone jumping to help her. She said quite calmly, "My late darling father told me one time, and mind you he was never overly religious nor ever wrong in anything he said," She paused, thinking of Bertram. "that there is positively a reason for everything. We should never question God's will. The way I see it, there are two fine men in Heaven, and I hope they have met."

Looking at her newborn baby and suspecting Susanne was somewhere in hiding, she addressed Isabella Rosatti first, who looked the most grief-stricken, and handed her the baby carefully. "Now you two dear Isabellas will have to be very strong," She smiled faintly while caressing her wet cheeks. "just like I was taught."

"I promise." She started to cry even louder.

"Alfredo and I gained our strength with poor Eugen."

What strength? Gabriella thought but replied, "I know."

Ingrid had the very same thought, knowing what Gaby and her family had to endure in Lindenfels, and Astrid came to her mind. "I have to send a telegram to your mother, Gaby. I hope they can make it to the funeral. Astrid and Andreas, I mean."

"Uncle Henry, I assume the coffin is kept closed. Tell them to give us a week."

"Why that long? Your family and the Rosattis will be here in two days."

"But I'd like to be there too. After all, he is, or was, my husband."

"Nine days bedrest is a must," he urged.

"Then tell me why our servants are working on the third day, regardless of their hard chores. What makes them so different from me?"

"Your upbringing, Gaby. You played the piano when they plowed the field. You skated and skied when they cut and carried firewood."

But her facial expression showed him that she was determined to go. "Please get me Susanne," she asked Ingrid. "I am not capable of breastfeeding under these conditions. Half milk, half water," she ordered.

"That's what I was thinking," Susanne replied.

"Aunt Ingrid, please press those roses in the *Jane Eyre* book. You are an expert on flower pressing."

"Happy to do it," Ingrid replied, very proud and stoic.

"It's the first book Lucas gave me for my birthday." She looked again at the surrounding family members, still shaken and sad, and said very kindly, "Please go home. I know you all need a good cry by yourself. I have Susanne with me. She promised to stay as long as I need her."

Susanne was elated. They kissed her goodbye with their best wishes for a good night's sleep. There was nothing else to add that would bring Lucas back.

~

Unlike a Reinhardt funeral, which was, with very few exceptions, a 'family only' affair, this one appeared to be one for an important statesman. The Rosatti family closed their restaurants in Locarno with a big sign on the door which stated, 'Funeral'. Gaby still looked pale and weak, but no one was able to talk her out of attending the long procession.

While most of the Rosatti women wore their long, black veils almost down to their knees until they reached the cemetery where the condolences took place, Astrid and Gaby wore small brim hats with netted veils which showed their beautiful faces. They were upheld by Andreas in the middle, whose arms were linked in his mother's and sister's. There was not a tear on either face, including Ingrid's. By now, they were all exhausted from crying in their own pillows. Some single Rosattis had thoughts of marrying the young widow, but then again, no one else could compare himself to the late Lucas Rosatti.

After the usual dinner, for which Alfredo opened his restaurant, a heated argument started among the men, as to why Alfredo bought a German-made car and not a Fiat or Bugatti from Italy.

"Because they are pieces of junk in comparison to a Mercedes or a Daimler."

"I agree with the cars, but don't agree with your insulting remark towards a Fiat or Bugatti … if one knows how to drive carefully," retorted his brother Marcello in fury. "I would have bought a Rolls Royce maybe later, but America sends us Fords at a better price."

"Thank God those so-called 'German women' went home so peace reigns," Henry Lebrun stated, ready to leave. "But I want to tell you that I am married to a former blue-blooded Contessa von Donat. Yes, a German like her sister, Astrid, who married an Austrian, Baron von Walden. Our Gabriella got the best genes of both families and she proved it during the whole week while under great strain."

Alfredo was eager to end the conversation. "Our discussion is closed!" He was more than happy that his relatives departed the same evening on a night train. It would be quite some time before he saw them again.

Astrid, Gaby, and Andreas cooed over the new baby, and in the presence of Ingrid they discussed Gaby's financial future. She would receive a monthly pension, and at the age of eighteen was already privileged to get her inheritance. She was pleasantly surprised, as no one had talked to her about it previously. "But I already got a nice dowry!" she uttered, flabbergasted.

"Oh, that was only part of it," Astrid said evenly.

"Then I can keep on living in this nice apartment?" she asked, still astonished.

"Not only that," Ingrid answered. "I'll pay for Susanne as long as you like. It's a pleasure, Gaby, and there is more where we come from."

"I read Germany has a new currency."

"It's about time. They paid for a loaf of bread in millions. It's the end of the black market," Astrid replied, hoping Austria's fate was not far behind. But all their money was in Swiss banks and, thanks to Ingrid and Henry, also wisely invested in real estate.

It was good to know that Gaby was completely independent from Lucas' family and, should she ever want to return to Vienna, with all her money she could buy not one but two nice villas. Andreas, too, was happy and decided to make his residency in Lausanne. He would be near Gaby and his little niece Isabella, along with his uncle and aunt, the Lebruns. Eugen, they were told, has to stay in a home, but they visited him on a weekly basis. Life went on as it had to.

~

After Astrid and Andreas' return to Vienna, she visited the Reinhardts, told them all there was to tell, and received lots of sympathy from Victoria and Philip, as they, too, loved Lucas.

Peter, who made his residency for 'Dr' in Salzburg, was heartbroken, not only because Lucas taught him so much, but their friendship was a solid one. Paul returned to Zurich for two years longer to become a 'Diplom-Engineer'. He loved Switzerland for one thing, also finding the studies much more advanced. The von Walden connection, however, made him always very uneasy, being still convinced that the 'ugly brat' was a drunk and easy prey. The rumors were still flying around in his small circle of friends. Even the visit of Rupert Foster had never really changed his mind, though it had made a big impression on Paul's sister Gisela.

Blumenfeld and Abbe Koch were forced to go, along with their sons, to court. Among many other accusations was slander. After lengthy questioning by the judge himself, both boys had no choice but to admit their lying. However, on their way home they laid their blame on Bertram and the 'von Walden trash' from Lindenfels.

Sam was another story. Shortly before his departure, he confessed to Ida and Martin Wertheim that 'once in a while' he paid a visit to Breuner's. "A young man like me just couldn't sweat out his physical desires, and a Jewish girl was out of the question; they would demand marriage. I would have married a girl like Gaby in a second, but she barely even looked at me."

"You want to stay in your own religion, Sam," advised his uncle, but Sam was just not that religious.

~

Martin Wertheim's traveling relatives finally went back to America. The arriving letters told them that regardless of their Austrian heritage, America is home for them. All of Europe is nothing but foreign.

The Wertheims visited Blumenfeld's hat store after hearing about their day in court. That also gave them the opportunity to tell him that his son Herbert, along with Abbe and their 'honest' nephew Sam, were regular customers at Breuner's.

"Vienna is the city of prostitutes with all Christian girls. Our Jewish girls would never do that," Blumenfeld replied proudly. "Which brings me to that von Walden girl—"

"That's why we came," Ida interrupted. "If we ever hear about you or your son lying about that girl again, you will regret it!"

"You mean those von Waldens from Lindenfels who couldn't make it?"

"What do you mean by 'couldn't make it'? They have been our closest friends from our Lindenfels time, when nobody wanted to be bothered with a 'damn Jew'. They are also the best friends of Philip and Victoria Reinhardt."

"But were never of my late client, Verena Reinhardt," Blumenfeld replied with a smirk.

"Times have changed drastically. She never liked your gossiping either, only your hats!" Ida answered with the same smirk.

"Don't let us get those von Waldens between our long-standing friendship," Blumenfeld pleaded, knowing their department store bought quite a few hats from him. Both Wertheims only smiled, never considering him anything but a businessman.

"In case you didn't know," Martin said wistfully. "that so-called drunken girl married a fine doctor from Switzerland. It was *he* who found her unconscious at Sam's party, brought her to the hospital, and was told that her drinks were tampered with on purpose so guys like your son could get the girl. Therefore, the down payment. All three boys and Bertram von Walden were in on it!" Blumenfeld's mouth opened in disbelief. "I have plenty of witnesses, including the doctors and police. They would love to testify against a Jew. I could re-open the case again."

"Don't do that, please. We went through a lot already."

"Well then have a good day, Mr. Blumenfeld. And as of today, we buy our hats somewhere else."

The Wertheims left, feeling quite satisfied. The von Waldens had endured a lifetime of being unfairly judged, simply for their lack of money. It was about time someone told that Blumenfeld the truth, so he would never utter a word again.

12

Rupert Foster still visited Astrid and Andreas on a regular basis. At present, they were sitting on the von Waldens' cozy terrace, sipping on a glass of lemonade, discussing the extremely hot July day. They never ran out of any topic or subject, yet Bertram's name was never mentioned. The von Waldens didn't care where he was, and Rupert, who knew the answer, cared even less. If anything, it was a relief not to face this scoundrel anymore who had deceived them in the worst way. Rupert felt neither remorse nor guilt, knowing he may have ended up in Steyr the way Bertram ended up in Grein. There was no doubt in his mind how carefully Bertram had everything pre-planned, never counting on a policeman's suspicions. His poor, dear trusting parents would be without their son who had survived the war, but Bertram would be nowhere to be found.

Astrid was in the process of thanking him for all those many unobtainable goods he brought again, when the doorbell rang. She welcomed Gisela Reinhardt, who said with great pride that this was her very first experience in making jam and she just had to bring some by to let them taste it! She also apologized for her interruption after hearing two men's voices.

Astrid asked her in, while praising her for her thoughtfulness and trying to make a proper introduction. Rupert stated quite nonchalantly that they had already met, and that he visited the Reinhardts' house again because of Bertram's disappearance. Astrid showed surprise, but Gisela told her the reason, still thinking how handsome he was and admiring his great physical appearance. He, too, couldn't help but notice her good looks and easy-going manner. After all, she was a Reinhardt. However, at present, she wore no ring. She gladly accepted the offered lemonade and joined the conversation about the extremely hot weather. "It must be awfully hot to be in uniform," she said to Rupert politely. He only said that he never gave it much thought, while Andreas claimed to receive many patients with heat strokes at the General Hospital, where he worked as an apprentice.

"I wish I had your brain," she replied clumsily, being sorry to have made that remark; after all, Rupert Foster was a Sergeant waiting to be accepted at the police academy.

"We are all meant to be and do something different, Gisela. I don't envy your daily task with those many deaf mutes, especially when you could be sitting idle." Andreas replied.

"Idleness at the Reinhardts' place is a deadly sin, you know that much. But be that as it may, I love my work."

Rupert said he loved his work too, looked at his watch, and said his parents were expecting him to help them with their flower beds. As usual, he embraced Astrid, who had each jar opened and tested by now, and said his good-byes to Gisela by expressing the hope to see her again, while tapping Andreas on his shoulders and saying, "So long, Doctor," with a smile.

"So long, Officer," was his reply, which both said always with tongue in cheek. It had become a joke between them for the last several years.

"Now there is a nice fellow, Gisela. What a pity you are one of the Reinhardts."

"I don't see that our name has anything to do with that," she replied sharply.

"Not the name alone, but what goes with it," Astrid said in return, while praising her homemade jam. "I took a taste of each one of them and can honestly say they all are very good!"

Gisela was happy about the compliment, but her thoughts went right back to her name and fortune. "Don't think for one moment that I won't marry whom I love, regardless of my parents' opposition. I have plenty of money of my own."

"Which may be another minus for a girl like you," Andreas interrupted. "Take a man like me, for example. There is no way I would like to have a wife who supports me with her parents' or her money. I'd rather work at the hospital for the rest of my life."

"Well, Andreas, you are the exception to the rule… and I am in a position to know that. Take, for example, Dr. Wimmer. His wife is rather common, but her parents own a butcher shop and their money enabled him to open a practice. Or Dr. Horner, whose rich in-laws don't even know how to spell surgeon, but they own a big farm. His wife is addressed as 'Frau Doctor' and everyone is quite proud," Gisela said with a sigh, with Astrid and Andreas agreeing, as they knew even more of those examples.

~

After she left, both felt strongly that she liked Rupert very much. And so did he, thinking about it while on the way home on the trolley. He just had her lovely face in front of him! Arriving at his small, newly purchased house, located near his parents' large one, he found the letter he had been awaiting anxiously. His first thought was that the young lady had brought him luck already. The police academy finally answered and wrote him that he was accepted. Knowing how happy his parents would be, he walked immediately to their place, waving the elongated envelope. While entering their large pantry from the garden, he looked at the calendar and it reminded him that it was one year to this day that Bertram disappeared.

As expected, his parents were quite happy, though they would now see less of him. For the next two years, it meant rigorous training and studying before he could call himself an 'Officer'. But he was willing to give it all.

~

September 2 was his first day, and he knew from many colleagues that his first duty was directing traffic, which would be a repetition of what he did three years ago, but so be it. He was told that he would be in the first district's commercial center, not too distant from the Reinhardt place, mostly known as *the* Palace.

As fate would have it, Gisela had to cross the street with eight of the deaf-mute orphans twice a day. Rupert and she had not seen each other since July 1, and both, although thinking of each other daily, had given up and considered another coincidental meeting as hopeless. The Reinhardts were the benefactor of other orphanages, and Gisela took, while staying in Berlin with her grandmother, a course for deaf mutes, which came in handy after her return to Vienna. It became unavoidable not to see Rupert Foster, who tipped his hat and smiled, in Gisela's opinion, more at the children than at her. He stopped the traffic, which consisted mostly of horse-and-buggies, with streams of bicycle riders along with repainted military trucks in any color available.

After a few weeks of his smiles, which she returned with a nod, she promised herself to see Astrid. Although she always had a weakness for tall, strong handsome men, somehow she felt this was an entirely different matter. He seemed not to care who she was, which made all the difference to her. Astrid was quite astonished that Gisela would confide such personal matters, but was glad to be asked.

"He is completely unattached. However, he was engaged during the war for about two years and, after his return in 1918, the girl was not only married, but had a baby boy. She never let him know a thing about it. The year of 1917, he didn't get a furlough, as they were in desperate need of medics, so he had quite a big disappointment."

"As you know, I was engaged not once but three times. How about that? My last one was our biggest embarrassment, as all invitations were mailed when father was told. Well, never mind. I am sure you know all about that. I had little choice but to live with my grandmother in Berlin. Of course, she lives in a small villa and enjoys an entirely different lifestyle. And you know what?" She smiled, gratified, "I liked it better! It was those strikes and demonstrations that worried my parents and made me come home."

"Dear Gisela, you were gone for years. It was about time you came back!"

"Now Paul is in Berlin keeping grandmother Lotte company, and he likes it as much as I did in Berlin."

Astrid continued to tell her all about Rupert's closeness to his parents, his taste in women and mentioned his newly purchased house. Gisela asked her to keep their conversation private as her parents would never forgive her. "Frankly speaking, I am not quite sure if I can forgive myself." While saying a hearty goodbye with an embrace, Astrid promised to say a special prayer.

"You do that, please, because it will take a miracle," she smiled before leaving, quite upbeat.

~

It was All Saints Day, November 2, and for Austrian and German citizens, it was a must to visit graves and, if possible, to put some flowers on them. Vienna, which had a huge, central cemetery, was overflowing with people since the war and its aftermath took lives by the thousands. And what would be more appropriate than for a volunteer like Gisela to take her brood of children, who were between three and six years old, to the graves of their parents. But for a big chore like this, she needed the help of a map.

To make sure no one got lost among the thousands of mourners, Gisela requested one person for extra help. Erika Landgraf, who taught at the same kindergarten but had no children with handicaps, was happy to offer her services, especially since her parents were out of town. Both had grown very close during the last few months and had much in common. While still looking for the last two graves, trying to get to the right location, a policeman, standing inconspicuously at their back, asked if he could be of any help. It was none other than Rupert Foster, who had spotted Gisela and her brood quite some time before.

"Oh, hello Officer," both girls said almost in unison. "As a matter of fact, we could use your help," Erika replied while Gisela looked in his brown eyes, her heart pounding all over again.

"Hello, Miss Reinhardt. I see there is no holiday for us," he smiled, seeing her perplexed look. In no time, he was surrounded by Gisela's children, who gave to 'their' policeman a happy smile. Gisela introduced Erika, while he nodded and took a closer look at the map.

"You are just a few feet away. Right over there." He pointed, shook each elated child's hand and said goodbye.

"Is he ever handsome!" Erika said once he was out of hearing distance. "But so was my former boyfriend, who not only cheated on me with my best friend, but I see him from time to time with other ones too."

"In my experience, it's hard to trust anybody."

"By the way, how come the policeman knew you, if I may be so frank to ask?"

"Through a mutual friend for one thing, a visit to our place a year ago for another … and I cross the Rotenturmstraße with the children. He makes the traffic stop so we are never harmed."

Both girls brought the tired children back and parted with a promise to see each other tomorrow. Gisela's thoughts were on Rupert. And, for the first time in years, his were on a woman again. "If she only weren't a Reinhardt," he told his parents that evening.

"So what?" his mother replied, who barely left her home and garden. But his father knew what his son meant and gave a very accurate description of the palace, as he remembered Christmas of 1918 quite well.

"I tell you Wilma, I have never been in a place like that before or after."

"Well our son has his own house. We help him to enlarge it, so he doesn't need a thing from that family."

"You don't understand, Mother."

"I do! It won't matter if she loves him."

To a woman like his mother, life was so simple and she never looked any further to make it complicated. She just couldn't comprehend Rupert's dilemma.

Rupert made his usual visit to Astrid and mentioned the short meeting with Gisela. Astrid could only think that her prayers were answered and volunteered more than he ever would have dared to ask. "Poor, sweet Gisela! She suffers from a low self-esteem, as she is the only one who never attended a university."

"Good to know," he answered, feeling rather pleased at the thought there may still be a slight chance for him. Arriving at home, with his mother tending to her flowers and garden, he had a chance to talk to his father alone.

"Son, you have nothing to lose by asking her to a fine cafe house. Clear your mind and go for it. That's what I did with your mother."

"You too?"

"Yup. Her family owned a large farm and I was a musician-turned-carpenter with no money, so to speak."

"Any opposition?"

"Until their dying day." He shouldn't have been surprised to hear it, having never met one set of grandparents. But since his father came from a very large loving family, they were never missed.

Erika and Gisela said their good nights when she saw a large man in a police uniform across the street. Rupert had an hour to spare before his night school and took his father's advice, agreeing that he had nothing to lose.

"Miss Reinhardt?"

"I thought it was you."

"Yes, it is me, alright," he emphasized with his pleasant, warm voice. "I came to ask you if it were possible that we might meet one day at Café Sacher over a cup of coffee and have a nice talk."

She was glad it was dark, so he had no way of seeing how much she blushed. "If you think we have something to talk about?" she questioned with a smile.

"Shouldn't we find out?"

"If you think so."

"I do."

"Alright… you know my hours, including Saturdays."

"Well mine are not that regulated, but this Saturday I am off duty."

She pondered for a while so as not to appear too eager. "Six would suit me fine, but I live near Sacher... I..."

"I know where you live, but I will be waiting here. By the way, here comes your trolley around the corner."

"You are more observant than I am," she smiled again.

"It's my job, Miss Reinhardt." He helped her to ascend with a light wave and a relieved heart. Arriving at home, she appeared still in a state of euphoria.

"You had a good day Gisela," her mother noticed with relish.

"Let's say a good evening for a few minutes."

"Can you be more specific?" her father wanted to know.

"I have a date Saturday evening at Café Sacher."

"Anyone we know?" asked her mother, quite interested.

"You may, as he was here with his father in 1918 at our open house, passing out cigarettes to the wounded soldiers." Both parents only looked at each other with a shrug.

"He was in a police uniform, as he had duty a few hours later. His parents have a grocery store in the ninth district and Peter, Paul, and some other friends remarked that they were the most generous ones to bring so much."

"Now I remember," Victoria said. "They came with the von Waldens."

"Right mother. At that time, I was so smitten with my former fiancé," she sighed.

"Is he still a policeman?" Philip continued to pry.

"Yes, but now he is enrolled in the Academy to get ahead."

"Ahead in that field means to be a Captain or a Major when you retire," Philip replied again.

"Who cares as long as one likes what he is doing? Not everyone can be an engineer or doctor," she said sharply, feeling defensive.

"Right you are, Gisela. He seemed, as I remember him, very handsome and authoritative."

"He still is, Mother."

Philip drew a deep breath. "You already had your experience with handsome men. And as for authority… well, so far no one has outdone me," he smirked, satisfied. Victoria gave her daughter a wink and told her to eat.

"Father, you were right. I took the liberty of asking Miss Reinhardt—her name is Gisela—to have a cup of coffee at Sachers. And she accepted!"

"Wonderful," he replied. "I am going to tell your mother!"

'Wonderful' was also the evening at Café Sacher; if one would have asked Gisela or Rupert to sum the evening up. The famous, cigar-smoking Anna Sacher greeted Gisela with a tight hug, gave them a good table, and Rupert knew at once that the Reinhardts were, without a doubt, some of her steady clients.

She was one of the most beloved Viennese, who served and treated everyone as her equals. Although the Café served primarily Vienna's nobility before the war years, it made little difference if a blue collar worker brought his wife or friend for a special occasion. She knew everybody and everything, but never repeated anything, regardless of her own observations. Among them were, of course, Philip Reinhardt's own reserved loge.

Gisela was surprised that he had suggested Café Sacher, but assumed that she was possibly only one of many girls he took there frequently. Anna Sacher inquired only about his liking and progress at the Police Academy and wished both a pleasant evening. Gisela found Rupert equally handsome in his tastefully matched civilian clothes, which itself was a rarity. Men just looked better in uniforms. There was not a moment of doubt in her mind that he had his connections. She wore a beige dress and coat with small red trimming, including a red French beret. Rupert not only found her very beautiful, but the first few minutes of conversation were totally honest and delightful. They discussed their upbringing, his one year in med school, which he flunked and then decided to be a medic in the war. His friendship with Bertram was mostly out of pity, though he was probably lying about his many beatings at the hand of his father Baron von Walden too.

She took her turn with her many years of schooling, never exceeding in anything, being the so-called 'black sheep' in a brilliant family. Her schooling in kindergarten was only considered a mediocre education, but her trip and time in Berlin was worthwhile, giving her a chance to communicate with deaf mutes. Both were good listeners and found each other's company enthralling. They were also hopelessly in love! There was no turning back now and Rupert used every opportunity to make plans to be together.

"How was your evening Gisela?" asked Peter and Victoria almost regularly, only to hear her reply that it was enchanting, as always.

Philip was more inquisitive and challenging. "How can you find this policeman so fascinating when he kept a friendship with that mysterious von Walden boy? His own father told me he was a perpetual liar."

"That's exactly what Rupert said. His parents took him in, feeling sorry for an abused boy. But now they would make him pay, just like Mrs. von Walden! Right to jail!" Philip was very relieved to hear that.

Gisela was off to the library with Rupert again and, if it was not discussing books, it was museums, or an opera.

"I guess we have to have a talk with her," Philip uttered shortly before going to work. "Gisela is a changed girl."

"About what, Philip? Does it bother you that our permanent black sheep is finally turning white? Take a look at the book she is reading. All classics and all at his advice? And as for her relationship with me, I am happy to say we are closer than ever."

"Well am I to understand that you would approve, let's say," he stammered, embarrassed. "of a marriage between a policeman and our daughter?"

"Why not? After three engagements with our friends' highly qualified sons, she deserves a happy marriage."

"How do you expect him to support a Reinhardt?"

"Maybe he does what Adam van Dreesen does with our Elisabeth! He gives her a thing called *love*!" Philip never dared to answer.

~

It was Christmas and the Fosters wore their Sunday best, but Rupert seemed to have a great variety of suits and to Gisela he looked more handsome as time went on. "It's only a tiny place in comparison to what you are used to, Miss Reinhardt," the father said, showing her the rest of the house.

"My father made all the furniture himself. Aside from remodeling the house, now he will hopefully help me with mine."

"I told you, son, it will be my pleasure."

All four sat down for dinner, which was nowadays a dream for most Viennese. Gisela praised her talent in cooking and Wilma replied that she got her first lesson at twelve.

"Oh, my God!" Gisela replied. "I was double your age and, aside from that, I was taught by my grandmother in Berlin with most items bought on the black market. And thank God we had foreign money."

"Are you trying to tell us you are older than twenty-four?" an astonished Wilma asked, but apologized immediately. "I gave you barely twenty" she said very sincerely.

"On September 10th, I was twenty-six."

An unbelievable 'no' was the result. "Mother is fifty-one, father is fifty-three, and today I am twenty-eight." Rupert laughed. "Now we finally got our ages established."

Now Gisela looked aghast. "If I only would have known," she said disappointed. "but I will make it up."

"Good Lord, Gisela! Just to have you at our house on Christmas day is more than a man like me can ask for," Rupert said fondly, with his parents wholeheartedly agreeing.

~

The gifts were unwrapped in the living room and Wilma took the 'snowdrops' from the dining room, putting them lovingly on their coffee table. Gisela screamed a loud, "Oh NO!" when she was the first to open a large box with a deep green, hand-knitted dress with small trims of off-white mink color garnishing that gorgeous piece of work. "I never... Well, I never in my wildest dreams would have expected that. It's absolutely... Well, there are simply no words for it!"

The Fosters were happy to see her so overwhelmed. "I love to knit while my husband works or is reading, and my son has to study or has lately 'dated' some wonderful lady we had the honor of meeting today," she smiled, tongue in cheek.

Gisela couldn't help but embrace her spontaneously. "But I've only known Rupert weeks and the size seems to look so perfect for me. Never mind the color and quality of wool and silk."

"In this time, I could have made you two dresses," she laughed. "as I learned to knit before I had to cook."

"What did I tell you, Mother? She is not only going to love the dress but us too!"

"I couldn't have said it better myself," she agreed. The books too were exchanged, and it was exactly what everyone wanted. Classics for the men and Gisela, light-hearted love stories for Wilma.

"Who plays the piano?" she asked after coffee and cake.

"I do," replied Rupert Senior. "Don't laugh, Miss Reinhardt. I always wanted to be a musician. I also play the violin, but with no money in my family and a doubtful income for my future, somehow, I turned to carpentry. Then I met my wife and we saw an opportunity to open a grocery store while I made our furniture and made some music for my wife, son and me in my spare time. Since I was never criticized, I felt I played well enough."

"Do you still play?" Gisela asked.

"Sure. One never forgets his first great love."

"My son and I are second and third … in that order!"

Gisela laughed at Wilma's comment and said anxiously, "Then let's play."

Rupert was surprised anew as they attended two musicals and she never uttered a word about it. They went from Christmas carols in which all joined in to sing along, to waltzes and classics, ending with Tchaichovsky's 'Tonight We Love'."

"How very appropriate," mused Rupert, watching her face redden.

"It's one of my favorites," she muttered, feeling a bit confused.

"Mine too," he smiled cheerfully.

"I have to be going now… as much as I hate to."

"We all hate to see you leaving but we understand. I hope your parents are not angry."

"Absolutely not." She promised a visit in her new green dress real soon and Rupert replied he would make sure she kept her promise.

Wilma was almost in tears, feeling she got in Gisela a daughter she never had. The white-haired giant, Rupert Senior, got up along with his well-trained German shepherds, who for some reason let neither one of the Ruperts out of their sight.

On the way to Gisela's house, Rupert told her not only how beautiful she looked in her red dress, but he was convinced that it was, for all of them, the best Christmas they ever had. Gisela responded without a single moment of pause. "Count me in too!"

"You mean that?"

"Absolutely. I will tell you about our routine ones some other time."

Shortly before arriving at the main street leading to their mansion via a sparsely lit corner, he hesitated for a moment before asking, "Gisela, in July of 1925 I will graduate. Hopefully by then my own house is made up to par. I got it for a good price because of its negligence with an old widow living in it and no relatives to claim it after one year of her death. But what I am telling you is…" He gulped nervously. "Well, what I am asking you is, will you wait for me as it is one-and-a-half years?"

"If you promise to wait for me too. You know very well what I am talking about."

"With greatest pleasure, as I wouldn't want to have it any other way," he smiled deliriously happy. "Here... it's for you," he said handing her an obvious ring box. "Let me put it on. The next one is a wedding ring!"

It was a flower-petaled emerald with a two-carat diamond in the middle holding them up; a very large piece of jewelry for her long fingers.

"My God, Rupert! I really don't know what to say," she stammered, once more astonished, when he gave her the first long kiss, and she had not the slightest intention to do anything other than to pull him closer.

When they departed, both felt like the happiest couple on earth. "I'm engaged!" she exclaimed in excitement upon entering the mansion's dining room."

"Again?" her family asked simultaneously.

"For the very last time. And we will get married right after his graduation in 1925."

"Oh," Philip replied, somehow relieved that it was not sooner. "By then... well, there is still much water flowing under the bridge."

"All right father. All I will have to do is prove you wrong."

"I am not in the business of being right or wrong. I just wonder how he will support you," Philip said sternly.

"He will have his own little house ready, which he recently bought near his parents' home on a fine street in the ninth district. He will also get a substantial pay raise once he graduates. Somehow, we will make it," she babbled while unwrapping her many books until she came to the dress.

"Look, Mother... all of you! His mother hand-knitted this for me. Isn't this something?"

"Oh, Gisela. That *is* beautiful."

All admired in honesty. "The very moment he told his mother about my figure and green eyes she got the wool for it."

Philip thought of their connection on the black market. But Victoria gave him a look he wouldn't forget for the near future.

"It was not too long ago that your own father admired my green eyes too. I guess in time things just change."

Gisela paid no attention, looking still at her ring, and showing it to her grandmother Lotte and brother Peter.

"By the way, I like your chosen one. And don't think for a moment I won't help you out."

"It's sweet of you, Peter," she replied with an embrace.

Victoria looked awestruck. "Gisela, you are my daughter. Did you think you would go into in this marriage empty-handed?"

"No, Mother, it's not me, but Rupert wants to prove something to himself. His father did the same thing and they live quite well. Frankly, better than I thought."

"Well right now a grocery store is a gold mine. I am sure they made their fortune, if one can call it that, by whatever they have with their son being a policeman"

"What are you trying to tell me, Father?"

"Let's just say, bartering is a common way of life."

Lotte was furious at her son-in-law's constant negative remarks about Gisela's newfound happiness. "If it were not for bartering on the black market, Gisela and I would have never survived with millions of other Berliners, or any other large city for that matter. Just ask Paul… he will tell you."

"Well, now I am wondering why Paul prefers Berlin to Vienna!" Philip fumed.

"The schools," Lotte answered, "as Vienna is in lack of them!"

"Father!" Gisela addressed him self-assuredly, as it was lately her habit. And aside from that, she wanted to get even for her father's open dislike for Rupert. "I don't understand why you are so much against bartering and the black market, which are the result of war. Every war is ugly, but you think nothing of it to make any kind of weapon of destruction and *your* industry is perfectly legal. Tell me what's worse, making cannonballs and shells to kill the innocent or trying to barter food to stay alive?"

"Amen to that," Peter replied, clapping his hands, with Lotte and Victoria exchanging glances in silence.

"I agree with you fully, Gisela, but don't forget that I inherited that dirty business. And so will Paul should there be a second war; although this one is supposed to have ended it all. Personally, I have my doubts. However, since the war's end, I was eager to make stoves, bathtubs, and any appliance my engineers could think of just to keep the factories open, while others close theirs for lack of work. At present, dear child, I could do nothing but relax in Italy with my invested money. Instead, I am at work every day like every other employee who is glad to have a job."

"I didn't know that, Father. I am very sorry."

"I didn't expect you to. But learn to think before judging your parents."

"Father, for the very first time in my life I found someone who truly loves me and it's not for the Reinhardt money."

"I know that, Gisela, and I am very happy for you and all of us. Believe me when I tell you there was always a reason when I interfered with your former fiancés. I am not easily fooled. The trouble with you is that you are not only pretty but wealthy, and that gives many fellows a reason to pretend. No doubt they loved you, but when I denied them some of our fortune, they were gone."

"That leaves just Paul and me. Never mind my brother, find someone nice for me, Gisela."

"I will try my very best," she smiled sincerely.

1925

13

The wedding was July 8, 1925, and, with the exception of Astrid von Walden who had played cupid, it was family only. And this time, family meant the Fosters. Ten people were attending and the Reinhardts' only contribution was their priest performing a short but touching ceremony.

It was Gisela's explicit wish to have a home wedding, as poor Mr. Foster never had a daughter. Victoria had two, but no wedding at her own house. From Elisabeth, she received mail on a regular basis; very informative but impersonal. The last letter explained the Boer War in 1899-1902 in South Africa. Then, she mentioned casually that she hoped her sister's marriage would be as happy as her own.

Wilma Foster not only did her own cooking and wedding decorations, but also set her house up like a garden. "I brought the outside in, Mrs. Reinhardt. Gisela had this wonderful idea," she mentioned so proudly. All Victoria could do was grin and bear it. Wilma Foster gained a daughter alright, but Victoria and Philip never acquired a son. Rupert was so distant, feeling a little inferior, but Peter and Paul loved him like a brother. At least something good came out of it.

It was Wilma Foster who crocheted Gisela's wedding dress of fine silk yarn.

"Imagine, Mrs. Reinhardt. She found a Paris fashion magazine and showed me the latest model of Coco Chanel. Well," she continued, "that designer is not famous for bridal outfits, but there it was, just perfect for our Gisela. I copied it to the last detail and she just loved it!" Wilma gloated.

"Mrs. Foster, I am afraid my daughter takes advantage of you. I really am," Victoria apologized.

"Nonsense. Knitting the dress for my sweet daughter-in-law was the happiest time of my life."

"Well then," she conceded. "if you feel that way, I shall stop worrying. I know how much my daughter loves you."

"Likewise, Mrs. Reinhardt."

Gisela chose Erika as her only bridesmaid and both made sure that their attire coordinated perfectly. Erika decided on light blue organdy that matched Gisela's bridal bouquet ribbons. Both wore flowered garlands and let their naturally curly hair down. It was extremely flattering and they both looked beautiful for this special day. Rupert chose Peter as his best man, as his father insisted on playing the wedding march, while still giving him a chance to see Gisela making her entrance on the arm of her elegant and handsome father, with Rupert waiting in the flowered archway.

Until this fateful wedding day, Peter never took notice of Erika Landgraf. He encountered her mostly on the tennis courts or ski slopes, always being astonished at her speed and endurance. She usually wore her hair in braids, held up with pins on the tennis court or kept it under a heavy knitted ski cap to keep warm. She never was permitted to join anyone's ski activity in one of those many skiing lodges, always in the presence of her older two sisters who were equally sportsminded. Since there were no brothers, they were, at a very early age, taught somehow to replace them. Sports were ingrained like good manners and discipline. Teo Landgraf was a feared principal in one of Vienna's private schools, expecting the same strict obedience from his daughters. Their mother was in a wheelchair due to a skiing accident.

But this time, Peter couldn't help but notice Erika, who looked every bit as lovely as his sister Gisela. He saw for the first time her blonde hair and blue eyes, aside from her clear, tanned skin. But since he was not unlike his father, with many short-lived flings behind him, he never let real love get the better of him, fearing that his carefree life would come to an abrupt halt.

No one knew why, but during the brief wedding ceremony there was not a dry eye. Even the giant Rupert Sr. took out his handkerchief several times while embracing the new Gisela Foster, with his son doing the same. Even the forever aloof Paul seemed to be moved, and Philip whispered to Victoria, "As of today, we lost a daughter without gaining a son." Victoria nodded in agreement.

During a delicious meal served at Vienna's own Augarten Porcelain, each of the men gave the required toasts, with Philip gulping several times. Paul was seated next to Astrid von Walden who told him about Lucas' accident as he started to inquire about him. All were taken by surprise when he confronted his family. "Why was I never informed?" But they knew within a split second that it also involved the 'von Walden brat', whose name he never permitted to be uttered.

"So, you see, Paul… there was my poor daughter with her darling child, a widow at the age of eighteen. Just imagine that!"

"How sad," he answered. "I hope she will find someone else." To himself, however, he thought, *"Wherever that ugly brat sets foot, some tragedy follows sooner or later."*

Peter not only sat next to Erika but was completely taken by her. Victoria and Philip took notice but never gave it a second thought, knowing his record with girls. However, they somehow felt sorry for Erika, as she seemed such a fine and sincere lady.

Rupert and Gisela decided to spend their honeymoon in Rupert's newly remodeled house, which they thought could stand up to any villa. The Reinhardts were pleasantly surprised with their cozy home which Rupert and Gisela had decorated together without a schilling of the Reinhardts' money. However, on their way home, they all agreed that she married an extremely devoted man with strong principles and a family who loved and adored her. They had no other choice but to wish them their very best.

Peter mentioned casually that he would love to date Erika, but was immediately told that all he would get her is a bad reputation. "Is that what I have?" Peter smiled.

"We both loathe her father," said Paul truthfully.

"Yes, and he hates us because my brother years ago made a very sarcastic remark," Peter said rather calmly.

"What happened?" his father wanted to know.

"Oh, it was when that von Walden brat sprained my ankle."

"You forgot to say 'ugly'," his brother reminded him in jest.

"When Professor Landgraf heard about it, he asked me to apologize for calling her that name as it was all my fault to begin with," he sighed.

"Go on," his father urged.

"I told him that we Reinhardts are not required to apologize for our opinions."

"You didn't, Paul!" his father said, firm and furious. "Your arrogance is well known, and it is not *us* at all, as I even apologize to my workers with you standing right next to me. I thought it would rub off some day."

"It has. They like me just as much as they do you. We are talking eleven years ago when I was still a boy."

"Poor, beautiful Gaby. If you could see her now."

"What of her?"

"The day she gave birth to her child, her husband died."

"So I was told by Mrs. von Walden, for whom I have the greatest respect. But there was also Bertram von Walden."

"Just stop it!" his father ordered, and not another word was spoken.

"Mother," Peter whispered before going to bed. "you have to admit, Erika would make an excellent wife."

"Absolutely. But what kind of husband would *you* make is the question," Victoria replied, worried.

1926

14

Despite opposition from Teo Landgraf, Peter and Erika went to Salzburg's famous castle 'Mirabell' to get married. It was the usual civil ceremony where many other couples flock to either elope or avoid a long, solemn Catholic ceremony. It was the exact date and hour when Gisela and Rupert had said their vows the previous year. The Reinhardts were there as they vacationed once a year in Salzburg, regardless of the circumstances. But Gisela and Rupert couldn't come, as she was expecting their first child in August. Neither Rupert nor Mrs. Foster would let her go anywhere without holding her hand to avoid a slip. The Reinhardts were not only overjoyed at the upcoming birth, but deeply touched by all the love their daughter received. "She seemed to blossom in her marriage like a beautiful delicate flower."

Victoria and Philip felt happy, too, because it would be their first grandchild who lived nearby, as their oldest daughter lived in South Africa and very little was mentioned about her children, other than how smart and perfect they were. Photos arrived once in a while, but none gave any resemblance to a Reinhardt. All were light blonde, long faced, and an exact copy of Adam van Dreesen. Their invitation to Holland to meet Adam's parents was always declined, giving a different excuse every time.

Not so with the Fosters, although they promised a visit with their newborn. Rupert Sr. was busy carving a cradle which would be a work of art and Wilma knitted enough for triplets. The Reinhardts visited there quite frequently and were always more than welcome, also getting to like each other more, much to their surprise.

Rupert's house could now be called a fine villa, surrounded by a beautiful garden. They hired a few hardworking foreign workers who were glad to be in Vienna again, being very disappointed at their own separated state of Italy. The former large country of Austria wasn't that bad after all, as people returned from other places to find work in Vienna again. However, the country had new money, called the Schilling, but the unemployment rate went higher as the weeks went by. All of Europe lived in a state of depression and the former Austrian citizen, Adolf Hitler, claimed to know exactly how to handle the situation, as Germany didn't fare any better.

The Fosters and Reinhardts adored and shared their new grandson, named Christian Philip, very much to everybody's surprise. "We didn't want a third Rupert. There is already enough confusion with two." Needless to say, both parents and families hoped for a few more. Life became peaceful and extremely content.

Even Philip was a different man. At the age of sixty, although still cutting a dashing figure, he seemed to enjoy family life. He visited the factories two to three times a week, always trying to keep his workers content, but for how long was anyone's guess. Paul, though quite different from his father in many ways, agreed completely with his father as far as the factories and workers were concerned. At the age of twenty-six, he acted and appeared older, and was quite proficient at helping his father running his business.

15

By 1928, Rupert and Gisela expected their second child. Peter and Erika were still on their honeymoon and lived in the palace with his own practice nearby. When coming home late due to some emergency, Victoria once took Peter aside, telling him frankly that she had a few detectives watching him for fear he would turn out like his father. And aside from that, she loved Erika just like the Fosters loved Gisela, as a daughter.

"Mother, dear, save your worries. If one is so lucky to have a wife like Erika, one has no need for anyone else." He left her standing awestruck. Once more, she was convinced that she had failed Philip in the bedroom, but then again, Peter may not have the same desires his father had.

To be rich and give elaborate parties was en vogue again. It really didn't matter how one made his fortune during the four years of war, as long as no one thought that one had profited through the black market. Vienna's once proud nobility was, in many cases, among the impoverished class, unless they owned a sizable amount of land. But years after the war and with new money since 1925, they came to realize that by serving the House of Habsburg with pride and dignity, one was only left with lots of memories and very little else. Of course, they got the usual bow and were addressed by their former titles when entering any of the café houses. There they met, drank their cup of coffee, and had a lively discussion about the 'good old times', and read the newspapers. The latest news was that Alfred Haas, the owner of Vienna's largest bread factory, would give a big party for his only daughter, Irene, after her long absence from Vienna. Frankly, nobody remembered her except that after the accidental death of her mother in 1915, the girl was sent to Switzerland to finish her schooling and, with the full consent of her father, went on to France to study art. She also took singing and acting lessons, the latter coming in handy. Since she was extremely beautiful with auburn hair, almost violet eyes, and symmetric features, there was never any shortage of suitors. Her slender body was the envy of many, as being lean became the latest fashion style. Aside from that, her father supplied her with a great amount of money. Simultaneously, although he claimed to love his daughter very much, he was in many ways glad to have her somewhere else, as he had, at times, not only one but two mistresses. Now that she was returning, he would throw a big party in her honor and then get her an apartment. After all, she was twenty-seven and still single.

He made a visit once a year just to keep in touch and had to admit that she was one of the most beautiful creatures God ever created. But so was her mother at the time of their marriage. Only later, he found out that her love went mostly to her horses and, until she was thrown off one and died a few weeks later, he vowed never to get married again, but to enjoy the single life.

He was, in one way, different from Philip, as he never set foot in a red-light district and changed his mistress the moment she expected a commitment. And so it went year after year until Irene arrived two weeks before. Now he had the obligation to introduce her to what was left of Vienna's high society, and was elated that she turned out not only beautiful, but had acquired style, refinement and knowledge in art, history, and five languages. It was, to her and her father, a great pity that Vienna's times had changed so drastically. Misery, unemployment, and uprisings were still all over the town. However, it didn't keep Alfred Haas from putting the upcoming party in the newspaper.

"Imagine that!" Dr. Peter Reinhardt said to his parents after arriving home from a very hard and challenging day of work. "Haas put his daughter and upcoming party in the paper."

"Why not? His brother is the owner of the Daily News."

"Oh, I forgot," he smiled, embracing Erika lovingly.

"Well, we lose nothing by attending," Victoria stated matter-of-factly. "He never missed one of ours."

To their surprise, even Gisela and Rupert received an invitation. But then again, Gisela Foster was still considered a Reinhardt. That she married well beneath her class was no different from Peter, or for that matter Elisabeth, who was a Doctor of Medicine and married to a missionary. "Strange family," her father explained to Irene. "but they all appear so happy."

"Well, is their other son attached?"

"Paul? No, he is waiting for the perfect wife. I mean, for a woman without a past."

"You are looking at her, Father. He would never find out about my life in Paris."

"If you don't mind me saying so, in the bedroom he would."

"After our marriage vows, it will be too late." Her father only smiled, hoping that Paul would show up.

~

The party was scheduled for August 3rd. It created a conflict only with Gisela's little daughter, who was on this day one year old. But since the party at the Haases' was

Saturday evening, the Fosters agreed to have their little birthday party the previous day.

"After all, my labor pains started much earlier anyway," Gisela laughed, and all the Fosters agreed. For a change, Paul had nothing on his agenda and promised to go, providing his family would attend. All of the Reinhardts did, including a very elegant Erika and Gisela on the arms of their proud husbands.

One couldn't help but notice Irene Haas immediately, who was not only stunning looking but dressed to the hilt. No one had ever seen anything like it, but knew immediately that it was pure Paris. The dress was navy with tiny golden ornaments woven in. She also knew to stand under a shiny crystal chandelier while presented to the largest crowd Alfred Haas was able to assemble. Philip was, as always, taken by beauty, his head already spinning while making plans. Paul, who had the reputation of being better off entering a monastery, was equally smitten by her elegance and perfect mannerisms. Alfred Haas hoped that he would be the one. Old money to old money was always his axiom, feeling it worked better, although his own marriage was a sham. He took great delight in watching Irene and Paul dancing the evening away and seeking out the Reinhardts on this fateful evening. Victoria was, in a way, relieved to hear how much Philip approved, should there ever be a plan for marriage.

"I would make it the biggest wedding Vienna would ever see!" Alfred Haas promised, very pleased at the prospect. "And you know we are both families who are not in need of anything."

Victoria answered only softly, "And you know, Mr. Haas, that we Reinhardts are not after anything either. My three children's happy marriages mean the world to me." Philip hardly paid attention, being completely preoccupied with beautiful Irene.

~

With the party behind them, each one, as always, had their own opinion. Rupert only complimented Gisela's appearance, keeping his opinion about Irene to himself. "Our parties are not so stressful... more at ease," Gisela replied. Both couldn't wait to be at home with their families. The Fosters had become Gisela's family a long time ago and she loved Rupert as much as he loved her.

Erika became Victoria's best friend and replaced Gisela in many ways. Victoria was a woman who always needed someone close to her, though she was not someone who confided easily. But Erika and Peter got Anette's apartment in the large mansion, decorated it their own way, and were extremely satisfied, as both in-laws gave them their privacy once Peter entered the place.

They drove home with Philip and Victoria, holding hands as usual in the backseat and talked about the party. Victoria said that Irene was very beautiful but lacked compassion. Peter agreed. "She seems to be a rather mysterious woman who would be hard to deal with. My Erika is honest, open, and easy-going. I could not handle anyone else, as my practice and the hospital are stressful enough."

"So I noticed," Philip replied. It was his only contribution on the way home, not even reacting to Gisela's comment about how smitten Paul was with Irene Haas, dancing with no one else. Paul arrived one hour later in his own car, telling Victoria that he thought, for the first time, that he was in love.

"Great!" she replied very curtly, and then Victoria wished him a goodnight.

Philip was already in bed pondering how to get this beautiful woman to his bedroom, knowing very well she had been around. A man like him had no problem spotting an easy woman playing hard to get. Paul will bring her by, and on one of those days there will be an opportunity to talk to her alone. To him, it was a laughable matter that Paul was so besotted with Irene, who had every man at her feet. He couldn't help but notice the envy of all his friends and contemporaries.

They dated as often as possible, she playing the part of a virgin, while visiting his father as often as he wished. Philip knew it was only a matter of time, and the fact that Paul was ready to marry her didn't change a thing. She was used to this kind of life and boasted occasionally how many lovers she had previously; among them, three brothers who never had any idea she even knew the other ones.

"Philip, I am extremely discreet when it comes to my love life. It will never come out." He was more than happy to hear it, as he had not the slightest intention of leaving Victoria. And those few affairs with mistresses lasted only a few weeks, as they all eventually looked for a commitment. That much, and only that much, he had in common with Alfred Haas.

He purchased a villa in the opposite direction of his factories and called it, 'Villa of Lust'. It was the perfect place, with a perfect partner like Irene, to make perfect love. And neither she nor he had the slightest intention of giving up something up both wanted so desperately. His usual red-light district was rampant with syphilis and he was without a woman until Irene appeared. And when it came to sex, both were devoid of any conscience, no matter how many promises they had to break.

On Christmas Eve, Paul presented Irene with a beautiful ten-carat diamond in her father's house, before they went to his own to tell his parents the good news. The Reinhardts were stunned, except Philip. But Gisela and Rupert came, so did Peter and Erika, who were amazed at Paul's fast commitment.

"My father was so overjoyed," she cried. "that he convinced both of us to have the wedding at Easter!" All were silent with a fixed smile, while a happy Philip exclaimed, "How wonderful! I'll bet he selected St. Stephan's Cathedral!"

"How did you guess, Mr. Reinhardt?" asked the actress, Irene.

"He told my wife and me it would be the biggest wedding Vienna will ever see."

"Poor, sweet man. He thought he would die without any grandchildren," she noted.

Watching her talking and tears running down her cheek while trying to smile simultaneously, Philip felt she was a greater actress than the legendary Sarah Bernhardt. To Paul's great surprise, no one except his father showed any joy when they wished them the best of luck.

When Victoria sat alone with Philip, drinking their usual glass of wine in front of the fireplace, she couldn't help remarking on how fast everything went with Paul, as it was so unlike him.

"Oh, he made it very clear to me that he had better move fast or he was going to lose her to someone else. This time it hit him hard. It was love at first sight for both of them."

"We should consult the Wilands in any case." Philip was surprised and asked what could possibly be the reason, with all of her wealth. "Some people can never have enough, for one thing, and if you noticed her wardrobe... jewelry... leather bag... it's the best of the best. We Reinhardt women were never that wasteful."

"I wish you and my two daughters were! And Erika too, for that matter."

"Peter, Erika, and I shop together. I only buy for her what Peter likes on her and you must admit, she always looks very stylish and beautiful."

"To tell you the truth, I only notice their happiness and wish the same for Paul's forthcoming marriage."

She only gave a slight nod but continued, "I hope they'll live in the Lindenfels castle as it stays empty almost all the time."

"Great idea!" Philip replied. "She is much like you in that matter, while I have to admit that neither our Gisela nor Erika show any interest, and both were never raised to enjoy giving orders. And servants without anyone to serve are an unhappy lot. They take great joy in being needed. That much I learned early in life from Mother, as Father hated to ask anyone, always thinking he was an imposition to them.

"What a wonderful and great man," Victoria sighed. "What a shame so many have passed away. Thank God for Erika," she added, before giving Philip his good-night kiss. It was nothing more than a daily routine.

1929

16

The date was set for March 30 and true to his word, Alfred Haas gave his daughter a wedding that no one was likely to forget. But once again, the Reinhardts were left without any kind of involvement and Paul reminded them in a gentle way that, after all, she was Alfred's only daughter and he would spare no effort and expense. Alfred Haas hired two wedding coordinators to take care of the details. Their plans included a lavish dinner for five hundred guests at Vienna's famous Hotel Imperial, which, among its many merits, was known for having the finest ballroom. After the long ceremony, which would include a high mass, the dinner and dancing would begin and end well into the night, making the newlyweds too tired for travel; therefore, a honeymoon suite was reserved.

Paul, his future wife, and father-in-law planned an elaborate six-week honeymoon, which included many places both had been in Switzerland, but never tired of seeing. It was the south of Switzerland with Locarno and Lugano at the top of their list, and Paul also wanted to meet his former school chums in Zurich again, to show off his beautiful wife.

Irene had the French Riviera on her mind and, of course, Paris.

The honeymoon was, of course, a gift from Alfred Haas, who personally made all the reservations and considered himself the happiest man alive. Paul kept insisting he would pay all the expenses, as Irene would be his wife by then and, aside from being wealthy himself, his father gave him both of his factories as a wedding gift, as at his age, Philip was getting tired of working so much. The truth was, however, that while Paul was working, Philip could be found in the 'House of Lust' playing.

So far, the only surprise at Irene's entrance on the arm of her glowing, proud father was the disappointing wedding dress from the French designer, Jean Patou, who, like others in the world of fashion, took the waistline away. Her dress, although from the finest white velvet, had a high neckline and was straight to the floor. She held a large bouquet of white lilies adorned with green leaves, her long auburn hair tied back with a velvet bow. Of course, her fixed, beautiful smile was directed at her father with a slight wink, showing how happy she felt.

"Not even one bridesmaid?" whispered several who were regulars at almost every big wedding. "Maybe she wants all the attention directed at herself." They agreed, and being informed about the coordinators, they knew Irene Reinhardt-Haas, as she requested to be called, had the last word on everything.

The lavish dinner made up for the lack of wedding attendants, and the variety of wines as well as the desserts were the best anyone could remember. After the reception, dancing began and it was repeated often how like her father she was.

Rupert and Gisela departed early, seeing no reason to spend more time with people with whom they had very little in common. Both wished Paul good luck, and Gisela added in a whisper, "You need it. She is too good looking."

"Don't be jealous, sister. You get better looking each time I see you," he replied, and she followed Rupert who said his good-byes to Victoria. Erika advised her brother-in-law to stay at the Hotel Danieli when in Venice, and Peter agreed.

"I really don't know if Venice is on our list, but there is always another year," Paul uttered, wondering where his wife was, as a few older friends from Lindenfels were ready to leave. Alfred Haas always was a charming and interesting man to talk to, and among his spellbound listeners was Victoria, who was only concerned with Paul's future. Although Irene was nothing less than sweet and kind to her, expressing how proud she was to be a Reinhardt, she couldn't help but notice her endless flirtation with every man in the room while dancing. Paul was in heaven each time they talked or danced together, but so were the rest of the men, including Philip.

Paul, feeling as though he had talked to everybody in Vienna, thought his new shoes were the most uncomfortable pair he had ever owned and, knowing their suitcases were up in their rooms, decided to change them. When he asked the concierge for the key, he was told his wife had picked them up a short while ago. *"So she has the same problem,"* he thought to himself until he reached the suite and heard talking with groaning. Turning white like a ghost, he opened the unlocked door, Irene having completely forgotten to lock it in her frenzy to let Philip in for a quick, shameless act, knowing they wouldn't see each other for the next few weeks.

"Oh, my God!" Paul stuttered in disbelief seeing the two nude bodies. "I married my father's whore!" Philip and Irene turned equally white, being completely at a loss for words. "So that's what I got for a... a... I will never be able to say for my wife! A dirty old man with a prostitute!"

Philip got out of bed, still shaking, and put his clothes on in a hurry quivering, "Paul... please. Not a word to your mother."

"Not because you ask me, but only because I love Mother!"

"I'll make it up to you. I swear I will," he stammered, still white, and left the room.

Philip didn't know how he descended the wide, red carpeted staircase, looked for Victoria who was still listening to Irene's father, not noticing his change of color due to the bright light. "There you are, Mr. Reinhardt. We were looking for you to say goodbye and to tell you, you have the most gorgeous daughter-in-law. We have known her father a lifetime," Regina Fiedler said ever so proudly. "What a beautiful couple," her husband joined in.

"Forgive me, but I don't feel well. Possibly ate and danced too much," he apologized, just in case they noticed any change in him.

"That's why we are leaving," Regina replied in a whisper. "One is not used to this kind of food."

"And wine," her husband smiled. "All imported from France."

"So I noticed," Philip smiled as well as possible, noticing his wife coming their way. They only waved, having said their farewells already.

"Don't you feel well, Philip?"

"I am glad you are so observant. I don't know if I drank, ate, or talked too much," he lamented. "but I am ready to go home."

"So am I, but we have to wait for Paul and Irene. We won't see them for a few weeks."

"You are right, dearest. I am going to talk to Arthur and Victor Wiland about something. Call on me if you see them."

"I will," she smiled.

~

Paul told Irene to get dressed, walk down with him, and behave like nothing had happened. She did it without uttering one word and he knew at once she had been in a similar situation more than one time. "I will explain later," she answered, completely in control again, while Paul didn't know how to get his needed strength without anybody getting suspicious that something was wrong. They arrived arm in arm saying their thanks, accepting all the good wishes until all but their parents were alone. She embraced her father heartily in tears and promised, loudly enough for the Reinhardts to hear, to make Paul a good wife. That jolly heavyset man also broke out in tears while quivering that he never doubted it for a moment. Philip and Paul never witnessed a better performance as she was in the process of giving the same promise to Victoria who only replied, "Marriage is hard work, Irene. It's a give and take situation, with women mostly on the short end of it all."

"I know," she smiled looking very sincere. "Paul and I will have no problem we cannot solve together."

"And we are hoping, of course, for some grandchildren one of these days," Alfred Haas smiled. "There are three people waiting to spoil them."

"You bet," Philip replied, and Paul started to hate him even more as he linked his arm in his mother's. "Darling, the servants are ready to put the place in order." With a renewed embrace, they said their final good-byes and wished them a good trip.

"What a day!" Alfred Haas said, shaking hands with both of the Reinhardts simultaneously.

"You can say that again!" Philip replied.

~

Arriving in their honeymoon suite, Paul lost no time in ordering Irene to sit down and give him some account of his future with her. "In my eyes, you are nothing more than a low-down slut who acted her way into the Reinhardt family. You probably went to bed with my father soon after we met. My only way of getting even with you is that I will never ever touch you. You are, as of now, free to do as you like, which on second thought, you would have done anyway."

She sighed deeply and said spoke candidly. "We were married in the Catholic faith and you have an obligation, Paul."

"Not after you broke yours a few hours later, Irene!" he fumed. "Which brings me right to another subject; you will be referred to by all of our servants as 'Mrs. Irene', in no way Mrs. Reinhardt!"

"Suits me fine. The moment I leave the castle I will be Mrs. Irene."

"Whatever… I will talk to my priest about the procedures of an annulment."

"Then I have no choice but to confront your mother."

He never replied and went in a sitting room which had the elegance and comfort of a salon. A bottle of champagne was in a silver cooler waiting for the newlyweds. Paul took it and put it in front of Irene. "Call someone and have a toast and a good night."

"I will as soon as we leave Vienna," she smiled and closed her bedroom door. A different and unusual Reinhardt marriage had begun.

Irene took a long, hot bath, but Paul didn't want to see her again. He undressed, put on his pajamas, took a sleeping pill, and went, teary-eyed, to sleep. *"What a day,"* he thought, thinking of Alfred Haas' words.

17

Right after her husband's unexpected accident, life for Gabriella Rosatti, formerly Gaby von Walden, came almost to a complete standstill. Only the baby, having never laid eyes on her father, seemed to be well-adjusted. The ever-present Susanne was happy to take care of little Isabella as Lucas' parents were incapable of leaving the house, or even holding the baby for that matter. Ingrid and Henry Lebrun were more concerned about Gaby, begging her to start a routine by doing something, as anything was better than staring at the four walls or the baby.

The change came during Andreas' visit two months later. He forced Gaby to take her skis and go for a few days with him to the Alps. That was the beginning of turning her life around. She also redecorated her nice apartment in the most tasteful way, thanks to the generous inheritance her mother sent with Andreas, while Aunt Ingrid and Rosatti insisted on paying for Susanne. And Lucas' monthly pension was quite sufficient to continue in a comfortable lifestyle. Her life became a routine with barely any changes the last five-and-a-half years. She wondered frequently if she had loved Lucas more than she knew during their short marriage, as there was never any shortage of love letters from some unmarried Rosattis, who after a few years of visits to Lausanne, just gave up on her.

By now, she was a very beautiful widow of twenty-four who had never dated anyone. Years ago, her self-imposed daily routine began first thing in the morning, enjoying the open food markets, picking only the best cuts of meats, cheese, vegetables, and fruits for a hearty meal which her little Isabella obviously enjoyed, as she was growing up fast and healthy. After lunch came a walk to the florist, then she continued on with her daughter to visit the cemetery for a prayer, then proceeded to the park's playground, watching Isabella play and make new friends.

Time permitting, Susanne would go along and if not, she paid a visit to the Rosattis or Lebruns before walking home. As time went by, both Rosattis became extremely devoted grandparents as well as in-laws. Somehow, they felt happy and relieved that their Gabriella didn't remarry as soon as the mourning period was over, as so many other widows did. Instead, she and Isabella went with her in-laws to Locarno to visit their growing family of Rosattis, who would spoil her little daughter.

Thanks to Aunt Ingrid's obsession with lessons of every kind for a little girl, Isabella was introduced at the age of three to skating and skiing, to playing the piano at four, horseback riding at five, and this year, swimming lessons at Lausanne's indoor swimming pool. Of course, a once a week visit to a fine café house was a must. She would learn how to sit straight and choose pastry and soda.

The Rosattis started to be on good terms again, one year after their disagreement about who built the best cars. They promised each other never to talk about vehicles again. The result was that Rosattis came to Lausanne with their newly improved Fiats, which gained in popularity or an elegant Bugatti, as for some of the well-to-do Rosattis, this was the car one just had to have. But Alfredo had just returned from Germany with a brand-new Mercedes-Benz to take his wife, Gabriella, and Isabella to Locarno to spend several weeks there.

He was sort of semi-retired, as the death of Lucas had taken away much of his desire to run the restaurant, so three years ago he made his former kitchen chef an equal partner, then enlarged the Rosatti-Torelli restaurant, not losing a single one of the regular patrons, but adding many more. It was still the best Italian restaurant in Lausanne.

Since the discussion of cars was taboo, they had to find a new conversation whenever the male Rosattis had their visits. Now it was Germany's new "messiah". As far as the Rosattis were concerned, Hitler was a little private from the Great War who was stirring up more troubles. But then again, they were Swiss first and foremost, strongly believing in the fairness of their founding fathers. So far, their treasured neutrality kept them out of many wars between other neighbors.

Astrid von Walden was now a devoted Christian Scientist, though her son Andreas, who was now a Doctor of Medicine, convinced his mother the necessity of hospitals and doctors. They arrived in Lausanne to stay with her ailing sister, Ingrid, therefore missing Paul Reinhardt's big wedding. After a few days, Andreas returned to Vienna and Astrid continued her trip with a visit to Gaby and Isabella in Locarno. Gaby still showed no interest in visiting Vienna, let alone returning. She and Isabella rented covered beach chairs, planning to spend a day there to do as they pleased. It was the middle of May and an extremely warm day.

Gaby, after swimming with her daughter, was still in her swimming suit, stretched out full length while reading Leo Tolstoy's *War and Peace*, which at times bored her. But since Aunt Ingrid insisted she read it, she felt today was as good as any, while from time to time glancing at Isabella's delight in building sandcastles. She kept a tiny metal water pitcher on the tip of the beach chair just in case the dry sand didn't give her the desired texture.

"Don't look, Mama," she said in Italian, which she spoke just as fluently as French, also planning to learn German in the near future.

"I won't, darling. I like surprises."

"It's one of the nicest castles I ever built."

"All of your castles are nice."

"But this time I won't forget the horse stables."

"Glad to hear that, sweetheart." No sooner had Gaby finished the sentence when a ball hit her almost finished castle. Gaby jumped up and noticed a man with his son running in their direction, while Isabella was still too startled to speak.

"Oh God, Madame, we are so very sorry. The ball just more or less went in a different direction." His son was equally embarrassed looking at Isabella.

"May I help repair the castle? I am so sorry too." Their French accent was obvious. He noticed that Gaby had the looks from a northern country; her light blonde hair, blue eyes, and light complexion, never mind the perfect slender shape he discovered with his by now lusty look.

Gaby observed that a young woman made large strides toward them, and assumed it was his wife. They all introduced themselves, still regretting the mishap, his wife bending down very kindly, assuring her that on a day like today too many people are on the beach to play ball.

Isabella finally found her voice after seeing all those nice people surrounding her. "I know it was an accident. I always build castles here, right Mama?" Gaby nodded with a smile. "I will build a new one tomorrow."

"Yes, you will. And since you are from France, maybe you have a few suggestions?" Gaby inquired, looking at their son Marcel. He appeared to be between nine and ten and seemed very well behaved.

"I have seen Chambord," he replied humbly, when his father added, "We live in Blois on the Loire. It's a special place to be if you love castles."

"How lucky can we get?" Gaby said to her smiling daughter. Marcel's parents returned the smile with an obvious sign of relief.

"I always try to build Versailles, but there is never enough space," Isabella uttered in sincere disappointment, with everyone trying to suppress their laughter. After all, to that little girl it was a serious project.

"I'll tell you what, ma cherie," Marcel's mother interjected. "Why don't we all go for some ice cream at a nice veranda café and we will design as best as we can all the castles we have visited."

Isabella clapped her hands and jumped for joy. "Please say yes, Mama!"

"Of course. All of us deserve some ice cream."

They decided at four o'clock in Café Rosatti, as any other place would have never been forgiven.

"See, my precious, now you can build even more castles. It was a blessing in disguise when the ball hit yours."

"Did I behave correctly, Mama?" she asked, concerned.

"Oh, darling, I was so very, very proud of you. I know how much it hurt you after hours of hard work, but I didn't even detect one little tear!"

"I am proud too," she said, embracing her mother who was ready to settle down with her book again. Isabella looked at her watch and asked with a plea, "Mama, we still have an hour to spare. May I give you a new hairdo?"

"And why not? You must have noticed how badly I need one." With a big smile she went to their beach chair to look in Gaby's handbag and fetched a comb. She stood spread eagle over her mother's small waist, took the pins out of her upheld hair to fit her bathing cap and tried to rearrange it, while twisting her face in the sweetest way. Isabella was once more in her glory. However, she couldn't help but notice a man sitting nearby in a beach chair reading his newspaper, while glancing from time to time sideways watching and listening, including the incident with the ball, for the last hour.

It was like a tonic to watch their behavior towards each other and towards the strangers who destroyed the little girl's castle. Paul felt it was his best day since his ill-fated honeymoon to Irene Haas. While in general counting the days for a return to Vienna, this time he wished for one day longer to watch the little girl rebuild again, while looking at her beautiful mother. But the next morning he would be on the train and he hated the thought of being close to Irene in a first-class compartment. Today, Irene was in Lugano, while Paul decided on Locarno, having enjoyed it the previous day. Unless there was an obligation to fulfill, each went his own way. He kept the promise never to touch her and she did whatever she wished.

~

Paris was her goal again and since she had permission to do as she pleased, she would take plenty of advantage. She longed for Philip, who counted the days for her return. So far, Victoria never gave Philip's glances towards Irene another thought. After all, he had to prove himself daily that he was still desirable, and in Irene he had found the perfect partner to make love and he was not willing to let her go.

Paul only cared that his mother never found out and Irene was just as adamant about her father. They just would go on pretending until the right time presented itself. Paul only agreed to an annulment and that takes six to seven years. She would occupy the left wing of the castle in Lindenfels, and he would have the rest of it. Their servants would neither care nor utter a word for fear of losing their well-paid and comfortable positions. Time would tell. It has always a way of working things out. Thank God he was very busy with his two factories, and he doubted that his father would ever visit as often as previously, but he would have to have a talk with him in the presence of Irene. He thought of so many things on the train while sitting, unfortunately, across from Irene.

"How will you explain to your mother that I am 'Mrs. Irene' and not 'Reinhardt'?"

"To avoid confusion."

"Ha! Erika is addressed as Frau Doctor, so where is the confusion? Both live in the palace. And I already observed she doesn't like me; neither does your sister Gisela or her husband?" He never gave her an answer, only partly listening to her endless chatter. His thoughts were still on the beach in Locarno with mother and daughter. He felt very guilty about it, as the mother wore the widest wedding band he had ever seen.

Still in front of his mind was how fast she put a flowered wrap-around dress on, with her daughter wearing an identical one. They went to meet the French people who invited them for ice cream. That same evening, he walked around Locarno, hoping to see them again, but it was in vain. Here he was, just married, after falling deeply in love with Irene, and now he hated her. And now he had fallen for a beautiful woman who was not only married, but had a child. He felt as low and cheap as he had ever felt and sincerely hoped his thoughts would leave him by the time he arrived home and went back to work, as lots of changes were awaiting him.

Philip Reinhardt and Alfred Haas were at the train station waiting for their arrival. He knew at once that his father came only after a sort of friendly persuasion from her father, whom he considered a very fine man. Both got along splendidly. What a pity his daughter and Paul couldn't do the same.

There were lots of embraces between Irene and her father, and Alfred Haas never noticed how cool Paul and his father were. Philip took all to Lindenfels to show the proud father his daughter's new castle. They left shortly after to leave the tired newlyweds to themselves. Paul lost no time in showing to Irene her wing. He chose her servants and told all of them to address her as Mrs. Irene. They bowed slightly but knew immediately that something was very wrong. Irene, who was raised with servants, had not the slightest trouble in taking over and commanding. She was kind, but she promised herself that she would earn their respect. No one talked, but everyone whispered when Paul decided to take the right wing, which was always his to begin with. As far as he was concerned, things were settled.

~

His father was in the factory by the time Paul arrived. Philip told him that besides the factories, his money from several banks was, with the help of Wilands, also in his and the company's name. He would never again bother Paul unless it was urgent business. Paul only nodded and replied, "I have been well trained to carry the burden. However, should there be some question in the future, I will call on you." Not another word was spoken. *"He can have his Irene back at any time,"* Paul thought, but refrained from telling him. Those two would carry on their escapades no matter what. He hated himself for his strong desire to see the Swiss mother and her sweet little daughter again and wished once more, with all his heart, that his thoughts would disappear.

~

The following day, Irene was in Philip's 'House of Lust' making passionate love as before. While having a drink on the balcony, she told him of her so-called honeymoon and Paul's own law for their marriage.

"I worried about it more than you will ever know, dearest Irene. That altar boy of mine should have entered the priesthood a long time ago. There was even a time when I thought he loved men. I was so relieved when he started to fall for you, but look what happened. Now that he mentioned an annulment... Oh God, if I only were younger... I would never hesitate to ask Victoria for a divorce."

"A woman like her would never give you one."

"I just wonder how long it will be before you fall in love with someone else. That's my biggest worry."

"Don't talk so foolishly, Philip. It hurts that you even entertain such a thought."

"Honest?"

"Of course. I enjoy our setup." And back to the bedroom they went.

~

Summer came. The Reinhardts went to Salzburg, taking Irene along without Paul, who had an enormous workload as unemployment was almost out of control. Every morning, he encountered long lines in front of his factories for any kind of work. There was none. Peter stayed only two weeks in Salzburg, but told Erika to stay longer as his mother felt so lonely without her. Rupert and Gisela were just told they would be parents again. Their third child would be due in January. Like Peter and Erika, they were still on their honeymoon, happily married.

By now, they all knew that Paul's marriage was a big mistake. They felt sorry for Paul, who visited his sister and brother alone or with his mother, who still had not the slightest idea about her husband and Irene's affair. Neither had Alfred Haas, who spent many afternoons at the Reinhardts' castle, giving the impression that he thoroughly enjoyed the marriage between a Haas and a Reinhardt.

While on her lonely honeymoon in Paris at the luxurious hotel, Prince de Galles, Irene met an Austrian businessman, who claimed to be legally separated and lived near Vienna, owning a hotel in the spa city of Baden. Since her return from Locarno, she had met the man a few times secretly while still carrying on the affair with Philip. They wrote each other frequently and, at the beginning of October, she became reckless. Philip felt that she had taken another, possibly younger, lover and when being confronted by him, she had the courage to admit it, claiming their love affair was going nowhere and her new lover was at least separated, had no children, and would ask his wife for a divorce. Philip was devastated beyond belief, crying like a little child. He had never seen a more beautiful body with snow white skin, little breasts, a tiny waist, and long, perfectly formed legs.

"I permit you to see your new lover from time to time, no matter how it hurts me," he cried. "as long as we go on seeing each other."

"I will think about it," she replied without emotion, and left. She had to hurry to meet George Adler at the train station, who already had a room reserved in Hotel Bristol. It was his usual hotel whenever in Vienna. The main reason for his trip was to take all his money out of Vienna's largest bank. A good friend of his was one of the managers, telling him most of them were inept and overextended themselves with poorly advised speculation.

Irene and George Adler met, had a bite to eat, and went together straight to the bank, took every schilling out, went to the hotel, made love, and she accompanied him back to the station with the promise to see each other once a week at Bristol's. He also mentioned that his wife lived a few miles away from Baden and there was no reason she couldn't visit from time to time. Irene liked that. She was, by now, utterly bored with her life and thought of traveling again, as Paul had barely spoken to her. They even took their meals separately.

True to George's prediction, the bank collapsed and the Viennese were not only stunned, but panicked. Each one ran to his own bank to take every schilling out, not trusting Austria's regime, who told the citizens a few years ago and quite frequently since then that, thanks to a loan from America, their country had nicely recovered. Everybody was in shock, including Philip.

The largest amount of Philip's money was given to Paul as a wedding present, and for his factories, which Paul deposited in Zurich while on his honeymoon. Philip had left the rest of it in the bank that collapsed. He arrived at home quite shaken, as he had retrieved very little from his own account. Victoria told him she had all her money in Switzerland and would be more than happy to give him any amount he needed. "After all," she added. "it was Reinhardt money to begin with. I had no idea your mother left it all to me and the children."

"Wise woman in that matter. She always thought a mistress of mine would end up with the Reinhardt fortune." He thought to himself that he would have gladly given Irene everything he owned, just to keep her until his dying day. As it stood right now, he was without a mistress and without money. But there was his wife again, not even batting an eyelash to give him everything he would ask for.

The following days he waited for Irene to show up, but it was in vain. He hated to make a visit to his own castle as he was informed about Paul's setups. To be seen there would doubtless give the servants a reason to put the puzzle together. He planned to go to her apartment, as it was not the first time he went there. She opened the door, looking at him as though she were seeing a stranger. "Oh, it's you, Philip. You can come in. I am alone."

"I'd just like to know if there is any hope of us being together again?" he said, almost in tears.

"No, Philip. I searched my soul and came to the conclusion that it was just an infatuation. Sort of two crazy, mixed-up lovers. It's over. I don't even enjoy seeing you, but will pretend at family gatherings like nothing ever happened. You are and were ever so right when you told me you were too old for me. Right now, you are eighty in my eyes. Like Paul said, 'a dirty old man'." With that cruel statement, she opened the door and let him go, but not before assuring him they were still family.

Arriving at home, Victoria told him how glad she was that Paul had put his money in a bank in Zurich. "Your trouble is," she continued. "you are too generous and always have been. I only wish you could have loved me as deeply as I do you." She put her arm around his neck, kissing him on his cheek. "Better shave, Philip. All our children are coming for dinner."

"I will, and thanks for your understanding all these years."

"Don't get sentimental. You are the one who was short-changed," she sighed.

He went in his bedroom, took the gun in his dresser drawer, and put it at his temple before pulling the trigger.

~

Upon hearing about Philip Reinhardt's suicide, most who knew him linked it to the unexpected bank crash, while the ones closest to him felt it was a love affair gone sour. Victoria, who loved this man unconditionally, had seen the many good sides of him and Paul hoped she would never find out about his liaison with Irene. She agreed with many of their mutual friends that it was due to the bank crash claiming all of his money that was deposited there. She felt she owed no one any other explanation. But she made sure he got a deservingly large funeral, something the Viennese thrived on, as the last ones were conducted only among the immediate family. Their own priest conducted the religious rites, with Irene being the only one without a tear. Her father made up for it, though, as he sobbed uncontrollably, counting Philip not only as a new relative, but also as one of his closest friends.

Paul held his arm around his mother, and it was up to Peter to give the eulogy in the name of his family. He kept it quite short, knowing that there were many present who knew about his permanent philandering. Rupert had his arm around Gisela and, as with every family occasion, they watched only the reaction of their children, who loved their grandfather deeply. Then came the Chief Engineer from Reinhardt's factory, who said that Philip Reinhardt was not just an everyday employer but a man who treated everybody with the same respect, be it the highest or lowest salaried employee. He never treated anyone as subordinate. He had only kindness and compassion for everyone, remembering the many who lost a loved one in the First World War. It all seemed like yesterday, and yet it was so long ago. Paul promised himself to give a speech tomorrow, as many worried about their jobs. The workers needed some assurance and some confidence. No Reinhardter would join the unemployment line.

His mother, along with the Wilands, would forge a plan until Austria is on its feet again. Since most servants were at the funeral, they had prepared the the food the previous day. The mansion was overflowing, and Paul was already taking charge. Victoria was very proud of him, knowing the House of Reinhardt would be in good hands. And as for Irene, they would deal with her depending on the circumstances.

1937

18

The scene would have made a pretty postcard that morning, provided anyone was wide awake enough to notice. The snow was whiter than white, the air clear and crisp and the sky its best shade of blue. But it was New Years' Day, and with very few exceptions, everyone simply had to sleep. The parties the night before had always been the gayest in Vienna, and who would have refused to attend 'The Reinhardts' party that put every other one in the shadows? As always, an evening at the Reinhardts' surpassed all others.

A young chimney sweep carrying the traditional good luck symbol under his arm – a paper mache pig, horseshoe, and a four-leaf clover equally made from paper – whistled a happy tune going from house to mansion making sure he missed no one's door in his territory. He knew the servants would be up regardless of their master's own good times the previous night, so he said a warm 'Happy New Year' and gave the usual picturesque calendar. But he also knew that there would be a schilling awaiting him, as it had been a custom as long as anyone could remember. And to alter anything connected with tradition would never enter the mind of any Austrian. Almost any, that is ... Paul Reinhardt being the exception.

It wasn't the money he minded, as he was known as the most generous one, but the last year seemed to be endless as he was anxiously awaiting his annulment, and the words 'Happy New Year' sounded like a farce. But even to Paul, this morning was somehow very beautiful; enough so that he decided to take his two horses he received for Christmas for a sleigh ride. *"Those Arabian beauties may be in front of a sleigh for the first time,"* he thought. *"but that may be better than standing in their stable."*

He made his own coffee and took a bite of a leftover bundt cake as he was not very hungry. Today the roads would be deserted, something he always appreciated. Like his own shadow, his Irish setter Bello was always right at his side and the household staff swore the dog understood every word. "Bello, you and I are going for a nice long ride and a visit, so you can play with your four-legged friends," he said, folding his napkin. The dog barked approvingly and perked his ears as Rosa the head cook and absolute ruler of Paul's kitchen entered.

"I am so sorry, sir," she lamented in her still strong Czech accent while donning her apron.

"There is no need to apologize, Rosa, just because Bello and I decided to get up a bit early to take my new horses out. And it is not the first time I have made my own coffee either. I know the party kept all very busy last night," he replied kindly. He got up, lit his pipe, and told her he didn't know when he would be back as he would visit the Wilands for a card game.

"Will you please tell Mother I will be back here to enjoy supper and talk about last night's party?"

She opened the door for him and promised she would, then returned to the messy kitchen to drink some coffee and wait for her helpers to get up.

Gaby von Walden stood in front of the open window admiring the beautiful weather. It was her first visit to Vienna in more than fourteen years, the main reason being the engagement of her brother Andreas to an operating room nurse he had known the last four years.

Theresa Bauer was everything a man like Andreas could ask for. Astrid always wondered why her son took so long to propose and ask her parents, who owned a small leather goods store, for her hand in marriage. But the excuse on her part was that, aside from being a registered nurse, she needed two more years to work with surgeons. As a Doctor of Medicine, Andreas understood only too well, and both were willing to wait. So, the von Waldens spent their New Year's evening celebrating too. Since Theresa was the oldest of eight children, it was quite a nice event, as Gaby and Theresa got along as well. And Astrid felt not very unlike the Fosters and Reinhardts with their sons' marriages. She gained a nice daughter, without losing a son. Also, Isabella, who was fourteen, had now many future relatives to spend the evening with, but hung mostly around Theresa like a big sister. Now she had decided to become a nurse too, causing the von Waldens to laugh, as she had chosen almost every available profession a female was fit for.

~

Paul Reinhardt was right; all the roads were deserted. If it weren't for the many crows looking for a morsel of food to find, no one would have known this place was inhabited. It was so peaceful and the hooves and sleigh bells were the only sounds on the glittering path. To his surprise, the horses took to the sleigh quite well and trotted in pleasing harmony. Bello sat close to his master, often looking up to make sure everything was all right.

They had ridden this way about twenty minutes when they heard some laughter. The voices came nearer as he turned the sleigh towards his friend's road. Now he could see clearly two girls throwing snowballs at each other. Each of them had a pile beside her, well prepared for a good fight, with the bare chestnut trees serving as shields. Both wore ice skating outfits and their skates and coats were hanging on a limb. Gaby and Isabella were having too good of a time to let the oncoming sleigh interrupt their game, and they kept throwing and giggling until the horses were halted, as the dog planned to catch a snowball too. Bello brought it right to Gaby and Isabella. Before Paul had the chance to fasten the reins and descend, mother and daughter were patting the dog.

"You are such a handsome and high spirited fellow and want to be playing too," Gaby said, bending down and scratching his ears.

"You know I love dogs, don't you?" Isabella lost no time and walked towards Paul Reinhardt, who didn't know how to explain his dog's behavior. He usually only reacted to his master's commands.

"I am so sorry, ladies. He has never done this before," he apologized, shaking simultaneously his finger at him. "Bello, what did you get me into now?" The setter understood this tone of voice and cowered guiltily toward him, putting his head on his master's boot. Paul smiled at his dog's old trick, finally looking at Gaby. Whatever he wanted to say, he forgot completely, taken by surprise at her beautiful face. He was convinced it was the same mother and daughter from Locarno, the very same woman he never got out of his mind, although knowing how unlikely it was. After all, she was a married woman with a young daughter. He went back several times to Locarno to find them again never knowing why.

Gaby, in turn, blushed at the intense gaze of this handsome man, being sure it was none other than Paul Reinhardt, the aggressive boy she hated many years ago. It took both several seconds to recover until he turned his attention towards Isabella, who talked a steady stream in the dog's defense. "Your dog would have never done it, sir, but he saw me holding the snowball meant for Mother, but sort of in his direction. Please don't punish him. Mother and I just love dogs, especially setters."

By this time, the dog was sitting up, holding his paw to Gaby who shook it gently while saying, "Glad to have met you, Bello. You are a fine fellow." She took their coats and skates, gave a small nod towards Paul, and walked away. He counted fast the years back to the beach, being completely sure it was the little girl who built a castle and fixed her mother's long blonde hair before putting their wrap-around dresses on and walking to the restaurant. Getting himself in control again, he finally answered Isabella's questions.

"I never punish any of my animals, Miss. Do you have a dog too?"

"Yes, sir, but she is in Switzerland. We are here for a short vacation." He felt numb at hearing this news.

Gaby called for her daughter, and feeling impatient, used her middle name too. Still being beside himself he only heard 'Marie'.

"Mother is calling, sir. I better run, but I will be here again this summer." She smiled, giving Bello a pat on his forehead. "Mother, wait for me!" she yelled as Gaby took fast strides. "Do you know what this man called me?"

"No, sweetheart."

"He called me *Miss*! Imagine that... for the very first time I was called a Miss."

"How nice of him," she replied, but chided herself for looking too long into his brown eyes. Aside from that, he was too handsome for his own good and he knew it. Like her mother always told her, he was the "almighty Paul Reinhardt."

He jumped up on his sleigh and leaned against his fur blanket. There was, once again, silence everywhere, no sign of a human being. Yet he knew the last encounter was not a dream, though he thought of her daily. He smiled at the young girl's cute French accent when speaking German. Her mother, on the other hand, had a fluent Austrian dialect spoken by the upper class. Of course, the wide wedding band was quite visible when she put her gloves on. He daydreamed of Locarno again and again, not noticing that his horses got restless and the Reinhardts' priest, Father Sebastian, stood beside the sleigh.

"Hello, Paul. Are you all right?"

"Never felt better. I am on my way to the Wilands for a card game."

"That's where I am heading."

"Alright, I'll give you a lift, though walking would do you some good," he jested, patting his well-rounded belly.

"By the way, Happy New Year, Paul," the priest said, looking strangely at him.

"Same to you."

"Paul, is there anything wrong? I mean, other than a few drinks too many?"

"I barely drank anything. You ought to know that. But please remind me to give Bello a slice of roast beef when we are at my place. You are eating supper with us."

"Gladly to the last question, but why roast beef?"

"Because he deserves some."

Father Sebastian looked at him more closely. "So you did have a disagreement with Irene. But how does the dog fit in?"

"He caught a snowball."

"Now I know you are sick."

"Not sick, but somehow very happy, though without a reason. No, forget that. Hell yes, there is a reason!"

"You said 'hell', Paul. That's not you at all. So you did have a quarrel with Irene?"

"Believe it or not, I barely saw her among the big crowd. I stayed mostly with the Wilands, that's why we made the plan for the card game."

"Well, something has happened to you no matter how you try to deny it. As a priest, I will find it out sooner or later," he said with a smirk.

"And I hope you let me in on it, as I am anxious to find out myself," Paul said, ringing the Wilands' doorbell. "Two hungry men need breakfast," he told the servant, who told them they had breakfast ready for ten.

"Good morning you two," Vera Wiland greeted as she entered. "What a beautiful party last night, Paul. So sorry we couldn't even say thank you and goodbye."

"Vera, what does it matter? We spent almost the whole evening with the three dozen Wilands who showed up."

"All of us came, you just lost count of us," Ludvig Wiland said, welcoming them.

"He lost count of his own life. I am telling you, Ludvig, he lost all his marbles. Something has happened to this man since I've seen him last."

"He may have heard something about the annulment and is not telling us."

"I wish it were true, as I am at the end of my rope," he sighed. "If it doesn't come soon, I will file for divorce."

They ate their breakfast and retreated to one of the rooms reserved strictly for playing cards, but Paul's heart and mind were somewhere else.

~

When Gaby and Isabella returned home from skating, the very first thing she told Astrid was, "Grandmother, guess what?" all excited.

"A nice boy asked you to skate with him."

"That too… but a very handsome man on a horse sleigh called me *Miss*!"

"I have to hear more about it."

"Wait until Mother comes out after changing her clothes." Then Astrid got the story with both girls talking about their snowball fight and Bello.

"That was Paul Reinhardt," Astrid replied, surprised that he talked to strangers that freely. "But then again, his dogs mean more… oh God, much more to him than Mrs. Irene. I told you all about their marriage already. By the way, before you leave, I'll introduce you to Mrs. Irene as she wants to purchase a villa in Switzerland. After her father's sudden death, she inherited what I would call a fortune, and wants to leave Vienna as soon as their annulment is legal."

"Is she still that beautiful?"

"Yes and no. She drinks a lot, Victoria tells me, and no one knows where or with whom she spends her time."

"And the so-called Almighty Paul?"

"I'll tell you more later," she promised, when Isabella said with a smile, "I know I am too young to hear certain stories. Happens to me all the time with grown-ups." Both laughed and the girl changed her skating clothes, having lost her interest in seeing the promised movie, which would play tomorrow too.

"Well, Irene tells everybody that Paul is impotent and should have been a priest. Before the Wertheims left for America, they became extremely close. I shouldn't be surprised if she, too, ends up in New York where they went."

"And the Silvermans?"

"Are going nowhere. They believe, like many Jews, that Hitler will never set foot in Austria."

"This is wishful thinking, Mother. I have seen those brownshirts greeting each other openly among themselves with 'Heil Hitler'. The Rosattis talk only about politics nowadays, and said it's only a matter of time before he enters Austria. There are so many illegal Nazis and Andreas told me Rupert Foster is one too. But it's all underground or they'll get arrested."

"Then our helpless Chancellor would have to arrest half of Vienna."

"Mother, why don't you come to Switzerland? I have enough space for you, and we could make up for lost time."

"Thanks, but Switzerland could be taken just as easily."

"Wrong, Mother. The Rosattis said it's Germany's own bank, knowing this mad man wouldn't respect their neutrality otherwise."

"It's possible. Everything is possible nowadays... but I have my many good friends here and don't know if they have Christian Scientists there."

They stopped their conversation, getting ready to prepare their lunch, when Isabella appeared again and said out of the blue, "I was just thinking, Mother ... I wish you would find such a nice gentleman as we met this morning. I really don't care for the Professor you are dating. He is so stingy."

"Isabella and I go to a theater or a restaurant with him and I always pay my own way." Astrid was still flabbergasted about her granddaughter's remark, but then again, she was fourteen, possibly knowing more about men than she lets on. Times had changed; girls matured earlier... especially Isabella.

Two days later, Irene called Astrid to set a date for a short visit with the soon departing Gaby. She wouldn't keep them long, knowing how valuable time is for a short visit between mother and daughter.

Gaby was very surprised, seeing her for the first time. She was beautiful and elegant, aside from being highly educated. *"No wonder a man like Paul Reinhardt would fall for her ... then get possibly tired,"* Gaby thought to herself, as she didn't believe the story about his impotence. The conversation was strictly about Switzerland, where she traveled very frequently, but somehow never made it to Lausanne. "Of course, I am even open for a trip to America. I am just sick and tired of Vienna for personal reasons." Gaby gave her the name of the finest hotel and invited her for a visit to her apartment whenever she wished to do so, giving her the address.

They spent almost two hours together without mentioning Paul. The visit would be during springtime, as she was departing for her usual skiing trip to Tyrol. "Do you ski?" she asked before she left.

"I would say quite well," Astrid replied for Gaby, who was known to say little on matters relating to her accomplishments. Gaby wasn't quite sure how to handle a woman like Irene, who was so very sure of herself. But then again, what is a visit once in a while?

For Astrid, it was a tearful good-bye, but they would see each other at Andreas' wedding in June or July; the date was tentative depending on his vacation. But the honeymoon would positively be in Switzerland, Theresa having never been anywhere else.

Paul had a long talk with his mother about his annulment with the possibility of a divorce. By now, Victoria would agree to anything just to get rid of Irene. The last straw was when she told the deeply religious Vera Wiland, who was standing next to her equally religious mother, that she agreed with Napoleon when he said that religion is excellent stuff for keeping common people quiet. Of course, she was quite drunk by then, asking the waiting servant to take her to the castle.

"Oh God, Mother. As you know, I just came from their place but not a word was said."

"Paul don't get upset. They knew her condition."

"But she will hear about it nevertheless, as I made an appointment with Ludvig for a divorce. I cannot wait forever for an annulment. I want her out of here! Father Sebastian is writing another letter and also going to the Archbishop. He may have more power and will mention how much we have done all these years for their institutions without being asked. Now they can return a favor."

"Reinhardts have given for generations, Paul, and I am in the mood to write myself that we would put a stop to it, but it would be the poor children who would suffer. Rome doesn't care!"

"Mother, I'd like to tell you about my plans this coming February. I made up my mind to visit Elisabeth and try to bring her and the family back for a few months."

"That would be really something. It's been almost twenty years since she left Berlin."

"I thought I could be of help to get their many children to come too. Adam would let her go by herself, but when it comes to his children, he is always giving me ten reasons why he doesn't like for them to travel."

"But first you have to get a visa, your shots, and God only knows what else."

"It's already taken care of. I also have very efficient people in the factory who were already with us before the war started in 1914. Can you believe that?"

"I can," she smiled. "I will soon be sixty-seven."

"You still look better than most at fifty."

"Thanks, Paul, but my mirror is not a liar."

He only laughed and continued. "Imagine having all our family together again." Victoria couldn't help but think of Philip. Paul did too, in a different way... despising him. "I told Peter and Gisela about it and they were so happy for me."

"I hope you can pull it off, Paul."

He left in good spirits until he reached the castle in Lindenfels. "Mrs. Irene," he called from his wing on the phone to hers. "come in my office."

"I am packing for my skiing trip."

"I didn't ask what you were doing. I have to talk to you. It will only take a few minutes."

She came reluctantly, knowing it was about Vera Wiland. There was little doubt his mother had told her favorite child about it.

"Sit down!" he demanded without greeting. "Before you leave, we have to see Ludvig Wiland about divorce proceedings. If you have planned to leave tomorrow, you will have to postpone it."

"Good God! I'll postpone this trip for a week if I need to!" she smiled cynically.

"And since you just mentioned God, you will see Vera before you leave and apologize for your unseemly remark about religion."

"I knew your mother— no 'Mrs. Reinhardt' to me— would tell you about it!"

"As of today, we only talk via the lawyer. Leave your forwarding address with him."

"With greatest pleasure." She smiled and left, only to come back to ask, "And what time does Mr. Reinhardt want to see me at the Wilands?"

"Ten-thirty sharp."

"Great! My own 'Happy New Year' has already started!"

"Get out!"

The following day, both signed all the necessary papers and Ludvig mentioned that he would also send a copy to the Vatican. "They may speed up the procedure because I plan to mention the Reinhardts' contributions to their church."

"I appreciate it," Paul said.

But Irene stated coldly that she would write a personal apology to Wiland's wife and explained the reason. "Vera never told me about it," he replied curtly before she left.

Paul told him about his planned trip to South Africa by the end of February. "I just have to get away, Ludvig."

"I understand only too well. Hopefully you can bring the family back."

"That's the idea," he smiled.

After almost two months of skiing, Irene was back just in time to see Paul as he was packing and ready to leave. But she wanted to make him furious. This time, she made an appointment with his office, knowing just what to say. "I am leaving for Switzerland so here is my address."

"What on earth would I do with it?" he said, tossing it aside.

"It's for the Wilands."

"Get it there yourself. I will be in Africa for several months as I want to wait and see what the Vatican does."

"That may still take too long for me!" she snapped. "I thought we signed for a divorce."

"I know we did. I'll take whichever comes first," he smiled sarcastically, and she saw her opportunity to get even as he never even looked up.

"I am planning to buy a nice place in Lausanne and leave Austria for good." A shrug was his only reaction. "Gaby von Walden is helping me to find the right place as she, too, left Vienna fourteen years ago and never looked back," she mused in delight.

"Well, well, well. Since you shared the 'House of Lust' with my late dirty, old man, any kind of brothel in the red-light district would be the ideal location for a couple of drunken sluts."

"You are sick!"

"Get out!" he demanded, his face reddened, and she only answered, "Gladly." After all, she got him mad and that's all she ever wanted before leaving. But she also forged another plan, hoping it would work.

19

Gaby and Isabella arrived in Lausanne late at night and took a taxi to their apartment. Both were so tired they fell into bed. The following morning was Sunday. On Monday, Isabella's school would start. The first visit was to Aunt Ingrid and Uncle Henry, who looked pitiful, having taken a severe cold. They were coughing constantly, and Ingrid suggested leaving the room as it was infectious. She, too, looked worn out, but was happy to have her two girls back.

After the exchanges of all the news, both decided to see the Rosattis. They were overjoyed but Gaby felt that something was just different in their facial expressions. It didn't take them too long to reveal their own news. They would leave for Locarno for good, as Alfredo was going on eighty. His wife, Isabella, had suffered for years with severe pain from arthritis and the warm weather would be the best, besides having all those many relatives to look after them. Gaby told them she may have a possible buyer for their house, but they had already sold it to a manager of Rosatti's Italian Restaurant. Tears were flowing from both sides, begging Gaby to reconsider and come to Locarno for good too. It was such a shock that she turned all colors, promising she would consider all options, but Uncle Henry was in poor health and what about Aunt Ingrid?

By the time the Rosattis had their moving trucks there, Henry was up and around again, also promising to think about a move to the sunny south. Ingrid didn't want any part of it, other than visits. After all, she was twenty years younger and loved Lausanne.

~

By the end of April, Irene called and Gaby agreed to meet her at the hotel. Both decided on an outdoor café and she talked more openly about her present situation. From the little she had seen of Lausanne, it was 'positively her kind of town'. Also, her French was perfect and, of course, the money was sufficient to live a good life. Both went to see Isabella's school and she was introduced to Professor Alain Rousseau, who was the head of the private school. Gaby had seen him from time to time, but mostly in the company of his domineering mother, who liked Gaby and even knew the late Dr. Rosatti, but always made sure nothing serious would ever come of it. So far, no girl was right or good enough for her forty-five year old son. But the truth was, she was a widow and Alain was the love of her life. She just couldn't and wouldn't live alone.

Gaby had no intention of getting serious with a man she could never love. In the many years of her widowhood, she had rejected richer and better-looking ones. Aside from his wavy red hair, he was too tall, too thin, wore thick black-rimmed glasses, and had otherwise a long, non-descript face. The Lebruns always considered him unattractive but extremely smart.

Irene, walking mostly by herself to find the right villa, came excitedly to Gaby, excusing herself for coming uninvited, but hoping that she would take a look at her new villa. It was, of course, in the best section of Lausanne and could easily pass for a two-family villa. But if Irene had the money, why not?

"I will also shop for antiques right here, as I am not attached to anything my father had and I sure don't take anything from the Reinhardts. They would get their lawyers after me for a safety pin, out of spite. So, Miss Gaby, I will start a new life. Of course, I get my own clothes and jewelry once the annulment or divorce is done with. My dear father, God rest his soul, had no idea about my miserable marriage and it was for him that I stayed with that monster all that time."

"How sad… losing so many years of your life."

"Well, to be truthful, I did whatever I wanted to do, so it was not all that bad in many ways. I lived in one wing of Philip's castle, and he never set foot in it, so I could entertain whomever I wanted. Whenever the Reinhardts had their own big parties, I was there just to give an appearance that everything was all right. Of course, many people whispered behind their backs, but why should I care if they did? His brother, Peter, and his wife were always nice; that's just the way they are to everyone. And his mother, who by the way hates me, loves Erika more than her own daughter, Gisela. Sounds strange, but it's true. Her husband is with the police, but I never cared what he does. He only looks at me with the greatest disrespect. But like I said, I don't care anymore. I am buying this house, will find me a nice husband, and live happily ever after."

"I wish you the best, Irene," Gaby replied.

In time, both went to play tennis. Isabella and her friends were at the same court but always in the presence of a coach. Irene took Gaby to go shopping for antiques in Lausanne's best stores and they seemed to enjoy each other's company. Even the Lebruns were always happy to serve them a good meal. Irene, of course, reciprocated by taking the Lebrun family, Gaby, and Isabella to Lausanne's best restaurants.

After seeing Gaby's apartment, she relied on Gaby's taste with every purchase for her large villa, be it for drapes, rugs or furnishings. Irene didn't miss Vienna, but by November, a letter arrived forcing her to return to sign some papers. No other detail was given. She asked Gaby to travel with her, as she planned to show that miserable husband of hers what a former ugly brat and a drunken slut looks like.

"How long will we stay?" was Gaby's answer.

"About a week."

"Good. I'll come with you, as at my brother's wedding in July there was no opportunity to see Mrs. Reinhardt, who had already departed for Salzburg."

"Don't tell me you like her?"

"Oh, yes. She and her late husband brought the long feuding Reinhardts and von Waldens together. She was always most kind and generous to us. Now, Mr. Paul Reinhardt was another story. I could and would never come when he was there. But the wedding was only a small family affair and we loved every minute of it," she smiled. "Then they went to my brother's and my favorite Jura mountains, with his wife proving herself quite a good and fearless climber. My brother insisted she is very much like me." They recalled the small party she gave in their honor, with Isabella spending her time in Locarno without her mother for the first time.

Andreas and his wife also met Irene for the first time, the woman one heard so much about. He was rather pleasantly surprised. Gaby also felt Professor Alain Rouseau and Mother should be invited, as they knew the Lebruns very well, so it would be a nice evening. Madame and Alain Rouseau were known for keeping their distance with most people, but once accepting an invitation, they surprised everybody with their dry sense of humor. Gaby still wondered if his mother noticed the exchanging of glances between them.

~

The next day was a party in Irene's new villa. This place compared to no one's as far as Madame Rousseau and Alain remembered. Both were taken by her wealth and being the perfect hostess. There was no time for another get together. The newlyweds had to leave, though they promised to be back by Christmas. "It's our tradition, and my wife and I love skiing too."

It didn't take long for Madame to inquire about Irene's marital status. After having been told by Gaby in only a few words that she is awaiting her annulment, Mme. Rouseau looked even further. The two-story villa would serve all three of them well, after having always lived in an apartment. In a good section, of course, but an apartment nevertheless. Neither of the two women had the slightest idea that Irene and Alain were already seeing each other!

~

Now both women, Irene and Gaby, were on the train to Vienna, anticipating a two weeks' stay, as the letter from Ludvig Wiland stated that Mr. Paul Reinhardt agreed to let her stay until December 31, 1937. "You know, Gaby, I won't stay a day longer than I have to; just long enough to get all my personal belongings out of there and shipped to Lausanne. You could stay in the castle, but given the circumstances, you may prefer your mother's place."

Gaby had a smile on her face when replying. "As you suggested, I'd like to see his reaction at the 'ugly brat from the despised von Waldens'."

"Don't forget that we are also 'drunken sluts'. I have to admit, before my trip to Lausanne, I got drunk on several occasions, just to embarrass him, for one thing, and I was so miserable for another.

"I am very proud of you, Irene. Alcohol gets you nowhere but deeper in trouble."

They arrived in the evening in Vienna. Irene took a taxi to Lindenfels and Gaby to her mother's place, who expected her arrival as Gaby had called her from Lausanne. As always, they had a lot of catching up to do and stayed up until the early morning hours. Andreas and Therese also rented an apartment nearby, as the uncertainty of politics and spreading of the Nazis left them quite insecure.

The first thing the entering Irene heard from her trusted servant, whom she took after her father's death, was that Dr. Elisabeth van Dreesen, her husband, and their five children had returned from South Africa with Paul, planning to stay a year.

"Suits me fine. We'll pack my things, I'll sign the papers, and we are out of here in no time. If worse comes to worst, we stay in a hotel in case something is wrong with the paperwork. You are coming with me, Regina. I hope you didn't change your mind."

"No, Irene, but I heard from some friends that Switzerland has gotten very strict with their visas."

"I know that too, but Gaby's married name is Rosatti and she is a Swiss citizen. You are with her on paper only. Switzerland is always short on servants. I bought a large villa, and put all my money in their bank, so there will be no troubles. And who knows, I may get married too, but keep it to yourself as only you and I know it." Regina put her hand at her heart and that was that. Irene could always trust her.

She called Gaby to tell her to enjoy the next few days with her family and informed her about Elisabeth and family's return, which Gaby already knew through her mother. "Regina and I are busy packing all my personal belongings with the shippers arriving in four days."

Gaby was relieved, as she was planning a few visits, with the first one to Andreas and Theresa. They were still in the process of getting their apartment ready, Gaby noticing a few things from Astrid as Theresa had a meager dowry, which mattered to no one.

Andreas and Gaby decided to go skating, as he was not sure his Christmas would be spent with Theresa's family. It was only November, but the snow was knee high and the weather ice cold. "At least the rink is not overcrowded," Gaby remarked. It was too cold for Astrid to go anywhere, so she sewed on Andreas and Theresa's bedroom drapes, from velour given to her from Victoria quite a few years ago. Also, the Wertheims had given Astrid many things which only needed to be sewn.

Andreas and Gaby danced to Lehar's waltz, 'Gold and Silver', for the first time in fifteen years, enjoying Vienna's ice rink. It was not as elegant as Lausanne's, but Vienna, too, has better ones in the first district.

20

Paul's Mercedes didn't start, and
never one for asking an employee for a ride, he took his usual
shortcut, thinking about the annulment and finally getting rid
of Irene for good, who in a letter to Victor Wiland wrote that
she was not asking for anything but her freedom, and to use
her former name of 'Haas' again, as no one was permitted to
call her Reinhardt anyway. He only confided to his sister,
Elisabeth, the real reason for the divorce, and also about his
encounter in Locarno, and their short meeting on New Years'
Day. She already called it his 'bedtime story' as he retold it
so frequently. Needless to say, a man of Adam van Dreesen's
caliber would never understand, and was therefore never
informed about anything, let alone finding Paul's bride on
top of Philip. Elisabeth, on the other hand, always knew her
father cheated. She claimed it was the main reason she went
to study in Berlin, being so ashamed after finding out from a
former girlfriend.

Quite a few people looked through the metal fence to
watch several pairs taking to the middle of the ice rink. And
Paul, feeling relieved after the annulment and in no hurry to
walk home, decided to be among the onlookers too. It didn't
take him long to spot Gaby wearing the same bright blue

dress he had seen her wearing on New Year's Day. By staring a bit longer, he felt numb once again. He noticed her dancing partner holding her tight and laughing happily while she was telling him something funny, equally happy. *"So that is it,"* he thought to himself, unable to walk a step further. It all felt too painful to even give it another thought. When the dance ended, both put their arms at each other's waist, walking up the bleachers to get something hot to drink while taking a rest. He was now sure her marriage was at least as happy as that of his brother and two sisters. He consoled himself by being happy for a woman to be loved as she deserved. But why was this chance denied to him? He barely knew her, never spoke a word, got a little nod, and yet he felt he had known her a lifetime.

~

"Paul, you poor thing. You must be exhausted," his mother greeted him. "I wouldn't be surprised if you caught a cold." The servant brought the food, but he ate little while his mother told him all about her smart grandchildren.

"Where is Elisabeth?"

"Both are with the children reading them a bedtime story." He couldn't help but laugh as his sister was always referring to his love story as one.

He also couldn't wait to catch her alone. "Paul, no matter what you tell me, something just doesn't make any sense."

"Which is?" he asked hopefully, not knowing why.

"There is no way on earth two blond people produce, if this is the right word, a black-headed girl with dark brown eyes."

"Alright... so there we have it again. Either her husband is in Locarno and she has a boyfriend in Vienna, or she is divorced. But this little girl, who is by now about thirteen or fourteen, has many of her mother's features. Oh God, what now?" he said, forlorn, wishing his sister a goodnight.

"Not so fast, Paul. The skating season just started. You point her out to me, and I'll find out the rest. In the meantime, I'll pray for you as hard as I can." He only smiled, repeating again his goodnight before turning in.

The following day, all the von Waldens were at Theresa Bauers' for dinner. Paul and Elisabeth looked for two hours in vain. Irene called at the Reinhardts' place to make an appointment concerning their annulment. Elisabeth answered, telling her kindly she wished to meet her before leaving. And the way she understood it, Victor Wiland would come to the castle in Lindenfels, 'visiting' another client too. Irene thought it to be a lie. Those Reinhardts just wanted to make sure she never even took a pen.

The date was set for the tenth of November. Irene knew it gave her two days to make it official, and as for meeting Elisabeth, she was not even interested but left the day open. Maybe the Reinhardts planned to give her an official good-bye party. She laughed when telling Regina about it. She felt a little shiver down her spine and after a severe headache, decided to go to bed early, blaming the last few hectic days for it. Just then, the phone rang. It was Gaby asking when to come, and after hearing from Regina that Irene seemed to come down with a cold, or that she was possibly too upset about everything, Gaby decided to take the next tram to Lindenfels. Paul and his sister were again at the rink.

The signing of the annulment was set now for 8:30 in the morning, as Ludvig Wiland had the next appointment at ten. Due to the heavy snow, Paul suggested he spend the night in his wing, which had more than twenty unoccupied guest rooms. Also, they could look carefully again at all the necessary paperwork, as Irene would soon depart for Switzerland.

During and after dinner, they listened to one of Adolf Hitler's many long speeches, which were by now heard on every station of Austria's radio. They talked about the former illegal Nazis who were by now seen quite openly and fearlessly in every district, giving their official salute with a boisterous 'Heil Hitler'. Even the police looked the other way unless there was a brawl in the making. The jails were over-crowded.

Irene's cold was worsening. Tea with lemon along with aspirin and bedrest so far had not helped and she was getting desperate. The last thing she needed was a runny nose and eyes while signing the papers. Regina, her fifty-five-year-old maid, suggested a tumbler of Slibowitz, a strong brandy made from prunes which, without fail, helped her late father.

"I am sure there is some of it in the Reinhardts' wine cellar, but I am too weak to go down myself. Will you go, Regina?"

"Gladly if Mrs. Rosatti goes with me, as I am afraid of mice." Gaby just came from the bathroom, having washed her hair. Irene told her to sit right next to her while signing the papers, more or less as a witness, but at the same time she would make the remark after Victor Wiland was gone and introduce Gaby as the 'partner of her brothel'. That would be her last words to him and she had longed for months to punish him for his remarks; now even more so, as she got to know Gaby and her family so well. This was her plan and she would see to it that it would have a lasting effect on Paul.

Irene insisted that Gaby wear her long housecoat which had a warm, lined hood to cover her wet hair, or she would take a cold too, the last thing all three needed. Off she went by herself, knowing what a bottle of Slibowitz looks like, a remedy most families keep in their household. Following the direction of Irene, still being in the possession of the cellar key until the next morning, Gaby knew at once she would be in need of a ladder, which were on each side neatly arranged in three sizes. The cellar was huge and gave the appearance of a fruit and vegetable store; potatoes en masse on the floor, wrapped cabbage next to it, with apples, pears wrapped individually in brown paper, net bags of dried fruit and all sorts of items hanging from the ceiling. On the shelves were enormous amounts of glass jars of marmalades and more canned fruits and vegetables lined up orderly and ready for use. Big barrels of possibly fat and sauerkraut stood around, just leaving enough walking space to get to every desired item. The wine bottles were laying with the dates and names in crates and Gaby finally found rows nearby which were full of spirits. She finally discovered her desired bottle of Slibowitz halfway to the ceiling. But it meant taking the middle size ladder to get to it. Regina stood at the upper stairs calling several times to ask if she was in need of help. "No, thanks," was her usual answer, but Regina was her standby anyway, just in case.

Paul habitually took his dog for the last walk of the evening, also letting him run, knowing Bello needed plenty of exercise while he took a slow walk along the castle. Suddenly he saw a glimmer of light from Irene's wing and by walking toward it, he knew it came from the cellar. His first thought was that she was drinking again, having a passion for their best brandy. His second thought was that she would take a few of his expensive ones to Switzerland, unaware that the packers for her several crates were there already, taking only her clothes and a few souvenirs from her late father's home. He decided to take the main side door leading to the cellar and with his tall boots with rubber soles to guard against slipping, he sneaked quietly up on her, recognizing her hooded housecoat. He planned to tell her that she could at least have the courtesy to ask for it.

The setter was right there and Gaby, being already in possession of the bottle, tried carefully to walk backwards, watching not to get a heel in the long housecoat. Simultaneously, Bello jumped and pushed his wet nose towards her slippers while his master yelled, "Why in God's name didn't—" He couldn't finish his sentence, recognizing Gaby who fell from the ladder, landing in the huge pile of potatoes and screeching "OUCH!" Her leg was in an awkward position, hitting a wooden plant, and she found herself even more embarrassed as the temporary satin sash which held the house coat together fell too, exposing her fully in her small, flowered flannel nightgown, showing her legs, and for the moment, she was unable to push her nightgown further down. Watching the scene from only a few feet away, he held tightly to the door, feeling as though he might faint at any moment.

Only a completely dumbfounded and long drawn out, "It's *you*" came over his white lips, looking for better words than his 'how', 'what', and an audible 'who'. Although still in pain and Bello licking her cheeks, she managed to pat his head with one hand. The dog paced back and forth from his master to Gaby, feeling that something was wrong. Once more, Gaby proved herself very strong in an adverse situation. Also, the well-rehearsed performance for the following day came quickly to her mind, while Paul felt he was losing his.

"No doubt you are wondering who I am, Mr. Reinhardt," she smiled. *"Only for the past eight years,"* he thought, but kept mum awaiting her answer. "I am that 'ugly von Walden brat'."

"Oh, no you are not," he countered, even more perplexed.

"If you say so. But let's call it even. I sprained your ankle more than twenty years ago and you broke my leg. Now it's *me* who can neither skate nor ski for the next few weeks. That should make you feel better!" He only gulped in total disbelief. "The other question would be what am I doing here?" His handsome face turned even whiter, knowing exactly why. "I found Irene a house in Lausanne and her maid and I helped with the move. And also with moral support, mind you."

Regina, who waited on the staircase for Gaby's return, recognized Paul Reinhardt's voice and ran upstairs to Irene's bedroom. "I think something went wrong, Mrs. Irene. I hear Mrs. Rosatti talking to Mr. Reinhardt."

"Oh my God. Seeing her in my hooded garment, possibly from the back, he doubtlessly thought it was me. There is no time to lose to set him straight." She didn't know how she got down all the steps in a hurry in her condition, but there she stood now, with a fur coat over her nightgown, watching Gaby still petting the setter, while Paul stood motionless by the door. She pushed him aside, running towards Gaby, and yelled "What has this monster done to you?"

"You mean Bello? He licked my heel when I descended the ladder. I got startled and here I am. I fell."

"Oh, I thought it was him as I wouldn't put anything past this man. Are you hurt?"

"Well, I think my leg is broken and hope it's a clean break," she replied calmly.

"WHAT?" She turned to Paul. "See what you have done?" There was no reply, just a look of hatred in her direction.

"I told you, Irene, it was the dog."

"Never mind poor Bello. It was *he* who let him in the cellar, seeing me on the ladder and suspecting that I'd steal a bottle."

"She was right, of course," he thought, though he would never admit it.

She still continued, enraged. "In case you don't know who she is, this is Mrs. Rosatti, formerly a von Walden. I am sure that name rings a bell with you. She is now my partner in a bordello, which we bought in the red-light district."

"Get out!" is all he could muster with his head spinning.

Gaby bit her lips, feeling how embarrassing the situation was getting one day before his annulment. And there was her own plan going up in smoke. She wanted to look her very best, and ended up looking the worst ever. But she felt, somehow, that he was in love with her. There was no other explanation for his behavior. Victor Wiland came in, hearing Irene screaming, and got the news from Regina, who was still waiting in the hallway.

"Please, Mr. Wiland, call a doctor right now," Irene pleaded and, noticing Regina walking behind him, she told her to bring a warm blanket in a hurry. Victor Wiland said he would call Peter since he spends the weekend in Lindenfels. "Good idea," said Irene, but there was still no word from the ashen-faced Paul, who forgot momentarily that Peter had purchased the Wertheims' weekend house.

Wiland came back, assuring everyone that Dr. Peter Reinhardt was on the way, adding, "I didn't even know the lady's name, but I did call you 'beautiful' who fell from the ladder."

"Thank you," Gaby replied. "Peter will have a good laugh. Many years ago, we went skiing with my late husband. I broke my leg once too."

That was a new shock to Paul. Victor finally turned to him, being startled at seeing him white like a ghost. Irene started to explain the situation but there was Paul again with his usual, "Get out or I'll throw you out myself!"

"Don't make me laugh. Ever since I came in, still quite sick mind you, you haven't even moved a step, neither trying to help poor Gaby nor calling Peter. But I imagine her condition is less important than your sprained ankle two decades ago. But then again, she is a von Walden and I imagine that makes all the difference," she fumed. "Good to see you, Peter," she said in one breath. "Look at our poor victim."

"Hello, Gaby. What happened?"

"I fell from the ladder, Peter, and diagnosed myself with a broken leg."

"Gaby blames the dog, but I know *he* had to bring him in the locked cellar door," Irene said, shooting venomous looks at Paul.

"Oh, Irene, accidents happen. It's not her first broken leg either. Why don't you all go out and let me see where it hurts?"

Gaby retold the story and Peter suggested an x-ray right away, calling for the ambulance in Lindenfels, but had to walk up to Paul's main entrance hall. Mrs. Irene and Regina went back to her bedroom. Even after her fall, Gaby still held the brandy bottle, giving it to Regina. Irene now started, for some reason, to get better, but her maid insisted on the 'medication' anyway, especially since they all went through hell to get it.

"Better get something for Paul," Victor Wiland said. "Take a look at him."

"My God, Paul. Are you that upset? I believe it was Bello running in front of you."

"But I was the one who opened the outside door thinking Irene is on the bottle again or was taking some to Switzerland. How on earth could I know she loaned the von Walden lady her coat? That was once my mother's coat; that's why I remembered it so well. I gave it to her for Christmas."

Once more, the ambulance came to the Reinhardt palace, and Peter insisted that he would go along. After they heard the ambulance leave with Peter yelling, "I will call you to let you know," Paul said only "thank you" and put both of his hands in front of his face stammering, "Why me?" and giving a short account of Irene's outburst to his friend, Victor Wiland.

"I felt I would die a thousand times. How did I not know *she* was a von Walden?"

"Paul, just be glad she didn't hit one of the barrels that stood so nearby. Her head would have split open."

"I was thinking about it the whole time standing there, just imagining I could have killed her."

"Why do I have the feeling of a lawyer, if you will, that there is a bit more to the whole incident than you let me believe?"

"There is and in time I will tell you."

"I thought so, because in all those years you never caved in."

"Well, frankly, I had it coming. Listen, if Irene is too sick tomorrow to come down, we'll go up to her.

"I usually never work on weekends, but made an exception for you and my other client."

Peter called from the hospital saying that it was a clean fracture on the right leg, but he would keep her in traction. Also, her left arm was very bruised.

"I hope you have her in first class."

"What do you think? I'll be by in a few minutes and give you something for your nerves. And tomorrow we'll talk."

"About what?"

"Come on, Paul. You will tell me. I am sure it's more than a broken leg." He hung up and was on his way back, leaving another doctor to put the plaster on her.

When Peter arrived, Victor retired. "We will see how Mrs. Irene feels, but I'll be ready anytime."

Peter prepared the pills, told him to take two in front of him, and he would be back the next morning too, making sure Irene's cold was not worse.

Gaby was given the best room at the hospital, usually reserved for the Reinhardts, as there were three 'first class' at the hospital. Her pain pills helped; she felt much better, but couldn't help having Paul's stare in front of her. He undoubtedly remembered her from New Year's Day, having, of course, no idea of who she was. Then came Irene's outburst of what he still thought about that 'von Walden brat'. It must have embarrassed him to no end. But somehow, she felt good about the whole incident, as she could love this man like no other. Feeling that it was fate, she finally fell asleep.

The following morning, Irene sent Regina downstairs, explaining that she was still too weak to walk down the stairs. However, next to her bedroom was a salon, and she wanted them to come up at the given time. Victor Wiland and a groggy Paul were more than happy to oblige. Both signed in a hurry and Paul left without taking one look at her, let alone saying good-bye. Victor Wiland explained a few things, among them that she was permitted to stay until year's end.

"What I want to know is how is Gaby?" After telling her the facts she screamed, "That monster ruins everyone's life! Now what?"

"Dr. Peter Reinhardt will see you later to make sure you two can travel when ready. Mrs. Rosatti will have to stay at least 3 – 4 weeks in the hospital."

"Oh, God! I have to see her to say good-bye for a while and settle the visa concerning Regina. She is sponsored by her as a maid. Mrs. Rosatti is a Swiss citizen."

"Since your maid has a visitor's visa, it doesn't matter whom she visits."

"I never thought of that. But that is why you are a lawyer," she smiled. They shook hands and both knew it was for the last time. Peter advised her to stay a few days longer in bed and by Wednesday she should be ready.

"The sooner the better. Paul and I haven't even exchanged one word. Can you believe that?"

"Let's just say you embarrassed him a great deal. Your outburst about the bordello was uncalled for. Ludvig and I feel the same way. After all, he didn't even know she was a von Walden when she fell."

"You Reinhardts always stick together. I, on the other hand, am all alone."

"Now that is not Paul's fault, Irene."

"I know," she replied guiltily. "I hope to see Erika before I leave. You two were the only nice Reinhardts," she said in tears.

"I will make sure Erika and you see each other one way or another," he promised in leaving.

Paul waited for Victor to descend from Irene's room to take him to his office with his sleigh. The roads were still not passable this morning due to the new snowfall. Both talked only about the weather and his setter Bello, who sat ever so proudly between them. Paul thought the dog had led him twice now to Gaby, but was incapable of thinking any further. Now the annulment was behind him and he felt free. He was glad to hear about Irene's plan to leave as soon as possible too. Although he permitted her to stay longer, he had no desire to cross her path again. He would stay in Vienna as he did most of the time, still having his bachelor apartment at his disposal.

The Dreesens occupied the guest rooms, and Peter and Erika, who got the Wertheims' weekend retreat after their departure to America, spent most of their time there, weather permitting. Victoria, after all, had a full house, but was still longing for Erika, considering her the favorite. Elisabeth and Adam, as well as their children, were reserved, doubtlessly missing South Africa and their friends already. Today they decided to have a snowball fight in their back lawn and Victoria suggested to water their tennis court for the parents to practice skating after twenty years and the children to get a chance to learn. When Paul entered the mansion, they all were ready to leave. "Uncle Paul, we are going to have a snowball fight!"

"Great!" he replied, but after Elisabeth took one look at him she knew something was wrong.

"You are pale, brother dear. I didn't think you would take the annulment that hard."

"I didn't. You will never believe what happened to me. After I get some sleep, I'll tell you."

"I can't wait to hear it."

"My God, son. You look like you've been to hell and back."

"Sort of. I need to sleep for a few hours and then you will hear all about it."

"Need some pills?"

"No thanks. Peter gave me some and they didn't do anything for me."

"Peter? How come he was there?"

"Mrs. Irene has a cold, so he brought her some medication. By the way, Mother, why did you give Mrs. Irene the velvet house coat I bought you years ago for Christmas?"

"I never did. She had one made because she liked it so much. She would be the last person I would give something you gave me."

"Well, now I feel better." He gave her a kiss and left for bed.

Victoria was lately in the habit of getting the phone herself after two rings, as the grandchildren made a noisy run for it before a servant had a chance. As always, she was happy to hear from Peter who related in detail what happened the previous day. "No wonder Paul looked sick, and I mean sick, when he came in. He went right to bed claiming he couldn't sleep regardless of your pills. I can imagine Mrs. Irene being at her best when she finally had a chance to confront Paul about Gaby. Well, Paul will get over it. Should I call Astrid?"

"She was informed last night from the hospital and I will call her now myself. By noon, the snow will start to melt and we did put Gaby in a first-class room."

"I hope you did. Maybe the weather will be better by tomorrow and all of you can come for dinner. I miss Erika terribly."

"She misses you too, Mother."

Victoria now called Astrid, who already knew and was, in a way, glad to have her Gaby a little longer. She informed Ingrid in Switzerland and, weather permitting, they would come. "I am so sorry, Astrid."

"Don't be silly. We both had nothing to do with it. It's not her first break either."

"I am so glad, Astrid, you don't take it as hard as Paul. He seemed to be devastated."

"Remind him that Gaby is so lucky to be surrounded by so many doctors."

"Since when is she for doctors again," Victoria thought, but answered, "Right you are. Aside from your Andreas and my Peter, Elisabeth and Adam are here too," she smiled and was glad that conversation was over; usually she would have answered, 'God will heal her' and talk no further.

Two hours later, Paul was still wide awake. He decided on a hot bath, a good shave, and something to eat. Coming down the steps, he found Elisabeth with her needlepoint, while his mother was telling the two boys and three girls a nice story about their Reinhardt ancestors. She was very surprised that Elisabeth had never as much as tried, while they knew all about the van Dreesens.

"Elisabeth, I have to talk to you. So glad we have our privacy, but first, where is Adam?"

"Helping the guys with the skating rink."

"Good." He retold what happened and she not only beamed with joy but embraced him spontaneously with a kiss. Paul had never seen her that happy. He only shook his head when she ran in the children's room, demanding they read their school lessons while she and grandmother have a talk.

Victoria was even more surprised when she learned about his encounter in Locarno.

"How could I tell you or anyone else, Mother? It would have made me not any different from Irene."

"Nonsense. You looked for love; she looked for a man… any kind of man, including your late father."

"How did you know?" both asked in unison, shocked.

"Because I had her watched. I confronted him and he said he had never seen a more beautiful body. 'She felt like pure silk.'"

"Oh, my God," they said, once more in unison.

"Does anyone else know about it?"

"If you mean the family, yes."

"Including Rupert?"

"He is family, isn't he? He, by the way, knew him even before he met Gisela, having had, at times, duty in the red-light district."

"So that's why he barely looked at him and never said more than 'hello' and good-bye'."

"Then how come you didn't leave him? Verena left you and us everything. Father didn't even get a pair of cufflinks. You are very rich."

"Because I loved your father and saw in him so many good qualities other men in his circle of friends never had. Aside from that, I hoped that we would spend our old age together. But let me tell you, as soon as he admitted to his affairs, I closed my bedroom door for good, knowing he would never change."

"Ha!" Paul laughed. "That's what I did with Irene on our wedding day."

"Like mother, like son," Elisabeth verified, smiling. "But now we need a fool-proof plan to get Gaby in our family. Then we all can live happily ever after."

"I should be that lucky," Paul replied.

"I am going to see Gaby. I want to meet her," Elizabeth stated.

"No, you won't!" said Victoria. "That's Paul's obligation."

"I'd just as well be dead," he uttered, red-faced.

"Do you try to tell me I raised a coward?"

"No, Mother. I just need time and plenty of it. I thought I'd go away for a while."

"So you are a coward."

"Mother, you don't understand."

"Like what, Paul?"

"Facing her after all the things I have done and said. You should have seen Irene in her role, recalling everything I told her about Gaby, and me having no idea who she was of course."

"Well that makes it even easier," said Victoria.

"I think the whole thing is so romantic," Elisabeth uttered joyously.

The following day, the white, beautiful snow turned to gray, ugly slush, but the Reinhardts loved it. They all came to Victoria's house to hear about Paul's love story. Of course, the usually quiet and serene Elisabeth called Erika and Peter, who thought to himself that he would try his utmost to bring them together. All excited, Erika called Gisela, who never kept a thing from Rupert or the Fosters. They all were overjoyed, knowing about Paul's sham of a marriage.

Gisela's children didn't want to come along for a visit as they did not get along with Elisabeth's five 'boring' ones. They were in every way so different, but it was carefully explained that they came from another continent. With five children there already, Victoria was rather pleased when Rupert and Gisela came alone. Paul had a good night's sleep, and, after dinner, the men went in their smoking room for a card game while the ladies tried to forge a plan on how to bring Gaby and Paul together.

21

Right after her arrival at the hospital, Gaby couldn't help but notice that she got treatment usually reserved for Reinhardts only. She was the only one who had the luxury to have a telephone. "Use it anytime at your convenience," the nun told her. "Dr. Reinhardt also left word to call your mother and brother." Astrid was more concerned about her sister Ingrid, who had Isabella, but she assured her that she stayed such long hours at school, had lots of homework, and they saw so little of her. However, they promised to surprise Gaby with a visit; she would talk it over with the Professor. Irene's cold was also mentioned, but that would be over in no time.

Gaby's first visitors were, of course, her mother, Andreas and his wife. They, too, were surprised about that beautiful room, already full with flowers sent by the Reinhardts. Gaby told them about the mix-up of the housecoat and the setter Bello with his elusive master who stood there in the doorway unable to say anything.

"Poor Paul," said Astrid. "I bet he feels horrible about it."

"Well, Gaby, we have you a little longer," Therese said sincerely.

"And if it took a broken leg, so be it," added Andreas with a big smile. "I think it's about time you came back to Vienna."

"I thought about it, once Isabella's school is finished," Gaby replied.

"We have good schools here too and we all can afford to pay for it."

"Andreas, I have money. But thanks anyway."

Peter made his entrance with some other doctors and they all agreed that her bruised arm was getting better and the traction could be taken away. Soon, she would be on crutches, and could perhaps stay with him and Erika, as they could set a special bed up for her.

Gaby smiled and replied, "I'd like that."

～

Professor Rousseau was more than happy to give Isabella all the time needed to visit her mother. He heard via phone about Gaby's accident and Irene's cold, and promised she would be on the train in a few days. Alain couldn't wait to see Irene and visa-versa. It was their very own secret. And Ingrid, who was given the responsibility to take care of Isabella in case of any emergency pertaining to Gaby, took no time in packing to leave Lausanne for Vienna. She kissed Uncle Henry good-bye, who reminded his niece to take the skates along. A nurse was on call to look in on Henry Lebrun twice daily to check his health condition, so off they went in the best of spirits and were met at the train station by Astrid, Andreas and his wife Therese. The weather, in the meantime, turned cold again and Isabella was happy having her skates along. They surprised Gaby to no end at their unexpected arrival. With Isabella at her side, she was taking a walk with her crutches while Astrid and Ingrid went to see Peter.

"Hello, sir. Remember me?" asked Isabella, recognizing the elegant man in the gray leather coat at once.

Pleasantly surprised about the encounter he said, "Of course I do, Miss."

"Isabella Rosatti," she replied, and he wondered where 'Marie' came from.

Gaby and he exchanged glances, she being completely relaxed, he being still upset but happy there was Isabella to do the talking.

"I assume you came all the way from Lausanne to see how your mother feels?"

"Yes, sir, and she is fine, and will soon be leaving the hospital. Right, Mother?"

"You know I caused your mother's fall?" Paul asked very seriously, looking at Gaby and Isabella.

"No, you didn't. It was your setter, sir... and I am glad you told me you never punish any of your animals." Both couldn't help but laugh this time.

"I have to talk to you one of these days, Mrs. Rosatti," he finally managed to say, thanks to Isabella's presence.

"I am not sure how much longer I will stay here," she replied, watching his facial expression change. "I will be staying in your brother's house, most likely."

"Oh," he replied with the most obvious sigh of relief, when Isabella spotted Astrid, Ingrid, and Peter.

"So sorry my daughter talks so much. I will have to remind her again."

"Mrs. Rosatti, please... I am delighted to have her helping me... you know what I am talking about."

"Yes, I do," was all she could say, turning finally to her room, expecting her visitors.

Isabella accepted Victoria's invitation to spend one night as her granddaughter and Ingrid permitted her to stay at the Reinhardts' castle.

~

Adam and Elisabeth's five children were raised to speak French, Dutch, and English. At the dinner table, they found Isabella very congenial, as she remembered each one's name immediately. The oldest girl, at seventeen, was called Wilhelmina, doubtless after the Queen of Holland. Juliana, fifteen, was named after the Queen's oldest daughter. Twelve-year-old Desiree had a French name but was named for the former Queen of Sweden. The oldest son was Adam III who, at ten, was looking very aware of whom the van Dreesens were in South Africa, and the seven-year-old, Gustav was spoiled and got his way with his sisters and brother.

Isabella conversed with each of them in French, never overlooking anyone. They all loved her for it and Paul was so proud that he said very frankly, "I am taking Miss Isabella tomorrow for lunch to Demels, with her mother's permission of course. She is leaving in a few days and I owe her one day of a good time."

"You will like Demels a lot, Isabella," Juliana verified, having been there frequently with her family.

She glowed but still looked at Paul, agreeing that she needed her mother's permission, which wouldn't be too hard to get as they had always talked about going there but never went.

"It's quite expensive," said Juliana.

"I have plenty of money saved," she replied proudly, causing the grown-ups to laugh.

Victoria, of course, corrected her. "Isabella, you are still too young to know, but whenever a young man or any man for that matter invites you, *he* has to pay."

"Excuse me, Madame. Not in Lausanne... except with my uncle. But when my mother and I go to a concert or a theater with my school's headmaster Professor Rousseau, he only pays his and we pay ours."

"Then he is not a gentleman," Juliana commented grandly, in the know-how.

"Really?" Isabella replied, astonished.

Adam laughed aloud. "Have you ever been asked out?"

"Many times, Father, but I never liked any of them."

"Our daughter is growing up, Adam," Elisabeth said wistfully. "Where have all our years gone?"

"I know. We spent them happy together," he replied lovingly. Victoria was still astonished that her daughter was still so much in love with the balding man twenty years her senior. But like she told her handsome Philip years ago, her children needed love.

The following day, Isabella, very proudly on the arm of Paul, entered Gaby's room asking for permission to have lunch at Demels, while his own voice failed him completely. "And why not?" she smiled sheepishly. "We've never been at this fine place before."

"I know, Mother; too expensive."

"I offered to pay," he said, tongue-in-cheek, somehow relaxing.

"Sweetheart," Gaby said to Isabella while opening the night table beside the bed, taking out her purse. "bring me a small box of truffles. Demels is known to have the best."

"Grandmother said they have the best of everything. But I'll take my own money and buy one for you."

"No, sweetheart. Here, take it."

"You should listen once in a while to your child, Mrs. Rosatti. Don't refuse her the joy of giving," said Paul with a wink and a smile.

"Is this man ever handsome," Gaby thought, but then imagined repeating her sentence when laying in pain on the pile of potatoes. "If you say so, Mr. Reinhardt."

He remembered this statement very well and bit his lips. "We'll talk about it this evening as there is so much unsaid which still pains me."

"Glad to hear it, Mr. Reinhardt." Isabella didn't know the extent of their conversation but was so happy both smiled.

"I'll have your daughter back at four... if this is all right."

"Yes, of course," she stammered, wondering about his plans.

~

The head waiter at Demels bowed deeply, not very unlike their own servants to any of his guests whenever a Reinhardt gave a party. They also got one of the best reserved seats. Isabella was all in navy blue except a white collar on her dress. After a short compliment, he was told her mother sewed everything, including the coat and her white beret. "She also designed it."

"What a smart mother."

"Not only mother; we are really the best of friends since my father died in a car wreck before he got to see me."

"I am very sorry," he said, feeling shame anew about his terrible thoughts upon hearing about it. But tonight he would clear up everything, hoping she forgave him.

The many lessons about behavior paid off, as much as she disliked Aunt Ingrid frequently for insisting on it. She ordered her menu like a lady and behaved like one. Paul was extremely proud of her, having no idea how good she felt to be in his company. On the way out, they went to the famous chocolate counter to pick up the ready-made, beautifully wrapped boxes.

"I always bring some to my family and there are now many of them who want something sweet," he sighed. "Also, my brother and his wife… a little box for the nuns who treated your mother so well… and no, I didn't forget your mother."

"For how much?" she asked honestly, fearing her own money wouldn't cover his taste.

"Miss Isabella, I caused your mother lots of pain, which I will explain some other time, so the truffles are on me."

She stood for a moment before replying. "My mother will never stand for it."

They walked towards a special shop which only dealt with skating outfits, and he insisted she get one, as her grandmother and Aunt Ingrid had told him she brought only the skates and could skate in her pleated skirt. He also wanted her skates transferred on new light gray shoes. He even noticed her loud heartbeat and she was, for the first time, lacking a comment, with only an astonished expression while deciding on a peach-colored dress.

"When I grow up and make some money, I'll pay every schilling back," she promised, and he knew she meant it.

He gave her the box of truffles in front of the hospital, assuring her his brother Peter would bring her at six to their castle again. "I have to ask my grandmother," she told him seriously.

"I did all ready."

"You did? What did she say?"

"Fine. She will be there with her sister too. You'll all have dinner together, then you skate for the five children and family."

"I don't know if I've ever had more surprises in one day."

"Why do you think I let you select a skating dress?" he smiled with a wave and left.

"Mother, I don't know where to begin!" she exclaimed, handing her the huge box of truffles.

"I said small, Isabella."

"I didn't even see it until now, myself, Mother. Mr. Reinhardt bought so much, saying his family loves sweets too. And Grandmother and Aunt Ingrid will have dinner there… I mean at the Reinhardts. Then I get to skate for the children from South Africa. Imagine all that, and Mr. Reinhardt bought me a skating dress and shoes to have my skates transferred. All in one day, I told him!"

"And?"

"He smiled and said at six Dr. Reinhardt will take me to their home, which is really a palace. I was there last night. Oh, my God, mother! Aunt Ingrid will faint. Gosh, why did you have to break a leg? You could be there too."

"One day you will understand that I had to break my leg so everybody can be there."

She shook her head. "I don't get it."

"I know, darling. Tell me more about your day."

"Gladly. It was the grandest day in my whole life!"

While she talked, Gaby listened only partly as Peter came by earlier explaining that Irene was, thank God, much better, and would come to say good-bye in a couple of days; possibly to his place as she would not face either Victoria or the rest of the visitors. "She will see you in Lausanne just in case things don't work out, but will call you anyway. And speaking about phone calls, she calls Professor Rousseau every day." Gaby was not too surprised. Irene loved charming men and the Rousseaus loved money. Irene will have a rude awakening should it ever come to pass. Mother and son are one.

~

Paul needed a quick meal before going to see Gaby and ate in the kitchen at his corner table, strictly reserved for him alone. It was his habit whenever he was busy. The kitchen help was in full swing too for tonight, but they loved it. Adam made it his practice to tip them well once a week. They never had it so good. At the exact hour of seven, Paul entered Gaby's room. "I see the nurses took your traction away," he stated, not knowing how to begin.

"Take a chair, Mr. Reinhardt, and make yourself comfortable. Also have some of the truffles my daughter bought me. I am sure she wouldn't mind." She smiled warmly at his worried face to break the ice. He looked from her to the floor and then to his intertwined hands, still not knowing where to begin his well-rehearsed speech. "Why don't we skip the encounter at the skating rink so many years ago?" Gaby urged, watching the uncomfortable predicament he found himself in, while finding herself more and more in love. His good looks came more from his mother's side, though his father was known equally for being handsome, but never without having mentioned his womanizing.

His dark brown eyes now looked straight at her, before he said uneasily, "Thank you. I'd like that very much, knowing we both were children at an awkward age."

"Yes, Mr. Reinhardt. I am sure my father must have told you that I was known as 'Gaby the tomboy'."

"Hard to imagine!" he smiled, it being one of his rare occasions to do so. "But there is more to it than that. I was raised... well raised is not the proper word... rather, influenced by my late grandmother about the 'dreadful von Waldens' who took some of our land in the sixteenth century." Both smiled at the few hundred years difference.

"I took those stories from my early childhood very seriously and was kept informed about everything your stepbrother, Bertram, did."

"There is much truth to it. However, my late father hated him since birth, because he had a miserable arranged marriage," she replied sadly.

"I feel for him," he replied somberly. "My father met your late father a few times and respected him highly."

"Thank you."

"Now I got off the subject for one of many reasons I came to see you." There was his sad look again.

"I have nowhere to go, so take your time," she smiled encouragingly.

"One of many times that I saw you and your sweet little girl was on the beach in Locarno in 1929."

Gaby's eyes widened and she gulped in disbelief. "How strange. My daughter, the one you call 'Miss Isabella' spends every year in Locarno, as my late husband's relatives live there. Once my daughter finishes school, we may move there permanently, as my aging in-laws retired there for health reasons."

"God forbid!" he thought, but said, "Don't laugh, but I was there on my ill-fated honeymoon and at the lowest point in my life, having not a single soul to turn to."

"Sorry," she said simply, not wanting to interrupt his thoughts again.

"But the, let's call it 'happy' interruption, came when I watched that little black-haired girl giving it her utmost to build a sandcastle. She was so intense and so engrossed, when a huge beach ball destroyed her work and I noticed you getting up and settling the matter in the kindest way possible."

"I remember it so well. That poor little boy was more upset than we were. We knew that the following day another sandcastle would make its entrance. I also remember that kind French couple who took us to their favorite outdoor cafe for ice cream, having no idea they were our relatives. We had the greatest time and the next day, four grown-ups built 'Versailles,' with Isabella being in her glory with so much help."

"I cannot explain until this day why I went back to Locarno year after year, at the very same spot mind you, just to see both of you again."

"You did?"

"Yes, and frankly I didn't feel bad because I was married, which as you well know was no marriage at all."

"So I was told."

"But I did feel bad because you wore the widest wedding band I have ever seen."

She laughed aloud. "My late husband bought it and wanted to make sure everyone else would notice it too."

"I cannot blame him. I would have done the same," he replied seriously. "Like I stated, I still don't know why, but never a day went by without thinking of you both. You cannot possibly imagine how the surprise encounter on New Year's Day, meeting you again, pleased me. You never aged a day; only little Isabella has grown tall."

"I knew who you were and thought how strange it was that you looked and talked so nicely to us. Then it occurred to me you had no idea who we were but had seen us somewhere."

"Oh, I was ready to find out, but you kept talking to my dog and left with a nod. I made a promise to myself to give the dog roast beef that evening."

She laughed. "You did? How nice!"

"Of course, a few moments later I was disappointed again when your daughter said you were here on vacation and her dog was in Switzerland. By the time I started to ask where, as I know the country quite well, I heard you calling 'Marie' and she started running."

"Well, she was named after my late husband's mother, simply because I loved that name, however, she knows if I call her middle name too she better be running."

"Did she ever," he smiled. "There I go again. I didn't know why, but the following day I insisted on a divorce, as our annulment had taken seven years already. Irene was enthused about it, planning to move to Switzerland for good." He looked abruptly at the floor again before continuing. "At the moment, I cannot bring myself to repeat my answer to her, including your involvement."

"You don't have to, Mr. Reinhardt. I was told everything there was to know about your opinion about both of us," she smiled.

"Oh, my God!"

"She came to our place asking me— by the way, it was the first time I met her— to help her find a house in Lausanne. She was educated in Switzerland and heard about the beautiful town."

"She may have been educated there for a while, but mostly got her experience in Paris."

She knew what he meant but didn't want to discuss it. "We became sort of friendly. She was very nice, and I helped her to find the villa she wanted. Then came the letter for a signature concerning your annulment and our plan backfired." Gaby giggled. "And there I wanted to be in my best suit and arrogant behavior when being introduced by Irene to you! Well, we both know the rest."

"The first night I didn't sleep, and with the exception of the second night being overtired, I still wake up every night dripping wet, still trying to come to terms with it."

"Well, it sure was a strange way to find out who I was," she smiled as he was trying to get some composure.

"There are no words to apologize... that much I know."

"Like my mother still says, things have a way of working themselves out."

"So does mine, but will they?" There, again, was this tense facial expression.

"Well they should. After all, you waited more than eight years just to see me again. Or, should I say my daughter and me, who by the way you spoil much too much!"

"I love that girl like my own child, never mind her mother." He was proud of his courage, but got up feeling he had kept her much too long and being also afraid of her reaction.

It took all her strength not to show how happy she felt. She knew she loved him more than he would ever realize, but also knew that everything must take its time. As he put on his camel-hair coat over his off-white turtleneck sweater and leather pants tucked in his boots, she could only imagine how many other women were now waiting in line to be asked out. The word that he was single again would spread around fast.

"Like I said a moment ago, I waited eight years just to see both of you again. I'd like to add that I am not willing to wait another eight to marry you."

"Mr. Reinhardt, you just got out of a marriage."

"Mrs. Rosatti, you know very well I was never in a marriage."

"Goodnight, Mr. Reinhardt. Give your family and mine my best."

"I will do that. Goodnight, Mrs. Rosatti." He re-opened the door quickly. "Remember, nothing less than a marriage will do," he repeated with a most sincere plea.

"Be sure to remind me from time to time, Mr. Reinhardt," she replied, with a joyous blush on her face.

"That wouldn't be enough for me. It will be each time I see you and I will make sure I will see you quite frequently, Mrs. Rosatti, especially now that I know where to find you. Goodnight again."

She wanted to ask him, "Even in Lausanne?" but the door was already shut.

~

Arriving at home in the happiest mood ever, he heard music and cheerful noise. The servants were clearing the table. The terrace was transformed to an outdoor café, to watch the skaters while sipping hot chocolate. Presently, Andreas waltzed with his wife, Therese. Erika and Isabella tried to match their steps and his sister Elisabeth was cheered on by Adam, trying after twenty years to skate backwards. It was a happy crowd, clapping their hands to the gramophone's music and the skaters' performance.

Paul was still deep in his thoughts of Gaby, enjoying his visit, tip-toeing in and standing behind on the terrace until his mother looked around and noticed him. "How did it go?" she whispered, getting up unobserved.

"Much better than I imagined as far as the conversation went. However, I couldn't ask her when she will leave for Lausanne once her leg is healed."

"Don't worry, it will work out. The worst is over. You have eased your mind," she smiled.

He looked at his watch and was surprised that he was only gone a bit longer than an hour.

"Where is Peter?"

"At the hospital. He told me Gaby will be staying with them as of tomorrow afternoon."

"Irene is leaving with Isabella and her aunt the following day; quite a burden off our shoulders. It's now up to you to win Gaby over."

"I started already by asking her to marry me," he smiled.

"Tell me you are kidding!"

"Would I do that with her? She was very understanding and forgiving."

"So is her mother and her brother."

"I don't remember him anymore."

"Never mind that. What was Gaby's reply?"

"To remind her from time to time."

"Now you see, she *is* kidding."

"She better not be, because I plan to marry her soon."

"Paul, all of Vienna will be laughing. Not only because your marriage just got annulled, but a von Walden and a

Reinhardt? You shouldn't have talked so hurtfully about her. I am happy about it, but wait a while longer."

"As for Vienna laughing, they laughed for more than eight years. And as for the harm I've done, I am partly forgiven. The rest I will make up once we are married." With this final and sincere statement, they walked towards the terrace.

"Hello, Mr. Reinhardt. Did you see me skate?"

"No, Miss Isabella. Will you do it again?"

"Gladly! I will waltz with my uncle."

"Please do."

Andreas, being informed about everything, and knowing how awkward Paul felt about an introduction via his mother, Astrid, or Victoria, took his own initiative and called, "Mr. Reinhardt! I am Andreas von Walden. Thanks for all you did for my niece."

"And I am Paul Reinhardt, the evildoer!"

"Never mind. Accidents happen," and off they went skating.

Paul took it upon himself to put Lehar's 'Gold and Silver Waltz' on again to the great delight of all spectators. Many wished the night would never end.

~

Irene called the following evening at Peter's place after being told by the hospital that Gaby was already there. She only wished her a speedy recovery as she was too busy to visit, having still some shopping to do. Neither Professor Rousseau nor Paul was mentioned, but somehow Gaby felt Irene sounded a bit nervous as she repeatedly said, "I'll see you in Lausanne and we'll talk more about it."

Isabella embraced each of the Reinhardts, thanking them for her good time, and promising to be back at

Christmas and telling the children they would meet her American girlfriend called Daniella. "In our school, they just call us 'Ella' and 'Bella' for short. Mother and all my relatives just love her! It's her fourth Christmas in Europe."

Everyone was looking forward to Christmas of 1937.

~

True to his word, Paul visited Gaby once a day with truffles and flowers, never leaving without asking her to set a date. Erika and Gaby became very close, as the three former Reinhardt servants were not to her liking to talk about anything other than the cooking or the household chores. Mostly, they were quarreling among themselves with Adolf Hitler and the brownshirts being the main topic. The former Reinhardts at the palace would have fired each one immediately for such talk, but times had changed drastically and were getting more dangerous as time went on.

Erika herself was in a very difficult dilemma, having been told by one of her sisters, who had to meet her in secret, that her own father was a fanatic follower of Hitler's doctrine, mentioning on several occasions that, should the time be ripe, Peter Reinhardt would be one of the first ones to get 'his'. Erika never doubted his intentions.

It was a leisurely, bad weather Sunday and as always, Paul was making his 'set a date' visit. This time, Peter decided to have Rupert and Gisela come by. Rupert had known Gaby since Bertram took him home. Gisela heard constantly about her, especially lately pertaining to Paul, and was anxious to meet her. Rupert embraced her with a lump in his throat saying, "Like the old saying goes, you have grown up very nicely."

"So did you, Rupert, as well as your taste in choosing such a beautiful wife. Glad to meet you, Mrs. Foster."

Gisela replied, "And you, Gaby Rosatti." She was just given a comfortable chair to support her leg, with Paul next to her, when the phone rang and the servant exclaimed, "It's Mrs. Irene, but I can barely hear the woman."

Erika took the phone instinctively. "Hi, Irene... yes, Gaby and I are all alone," she said, causing the still astonished guests to be quiet. "Well, Peter will be here in about an hour. Sunday duty, you know." All gave her the sign of agreement, knowing that if they told her about a cozy get-together with three of the four Reinhardt children present, she would never talk.

She handed Gaby the phone, sensing a kind of urgency. "What a surprise, Irene. Sorry our connection is rather poor. We'll just have to scream," she replied, looking around the table for understanding. They only smiled.

"I feel so very badly, Gaby, but Alain Rousseau and I have fallen hopelessly in love. We want to get married very soon and I wanted to be the first one to tell you, knowing it would hurt your feelings," she sighed. "I didn't want you to hear it from Isabella or the Lebruns first."

"Irene, what makes you think you hurt my feelings about a man I never cared a thing for one way or another, and neither did he. That man was my daughter's professor and happens to be the schoolmaster of her girls' lyceum. His mother is my aunt's friend and we all love music."

"Is that all?"

"Yes, that is all, Irene. He and his mother are looking for someone unattached with money. I have a daughter and although she is my everything, as far as those two are concerned, she is only his prize pupil as long as we pay."

Irene sighed in relief. "I was told you loved this man."

"You are joking! Why would I care for a man who looks like him? Just the thought of holding his hand other than in greeting gives me goose bumps. Never mind anything else."

"Well, between you and me, he is the best lover I ever had."

"How would you know?"

"Because we are in bed everyday, putting our experience to work."

"You do? You are? *Yuck*!"

The last short sentences forced somehow Gaby to look up, only to find the three men nodding their heads in unison which meant 'yes she did' and then some. Gaby's face turned red, noticing Gisela and Therese's hands in front of their mouths to contain their laughter.

"Poor Gaby, you will never know how much you are missing."

"I'm not missing a thing, Irene! Anything else?"

"May I have Isabella as flower girl? It will be a lavish affair, even the second time around."

"I don't care about your lavish wedding. My daughter will never be permitted to act as flower girl. The professor has a whole school to choose from. Our morals are well above his and yours!"

"So you are jealous and bitter."

"If you think that, you are sick. Goodbye and good luck!" And she banged the receiver down.

"So sorry, but you didn't hear the other end of the line. Especially the accusation that I am jealous."

"Don't get upset, Mrs. Rosatti," said Paul. "Isabella told me in confidence that the girls call Professor Rousseau 'Warthog'." They all burst out in laughter.

"She did? Well my aunt and I call him that too. But I would never tell Irene, for fear the girls would get bad grades in return."

"Let's eat," Gisela said cheerfully and, looking at Erika, continued. "I am forever grateful that you said you two were alone. That was the best entertainment we ever had."

"Well, I felt the urgency in her voice and wouldn't have wanted to miss it myself. The Warthog and she are getting married at Easter time. The rest you have probably figured out for yourself."

"As men we did, Gaby dear," said Rupert, looking at his wife and Erika. "And believe me, those two sly women of ours did too."

Peter gave his wife a slight pinch. "Now Irene is soon a 'Frau Professor', my lovely Erika is 'Frau Doctor', my dear sister Gisela is 'Frau Police Captain'," He laughed, thinking about Austria's fascination with titles bordering on absurdity. "How about you, Gaby?"

"Irene got the best of you too, Peter," she burst out in laughter.

"No, I am dead serious. Isn't it about time that after fourteen years of widowhood, you should be called "Frau Diplom Engineer?" He smiled speculatively with Paul's and Gaby's faces turning crimson red and Rupert starting to applaud, followed by the rest of them.

Paul, finally looking at Gaby's joyous expression of surprise clapped the loudest. "Thank you, brother. I couldn't have said it better myself."

"I will think about it," Gaby smiled.

"For how long? I have known you for eight years."

"That's where our problem lies. I, on the other hand, have known you barely a month."

"Don't be silly, Gaby," Peter intervened. "You have known each other since childhood. I was there. Remember?"

"And I thought you were trying to help me, Peter," Paul mused.

"So when is the wedding, Gaby, now that we are on the subject," Rupert inquired seriously. "Neither one of us has any intention of leaving until you set the date. Not only are you outnumbered by five to one, but remember your leg in case you want to run. The way I see it you are in a tough spot." Paul looked at him and winked. "Not only that Gaby, but as a man of the law, I am Paul's witness should you dare to retract."

Gaby shook her finger. "Wait until my cast is off. I'll get even."

"How much longer Peter? You are the doctor," Rupert continued.

"About three weeks," Peter laughed. "The Academy sure taught you persistence."

"What I meant to say—" Gaby started.

"I know exactly what you meant to say, Gaby, but it didn't involve the marriage date."

"Thank you, Rupert," Paul smiled gratefully, reaching for Gaby's hand and squeezing it tightly.

"Alright. I'll talk with my mother about it today."

"I thought you were over eighteen," Gisela joined in laughing.

"Gosh, Gaby, it's going to be a family affair only. Adam will give you away. He is old enough to pass for your father. Peter is Paul's best man. I'll stay on the other side with a loaded gun in case you change your mind, right Paul?" Rupert proposed.

All laughed with Paul saying, "I always knew you were a good brother-in-law."

"You may get some roast beef too," Gaby replied, thinking of the setter, causing Paul to laugh aloud, taking her other hand.

"We are waiting," Erika said with a show of confidence.

"Alright, alright. We'll get engaged at Christmas."

A round of applause followed, with Rupert again prodding. "Gaby, I love the idea about your engagement, but Paul needs a date for the wedding."

"Like I told him, he just got out of one," she smiled at him warmly.

"Like I told you, I was never in one," he responded quickly. "Mother chastised me for saying those awful things about you," he said, his face tense as usual.

"What does Mother know?" Gisela laughed, thinking how she had endured their father's countless infidelities.

"Right, sister. What does she know?"

"Well, Isabella has Easter vacation and I wouldn't get married without her. She loves Paul... and I may just as well say it... after our first encounter on New Year's Day, she told mother and me, 'Why can you not find a handsome man like this?'."

"Which tells me how smart my future daughter is," Paul acknowledged. "She will be a Reinhardt as soon as we are married, as her late father never knew her and vice- versa. Is that all right with you, Gaby?"

"Of course, it is... but we have to keep it a secret until her tests are done or she will think of nothing else and flunk them."

"So what?" Rupert shrugged with indifference. "We have good schools too. You, yourself, went to one of the best. Isabella needs to be near her parents anyway."

"I agree. She and I have rarely been separated, but there is still so much to do as I have an apartment too," she replied with a frown.

"So, when is Easter?" Peter inquired, rubbing his hands together.

"This year, in February!" Rupert laughed.

"Easter Sunday is March 30, as Isabella arrives the 26th. I know this for a fact as I was supposed to come too, but as of now, I have to change certain plans."

"I'll help you anyway I can," Paul promised solemnly. "As our mothers used to say, things have a way of working out. I cannot wait to see my mother's face," Paul smiled happily.

"And mine."

"If I may suggest a little change," interrupted a serious Rupert. "Why don't I ask my father to give you away? Though he considers Gisela a daughter, she had at our wedding her own father."

Gisela was in tears looking at Paul. "He knows so much about you."

"And possibly cannot stand me."

"You know better than that, Paul."

"Just kidding."

"What a great day! Let's open a bottle of something," Erika suggested, getting up and making her rounds kissing everybody, starting with Gaby. Rupert got kisses left and right; after all, he deserved them. A servant brought a bottle of wine and they all toasted each other. The moment Astrid and Victoria heard about it, they kept the phone lines tied up. Some friends were happy, some extremely surprised, some disappointed, but no one was happier than Aunt Ingrid and no one more enraged than Irene. She just had to warn Gaby before it was too late. Once more, a call to Erika's home was therefore necessary. "Gaby!" she screamed, after Erika heard her demanding voice and passed off the phone. "Is this a joke or what? Alain tells me that an ecstatic Ingrid told him you are marrying Paul Reinhardt."

"Yes, he asked me a few days ago and I accepted."

"You cannot be that desperate. He is an impotent wife abuser! I was married to this heartless monster until my dear father died, because he didn't believe in divorce."

"But he believed in mistresses," Gaby interrupted.

"Well, to each his own."

"That's what I am saying, Irene. If my marriage had caused me to suffer that much, I would have divorced the man, never mind the opinion of my father."

"You surprise me again, Gaby. But coming back to Paul, please don't marry him."

No sooner had they hung up, than Irene called Paul at his factory. She was very short and repeated that he was nothing but an impotent wife abuser.

"One more call to Vienna and I'll pay a visit to the Professor in Lausanne. And don't think for a moment I'd go back on my word," he replied. Irene hung up, threw herself over her bed and cried.

The very moment Paul told his mother that Gaby and he planned to get engaged at Christmas, she went to her jewelry chest and looked through all that was in there for the first time in years. Since Philip's suicide, she wore, with rare exceptions, a few of her favorite things which she kept in a box. Now was as good a time as any to start giving away some of her inherited and accumulated things, putting the many little boxes on display and letting each one choose to her own liking. It would make a joyful Christmas day when she would have all her relatives there. Of course, there was

Elisabeth, who abhorred anything large, be it diamonds or other stones unless Adam gave them to her. And he, in turn, made sure it was befitting for a missionary wife. But she had three daughters who might be delighted.

So far, Gisela had received, for every special occasion, a piece of the beautiful gems but there was always a question of whether or not Rupert would approve. He had seen them as family heirlooms, his parents never owning nor caring for such things, of course. But Gisela had two daughters too.

Erika had a taste for pearls. She had to dress up frequently for the sake of their parties and always took the advice of Victoria.

Now it was up to Gaby, Isabella, and Paul, should he have a family. While going through everything carefully, she also found Stephany's priceless collection of necklaces, bracelets, rings, earrings, and pins. And among them, she found Verena's 52-carat diamond ring that she never wore because Hannes thought it too large for her small hands. But Gaby had long, slender fingers, just where a ring like this belongs. Victoria couldn't help but think back to when Philip presented her with one for her engagement. How happy she was and how little she knew then.

"Paul, I got the pear-shaped one, and also a scalloped necklace with it. This is the finest ring and I want you to give it to Gaby for the engagement." Like his father in 1895, he asked the same question. "Are you sure you want me to have it?"

"Who else is there? Thank God, Irene never got even one pin from me."

"Mother, she left behind the engagement ring and whatever else I gave her before our marriage in a box."

"Really?"

"The ring was only ten carats and she expected more."

"Well, maybe her new love will come up with one better than ten," she laughed.

Paul, now in possession of the gem, told his mother about Irene's second phone call, and also that she had harassed Gaby with the same lie.

"Poor thing. She never will believe her."

"I was thinking, why don't I give her the ring a few days early. Christmas will have so much activity and all will be lost in the noise. At the same time, I don't like to take the joy away from the young Dreesens, who will have Christmas in Vienna for the first time."

"I think this is very thoughtful. Why not tomorrow as we all go to see the Nutcracker," she smiled. "Peter and Erika are coming as well, so there is your opportunity."

"Great! It's just a week before and she will be so surprised at the beauty of it."

"And for Christmas, you give her the rest of the matching diamonds. She will be the only one who can wear them as they should be worn. I shouldn't say this, but with me fading away, there is only Gaby."

"Don't forget Isabella."

"How can I? But she is still too young for certain pieces. What a fortune Otto spent on Stephany alone! Then there were Lillian Essler, Anette and Verena who also cared very little. And as for me, I would have traded everything in for a faithful husband," she sighed.

"And I made a mistake in choosing the wrong wife," Paul grimaced.

"And she could possibly have ended up with everything. But now she has a tight-fisted professor!" laughed Victoria. "And don't forget his mother. Astrid described her well to me."

"Was anything said about my engagement?" Paul wondered.

"Yes, but I wouldn't let your head swell up, Paul," she smiled.

Gaby was playing the piano when a servant let Paul in. Somehow, she was sure he had gone with the family to see the ballet. "Why didn't you go, Paul?"

"This is my first opportunity to be with you alone since our visit at the hospital. Don't stop playing, please. I love to hear the piano."

"Well then, I may just as well give you an earful."

"You would have made a fine pianist, aside from being beautiful."

"Possibly, but I'd rather have Isabella."

"Yes, one just cannot have everything. Like me, for instance."

"You had your share of sorrows."

"Gone. Gone forever, unless you've changed your mind about marrying me."

"Why on earth would I do that?" Gaby queried.

"Irene's lies." Paul frowned.

"I know that she is simply jealous, or she wouldn't have called. Next time, I'll tell her ever so proudly, 'You got what I didn't want, and I got what you couldn't have!'" He laughed.

"But I imagine there are quite a few men that I could tell the same thing, Gaby."

"And more women, Paul. Don't sell yourself short. I will be the envy of Vienna," she smiled, stroking his cheek with the back of her hand.

"You took your wedding ring off," he said, elated, taking her hand and kissing it.

"I thought I might just as well give my finger a rest since I get one next week from you."

"Wrong," he smirked, reaching in his jacket. "We... but mostly I, decided to give you the ring today. I didn't buy it, as it is a family heirloom, possibly never worn and stored for years for the *right* Mrs. Reinhardt."

"Oh my!" she exclaimed, enraptured. "I've never seen anything so beautiful."

"To tell you the truth, neither have I," he said, looking at her astonished face, taking it between his two hands and kissing her with the ring on her lap. "You meant the diamond, Gaby, but I meant you."

"Please put it on my finger, Paul. Make it the happiest day of my life."

"Gladly. The ring was made for your hand."

"Paul, as much as I love and treasure this, any ring would have been perfect."

"I know that, Gaby," he whispered, embracing her and kissing her again. "It's the happiest day of my life, too," he said, visibly moved. "You are permitted to cry," he said in a quivering voice. "providing they are tears of joy."

Now Gaby put his face very close and returned his barrage of kisses. "If only my leg was not in this long cast, I would sit on your lap, Paul."

"That can be arranged," he replied lifting her up and carrying her to their comfortable couch.

~

He had left before Erika and his brother returned, but Gaby was wide awake and still on the couch when both entered.

"I don't know why, but I thought you would be in bed by now," Erika mused.

"I would have, but look," she said with her arm stretched out. "Just look at this. It's my engagement ring."

"Congratulations, Gaby!" cried both ecstatically.

"Three months and I am a Mrs. Reinhardt too!"

"It may be even earlier than that, providing you want all the family together. Adam wants to leave right after New Year's."

"Oh, God, why?"

"Too many Nazi demonstrations. He is afraid of being a foreigner."

"That bad?"

"To him it is. Don't forget, he has his five children here. He will travel to Holland to see his family and be on his way," Peter announced.

"And Elisabeth, along with her family?"

"She said yes to everything. Adam's word is the law."

"But they will come tomorrow for dinner. You will like them," Erika said fondly. "Gaby, I am so happy for both of you. And I know that ring is an heirloom like mine. A dozen years ago, I had the chance to choose from a large selection with Peter insisting on this one."

"I have always looked at yours, as it sparkles so brilliantly, though I told Paul I would have been happy with anything."

"Well, your shape was not for my hand, though mine is over twenty carats."

"Good heavens!"

"But like you said, anything would have done for me too." They embraced each other with their usual goodnight wishes, Erika supporting Gaby who, with her two crutches, went in her bedroom, staring at her large ring for hours before she finally went to sleep.

~

Arriving at home, Elisabeth and Adam discussed with Victoria their early departure due to those openly demonstrating brownshirts. Victoria looked disappointed. "Since 1865, the Reinhardts have never held a wedding with all the family together. And as far as those demonstrations are concerned, they are mostly illiterate fanatics with very little else to do. It certainly will pass."

"It will not pass, Mrs. Reinhardt. I read Hitler's book that he wrote while in prison and his plans are very clear. He will get Austria one way or another. That evil demon will stop at nothing. Just think of the Russian Revolution which started twenty years ago."

"Right you are, Adam, but we are not Russia."

"You mentioned illiterate fanatics; between that and being without work and hungry, they will always look for a so-called leader, never mind the false promises."

"But will you think about it, Adam? Gaby's cast may be removed by year's end, and the way Paul feels, he would get married the same day. Today he gave her the engagement ring while all of us went to the theater."

"Great!" Elisabeth exclaimed.

"I cannot wait to meet her," Adam said. "after hearing endlessly what my wife refers to as his 'bedtime stories'. I guess I am anxious too."

All the van Dreesens were quite taken with Gaby's beauty and her gentleness. Even Adam, who only dated dark-haired girls, with Elisabeth being his first choice of brain and beauty, had black hair like all the Reinhardts. But Gaby was something else altogether. "Now I understand Paul completely," he whispered to his wife.

No one made any fuss about the exquisite diamond and Gaby felt they must have seen bigger ones. After all, South Africa was the country for it.

The children had the best table manners but lacked personality. Each one had a rather long face, uneven features, and light-blond hair with watery eyes. Not a trace of Elisabeth's beauty, of whom Victoria stated that she looked better at forty-one than when she left at eighteen for Berlin. But all in all, they were a pleasant and happy family. Politics were never mentioned, as she had twice mentioned Erika's dilemma with her repugnant father and the hate he had declared against the Reinhardts. Otherwise, it was an uneventful evening!

~

Isabella, along with Daniella, arrived with several large suitcases and skis, feeling extremely happy. They were met by Paul and his big sled four days before Christmas, planning to stay with Astrid. Isabella embraced Paul and said, "Soon I will be able to call you 'Papa'."

"Yes, and I will have to leave 'Miss' out completely," he smiled.

"This is my best friend, Daniella, and so far she has had three fathers, liking not one of them," said Isabella, who was in her glory about all she heard from her mother. As far as she was concerned, her greatest wish had come true.

Despite a few changes on Christmas Eve due to Paul's engagement to Gaby, Isabella and Daniella spent the day with Astrid, but had the traditional meal with the Reinhardts. And Astrid decided to have dinner with Andreas' family, whom she enjoyed more than holding a conversation with Adam, who tried to convert her to Lutheranism.

~

Christmas Day was the most wonderful time for Victoria and everyone else present. But somehow, she felt it would be the last one where all her loved ones were together. Even Rupert's parents came, and Gisela talked her in to taking a few conservative pieces of jewelry. Gaby was able to walk with a cane and looked as beautiful as always in a hand-embroidered dark blue dress. Her gifts were many and she trembled at the thought of them. Isabella and Daniella were included too, but Gaby made the selection since neither one of them knew about value, but like the largest stones. Elisabeth gave her own girls a lesson concerning the many Tourmalines which came from America. Their colors were exquisite and each of her girls showed great interest. Adam was engrossed with Paul and Gaby, so it was the perfect opportunity to let her three daughters take whatever they wished. Victoria made it very clear that whatever was on the table could be taken by anybody. She put out for Gaby and Isabella many priceless scalloped necklaces of marquise-shaped diamonds, be it sapphire, Burmese rubies, or emeralds. She gave Astrid a natural, black south sea pearl necklace with matching ring and earrings, and the latter spent most of the evening crying and admiring her treasure. Her son Andreas got a rare pocket watch and Therese had the choice of anything on the table.

Victoria helped Isabella and even Daniella to pick out a few good gems despite Gaby's objection. Daniella had a passion for earrings and Isabella for bracelets. Since Andreas' in-laws didn't come, claiming the family was too large, Victoria, with the help of Therese, made sure they would get their share too.

The evening ended with more good music, food and wine, and Elisabeth's girls begged Isabella and Daniella, as well as Rupert's children, to skate. "After all," Elisabeth replied. "once we are back home, no more skating."

The girls were only too happy to comply, Rupert's girls being in awe of those two Swiss-trained girls. "Mother, when Isabella is our relative, can you ask her to teach us?"

"You have to ask her yourself," she said in reply. Gaby, overhearing their plea, told Gisela once the cast is off a week, she would be on the ice again and they soon would skate like Isabella and her friend, as she would be their coach.

"I told you," Gisela smiled. "You know Gaby, the Swiss schools also taught them to be very humble. I like that."

"My God, Gisela! You, being one of *the* Reinhardts, talks to me about modest and humble? You are all the best examples of it."

"Thank you, Gaby and welcome to the Reinhardts," she smiled sweetly.

Everyone left for home in the best of spirits, having celebrated the best Christmas Day ever. Each one carried many gifts including priceless ones from Victoria's collection. Austria was about to change, and not for the better either.

1938

22

Gaby's and Paul's wedding date was set for March 22, exactly a week before Easter. They would honeymoon in Switzerland, and at the same time take care of her little place, possibly letting Susanne live there so they could visit anytime at their own convenience. Isabella didn't even have to think about leaving school, but promised to finish the full term until July.

Adam and family were already packed to leave, warning each one over and over again to do the same. Things went back to normal. Erika and Peter moved back in with Victoria as they promised her. She would never live in the mansion without one of her children being with her. Servants were, nowadays, not the same as in the good old days. Aside from that, she was told by Rosa, the cook, that there were many quarrels among them involving politics. Being very well informed on what had happened since Hitler and his followers took over Germany, many of them among his infamous Gestapo, she refrained from any interference.

Gaby, with her cast off, stayed with her mother, but both made many visits to Victoria or the Fosters, young and old, as well as Andreas and wife. Peter prohibited her strictly from staying at the skating rink and Paul agreed. Erika was there to go for walks, weather permitting, and talking mostly about the forthcoming wedding. For Gaby, the time went fast, for Paul at a snail's pace. He made sure he would see her once a day, no matter where. His workload was quite heavy. He had to instruct his engineers about many details in order to have an extended honeymoon beginning in Switzerland, followed by Italy and France.

Elisabeth and Adam wrote from Holland quite frequently, with their departure to South Africa scheduled at the beginning of March. All preparations for the nice wedding were in full swing, and the guest list included Andreas' in-laws, with their large family, to make up for the absent Van Dreesens. Isabella was again permitted to leave school ahead of the official Easter vacation, as she was Gaby's maid of honor.

Daniella, caring little about her school time, beseeched Isabella to take her along, having never attended a wedding in a castle. Besides that, she loved the Reinhardts and von Waldens, and wrote to America about her wonderful Christmas time. They wrote back that they would see her this summer, and maybe Isabella could spend time with them in America.

The first weekend in March, Irene called Astrid, sounding extremely upset, begging Gaby to call her at any time, day or night, but implored her never to mention it to anyone. Gaby returned from her visit to Victoria's place as Paul took residence in two of the many guest rooms. "Gaby!" Irene cried. "I am pregnant and Alain refuses to marry me, claiming it's not his child. I swear, I never saw another man, never mind go to bed with one. Alain has the key to my house and comes and goes as he pleases."

"No, Irene. It's not that at all. It is how will he tell his mother. That is the only question there is to it."

"Well, I am three months pregnant according to my own calculation."

"Well, what did he suggest?"

"An abortion right away."

"And how do you feel about it?"

"I don't want to lose him."

"Do you want me to talk to him or his mother?"

"God, no! Then it would be really over. I just wanted to talk to someone and have only you I can trust."

"Irene, with your money, I would have the child, throw Alain out, and being so beautiful, you will have a man who is deserving of you in no time. This is my honest opinion and I want you to think about it."

But Irene didn't. Alain gave her the name of a doctor, admitting she was not the first one he sent there, and their wedding would be as scheduled. She took his advice, got it 'over' with, and was sent home, still bleeding, via taxi.

Her maid, Yvette, saw a snow-white, sick woman entering. She took her to the bedroom, undressed her, and saw all the blood. Having been through the same thing herself many years before, she immediately called a doctor who put her in the hospital at once. The doctor followed the ambulance and explained the situation in the emergency room. Upon awakening, she was told that she would never be able to have any more children. However, if she wouldn't give the abortion doctor's name, *she* would end up in jail.

"Gladly!" she said, being furious after Yvette told her that Professor Rousseau had never even bothered to call, let alone come by the house. "It was Dr. Eberti, and I was sent to him by Alain Rousseau."

"You mean by…"

"Yes, the professor from the elite girls' school."

"Well, well."

Dr. Eberti went handcuffed to the police, admitting his friend Alain had previously sent him some clients. If he had to go to jail, then stingy Alain, who made the woman pay for it, might just as well be in the same boat.

It was the biggest scandal in Lausanne for weeks to come. Irene sold the house to a German Jew in a hurry, who offered much more than she paid for it, being grateful he had the connection to escape Hitler's Germany via Italy. She left for France, but not before Mme. Rousseau set her straight.

"It took a harlot like you to finish us. But believe me, you will pay like my poor son. Remember, what goes around comes around."

~

With the rehearsal dinner behind them, which Victoria had hosted in her mansion, they all went to bed late, promising themselves to sleep in. But it was not to be. They all awoke to the loud screams of "HEIL HITLER" the next day.

It was March 13, a sunny Sunday with the Austrians going and coming from their traditional mass. The streets were full of brownshirts, among them also black ones with silver death skulls on their uniforms. The new Nazi government in Vienna declared on the radio that Austria was now a province of Germany, and both armies joined together were now called the Wehrmacht. Vienna and most cities in Austria never experienced more shouts of joy. Citizens appeared in brown shirts, marching the main streets with their outstretched arm giving Hitler's salute. Many Viennese lost no time in plundering Jewish stores and putting 'pigs' signs in front of their store windows.

The Reinhardts, too, were visited by some of their former employees and servants, telling them they had belonged to the Nazi underground. The Reinhardts were extremely careful not to get caught in their well-spun web. They pretended to be glad to see them again, telling them also about Paul's forthcoming marriage to Gaby.

"Well, how lucky can you be Miss von Walden," they said cheerfully, never knowing her other name. "You came back from Switzerland just at the right time. Now you are a German."

"Yes," Gaby smiled. "Unfortunately, I have a dual citizenship, half Swiss and half German," she laughed.

"You will make a fine German wife and give Mr. Reinhardt many offspring. Our Führer loves children," the former manager of the Reinhardts' vineyard said happily.

"I hope so," Victoria replied. "I wish all of you had more time to spend with us, talking about our old times together."

"Madame, I hate to disappoint you, but I threw my old times overboard. This is a new beginning for all of us."

"Well, I am glad to hear that. As you know, I came from Berlin to marry a Viennese, and now I am a German again." That statement shut him up, as he had forgotten all about it.

"Heil Hitler, Mrs. Reinhardt." They saluted and left.

"Father, please, you cannot do that!" screamed Erika at the top of her lungs, when three Nazi brownshirts came for Dr. Peter Reinhardt, taking him to the Gestapo's headquarters to question him about why he lived on the weekends at the former Wertheims' house.

"It has always belonged to the Reinhardts, his great-grandfather only rented them the house," Erika screamed again.

"Which shows that the Reinhardts were always Jew-lovers." And a shaking Peter was forced to walk with them, being thrown on a truck full of Jews.

"Oh, my God!" Erika cried, calling Gisela on the phone as she didn't want to upset his mother, Victoria. She remembered now that Gisela was once very upset when Rupert, after many meetings, was confronted by her as to whether there was another woman. He had no choice but to confess. "My biggest vice is that I always had to belong to a party. Maybe I wanted to be more than I am."

Erika and Gisela were like sisters who confided in each other. Now was the time to get help for Peter. "Gisela," she cried while being happy to have reached her at once. "My father kept his word and he and two other Nazis picked Peter up, taking him to the Gestapo's headquarters."

"Does my mother know?"

"No. I thought I'd call you first."

"Good. Here is Rupert. Tell him what you told me."

Again, she felt relieved to have found him at home. Rupert changed his facial expression after hearing about it. "Calm down, Erika. I belong to the SS, which is way above the SA your father belongs to. I have a secret code and will call there at once. Aside from that, I am already in my uniform bringing some large flags to the Reinhardt palace, as well as to the von Waldens. I am on my way after this phone call." And turning to an distraught Gisela, he said, "I told you I would help your family one of these days." And with that statement, he was gone.

Gisela looked at their flag, already placed that morning with a big swastika on it. Looking also more closely at Adolf Hitler's large photo she whispered to herself, "I'll be damned. A little private from Austria."

She walked with her children a few houses down to the old Fosters, who were more stunned than jubilant, never having suspected their son's involvement. "I see it this way, Mama. Rupert has a chance to do a lot of good for the people he loves. My family and the von Waldens are only two of them. I am now wondering about Andreas' in-laws and their little leather goods store. I hear on the radio that the mob is breaking lots of store windows. They are running wild with their newly acquired armbands."

"We have known so many nice Jews. Where will it all end?"

"Well, the Bauers are not Jewish."

"Thank God for that."

It took Rupert no time to arrive from his ninth district to the first. He hated what he saw, but first went to the office asking for the SA, Teo Landgraf, who took Dr. Peter Reinhardt for questioning under false pretenses. "His only crime is to be Teo's son-in-law."

"You're trying to tell me he's one of *the* Reinhardts?"

"Yes, and in case you don't know it, I am married for thirteen years to their daughter."

"You don't say," he replied, flabbergasted.

"I also met on several occasions Heinrich Himmler, who will arrive with our Fuehrer in a few days."

"So I was told," he said, somehow uneasy, knowing very well the difference between the SA and the SS. "There is our third roundup and possibly the man you are looking for."

The SA leader pointed towards the door. Rupert turned around and noticed Peter at once, though he was tending a nosebleed. "Peter, can you point out the man who hit you?"

Peter thought for a moment that he was dreaming after having taken a few beatings and kicks with boots on the way to the headquarters. *"Rupert in an SS uniform?"* he wondered, but was more than happy to encounter him. "There he is. Erika's father, who hates every Reinhardt."

"Happy to meet you at last, as I heard so much about you. In case you don't know me, I am Rupert Foster, Captain in our Waffen SS." He watched the man shaking, his face turning every color possible, and at a loss for words.

"I expect to be saluted by any SA man," Rupert said harshly. He did it at once without uttering a word. He was tongue-tied on top of it. "Just in case you still don't know who I am, I am Dr. Reinhardt's brother-in-law, married to his sister. As a matter of fact, Erika and Peter met at our wedding. How is that for a coincidence?" Still no answer, but a gulp of disbelief, looking quite afraid knowing he had had it.

"Peter, sorry for the misunderstanding. My car is outside. You cannot miss it with the insignia of the German flag on it. I'll give instructions on what to do with the man who had you picked up for personal reasons. We cannot have such incompetence in our Führer's party. It gives us a bad reputation."

"Yes, Captain Foster," the SA man saluted, being very afraid to cross him.

Rupert left the place hearing many people still screaming, only to walk on the street to experience their loud 'Heil Hitlers'. Girls were kissing the newly arrived German soldiers, who were utterly surprised at their enormous reception. No one expected Austria's welcome to the extent of going to the extreme.

"My God, Rupert, did you steal that uniform or what? Never in my life have I been so happy to see a black shirt. Erika's father gave strict orders to break every bone in my body so I could never function as a doctor again. The way I saw it, Paul would have been the next one. As of tomorrow, he has him watched at his factory to see if he says 'Heil Hitler' or not. Imagine that. I am sure Gaby will go back to Switzerland."

"No, she won't. I told my Gisela that I will play it very smart and can do a lot of good."

"Well, you started with me already."

"And helped the Silvermans a few months ago. I bought their house, with the promise to return it should they ever want it back. They left with the van Dreesens to Holland and are on their way to America, as the Wertheims sent them their affidavit."

"I never heard a thing about it," he said, trying to sit up straight.

"You never will. They are on a 'visit' to America."

"I liked them a lot and now he and she would be scrubbing sidewalks, and be kicked and beaten for it."

"I swear it, Peter. I had no idea when I joined the party it would end up like this. We used to bring people food and clothing and at Christmas time, plenty of toys for children. I loved it."

"Whatever, Rupert. We all know you are a good man. Now you have a chance to prove yourself to be even better. You got a fast start already with me. God only knows where or how I would have ended up. You should have seen poor Erika pleading with her SA father. I will never forget the agonized expression on her frightened face."

"I assure you, Peter, he will never come back, because if he does, there is no telling what he will do next." Rupert couldn't help but think of Bertram.

They arrived at his weekend place in Lindenfels, with Erika looking anxiously out of the window. She embraced Peter, still crying, with her eyes red and swollen. "Thank you, Rupert. You saved the life of the kindest person in the world."

"You tell me nothing new, Erika."

"Oh my God, Peter. They beat you up. I am so ashamed of my father."

"It's not your fault. Who could have known?"

"Yes," Rupert said thoughtfully. "Who could have? Now, I am going to put flags anywhere a Reinhardt, von Walden, or Wiland lives. The first few days will be crucial, as the young and unemployed will wear a band, pretending to have belonged illegally to the party and use their power to get even with anyone they encounter. Believe me, it will die down, as all the real underground Nazis know each other and carry a card."

"What a difference a day makes, Rupert. I can never thank you enough."

"Forget it," he said, and left knowing there was still so much to do. But first he must see his wife and family. Everything else could wait an hour. It was not even noon.

～

"How about my brother Peter?" Gisela asked anxiously.

"I got there just in time."

"What kind of a father would do that?"

"Well, he is on his way to a concentration camp. That's what he had planned for Peter."

"NO!"

"Don't mention a word to Erika, please."

"She wouldn't have cared if you killed him. She called me back... that poor thing."

"I have a few calls to make to secure the Reinhardts' mansion and Paul's factory."

Gisela sighed. "People are dancing in the street. Can you believe that?"

"I have seen it myself. I hope they all get a tour of the Gestapo headquarters. It would make their heads spin."

"My God, Rupert. What next?"

"I wish I knew. Believe me, I would feel much better."

"Or worse!" she replied, leaving him to do his work. *"But what work?"* she thought in dismay.

～

It seemed like all of Vienna had gone crazy one way or another, so Paul went to his factory just to make sure some hoodlums were not there. No one was, but on his way home he had to make a dozen detours just to arrive at his own place. While driving, he thought mostly of Gaby. Will she change her mind and return to Switzerland? He imagined that quite a few phone calls were being made, declining to come to her wedding. What about Isabella? Will Aunt Ingrid let her leave? And there was Irene, who was possibly laughing her head off, having left at the right time to marry a Swiss professor. Well, this time Paul was wrong on all accounts.

"Where is Gaby?" he asked his mother, embracing her.

"Talking to Erika on the phone."

"Did she mention anything about leaving?"

"Leaving to where?"

"Switzerland... with all the commotion going on."

"Paul, she just tried the dress on for the wedding to let me see it. She loves it and so do I."

"Oh, good," he said with a sigh. "Has anyone called from Switzerland?"

"No, but I imagine all lines are busy. Only Rupert called, and he will get us flags out to save us from harassment until the disorder has calmed down. Hitler and Himmler are supposed to arrive in a few days. Better close down your factories on those days."

"Hello, Paul," Gaby said cheerfully, hiding from Victoria and Paul what she just had learned from Erika.

"I had more than two hours of detours. So sorry, Gaby. I was so afraid someone would call from Switzerland and tell you to return."

"Now that would be silly a week before my wedding. My relatives may be afraid to travel, but it won't change a thing."

"You have not the slightest idea what all came to my mind," he lamented. "What poor timing."

"How was anyone supposed to know?" Victoria joined the conversation, looking at Paul's distraught face.

"Gaby, I suggest you call your mother and stay for one or two nights in one of our guest rooms."

"Good idea. I have to wait one hour until her prayer meeting is over."

Paul also hinted about their own servants' affiliation with the Nazi party, as one just didn't know who was who. "I forgot to tell you, some of our former servants were already here this morning to pay their respects. All in brown shirts, which to my little knowledge is the SA." The phone rang and it was Rupert, who was on his way to the mansion. "He has to talk and explain a lot. Also, we shouldn't be surprised to find him in the SS uniform." Victoria tried to prepare them as much as possible.

"The world has gone crazy, Mother. Rupert will be here shortly in a black shirt?"

"Knowing Rupert as I do, there is a reason for it. Let's see what he has to say."

And there he was with flags and another SS man, who was his chauffeur, waiting in the car after he opened the door for him with a salute and his boots clicking.

"Lord have mercy!" Victoria greeted him, and their old doorman nearly fainted, not knowing what to do. He was not even able to announce Rupert properly when Victoria, Paul, and Gaby met him halfway.

"Now we have seen everything," said Paul.

"Possibly... but not heard," replied Rupert and he then began with his story, starting with the frantic call from Erika and including the departure of the Silvermans with Adam and family, including Isaak Wertheim who helped with the real estate transaction. Now it was Rupert's house until their return.

"The Wertheims had an affidavit for him too. Everything was mailed to the von Waldens. Her son, Andreas, and his wife took the Silverman's apartment."

The Reinhardts were astonished. Gaby held tightly to Paul's arm, as he was concerned about the Wilands who were strict Catholics.

"Paul, it doesn't matter what anyone believes, but I can help more people in my uniform than out of it."

"There is no doubt in our minds," Gaby answered sincerely. "You have done it all your life."

"Please call the Wilands so they don't have a heart attack seeing me!"

"I will go there personally, as one never knows if they listen in on certain people," Paul replied.

"Ha! You are smarter than I am," Rupert acknowledged before leaving. "Watch your servants. They have seen me in uniform. It will tell you a lot," he whispered, walking down the steps.

"Thanks again."

23

The wedding took place in the evening at the castle's chapel as scheduled. For Paul and Gaby, as well as Isabella, it was one of the happiest days of their lives. Aunt Ingrid came with Isabella and Daniella, regardless of the newly arisen change in Austria. After all, two were Swiss and one an American. They were treated by the German border guard with the utmost courtesy and not even asked for their reason to visit the new 'Ostmark'. They were more clever than that. Why would anyone from a neutral country want to stay longer than necessary?

It was still family only, but the Lindenfelsers were equally as stunned as the day when Austria ceased to exist, becoming now a part of Germany. What next? Paul Reinhardt with the former Gaby von Walden? They wished Paul the best, knowing his marriage to Irene was a sham, but it didn't take their servants very long to reveal the true circumstances, which all the ladies of Lindenfels found truly romantic.

Gaby, of course, was consulted, but her own mother refrained from interfering as Victoria pleaded with her to give her and Paul the joy of paying. "After all," she said sincerely. "Gaby and Paul deserve it."

The men would all wear the same black suits in a timeless design. Gaby would wear, like the rest of the ladies, light wool, considering that it was the time of year where chill is always the norm, regardless of the heated chapel. Since it was Gaby's second marriage, she suggested a delicate blue wool with a wide pleated cummerbund in heavy satin, small ruffles leading to a high mandarin collar, and fastened by a large sapphire and diamond broach. The skirt descending from the cummerbund would be more heavy ruffles to enhance her small waistline. The sleeves would be long and straight. Gaby would wear only her matching bracelet which had the same size of sapphire, each one again encircled by diamonds.

"I have spent over thirty years designing for Mr. Charles Worth, but I have never seen a more beautiful selection of attire, given the size of the wedding," the coordinator stated sincerely. "Mr. Worth will be enormously happy."

Isabella, as the maid of honor, wore the same style in off-white. Daniella, who insisted on being in charge of the four little flower girls, also demanded the same style in dress, but took the lightest shade of watermelon. Her little flower girls were in off-white satin with velvet sashes and big bows in the back. Then came the attire for the younger three wives. Erika was in a light sea green suit with the same color satin blouse. Although not ruffled, it showed the mandarin color with an emerald pin. Gisela was in a delicate antique rose and Therese in light apricot. All had the same suit and blouses, planning to look like spring flowers. Their headdresses were made from pleated satin just large enough to cover their hairstyle. They had their chignon arranged the way Gaby wore hers.

Then came the older set with darker colors and off-white blouses. No one objected to the collar with pin. Victoria wore deep emerald green, Astrid wine red, Ingrid cobalt blue, Wilma Foster dark violet, and Mrs. Bauer a beautiful bronze color. It was the first suit the House of Worth made in this new tinge.

Paul was nervously looking around, but extremely pleased at the arrangement pertaining to their wardrobe, while enjoying, like everyone else, the beautiful organ music. But what pleased him beyond comprehension was that Aunt Ingrid, his soon-to-be daughter, Isabella, and her American friend, Daniella, came along, ignoring the newly-arisen political changes in the 'Ostmark', formerly Austria until a week ago. All made sure the wedding of Gaby and Paul would not be marred, regardless of the circumstances.

With the priest entering and taking his place behind Paul, the organ started to play the traditional wedding march while an exquisite looking Gaby, on the arm of Rupert Foster, Sr., walked down the aisle, only to notice a visibly moved Paul, almost in tears. The priest made the ceremony short, less religious to his own surprise, after being told that Rupert the SS man rescued his brother-in-law, Peter. He didn't want to risk having to be rescued. But it was a Catholic wedding nevertheless and had to be conducted as such. Paul omitted the high mass, however, having had one with Irene.

The priest, being a friend of Paul's, remembered very vividly their sleigh ride to the card game, calling him crazy when Bello would get roast beef. He spoke what he felt should be said; that mature love means liking as well as loving, and is quite frequently love at second sight. All present could vouch for that remark. He also emphasized that love is sure, is giving, and always wants the very best for you. He ended by saying he felt more than honored to share their newfound happiness with them.

By the time he pronounced them man and wife, after Paul retrieved an even wider wedding ring to put on her finger than the previous one from Lucas, there were no dry eyes in the pews. It was Daniella's turn to let each of the girls give a small bouquet of orchids according to their color of suits, as the surrounding guests came up to congratulate and to admire her gown and the garland in her hair, made from tiny blue orchids held by a light blue veil which reached to her shoulders. Paul and Gaby felt like the happiest people on earth.

There was no dancing as it was the week before Easter, but the table setting eclipsed all previous ones thanks to Wilma Foster's talent in arranging flowers. Everybody fully appreciated the beauty and rare colors of orchids. The Reinhardt family made the new Bauer family quite welcome, thanking their youngest seven-year-old son for being the ring bearer.

"You know Paul," Victoria whispered to her son. "I enjoyed this wedding more than the last one with five hundred and some guests."

"No comparison, Mother. And that goes for my heart too."

A liveried servant was commissioned after the lengthy dinner to show Daniella the castle, pointing out many paintings, furniture, and tapestries of great interest. After all, she may soon leave for America and never be back. The men discussed politics, Peter and Rupert being the heroes. Rupert, although in civilian clothes, knew immediately on whose side their servants were on.

"I am sure they know about you in the SS and our Nazi flags should tell them something," Paul replied. "I had to do the same in my factories. It pains me to return their stern look with their outstretched arms to say, 'Heil Hitler,' but I would lose almost all my best engineers and workers. I feel powerless for the first time in my life."

"It will pass," Peter calmed his brother, knowing it would take quite some doing.

"I hate to talk about politics on the happiest day of my life, but tomorrow Gaby and I are leaving. Don't think for a moment I don't take my workload with me."

"I'll have your place watched, Paul, as well as the castle and this palace here. My orders come from Berlin now, which is, at the moment, quite a blessing. Or is there another word for it?"

The doorman announced the photographer.

"Finally!" some said, their children getting restless. Gaby went for Paul.

"My dear husband, the picture taking is about to begin. The poor man is late as he had to take many detours."

"How well we all know," Paul replied, apologizing profoundly for leaving her alone, but since they would be leaving tomorrow, there were quite important matters to be discussed.

"Believe it or not, we ladies had the best time."

"And I was shown this beautiful castle," said Daniella and Isabella, who joined her later with the flower girls.

With the picture taking behind them and the guests gone, as well as Victoria, Erika, and Peter back at their palace, Paul and Gaby were finally by themselves.

"I have attended many weddings, but have never seen a more beautiful, lovely, charming, and radiant bride. Gaby, there are just not enough words to praise you."

"Same here; only for a man, the words have to be different," she smiled.

"Let's have a toast to each other. I was so happy each one had only a few but heartfelt words to say."

"Same here." Neither wanted to mention their first marriages.

"I had a honeymoon suite reserved at the Hotel Imperial for our first night, before leaving for Switzerland. I also planned to arrange a lunch for our families, but it had to be cancelled as the Germans took temporary possession to have a place for their High Command."

"Thanks, Paul, but a honeymoon in a castle is nothing to look down on. Especially if one is married to the owner." She smiled happily.

"Here is to our happiness," Paul said, touching her glass.

"Same here," she replied.

He carried her over the threshold in the section he occupied, and strangely enough, Irene never had set foot in it. It was a breathtaking, beautiful salon, with flower-painted panels from Stephany's and Otto's time. But he lost no time in showing her to her dressing room before going to his. A few minutes later, they met in the huge master bedroom with angels on the ceiling looking down. It didn't take Gaby very long to realize she was not Paul's first encounter. And it took just as little time for Paul to notice that Gaby had taken no lover since the death of her husband. The life of Gaby Reinhardt had finally begun!

~

They left the following afternoon after a few more goodbyes, and would see Isabella, et al in Lausanne. They drove in his Mercedes, making their first stop by evening in Salzburg, where two places carried the Reinhardt name. They opted for one night in their chalet and the second in the villa 'Karl Reinhardt'. He refrained purposely from bringing up the past with very few exceptions, as the Reinhardts were somehow always intertwined with the von Walden name. Therefore, very little of Verena's own hideaway chalet called 'Full Sunshine' was mentioned.

A few days later, they left for Switzerland to the town of Locarno. She wanted to visit all the Rosattis, and he looked forward to sitting at the same place where he fell in love almost nine years ago. The border of Switzerland was a sad sight as far as the Jews were concerned. Without exception, they were all turned away. Gaby showed her Swiss passport, and Paul his still Austrian visa and their marriage license. They were pleasantly surprised by the kindness of the new German border guards, who mentioned very casually that upon their return they would have to get German passports and why not pay their own beautiful country a visit too. Paul replied that he had studied in Berlin and lived there in the lean years. The guard lit up like a Christmas tree and called his partner over, as he too was from Berlin. They had a nice, long chat about Germany's great future, guaranteed for the next thousand years. Then the border guards wished them a happy honeymoon.

Once well away from the border and in Switzerland, they found it hard to believe what one former downtrodden Austrian laborer had accomplished. He hypnotized his people. "Did you see all those forlorn Jews, Paul?"

"How could I not?"

"I was already getting upset in Salzburg. How can people do that?"

"The Wertheims and Silvermans were very lucky."

"We loved both families," Gaby replied.

Arriving in Locarno, the Rosattis laughed and cried simultaneously. There was her former mother and father-in-law, looking Paul over and telling Gaby that after fifteen years of widowhood, it was high time she remarried, as one child was just not enough."

Paul put his arm around his wife and agreed. "Those are exactly my thoughts, even though I love Isabella like my own daughter and with your permission I would love to adopt her."

"Of course, it is all right. Our son, Lucas, would have loved the idea. You almost look like him."

Gaby knew better, but let it go at that. After all, Paul had black hair, brown eyes, and a healthy suntan, which made him look more Italian than Lucas, whose complexion was rather light. They showed a slight disappointment on their weathered faces after hearing of Paul's reservation in Locarno's hotel Il Palazzo, but when he told them he had stayed there every year since 1930, they fully understood. Little did they know he came at times twice a year in the hope of seeing Gaby again.

"But you will at least eat with us whenever it suits you."

"Gladly," both agreed.

But with each meal, the invasion of Austria by the 'low-down warmongering Germans' was brought up, and Paul was asked frequently, "Why don't you stay in Switzerland?"

"Because I have my family in Austria. I am especially concerned about my mother, who is a widow." That was the only reason which made sense to the Rosattis. Family always came first. Had Paul even mentioned his materialistic belongings, he would have been condemned to hell.

Gaby and Paul took full advantage of the hotel's tennis court, horseback riding and swimming, always meeting at the place where he had spotted her and Isabella. After a week which included lots of sightseeing at that little piece of earthly paradise, he decided to call home. They were so glad to hear from him, never suspecting them to start their vacation in Locarno.

"Yes, Gaby and I are still here. Today is only Easter Monday. Isabella and her friend have still a week for respite."

"They are leaving Thursday, enjoying Vienna despite everything."

"So what's the urgency, Mother? You sound upset."

"The word is *uneasy*, as I am told on a daily basis that quite a few German officers and civilians are visiting your factories regularly, despite being told you are somewhere in Switzerland on your honeymoon."

"If that is the case, Gaby and I will drive tomorrow morning to Lausanne. She will stay and settle her things while I drive to Vienna. I cannot neglect my work and what else is going on. God only knows what their plans are. I'll see you shortly." And with that, he hung up. Gaby told him to leave right away with the car. She would stay a night and would take a train to Lausanne the next day, arriving in Vienna as soon as possible.

"I know I have the most understanding wife," he acknowledged, embracing her tightly.

"And the same goes for my husband. I just have to take care of my few things in Lausanne."

"Until Vienna!" They embraced each other again, again, and again. He could never get enough love from Gaby.

She explained the circumstances to all the Rosattis, but this time they did not understand. "He is stupid. His factories could have waited. After all, he was on his honeymoon."

"I begged him to leave, as the Germans are in and out of his place like it's their own. He talked with his mother last night. All telegrams went to Lausanne, and I am taking the train to Lausanne tomorrow."

"Gaby, we mean it when we say you and Isabella are Swiss citizens and a nice man like him can find work anywhere."

"Thank you. It's good to know."

Gaby arrived at the Lebruns' place, where her Uncle Henry was waiting for Ingrid's arrival. He, too, could not understand why they didn't start out in Lausanne.

"He made reservations a long time ago in Locarno."

"Why?"

"Because he had seen Isabella and me for the first time on the beach and went every year thereafter."

"Oh, I forgot all about that."

"Well, he didn't."

"And the Rosattis?"

"Thought he looked just as Italian as Lucas."

"Only much better."

"I thought so too." Gaby smiled. "They also offered to help him in case we all want to stay in Locarno, in lieu of the German occupation."

"There is always Lausanne too."

"I know that."

~

Victoria was overjoyed to see Gaby return in such a hurry. Paul had just left hours before with some officers in a staff car straight to Berlin. He told her all the talk he had with Gaby and she was ecstatic to visit Berlin again. She hadn't been there since the death of her mother. The Kronthalers had moved to their country estate, where some relatives took care of them as both were old and sick.

Victoria and Gaby left on a sleeper train, preferring to travel through the night and arrive refreshed in Berlin. There were no worries about leaving Vienna with Erika and Peter supervising the mansion, and should there be any problems, Rupert would set everything straight. They were surprised to be met by Paul, who took them to their beautiful hotel and left again with the promise to be there around six.

During their first day of excursions, they were surprised to find those many billboards recommending highly the many musicals, operettas, and plays from Vienna, with their best actors performing. Also, the movie houses with a silly Viennese theme were sold out. One could honestly say that Vienna was 'in'.

~

Paul was shown around most of Germany's large industries, starting with Siemens. He was not quite sure whether it was to intimidate or impress him. As a Reinhardt, he was neither. He let them know in the politest way possible that he had visited the place with his late father during the first World War. "I studied in Zurich and Berlin to become an engineer."

"And a Diplom on top of it. Believe it or not, we know a lot about the Reinhardt corporation," one of the generals smiled. Paul had never any doubt about it. "Your late father manufactured ball bearings. Now you will convert the same place to do it all over again. It shouldn't be too much trouble, as we found many items which are of great convenience to make a fast transition."

"Why the urgency?"

"Our Führer will give all those many unemployed Austrians plenty of work. Germany is going to be great again. The unfair Treaty of Versailles will end up in the gutter where it belongs."

"And Germany will start a war," he thought, but kept listening to more of Hitler's plans while visiting another war factory in full swing. He thought momentarily of Switzerland and all their tranquility. Then he had to give his oath for the utmost secrecy.

After four days of intensive tours in above and underground factories, Paul was told that in two weeks he would receive orders from Berlin. "In the meantime, enjoy yourself."

For five days, they did just that. Victoria and Gaby went on a shopping spree, aside from a few sightseeing tours. Now they would enjoy Paul. On the last day, he had an idea. He got written permission to purchase any German-made car. To him, it was funny as all he had seen so far were Mercedes; Opels were produced by General Motors. His thought was to surprise Gaby with a wedding gift since their time was cut short, and there was no occasion to give her something special.

"Why don't you two girls do some more shopping the last day and I'll do mine?"

"We didn't forget anybody," Gaby commented. "We had a list."

"So do I!" He smiled and left, only to return two hours later with a shiny black Mercedes.

"You two had too much luggage, for one thing, and for the other, Gaby never got a wedding present from me. So here it is, dearest wife."

She was amazed and tears came very easy. "Paul, I don't deserve all this."

"All you have to do is learn to drive it so we can see each other more."

"Mr. Paul Reinhardt," she smiled tongue-in-cheek. "are you talking to me?" Victoria started to laugh, too.

"Yes, Gaby, to you, as my mother has no intention to learn now, my dear."

"But I have been driving Uncle Henry's car for the last eight years," Gaby added brightly.

Now he looked flabbergasted. "Why didn't you tell me?"

"There was never any reason."

"Now I wonder what else she does or knows I am not aware of?"

"Nothing I can think of," Gaby smiled.

"I could have told you, but the name of 'von Walden, the ugly brat' was a taboo subject," Victoria thought to herself, chuckling.

The last evening in Berlin was spent at their state opera to see Puccini's *La Boheme*. Victoria and Gaby bought long dresses just in case. Both looked stunning. Victoria could have passed for the middle fifties and Gaby looked not a day over twenty-five. Paul felt proud to take his two girls out. Soon there would be three. Isabella had told him in confidence that she had no plans to return to her school in Switzerland, but would enroll in the finest one in Vienna.

Summer vacation started and Isabella was met by Gaby and her mother in Ingrid's place. Paul was presently in Germany's Ruhr area, where their industry was the busiest. He toured the Krupp factories, about whom he had read every word written. As usual, he was sorry about the ongoing war production but could do little about it. Gaby and Astrid planned to stay a week, knowing they would possibly have their last talk with lovable Uncle Henry, who was going downhill by the day. Then what? Ingrid would be alone, and without Henry it wouldn't take the Swiss long to consider her a German. Austria was now her Germany again. Should she sell and move in with her sister in Vienna? Or go back to her few living relatives in Baden-Baden, a health spa for the rich? "It's up to you," Astrid advised. "But first, pay them a visit."

Daniella would return with Isabella. Her mother and stepfather would come at a later time and take Isabella for a month to America. Gaby had known Daniella's mother under two different names the last few years. First, she was Mrs. William Thornburg, a lawyer's wife living in New York City. Now she introduced her new husband as Chris O'Hara, a kind, slightly bald and red-haired banker who worked and resided during the week in New York, but they had places in Connecticut and Florida. "One just cannot live always in the same place. I personally need excitement," Gaby remembered vividly being told with her rather snobbish attitude.

After hearing at that time in 1932 about Gaby's nine-year widowhood, her mouth opened with an unbelievable expression. "My Lord! You don't smoke, you don't drink, and above all, you don't date. What on earth do you do?"

"Everything else," Gaby laughed.

"My Lord," she repeated. "what else is there?"

"You would be surprised."

Since she barely talked about motherhood and left Daniella completely in the care of the school, seeing her once a year mostly to explore Europe, Gaby had not too much in common with her, except the required conversations after the meeting with their own child's teachers.

The O'Haras had already made two weeks' reservations in Hotel Bristol, which was not too far from the Reinhardts' place. They arrived a week later, called Daniella at the Reinhardts and were told the girls were playing tennis. Victoria took the phone and invited them to have dinner the following day.

They arrived via their own rented 1934 French Citroen, which they would return in Le Havre. Chris O'Hara had his connections via his bank in New York and it was another reason why Anne had stayed with this rich widower for two years. She considered herself very flexible.

Even the social-climber Anne O'Hara couldn't believe her eyes when greeted by a liveried doorman and entered Reinhardt's palace. She was told by Daniella about the wedding in the castle with her being the main flower girl, but since Isabella was the 'only' bridesmaid, Anne paid no more attention to it. Now she encountered a palace she had never seen before. Even the usually spoiled Chris O'Hara, whose life consisted of entertaining and being entertained, was now in awe. A servant offered a variety of drinks when Victoria, Gaby, her daughter, and Isabella appeared, all impeccably dressed for dinner. But so were the O'Haras, more or less to let the Reinhardts know that if it's money, 'we got it'.

Gaby told them that they also invited her mother, Astrid Walden, whom Anne met fleetingly and couldn't remember at all and her brother, a doctor, with his wife. They all spoke English, she assured them. With a drink in their hands they got a tour through the place, being always more impressed as both O'Haras understood 'old money', she being from America's 'old society' by the maiden name of Woodward. But her biggest envy was always Gaby's flawless beauty and polite behavior; a lady from top to bottom. Anne was like Irene. With all their money, they never achieved it. By the time the tour was done, Gaby's family had arrived and one had to wait for Gaby's husband, who apologized for being late, as usual.

If Anne was surprised before, now she was speechless. Never before in her life had she encountered a more handsome man. Well, he was worth waiting for. Gaby got everything she could ever want. Those guys were taken, always taken. Andreas looked a lot like Gaby, but for her American taste, not 'sexy'. Therese and he made a nice couple, but Gaby and Paul were the most extraordinary ones she could ever remember.

The conversation was, of course, the invasion of Austria by a former Austrian. Both O'Haras were very well educated and informed. They would see Salzburg, but skip the famous play, Everyman, because they had tickets to sail on their favorite ship, *Ile de France.*

"And what will you do, Mr. Reinhardt? Stay in that so-called great Germany, while they prepare for a war; a war that will surpass all previous ones?" Chris O'Hara asked.

"I was born and raised here. I love Austria, and I hope it will never come to that," he winked at him.

Chris O'Hara changed the subject fast, knowing he went too far. A good dinner and bad politics is a poor combination. "Can we take Isabella to Salzburg? Of course, we are still staying for about ten days in Vienna."

"Then you should see our countryside," Victoria suggested.

"Please show my mother and papa the castle you got married in. Please!" pleaded Daniella sincerely.

"Only if it does not interfere with your family's plans," answered Gaby.

"A castle never interferes," replied Anne in a hurry. They set a date. It was the same thing all over again. Sheer astonishment… if anything, more so. No tennis court because it would take some beauty from their well-maintained garden and shrubs, as well as the magnificent fountain. But there were riding paths which Isabella and Daniella used daily with several Irish setters beside them.

Daniella almost hated the idea of going home, though she had the best of everything except love and a harmonious home life. Anne and Chris O'Hara fought a lot after a few drinks, she always claiming his Irish temper, he claiming her constant flirtation.

Isabella told her mother about it, having never witnessed a quarrel except among the Rosattis, who were disagreeing constantly for the sake of disagreeing. But now that the time came closer to the departure for America, she had second thoughts and was already homesick even before leaving. But so was her family. The Reinhardts wanted Isabella with them in Austria, regardless of the occupation.

Europe's famous Circus Krone was in Vienna for two weeks, and with both girls attending the same riding school, they wanted to see the equestrian performance in the worst way. Daniella begged her own mother, as so far, they were royally entertained by the Reinhardts constantly. And Isabella was even more a horse lover than anyone else she knew. But it was to no avail. Vienna's theater showed 'Dances of the World' and Anne insisted she would rather attend that. Chris O'Hara was more a horse than dance lover but had to give in, promising to take them some other day.

"Your mother doesn't care that much for horses, so we'll go alone."

But the Reinhardts settled the girls' plea very easily. They all were horse lovers and saw the circus whenever in town. Also, the children of Gisela and Rupert wanted to see the little zoo of elephants, monkeys, and to the Reinhardts' dismay, the caged lion and tigers who performed with greatest discipline. Paul and Gaby, after hearing about it, invited themselves and would bring both girls with their car. Everyone was happy again, as the O'Haras never cared whom Daniella was with as long as she was safe. Victoria didn't want to leave Erika alone, as she didn't feel well the last few weeks, disliking the heat.

Once in the huge tent, the family split up, having more than an hour to spare before the opening. "Isabella, look at this beautiful horse on that rotten leather line. It limps so badly when trying to walk." It took her barely a minute to diagnose the left leg as broken, also the right one badly swollen. "Possibly from an infected hoof," she lamented, almost in tears.

"How do you know, Isabella?"

"Thanks to Aunt Ingrid's lessons. It included not only riding and horse jumping, but also the anatomy of one."

"Wow!"

"Wow is right! I was questioned vigorously about those beautiful and useful equine species which can be traced back to about sixty-million years."

Isabella was beside herself from the out-of-the-ordinary beauty, trying slowly and gently to get nearer, but the horse neighed loudly, standing on his hind legs.

"I've got to get my papa," she said with pride. "Please stay with the horse." Daniella agreed happily, still admiring the golden color and long white tail and mane. Isabella looked franticly among the large crowd until she saw Paul and Rupert strolling alone.

"Papa," she pleaded in tears, "will you please come and take a look at this forlorn horse? It's the most beautiful creature I ever laid eyes on."

"Oh... and I thought ours were nice," he smiled. "May I ask my new uncle to come too?"

"I rode many horses during my duty as policeman."

"Oh, you did? Well, then you will understand me better."

"The way you looked, I thought a lion was on the loose," Paul teased when they arrived.

"Oh, what a rare beauty," he exclaimed, knowing it was unmistakably a Palomino.

"They'll pay for it," Rupert said furiously, "and I will personally see to it." He disappeared, not waiting for Paul's reply.

"Papa, what do you think?" she asked, now visibly in tears.

"That poor horse needs a veterinarian right now. Dear Isabella, it is sheer coincidence of course, but this horse color is called 'Isabella', after the Queen of Spain, who loved the color and encouraged their breeding." Isabella turned white in awe.

"What happened to you, Isabella?" Daniella asked noticing her change.

"I love that horse so much!" she cried when Rupert appeared with a gypsy, who took barely a look at the horse.

"We have a show to go on now," he said very annoyed. "I cannot be bothered with this." He then tried to leave.

"Where is the manager?" asked Paul angrily.

"How would I know? He is busy with the show too, I imagine. We cannot stand around like you."

That did it for Rupert. He took his arm with a strength the gypsy had rarely experienced previously. "Look here," he demanded in no uncertain terms. "Here is my badge, as I am with the SS. I am sure you heard about us."

He shook his head up and down and stammered, "Come with me and I'll get you the boss. I am only a stable boy."

"Who lets horses die!"

"No! We called for a veterinarian already."

"Don't lie or I'll take you with me."

They arrived at a trailer, and this time, Rupert had his identification ready. "I am checking on this horse outside your tent, and I want some answers."

"What horse?" he asked, equally scared.

"The light one with the white tail," the gypsy replied uneasily.

"The one with one broken and one infected leg, among other negligence."

"I told someone to call a vet."

"And no one showed up? Is this what you want me to believe?"

"No… I am too busy with other details."

"Is the horse for sale?"

"Depends on the offer," he said in a hurry.

"Give me a figure and don't forget the vet bill."

"Is it for you?"

"No, for my brother-in-law's daughter, who stayed with the horse crying her eyes out. By the way, her father knows horses."

"Is he there?"

"Yes," Rupert answered sharply. "We all wanted to see your horses perform. Some of our families are already seated, but I won't leave until something is settled, even if I have to bring a few more of the SS in. We don't fool around."

"How well we know," he thought, and left with Rupert.

Paul, seeing this, knew he could make a deal. That sick horse would be slaughtered and used for a meal. He would offer twice the amount.

"We called a veterinarian," he said without introduction, and both men knew he lied. "Here are your tickets girls, why don't you go in and tell my sister what happened. We will be there shortly."

Isabella wiped her tears and said, "We ride horses too."

"Well my daughter is performing shortly, and she is the top of six girls in bright pink."

"Thank you," both said, elated, feeling they knew a circus rider.

"So, your daughter cares for this horse?"

"No. My daughter, Isabella, is in love with that poor neglected creature and I'd like to make a deal for both of us," Paul replied.

The man looked at the floor. He didn't want to be too expensive, knowing the SS guy was capable of doing anything. Quite a few of his gypsy stable boys had already disappeared since the Germans took over. "Since you seem to know horses, you must know her descendants are called after Don Juan de Palomino," he bragged.

Paul smiled and replied, "Since I do know horses, there is another version in my books. The name may also be that after the golden Spanish grapes. And aside from that, the truth is that the color is called 'Isabella', after the Queen of Spain, who encouraged their breeding. It can be only two or three shades lighter or darker, like this one."

"I didn't know that," he admitted.

"Well, since my daughter's name is Isabella, you can see why I'd like to get it for her, as it is not much use to the circus anyway."

"I assume you have the money for the doctor and a stable or two."

"Correct on both accounts."

He paused and tried to count in the new German money. "How about five hundred and fifty marks?" Paul and Rupert were speechless, having expected three times the amount, since Isabella was later able to open the mouth of her beauty, and it was still a very young horse; three or four years at the most. "I am not a cheating man," he replied, business-like. "What is your connection to the circus?"

"I am in charge of our horses and their riders. I was one of the best, myself, until I got too old. I am staying because I trained my three children, two on trapeze and one on the horse."

Paul could only imagine what it was like to live in a trailer with nowhere else to go. "I am driving home and will come back with the money, truck, and horse trailer, and a veterinarian. I don't want the animal to get hurt. In the meantime, get her a bucket full of water.

"Yes, sir."

"And I'll give you more money. Do what you want with it." His happy grin was obvious when Paul left in a hurry, called his veterinarian, Dr. Steuber, took three of his stable boys with a bag of oats and returned.

It was obvious the horse was never whipped but rather neglected. It took the bag of oats happily, and the empty water bucket was noticeable. Dr. Steuber said, after he examined both front legs, that within a few weeks, it would be as good as new. The price for the horse was unbelievably low, as this breed would easily fetch three thousand marks, even without papers.

Since Paul had no intention of breeding, this was fine with him. It would be strictly Isabella's own, and he hoped sincerely she would change her mind about the trip to America. He gave the man one thousand marks and said kindly, "You and I know the horse is worth more. Whatever you do with the money is your problem. I have witnesses and showed them the money I will give you. I expect no foul play, even if the horse was stolen."

"It was not! We got it two weeks ago from a small circus who went bankrupt. All together, we got four horses and we, too, got a good deal. Besides that, I was scared of that SS guy and wanted to get rid of both of you, not knowing if you are undercover too."

Paul laughed. "No, I am Paul Reinhardt and own many Arabians, thoroughbreds, and Clydesdales. This horse will be pampered and spoiled by my daughter."

"That's another reason I sold it so cheap. My daughter sleeps in the horse stable so no one would mistreat them. Gypsies are cheap, but can be cruel at times."

"How well I know," Paul finalized, hoping the man kept the money. After all, he was a well-deserving one, short-changed all his life.

Paul was coming in when the clown entertained. Gaby took his hand, squeezing it. "You are too good to us. Rupert told me, but Isabella has no idea. She thinks you went for a veterinarian," she whispered.

"I only hope it also takes care of her trip to America. I don't have a very good feeling about it. That woman may be a member of America's aristocracy, or anything else for that matter, but she is neither a wife nor a mother."

"I always felt that way. I never got close to her, but I love Daniella."

"You think they would let her spend the summer with us?" Paul asked.

"We can try."

The funny clowns with their loud trumpets and even louder drums had now disappeared, with tigers making their entrance. All visitors were captivated by their performance. Isabella, however, still thought of the most beautiful horse in the 'whole wide world', driving Daniella insane with her comments.

"My God Isabella, we have the same ones in America. You will see."

"Not like this one," she countered.

When the show was over, Paul and Rupert whispered between themselves, and all wished each other a good night. Isabella, however, insisted that her family, especially her mother, take a look at the horse.

"Isabella, Rupert and I made sure a vet would be called, so I stayed here until one arrived. Why do you think I missed more than half of the show?"

"Oh." She got excited. "What did he say? Can he help her?"

"In a few weeks, she will be as good as new. He took her to his own horse clinic and I offered to pay the bill."

"Thank-you, Papa." She reached and patted his shoulder from the backseat of their car.

Paul drove from a different entrance to the castle, so there would be no way Isabella could spot the light, knowing Dr. Steuber would still be working on the horse. Isabella was still talking about it. "Mama, did you know the color is named after me?"

"No darling, you have to explain yourself better."

"Papa, please tell us again."

"Gladly."

Daniella gave a deep sigh. "I didn't know you were *that* horse crazy."

"Well, I love Papa's horses, but there are so many of them."

"You told me you loved Lippizaners the most."

"Of course, look how they jump the capriole."

"Isabella, it can be taught to most horses of Spanish descent."

"It can?"

"Oh, no," Daniella lamented.

~

Paul got up very early to take a good look at the patient. Dr. Steuber left a note, explaining in detail what had to be done. He reset the left leg, now in a heavy cast, lanced the right one, now in a lighter plaster bandage, and as it also had worms, he would see the horse the following afternoon.

The stable's headmaster greeted him, telling Paul about the instruction, also that the Palomino was heavily sedated while all the procedures were done. Like everything else, the Reinhardts kept him busy. They hated a change with people that worked well together. Dr. Steuber, like the stable master, had served them for more than twenty years.

He planned a leisurely breakfast and walk with Gaby and Isabella to the stables. Both wanted to witness her reaction. The O'Haras left a message that, around 9:00 a.m., Daniella would be picked up to do more sightseeing. Since Isabella had already seen the places they had chosen, she declined to go along. Isabella wanted her Papa to take her to the animal clinic.

"And why not?" he smiled at his wife. "I've taken the day off anyway, but first let's look at our stable, as one horse may need some attention from the veterinarian, too."

They strolled arm in arm in their Austrian dirndls, starting purposely at the back of the stables, knowing Isabella's horse was in the front sickroom. The stable boys greeted them, already fully informed by their boss about the surprise.

"Mr. Weber," Paul addressed him as they walked along, "would you know of any breeders who sell Palominos?"

"You mean a mate for ours?"

Isabella laughed. "Ha! I hate to contradict you, Mr. Weber, but Papa doesn't have one."

"You must be kidding, Miss Isabella. He just never told you."

"He didn't have to. I would have seen it. After all, my friend and I have been riding every day for the last two weeks."

"Where do you take the horses from?" he asked, walking and playing along.

"My friend takes Nelly and I ride Gitta."

"Well that explains it. One takes number eleven, and the other, number eight."

"And no one ever looked at number two?" Paul, Gaby, and Mr. Weber laughed, almost upon it, when she saw the golden horse face with a white front mane and a small white stripe blending in with a pink one between the nostrils. She stared for a moment, in shock, looking from one to the other, and put her hands in front of her white face and started to cry, leaning from her Papa's chest to her mother's.

Gaby, like her own daughter, had tears running down her face too, while a glowing Paul and his stable master were astonished, never having witnessed an emotional outburst quite like this. It only happened when a horse died.

"Come in her stall and I'll tell you more about it," Paul said, after stroking both of his girls' hair. "It will take several weeks for the legs to heal. Then you have to walk her several times slowly until she starts running on her own. She was a former circus horse; she may have been trained or not. I don't know any more about it, Isabella. And this is my present to you for being such a fine daughter, making your parents very happy." Gaby cried even more. "Here, dear wife," he said giving her his handkerchief. "Why do you go without one, knowing this would happen when Isabella saw the most beautiful horse in the whole wide world?"

"Oh, Paul. Never ask me why I love you so much."

"We!" Isabella interrupted, patting her horse's neck. The stable master had the happiest grin ever.

"Mr. Weber, try to get me something sour. I've had too many sweets for one morning."

"Let me tell you something, Mr. Reinhardt. If anyone deserves even more of it, it's you."

"Thank you, Mr. Weber," Gaby said happily.

"I will see to it personally that we never run out of it."

"What a fine day," he thought to himself, returning to the stable boys who had just arrived, one by one, to see the 'Miracle Horse'.

"If you don't mind, I'll sit here until lunch, picking a name for her. It has to be fitting and unique. Also, I will tell the O'Haras I am staying in Vienna. The horse needs me. Daniella has lots of friends in America."

"As you wish." Both were elated.

"Well, I cannot ask her to watch me take care of my horse."

"That wouldn't be fair, Isabella."

"Aside from that, Uncle Peter said New York and those other places they named are extremely hot during the summer. He never experienced anything like it."

"He told us that too," Paul replied soothingly. "You will have to tell the family very soon."

"Today, Papa. They will understand. I can always visit once I am out of school. Then my horse and I will already have a strong bond."

"I agree," replied Gaby. "We all may go there someday. Papa might like to see their industry." They all smiled at each other and left.

~

When the O'Haras came home exhausted from touring the city, disgusted to see so many SS, brownshirts, and military walking in the same places and Jews still being rounded up, they decided to pass over Salzburg and leave for Switzerland until their departure to Le Havres pier. Letters arrived from their friends and family, advising them that America had become anti-German again, and certain friends were not looking forward to meeting Isabella, who was, after all, a German now.

"Damn it," Chris O'Hara cursed. "What do your stupid friends know? The Reinhardts put everyone else we know in the shadows."

"What can I do?" Anne agreed.

"We'll just have to take her to some other places. The girl speaks good English."

"What will I do?" Daniella cried. I'd rather be with the Reinhardts than back with you, listening to your quarrels."

"We cannot have that. I am already told by some of my friends and family that I am a poor mother, keeping you for five years in Switzerland."

"Those damn friends of yours are all you are ever worried about! Never about us!"

"Chris, shut up. You have had too much to drink."

"No, I haven't, but I consider my wife the biggest 'nothing' there ever was. You'll pay for it once we are back in New York!"

"You both be quiet!" screamed Daniella. "When I go back, I'll live with my grandma."

"Which one?" asked both in unison.

"Grandma Rosemarie O'Hara."

"There!" Chris stated grandly. "There you have it. Smart girl."

"Smart, my foot! Your relatives came from Ireland because of the great Potato Famine. Mine arrived on the 'Arabella'!"

"You never did want to find out *why* they came. Like the saying goes, 'Dukes don't immigrate.'"

They would have argued more if a phone call hadn't stopped them. It was Isabella asking to speak to Daniella. She was surprised at Anne O'Hara's huffy voice and mannerism.

"Hi, Isabella. I would have called you anyway as soon as my parents stopped their quarreling." Chris and Anne looked at each other in disgust. "Oh, your Papa got that injured Palomino for you? That's great!"

Isabella went into the details of her surprise then told her very honestly why she couldn't possibly leave, as the horse and as she needed to form a bond first. "My parents and I may visit America in the fall of next year, as Uncle Peter said August is very hot."

Daniella didn't know if she should be glad or sad, having just witnessed their disagreement over a German. "I understand, Isabella. I am so glad *you* have such nice parents," she said quite sarcastically. "Maybe by next year everything will calm down. And spring or fall will be a better time. We'll see you tomorrow." She was now in tears.

Anne O'Hara took the phone, saying she heard all about the horse, and could she please speak to Gaby or Paul. Gaby took the phone and accepted an invitation for dinner at Bristol. "Bring your husband's brother and his wife and your mother-in-law. We are leaving the following day."

"To where?"

"Switzerland."

"Oh… because the Reinhardts have two beautiful places in Salzburg you could have stayed at."

"No, but thanks anyway."

~

They all came dressed fittingly for the occasion in one of Vienna's finest hotels. As always, Anne O'Hara wore too much jewelry. She was a dark-haired, beautiful woman with blue eyes and great sex appeal. Daniella looked very much like her mother, unlike Isabella who could pass for Paul's daughter easily.

The conversation was strained as both O'Haras explained why they had eliminated Salzburg and were leaving for Switzerland. "It will not be a good end," Chris O'Hara predicted, advising them to leave.

"The Reinhardts have their roots in Austria back to 1509. We love our place and country. Of course, we realize all the wrongs as well," Victoria replied.

"Mr. O'Hara," Peter finally joined in. "I was at Atlanta's famous Emory University and visited also Danielsville in Georgia to see where Dr. Crawford Long lived, among many other places where the Civil War took so many lives."

"We wouldn't dream of visiting the South. We are strictly from and for the North," admonished Anne.

"Nevertheless, I was astonished, as were many of the northern students, I may add, about the separation of blacks and whites. Don't you agree?" He directed the question to Chris.

"No, and there is nothing I can do about it."

"Same here. We disagree with everything the man in Berlin stands for, but being lucky enough to have been rescued from the Gestapo's headquarters once, I am not about to risk going back again." They were astonished at Peter's remarks and experience.

"I agree, Dr. Reinhardt. That's why I am saying to leave. I personally will do all I can." They knew he meant it and thanked him.

After a few artificial niceties, the evening was over. Both girls cried bitterly at their good-byes; the grown-ups shook hands. Somehow, the Reinhardts were sure, should they see Anne again, she would have another name.

1939

24

Ever since Philip's suicide, Victoria took to her daily diary with the same vigor that all Reinhardt women did before her. Once again, she listened to the many sounds of Vienna's church bells, including the loud Pummerin, remembering the year of the turn of the century, 1900. She still could picture Verena holding her little Elisabeth and telling her stories about the bad Turks and the 'dreadful von Waldens'. She rocked the cradle with Gisela while she put Peter and Paul to bed after a good dose of milk.

Hannes and Philip visited the Esslers' New Year's party, only to arrive quite early and Philip confessed to her his many infidelities, promising solemnly that he would seek help. Of course, there were also two operations ahead of her. And then came a slightly intoxicated Anette, and both became the closest friends until her dying day. All this seemed like yesterday and yet it was so long ago.

In the meantime, two new generations were added, although so far, only her two daughters had given her grandchildren. But now the tide seemed to be turning towards her son's direction. Peter's wife was, following two miscarriages, expecting her first baby after thirteen years of happy marriage. And Gaby told Paul on Christmas Eve, after they went home, that she was three months' pregnant too. Paul was so elated that he talked the following few days of nothing else. Isabella predicted a baby brother and her main concern was, once again, the proper name. It took her two weeks to get a name for her Palomino, Lillian. No horse could have been more worthy to be called Lillian, after the ultimate horse lover Lillian von Essler.

But now they were all gone. Gone forever like her beloved mother, Kurt, Verena, Hannes, and those wonderful Kronthalers, who were still alive but completely unaware of their surroundings. But so were some of the Wilands. There was, however, a big difference with that family. They produced son after son, waiting desperately for at least one girl to make her entrance. And without exception, they all studied law. There was always a Wiland Senior, Junior, or a Wiland the Third. And then there was also that 'Mrs. Irene' she would love to forget, because Philip's last days were linked with her. She was now married to an old and wealthy French jeweler.

This New Year's Day of 1939 she would have to contradict her late mother Lotte, who constantly told her that, 'the more things change, the more they stay the same.' Maybe in your time, Mother, but surely not in mine. Or, for that matter, my children's and grandchildren's. And those changes have taken place so rapidly that no one, including me, can keep up.

"Our beloved Austria was taken over last March by Germany, and we are now called 'Ostmark'. The beautiful city of Vienna is nothing more than one of many large cities in the east. So far, the Germans behaved well, however, they are made welcome. The same thing happened last fall when they entered to free the Germans in Czechoslovakia. However, how the Czechs themselves feel is another story. They were sold out without any of their own people being involved. And the former Austrian loafer, Adolf Hitler, is, if anything, a hypnotist who bedeviled all of his followers. George Bernard Shaw's quotation that 'Words are the most powerful drugs used by mankind' comes once again to pass. So far, Hitler has created the feared Gestapo, who enjoy torturing, killing, or putting the Jews on cattle trains to God only knows where. Then there is the infamous SS in their black shirts and dead skulls as insignias, who are no better than the Gestapo. We also have brownshirts who are calling themselves Nazis, though they have less power but are by no means kinder. Paul is convinced we are shortly heading toward a war, and with his many contacts in Berlin, he is in a position to know."

~

Being presently all alone, Victoria took a cup of cider and started to go through all the mail before discarding some of it. Still to her utmost astonishment, both O'Haras wrote more than anyone had ever anticipated. They also mailed many parcels from New York's finest stores, with expensive and selected items which were very useful. Beautiful and warm housecoats were only some of them. They also apologized individually for their rude behavior at Hotel Bristol and explained that those were very unhappy times as their marriage was falling apart. Once arriving in New York, they had separated. Daniella was in a prestigious boarding school, staying during the holidays with Grandmother O'Hara and her stepfather, since he was the better one of her parents. Anne already had a new boyfriend, which in her circle of socialites was easy to get. This one is related to many of the 'Who's Who' in New York.

Victoria only shook her head smiling, never caring about 'Who's Who' in Vienna, which was not the case with many of their acquaintances. The Reinhardts were above caring, and many suspected they were not only very secure but made their own manners and laws. Their fortune allowed them to be totally honest and no one ever questioned how they got rich, as not one of the Reinhardts was ever considered idle. Isabella, the young addition to the

Reinhardts, remarked that her relatives in Switzerland had a schedule for giving her no more than an hour of rest. 'Knowledge needs constant hard and persistent labor.' It was a small engraved plaque standing on her writing desk.

Peter, too, had a pleasant surprise from Chris O'Hara, which Victoria felt noteworthy enough to write in her diary. He was apologizing for not knowing who Dr. Crawford W. Long was. He read up immediately upon his arrival only to find out there was a statue in Washington. He was positively the inventor of ether! "But," he added with humor. "I am only a banker, and should you ever be in need to know all about J. P. Morgan, I am in a position to help you." Before his departure for America, he left a fine collection of San Francisco ten and twenty-dollar gold coins from the late century, enclosed in a special glass and wooden case with Ingrid Lebrun in Lausanne, knowing she would visit her sister, Astrid, and the Reinhardts too.

The Reinhardts were aware of Anne's highly valued ancestry arriving via the *Arabella*, while Chris O'Hara's arrived in 1847 during the famous Potato Famine. He was the one they admired most. His brave parents came with six children, had four more in the New World, and each one became a learned and prosperous immigrant at a time when signs in New York windows stated, 'Irishmen and dogs not allowed on the premises.'

Chris talked frequently about his loving family and how Anne's insult hurt him very deeply in front of strangers. So Peter had a fine wooden etching done on a special piece of oak from a young American humorist by the name of Ring Lardner, stating ironically that, 'The family you come from isn't as important as the family you are going to have'. Chris O'Hara was as happy as he was proud. Although every bit as Irish as they come, there were no skeletons of drunken Irishman in his closet. It was more than his wife could say.

Daniella wrote that she was more than happy to live with the O'Haras on Long Island as her own mother showed more interest in how her seamstress made her look and how her hairdresser made her feel. "Never did she ever waste time or money on me." All the money came from her father and stepfather. Isabella's surprise from Daniella came in the form of a beautiful painting. She was standing face to face with her Palomino. She was overjoyed and had the frame handmade by a Reinhardt employee, who took great pride to in making something so special for Isabella. The family gave her all the necessities for riding including a leather jacket that matched Lillian's color.

Victoria was now too tired to continue with her diary. There was always tomorrow and for one late night, which had turned in to 2:00 in the morning, she had done just fine.

February 17 was one of their happiest days, for Erika finally gave birth to a baby boy who weighed almost eight pounds, was healthy, and named Hannes Paul Reinhardt. Peter and Erika would make sure that there would always be a Professor Reinhardt at their own hospital in Lindenfels. Victoria was only interested in his health, and expressed the hope that his parents would only guide him once he knew what he wanted. They agreed.

Gaby and Paul's baby was due at the end of June. Secretly they hoped for a boy too, but never mentioned it. The baby's health was their first concern, and Paul was worse than Peter. He took the right wing of their castle with a staff of four at his office so he could check in on Gaby all day long and take her on walks in their beautiful garden. He would also make sure of her proper rest and whatever else Peter advised him and Gaby. Like Erika, she would give birth at their own hospital. It became more and more the wish of women over thirty.

Gaby would be thirty-four in July while Erika was two years older. Isabella still predicted a boy and, according to her talks with Victoria concerning the Reinhardt family tree, it was Robert who bought and left Philip the factories, which in turn belonged to Paul. Her mother liked the name after hearing the story about it, and both gave Paul the choice of his middle name. No one ever considered a girl except Gaby, who would name her Elisabeth and call her 'Sissy' after Austria's last Empress.

But when, on June the 21st, Gaby too gave birth to a boy, Paul and Gaby decided between themselves that it would be Robert Maximilian, going back to the eighteenth century. Not only was Paul extremely happy, aside from Gaby as he weighed almost nine pounds, but Isabella jumped for joy. "I finally got a baby brother!" Of course she had to run from the hospital to the horse stable to tell Lillian all about it. Even Lillian neighed, and she told everyone about it who would listen.

Isabella decided to become a nurse in the operating room. She claimed she was not cut out to be a doctor as she had too many other interests. But she would make an excellent nurse, Peter being a surgeon, her Uncle Andreas a doctor, and his wife Theresa with a diploma as an operation nurse. She would take advantage of their knowledge and study with all of them. She had even forsaken her vacation, like all other Reinhardts, to Switzerland and Salzburg, as Lillian was, as always, badly in need of a companion. Once the horse was up and around, she had shown Isabella how many tricks she had been taught. Anytime she wanted to ride her bareback, she went down on her front feet. Seeing her rider arriving with the saddle, she stood still, expecting to be mounted.

Both new mothers, Erika and Gaby, would meet in the castle, as Paul once again had the last word on his son, Robert. Every weekend, the Foster clan would drop by, and Lindenfels became a haven for children of any age. The Reinhardts' castle builder, Albert, the famous architect, and his son, Otto, would have been very proud of their foresight. And their beloved Stephany would have it once again be called 'the Garden of Eden'.

The long-suspected and unavoidable finally happened. Germany invaded Poland on September the 1st and the Second World War had begun. Although France and Britain issued an ultimatum for an immediate withdrawal, Hitler refused and, as usual, blamed the other side. Both countries had little choice but to declare war on Germany, along with a few other far away countries like Australia, India, and New Zealand, who were, as far as Hitler was concerned, of little significance. America, however, declared its neutrality. Once more, Victoria tried to remember the First World War, as it was only twenty-five years ago, and was not surprised to find many among the young men marching below singing and showing the same confidence and enthusiasm. After all, they too would be home by Christmas.

~

Poland was completely unprepared, and the German soldiers were not only well-trained but merciless. Russia would also get involved, as Stalin had secretly made a deal so that he, too, would get his slice of land from Poland. Stalin, like many others, would be fooled into believing all would be over soon. They didn't know Hitler. The Reinhardts' place began, once more, to be without young help.

Their parents cried bitterly, having the war of not too long ago fresh in their memories. But their sons smiled and were convinced they fought to gain a 'thousand-year long realm'. By the end of September, Poland had a provisional government as Hitler renewed his friendship with Stalin after a swift win. But Poland had two thousand soldiers and ten thousand civilians dead, nevermind the destruction. Their prisoners were now marching towards Germany and towards the 'New Ostmark'.

When Isabella heard at her school that soldiers were rounding up horses, as the war may still not be completely over and the German troops needed, aside from hundreds of cars and trucks, thousands of horses to support their new undertaking, she almost fainted. No way would they take any of their Lippizaner thoroughbreds or, God forbid, her prized possession, Lillian. She rushed home, completely out of breath, and in a condition which worried even the servants, as she usually made her entrance with a big smile. But not this time.

"Mother!' she cried. "The soldiers will take our horses! I was told that in school by a girl whose parents' horses are gone!"

"Isabella, please catch your breath. Papa and Rupert already thought about it and have made the necessary arrangements. They didn't even tell me of their plans, so if asked by a Nazi, I could never give any other answer than 'I don't know'." Her sigh of relief was quite obvious. "And as for your horse, Isabella, Papa will try to do something about some of the many entrances and have your Lillian hidden safely in the castle. How does that sound to you?" Once more, she put her hand in front of her mouth and cried. "Isabella, you have to learn to cry properly, if you have to show your emotions that way."

"Is there any other?"

"Control, dear child. I am surprised the schools in Lausanne or Aunt Ingrid didn't teach you better."

"They did."

"They did?" Gaby asked doubtfully.

"Yes, but I failed, and I think it's the only subject I ever failed."

"Well, then. I like to think as you get older and more mature, the problem will solve itself."

~

She was permitted to hold her little baby brother and Gaby told her, while searching for Isabella's own baby photo of 1923, that she looked exactly like Robert.

"Mother, will you have another one?"

"Of course, if it is possible." Isabella smiled, very pleased about it. "You, of course, will think of a name again."

"Only if you would like it."

"Well, I have a secret for you if it's a girl."

"I will not interfere, Mother, because I think Isabella is a beautiful name."

"I think so too," Paul replied, coming from his office almost next door, kissing his wife, his daughter, and taking his son from Isabella.

Her horse story was discussed, and her Papa got a few extra hugs and kisses for his idea about hiding Lillian, whom she was about to ride. Arriving at the stable, she saw quite a few empty places among the Arabians. She knew, for the moment, those Lippizaners would be safe.

1940

25

Rupert Foster was never happy about his so-called promotion from an Austrian police Captain to one in the Gestapo of the Ostmark.   The Polish war was behind Germany, but he knew Hitler had plans for more conquests with the war factories in full swing and the training of new recruits in full force. There was no sign that, with only one occupied Poland, Hitler would be satisfied. All of Europe awaited their fate, as rumors were spreading that France would be next. Between the Reinhardts, they called the invasion of Poland a calculated robbery. So far, the first prisoners went mostly to Germany, but the New Ostmark was not far behind.

Paul received a few elderly men who had possibly fought during the First World War. They were supposed to replace his young skilled workers who now wore a uniform. It would be a joke if it all wasn't so very sad.

Little Hannes Paul was one year old. Peter and Erika were so happy, and they hoped for an addition soon. They wouldn't worry about a son anymore; a healthy girl would do just fine. It became quite a nice celebration with Gisela's children making the biggest fuss over him. He had quite a few handmade toys that he couldn't as yet figure out until he found himself on a rocking horse. 'With love from Isabella', of course.

Wilma Foster came with a hand-knitted outfit. "She never puts her needles down since Rupert married a Reinhardt."

Looking around, Victoria agreed, seeing all the grandchildren in handmades. "If Mama weren't so happy while working, I would make sure she would be left without wool!"

"And live miserably, my dear child?"

Victoria never understood, after all those years, how much love they had for each other. She always felt Gisela thought of Wilma Foster as her own mother.

Isabella had, of course, a name for the yet unborn baby. "Richard for a boy and Raphaela for a girl."

~

When her little brother Robert was one year old and had the very same party with the very same guests, it was the day France officially surrendered to Germany. The signing took place in a railway car in Compiegne; the exact car and place where Germany surrendered twenty-two years previously. It was the sweetest revenge Hitler and his staff had experienced so far. He made sure all his Generals took notice of the erected granite plate of 1918.

The newspapers wrote every day of more victories, while the radio constantly played Germany's march, only to be interrupted by more triumphs. The song, "Today we own Germany and tomorrow the whole wide world" became a daily creed. Nothing could stop their brilliant Führer, especially after the loss of Dunkirk by the British. Italy declared it would fight on the side of Germany, and as long as they didn't oppose Hitler's planned conquests, that was good enough for the Germans. Italians were not to be trusted, as many still remembered the previous war.

This time, the Reinhardts' factories, fields and vineyards were worked by prisoners from many lands, except for the horse stable. No one had met Isabella's approval, and the stable master had little choice but to agree. Those chores fell on a few kind Reinhardters who were too old to go to war, not unlike some of their horses who were left behind.

Isabella had the same busy schedule which included an early morning breakfast in the kitchen with Rosa, who was of Czechoslovakian descent. The Reinhardts considered her the most trustworthy servant. Then Isabella went to feed, stroke, and talk to her Lillian, rushed to school, ate lunch with Uncle Peter whenever possible at the hospital, and started her work with old patients until it was time to leave. Supper was taken with Mother, Papa, and the baby. All went for a walk to the stables, with Isabella riding, while Paul, Gaby and little Robert continued their walk.

On any given warm evening she would do her homework next to the horse, then rush to her ballet lesson, play the piano, take a bath and start the next day all over again. Saturday evening was reserved for her parents, as Papa always made plans to take his ladies somewhere. It was the highlight of the week for all three.

~

Several letters arrived from South Africa, and Adam van Dreesen was furious that Germany, in order to reach France, occupied Belgium, Holland, and Luxemburg on the way. His parents, although so far safe, were beside themselves. He enclosed for Paul and Peter a note reminding them of those immortal words from a British statesman in the eighteenth century that 'the only thing necessary for the triumph of evil is for good men to do nothing'. He underlined 'good men' and 'nothing'. Peter and Paul wholeheartedly agreed, but couldn't state that in any letter to the van Dreesens, knowing that South Africa had declared war on Germany and the mail might be censored.

A letter also arrived from Ingrid Lebrun who was now a widow, traveling with her Swiss passport between Vienna and Baden-Baden and, after long soul searching, decided that Lausanne was the place to be. She decided against Locarno, as the loud and lively Rosattis were not quite to her liking. However, she did visit Lucas' parents from time to time, who lived near the town with more subdued relatives.

Irene had written several letters to Ingrid asking her to secure a visa, as the Swiss consulate was swamped with people. Ingrid never replied, knowing it would only cause problems. Now Irene's old wealthy husband was bedridden, and she had no choice but to stay in France. Irene, with her fluent German, had free rein to date German officers. He was from Berlin, promised her a marriage after several enjoyable nights, and helped to dissolve her short-lived marriage. The new government, although pretending to be anti-German, was only too glad to oblige a German Major. Her former French husband took up with his nurse, to whom he left all his money.

~

Erika gave birth to a girl on July the 4th, which was Gaby's birthday too. It was a double celebration and Erika and Peter decided on 'Victoria Charlotte'.

Isabella was distracted as she fell in love with one of the young Wilands, who was on furlough after becoming a certified pilot, flying a Messerschmitt 109. The Wilands gave a party in his honor, and no party was complete without some Reinhardts. It was Isabella's first time to be invited to the Wilands, although the older generation came frequently to the Reinhardts. Gone were those times when Lindenfels was one large family. Now, distrust and fear had taken over since

Hitler took Austria and turned it into a totalitarian state, where one could be on the way to one of those concentration camps in a hurry for any opposition to the present regime.

Nicolaus Wiland, called Nico since his return from his study in France, was an extremely intelligent and good-looking young man. Even more so in uniform, Peter and Paul thought, but that was the norm.

Of course, a Reinhardt would be a good catch in any case, but Isabella was one through her mother's marriage. Lindenfels was still laughing about a Reinhardt-von Walden union, since everyone knew the history. And the rumor was that Paul was extremely jealous of Gaby, having his office right in the palace where he could keep an eye on her day and night. Some went even so far as to pity her for being a prisoner in her own place.

Among the older generation, the subject was war, though very carefully worded. The young ones believed that peace would be here soon, as they practically walked through every country. They got their enemies by air, sea, or cannons, but they got them.

Of course, the conversation wouldn't be complete without Lillian. Nico wanted to see the horse before his departure the following week. However, he wanted to see Isabella sooner... like to a movie on Saturday night.

She would have to ask her parents, and Nico felt that with him being a Wiland, there would be no opposition. He was not known for making the rounds. To most girls he was a bore, talking constantly about flying and the First World War aces. Not exactly what a young girl likes to hear.

The old and middle-aged group talked about the disappearing Jews, especially their former stores and the new owners. Although they only knew from hearsay that the Wertheims were safe in America, they missed the stores of Mandelbaum, Friedmann, and Feinstein, as they had good quality and most merchandise came from France or England.

"Mother, don't forget the many bankers like Herzig and Kohn who practically stole the poor population's money."

"Oh, Nico," she replied. "there are some greedy Christians too."

"Not like the Jews, Mother," he insisted, and all guests knew where they stood, commenting no further.

Nico and Isabella had several dates, went to a movie, and a concert where she had to endure the music of Wagner, which she hated and he loved, and went one time to the famous Sacher Café. Always being impeccably dressed, he in uniform, they, like her parents, made a dashing couple. Both were sure they were in love, especially after he thought Lillian was the best-looking horse he had ever seen. Both sides of parents took it in stride, and they shared their first kiss on the day of his departure. It was her first one, in any case, but she was sure not his, as some experience was apparent.

They would write each other, that much both knew, but otherwise it was Isabella's first real romance and she took it very seriously. He carried a photo of her in his wallet and took a look at it from time to time, even when having a good time in a bar in Aachen, the town where he was now stationed.

A good time for him never meant with girls. It was always with his buddies, who loved the fighter planes as much as he did. Girls who visited unescorted bars were to be avoided, like his father told him. They were easy prey. Being a Wiland, he knew better, as his father fought in the first war and told him quite a few stories he wouldn't dare to repeat. Of course, he omitted his own involvement with some very willing French women. After months in trenches, who could have blamed him. But he was talking to his son and there lay the difference.

1941

26

On March 15, 1941, First Lieutenant Nicolaus (Nico) Wiland arrived on the French west coast and had an APO number. He wrote faithfully at least once a week to Isabella. So did she, even if there were only a few lines, as she was preparing herself for exams on July 2. She would be a certified R.N. in the operating room. With all the help Uncle Peter, Andreas, and Theresa gave her, she was still nervous; not in failing the test, but to pass it with the highest marks possible.

On June 21st after celebrating, in style, Robert's second birthday outdoors in the castle's garden, Isabella took him for a ride on her horse, which he caressed each time he had a chance. Both rode side saddle, and Paul was right next to them just in case. It seemed Robert would be his only son. But he was happy with it.

The following day, all of Germany heard via radio that Hitler and the Axis powers invaded Russia, along an 1800 mile line from the Arctic to the Black Sea. It was the greatest military attack in history.

"It is the beginning of our end," Paul replied sadly. "If he thinks he can pull another Poland or France on them, he is just as mistaken as Napoleon was. They overlook Russia's main 'General Winter', who freezes everything mercilessly to death."

Gaby only replied that she was glad not to have anyone so close to her who would qualify. But then again, for many people like Rupert, the real cruel war may just be starting. Rupert was now a Major in the SS and had a secure office job with much power to help even more, should it become necessary.

Isabella was third in her class of sixty, but four hundred RNs who were to be stationed anywhere, also graduated.

~

Two weeks later as she was leaving the hospital for the evening, she had a great surprise. Nico was standing by the door. He had four weeks leave and wanted to spend as much time as possible with her. Uncle Peter promised to do his best to give her time off, but it was not to be. The first wounded soldiers from the eastern front arrived, making more work than ever and involved overtime, too. Nico was more than understanding. He left the dates totally up to her, knowing how tired she would be. As for his flying, he never mentioned which town in France, but said it was somewhere in the northwest, as the flights to England took place day and night. There was nothing he loved more than being a fighter pilot. "And as for the girls," he smiled when asked by Isabella in jest. "Can you imagine a man like me going out with a street walker?"

"Absolutely not!" she agreed, smiling.

They went to see the Rupert Foster family. Seeing him in his SS uniform and his children in Hitler youth outfits impressed him. The talk was, of course, about the war and the stupid Russians who need to be told by Stalin, a former farmhand, what to do, while believing everything.

Isabella and Nico visited many of his relatives and it was now understood that he was very serious about her, and an engagement was just a matter of time. Knowing he would leave in the next few days for the western front, his mother gave him a two-carat diamond ring from her grandmother. He knew it was a great honor, as it was a family heirloom.

Isabella heard about it via her parents, who were only concerned about her love for him. Otherwise, Nico Wiland was a very respected young man who had studied at the Sorbonne in Paris and planned to practice law until Hitler took over Austria. Then, seeing the disciplined military and knowing of Germany's help via planes in the Spanish Civil War, he decided to follow his secret love, 'flying'. His parents were extremely disappointed, never having much use for those noisy mechanical birds, but had no choice but to give in. He was otherwise a model son. Nico was twenty-six, tall, and considered by many to be very good looking. And the waiting for the right woman was now over for him

He would always be able to support a wife. He inherited a great sum, ironically from a man who served, like many of his relatives, the Reinhardts. It was their money, which now became his. But Isabella loved him the way her mother loved Lucas Rosatti, though Gaby never shared her secret with anyone other than her brother.

"Mama, Nico is leaving in four days and wants to give me an engagement ring. He loves me like he never loved any woman. As a matter of fact, he told me he barely dated anyone and after a kiss or two, he knew it was over because he never felt anything."

"And with you? How do you feel after a kiss or two?"

"Mother, in my own way, I love him. Yes, I do feel good when he holds me, but I was never held or kissed before."

She thought about her own situation with Lucas. "We will talk to Papa about it."

"I am the wrong person to ask as I hate to talk about my first marriage, and the one to your mother is heavenly, although I know she doesn't feel that way."

"How can you say that, Papa?" she asked, surprised.

"For one thing, I am an insanely jealous man, without any reason for it. I know it hurts her, but I am trying hard to be a less possessive husband." That was news to Isabella, never giving it a thought why her mother always had to wait until her Papa came home to go out.

Gaby smiled sheepishly. "You may not believe me, Paul, but after three years of marriage I started to get used to it. And I know you will take any spare time to take me anywhere, as long as you can be with me."

"I think this is very nice of Papa. The real trouble is the war, Mother. I see it with me; so very little time for anything. But speaking about the engagement, I could be falling in love with him in time and I told Nico that last night, but he said there is a big difference between that and being in love, which he is with me very deeply."

"He is a fine young gentleman," Paul assured her in honesty. "I know the Wilands better than anybody. They don't come any better."

Gaby nodded, thinking once more of Lucas, wondering how everything would have turned out. They would have been married almost twenty years.

"Should we have a little engagement party?" Paul asked. "Just his parents and us."

"Papa, that will never work even though it's very sweet of you. The Wilands are a large family, and there are the Reinhardts and von Waldens with so little time."

Paul agreed. "We will give one on his next furlough. How about it?" Gaby assured her that it would be fine, and all was settled.

Isabella received her ring one day before his departure, but not before he asked the Reinhardts for Isabella's hand in marriage. They were happy about it, but Gaby still missed her daughter's 'glow'.

~

The daily propaganda about Germany's victories against the Russian giant continued, as did the air war over Great Britain. Germany was still on the go. Letters arrived almost weekly from Nico, along with photos in front of the Eiffel Tower, as he got a three-day pass.

Strange as it seems, he loved the French, spoke the language fluently, and bought many bottles of fine perfume, gloves, and even a watch of pure solid gold for Isabella, mailing it early for Christmas with a note that read, 'DO NOT OPEN UNTIL DEC. 24'. He also explained to her the difference between the Marshal Petain and Vichy governments in France. She replied that she was glad to read that he held no animosity against the French, as they were just as good or bad as many Germans. Nico took it for granted that she spoke with his mother, and she did.

~

On the eighth of December, President Roosevelt called on his Congress for a declaration of war on Japan, as Japan's Air Force had attacked, the previous morning, the American fleet stationed in Pearl Harbor. He called it, "a day that will live in infamy". Three days later, Germany and Italy declared war on the USA and America declared war on them. Most Germans were pre-occupied with Russia's terrible winter and how their sons, husbands, or fiancés would survive. Still, so many fanatic Nazis spread the rumor that Germany was in the process of developing some secret weapons which were so powerful that they wouldn't have any trouble reaching America too.

Nico Wiland wrote regularly to Isabella with the greatest confidence of a sure victory. Germany against the whole world!

For the last few months, many of those skinny, ragged, and worn-out prisoners from Russia arrived by the thousands. How they ever made this long, awesome journey verified their strong stamina, having been through much hardship throughout their lives. They came just in time for harvest, with every available young man by now in uniform, possibly fighting in Russia. The Reinhardts, although extremely careful, made sure these Russians got a little extra food rations, while their guards were invited to eat with the servants in a section reserved for them. Also, a few glasses of wine got the guards in a better spirit before rounding up those 'poor devils', as the Reinhardts called them, and bringing them to their wretched barracks.

Isabella took her ballet teacher who had a Russian name, Olga Platikova, into the castle not only to continue with her ballet lessons, but to teach her Russian. She didn't know why, knowing quite a few languages already, this one would be a new challenge. She found two Belgian prisoners who understood much about horses and she trusted them with Lillian, who had a special added room for her well-being. But mostly it was because Isabella was paranoid that someone would steal her. The three old Reinhardt stablehands were quite relieved about the new arrangement, as by now their bones were already aching.

Food and clothes rationing made their entrance and, to Paul's amazement, Gaby took charge of many things previously meant for managers. She ordered their many beautiful flower beds to be replaced by potatoes, cabbage, and carrots; anything edible. Victoria and she, along with their household help, looked ahead when it came to food, remembering the value of it from the first World War.

Whatever there was available in canned goods was sent to the troops. By now, very few countries were neutral and none of them were willing to take Jews. They went from port to port to find a ship, hardly ever in the destination they hoped for. Switzerland turned them back to their borders to keep their neutrality, and the German border guards were always there waiting. They stole their valuables before rounding them up for a cattle train ride to a concentration camp. Isabella was frequently asked why she wouldn't return and sit the war out. "I have my family here and would feel like a traitor. One has to take the good times with the bad."

~

German Commanders started to pull troops back before reaching Moscow, giving the cold weather as an excuse for one reason. But Josef Goebbels, being the minister of Germany's propaganda, claimed it was their new strategy. He was their best spinmaster and had a positive answer, no matter how obvious the defeat. Leningrad was under siege, people starving by the thousands. Even their late arriving food was never enough. And Christmas of 1941 was anything but a holiday.

The Reinhardts invited only Nico's parents and Father Sebastian, their family friend. After a short prayer before a rather plain dinner, and once leaving the table going to another room, Gaby took him aside and told him what was on her mind.

"You know, Father Sebastian, it seems to me that the Church and Germany's dictator work hand in hand. And needless to say, it's not the first time in history either. You Catholics tell your families to have as many children as possible, and a dictator like Hitler takes them to have them killed."

The priest was stunned. "I have never questioned the Law of God."

"Therein lies our difference. I have."

"Mrs. Reinhardt, people make war! Life has become so disheartening and our hands are tied. And if we, or let's say 'I', would say what I think, I would be sent where other religious people are, sent right along with the Jews or the Jehovah Witnesses. Maybe I am not that brave. As long as they let me preach in my church and do good in my own way, I feel many people are better off."

Gaby understood his meaning and was sure many Viennese were hidden.

1942

27

Chris O'Hara read his morning papers while eating breakfast. He was a happy man, as he had just returned from San Francisco after witnessing his daughter's short civil ceremony. He loved her chosen husband like the son he never had, not because he was Irish and worked in his bank, but he knew Daniella and Thomas were totally in love. Though the family background was to his liking; a hard-working family who immigrated two generations ago, with his father working himself up in the management of an insurance company in Hartford, Connecticut.

Thomas Buchanan III asked on Christmas day for his daughter's hand in marriage, which had to take place no later than January 3, as he was in the Navy and ready to be shipped out. They decided to make the trip to San Francisco together while Thomas' own family was unable to travel for a week on such short notice. One trip took three days.

Right after the nuptials, he took them to dinner and returned a few hours later on a sleeper train to New York. Arriving at home, he was in such a jovial mood that he decided to give his forever pleading former wife the approval for a divorce. She was spending her winter in Palm Beach, hating the cold weather in New York. Now she would be free to marry the equally anxious, divorced stockbroker who also resided in New York. His two teenage children lived with their mother in Philadelphia, seeing their father on rare occasions.

The man in Anne's life was Frank Leitner, which sounded as German as one's name could get, yet he prided himself on being Austrian. But since Austria was now Germany, it made little difference. However, he was the fourth generation of naturalized Americans and owned real estate on Long Island and in Miami, so it didn't really matter. This time, Anne claimed she was marrying for love only.

"Speaking of love, Anne," Chris responded, angry that she never inquired about Daniella, who had told her mother about her marriage. "Daniella is now married to Thomas Buchanan."

"When did that happen?"

"Four days ago. I went with them to San Francisco for a short ceremony. They wanted to make it legal."

"I hope they are happy."

"No doubt about it. Her husband calls her 'Dany'. Very Irish, I would say," Chris O'Hara laughed in pride.

"To me she will always be 'Daniella'," Anne replied sharply. "Her friends from Switzerland already called her 'Ella', as each one had a pet name. How many names should my poor daughter have to endure?"

"Now Anne, 'poor' is the last thing that daughter of yours wants to be called right now. She is very happy and for all the right reasons."

"Good. And thank you, Chris, for being a better father than her own ever thought of being."

"Thanks, Anne, for letting her make a choice. My mother calls her 'my favorite grandchild'."

"I will write and mail her a wedding gift."

"That would be nice." With a mellow good-bye, both hung up.

~

Though Chris O'Hara was as anti-Roosevelt as they came, this time he agreed with his State of the Union address, that America would not fight isolated wars. Since Berlin and Tokyo started it, his angered soldiers would finish it for reasons of humanity. America, like many other countries, was fully mobilized to fight from English soil their common enemy, which was now Japan and Germany. But his present and main concern was Japan. They still continued to bomb any ship, freighter, or cruiser in sight, seeing America as a weak enemy, ready to be fought.

While the President was speaking, Navy Lt. Thomas Buchanan's own submarine, *Canopus*, was leaving San Francisco and heading towards the Philippines. And Dany was on her way back to New York. Father and daughter talked about many things, including Europe, and also that her mother and he had made some sort of peace by agreeing on a divorce.

"I thought Catholics didn't do that."

"Well, I for one will never remarry, and your mother, who was previously married, had a proper annulment and thus I was able to marry her. But this time she is marrying a divorced Protestant with two children." Dany was too tired to answer.

~

The R.A.F. and German planes flew day and night on their missions, and so, for the last several weeks, Isabella received no mail from Nico. Then, by mid-May, a letter arrived from England. He was shot down near London and captured. His left arm was severely hurt and might need to be amputated. He had been treated very well and hoped for a speedy recovery. However, he would be a P.O.W. until the war's end. Considering that he could have been shot down over Russia, she was sad but relieved. So far, the 'Ostmark' had been spared any bombing, but Germany got heavily hit by the British bombers, Halifax and Lancaster, whose bomb loads were quite heavy, especially in compare to the Russians.

Air raid shelters were now a daily must. And there were still the many wounded soldiers arriving from Russia with the war being fought stronger than ever. They were determined to get their own captured homeland back. Leningrad was still under siege. No telling how many thousands more starved to death. But so far, there was no sign of surrender. Also, General Erwin Rommel was fighting in North Africa with the Italian army on his side and was expected to win at all costs. The Germans and their Allies were by now so thinly spread that many generals doubted Hitler's strategy, but kept mum in order to stay alive. Regardless of anyone's opinion other than the Führer himself, nothing would change.

At the beginning of September some Soviet planes attacked Vienna, Breslau, and Budapest but did very little damage. The Nazis excused it as an attempt to show strength while Germany was in the process of taking Stalingrad.

～

It was a long and tiresome day, and Isabella walked slowly home, trying to relax when she heard someone moaning in the nearby field leading from the hospital to the castle. Since no lights were permitted anywhere, as all of Germany was in a total blackout, she had to make use of her green flashlight and follow the sound. She found a young girl squirming around, trying by herself to give birth to a baby. Taking a close look, she saw the Star of David on her blouse and took it off in a hurry in case a soldier walked by. She helped with the birth and promised aid immediately, telling her where she lived. She still remembered the girl's sad smile.

She wrapped the newborn in the blouse, put her white apron over it, noticing that the baby barely made a sound, but left it near the mother. She found the night watchman, who had conveniently dozed off, awakened him and explained the situation. Although half asleep, he said, "We better wake up Dr. Reinhardt. Your parents are leaving very early for Wiesbaden."

Isabella had forgotten all about it and rushed to Uncle Peter, who had just arrived. He ran for a bedsheet and towels, with Isabella showing the way. There they found the woman dead. Although the baby still kicked, it gave only an eerie sound. But Peter was determined to save his life; Jewish or not was, to him, of no consequence. He brought the little boy to the hospital, confiding to a nun the truth.

"We will put the child in a crib and look him over, but his dead mother is another story. I am not worried about her, of course, but about *you*, Dr. Reinhardt. Her shirt will be taken care of, but how to bring her in?"

"I'll get her, or better, drag her. You get a hospital gown and have the paperwork ready."

Peter left again, while the baby was cleaned and wrapped in bunting without ever making a sound. However, he took to the milk bottle very eagerly and the nuns suggested a few days longer for observation. "Father Sebastian will christen him, and Dr. Reinhardt will think of a name. The dead woman will be unobserved in the morgue as it is overflowing with bodies. Only the mortician or pathologist may question us in the morning as to how we got her."

When he was told the girl was found in the nearby field, the mortician only said with a smirk and a shrug, "Ha!

Another harlot trying to give birth by herself. Our troops' pastime seems to be to impregnate those pick-ups." With a few scribbles in disgust, he handed her body to another nun. "It's all yours, Sister," he remarked aloof, never inquiring about the newborn. The unknown Jew had to be buried among Christians. Only a little cross without a name adorned her grave.

The little boy was a picture of health except for never uttering a sound. Peter and Isabella were quite proud of their accomplishment, regardless of the mother's death. She and the baby were spared from a worse fate. Since his facial features showed nothing out of the ordinary, there would never by any questions.

When Gaby and Paul returned a week later from Wiesbaden, both listened in awe about that little 'miracle child', as Isabella called him. By now, with all young servants in uniform, the Reinhardts had again the luck to have the old tried and true ones left, who could be fully trusted as they served their lifetime with them. They would raise the child, as there was no chance that after the war someone might claim him. As for the Jews still remaining in Vienna, they were confined to a district called Leopoldstadt, and it was still a puzzle as to how she had walked the long distance.

Paul was happy for more than one reason. Gaby would feel needed, and so she wouldn't mind staying home. She wouldn't venture to the city so much to take Robert, who was three, and loved to play in Vienna's parks with children his own age, rather than with his parents in Lindenfels. Paul was still an insanely jealous man, loving his wife even more than back in 1929 when he first laid eyes on her. At that time, he didn't allow himself to go that far, as she was obviously married with a little child, or so he thought.

After four years of marriage they were still on their honeymoon. Their only son, Robert, was told about a sick baby brought to them because there was an older brother who would take care of him. He was very proud to be part of it. There would be a christening in Lindenfels' chapel, with Father Sebastian doing the required task. The priest, of course, was happy to have a new member. Isabella, after carefully reading the Reinhardts' diaries, decided on 'Karl Otto', a very proper and worthy name. All had thought of 'Kurt', matching her horse 'Lillian'.

"That name is reserved in case she ever has an offspring."

"Now why didn't we think of that?" Paul laughed heartily.

~

Daily life became harder with so many countless dying or wounded, the fighting still going on all over Russia, with Stalingrad the name most mentioned, either on radio or in newspapers. Rupert heard, after his last visit to Berlin, that Hitler was furious that the Russians wouldn't lay their weapons down and surrender. And every day, other countries declared war on each other.

~

There was still the war fiercely fought in Africa, with more wounded arriving, and Isabella was at times too exhausted to write to Nico. He was out of the hospital, and his left arm did not have to be amputated but otherwise it was of no use to him. "My arm just hangs down and it was quite a chore to learn to dress myself in those ragged P.O.W. clothes." He was still very much in favor of Hitler's cause. "In the end we will win!" he usually ended his letters, and Isabella was always surprised that the otherwise heavily censured letters let his slip by.

Otherwise, it was still more of the same. Fighting battles, victory or defeat. Germany's friend and ally, Japan, was more and more in the news with its overall win against America. And as usual, the British R.A.F. and the German bombers were doing their best to destroy as many industrial facilities as possible, also taking the lives of thousands of civilians simultaneously. It was not too long ago that the German Commander Herman Göhring made the statement that no bomb would ever fall on German soil, or his name would be Maier. It had been Maier for quite a long time now, with much more to come. It seemed the British R.A.F. paid little attention to whether Göhring or Maier was in charge; they just kept on loading their bombs.

The latest of many of their propaganda speeches was the great success of their submarines, which were judged and glorified according to the tonnage they sank. The loss of their own was, as usual, kept to a minimum. Winning was still the only thing that mattered to Hitler and his followers, though many more doubted his strategy. Father Sebastian made his rounds, visiting every family who had lost a loved one, had someone missing, or in a field hospital. The late Anette's former erected monument had to be enlarged, as the list of fallen soldiers grew by the day and the P.O.W.s worked on it with greatest pleasure. After all, they lost their own land unless it was occupied. Paul's factory worked day and night to keep the orders up as much as possible. His prisoners came from France, Belgium, Poland, Yugoslavia, Czechoslovakia, and Russia.

~

Little Karl Otto was the 'darling' of the Reinhardt household. He only smiled whenever looked at, which was more than frequently. Gaby and Robert went for daily walks on the castle grounds, which looked more and more like a large potato field. In that way, it fitted with the rest of the Lindenfelsers' mansions. They watched Isabella ride and jump on her off days, which became less and less frequent. They also noticed that Karl Otto lacked hearing. Isabella decided to take a course on deaf mutes as Gisela suggested, and once again she had an ally to help her. Gisela visited the Reinhardts' place very frequently, as Rupert sent many unobtainable spices to Victoria and Astrid. It seemed just like yesterday that they were doing the very same, and yet it was so many years ago.

~

Although the new year of 1943 had begun with fewer bells ringing it in, one would have never known it was a significant day. And the bells which Hitler's factories melted down to make canons and other weapons with it were not the only reason. The war had started to take a turn for the worse.

The town was deserted of young men unless they used crutches or showed other signs of disabilities. Many were also blind and found, with the help of Red Cross volunteers, a chance to be taken to the opera house or concert halls, which were still kept heated and open like during Vienna's peace time. Some Germans insisted it was their own Minister of Culture, Joseph Goebbels', doing, but they were quickly rebuked. Even after the end of 1918, prized Lipizzaner horses were put in front of coal wagons to keep cultural places heated.

On January 27, America made its own air raid over Germany for the first time. The town was Wilhelmshaven and known for its heavy industry. Hitler and his generals knew it was their 'All-American' first, but surely not their last. Many feared the worst was yet to come. The only way they could retaliate was with their fighters and heavy anti-aircraft. So far, the V2 could not hit that long a distance.

Stalingrad, despite Germany's best efforts, was now in the hands of the Russians. Although General Paulus surrendered on the last day of January, it took the radio and newspapers a few days to announce it. Germany also took a three-day period of mourning while the Soviets advanced on all fronts. And there was still Rommel fighting in North Africa.

~

Rupert Foster got orders for a transfer to Berlin. It was another office job, but somehow, he was glad to leave Vienna. Many of his friends, who had returned wounded and would be sent back to the front again, avoided him. He was a pro-Hitler SS officer who had never seen a day of battle. They may also have seen the SS in action, assuming he was capable of the same violence. He served gallantly in the first war, but this time, Hitler made it a slaughterhouse and he had no way of leaving his SS outfit. However, he was permitted to take his family with him. Gisela, who spent quite a few years during Berlin's worst times, was somehow glad to see a different city. The old Fosters refused to go with them, though their promised Berlin villa had plenty of space. They would be better off staying in Vienna to look after Rupert's place since they were heartbroken. But so were the Reinhardts and von Waldens. SS or not, Rupert had saved Peter's life when Teo Landgraf wanted every bone in his body broken.

~

While Isabella had a chance to play with her two little brothers and had a nice talk with her mother on many subjects, she was needed by a crying, barely understandable Mrs. Wiland, according to a servant.

"I'll bet her husband got worse, Mother. I am taking the bicycle and will be back in a hurry."

"Here," Mrs. Wiland said, noticing Isabella's arrival from her open window. "Here," she repeated, shaking and handing her the telegram. It only stated, 'We write to inform you with deepest regrets that Lt. Nicolaus Wiland, P.O.W. in England, is dead'. And, of course, there was the usual 'Heil to our Führer' at the end.

"The only way he could have died is in an air raid by our own bombers," Isabella stammered, her face white like a ghost with tears streaming down.

"We will never know, will we?" Nico's mother replied, crying bitterly.

"May I please call my parents?"

"And why not? They loved my son too."

Isabella had her own thoughts about it. Although they considered him nothing less than a fine young gentleman on the one hand, he was still a loyal Nazi on the other, and the Reinhardts abhorred the Nazi ideals. Paul only answered her via the phone how very shocked he was to hear about it, and only told Gaby his real feelings.

"As a lawyer he would have been a good one like the rest of the Wilands, but otherwise, I felt Isabella was too good for him." Gaby agreed.

Isabella took Nico's ring off and returned it, as it was a family heirloom. Mrs. Wiland didn't object. She only cried, lamenting that her ailing husband would be soon in the grave too. "Then I will be all alone. All my relatives have so many sons except me, and theirs are still alive," she uttered with envy.

Isabella could have told her that Nico was only one of many she dealt with in the hospital on a daily basis, and many of them were not even Nazis like her Nico, just drafted.

"Well, Isabella, you are still young and beautiful. You will have no trouble finding a husband."

"I don't want to think about it, Mrs. Wiland," she replied in parting.

Upon arriving home, all servants were standing near the radio, hearing that General von Armin surrendered his African Corps to Field Marshall Montgomery, and over 200,000 prisoners were taken. It was followed by the march music as usual. "Today we own Germany and tomorrow the whole wide world." Hitler planned to put more troops in Russia. For him, it was only a normal day.

~

In New York, Mrs. Frank Leitner had lunch with her husband at Schraft's when she told him that she finally got a hold of her good friend Kathryn McAllister and both would meet, as they always did, at Luechows Restaurant on Fourteenth Street.

"But Anne, dear, why not Tavern on the Green?"

"Because it's a very special old restaurant. I would even go so far as to say Manhattan's oldest and it serves the best apple cake right out of the pan."

Frank only shook his head and asked her to bring those friends someday to their own house. He was looking forward to meeting the McAllister brothers who were bankers and financiers, also owning real estate by the thousands of acres in Virginia, where they kept their priceless thoroughbreds. He, being a stockbroker and owning a seat on the exchange, knew all about money. And the McAllisters were old money, like his present wife, Anne.

Although both women had not seen each other for three years and their age difference was twelve years, with Anne being the younger one, they had not only much more in common than with anyone else, but both could be trusted with any secret, never to be shared with anyone. After their greeting in tears, as always, Anne started to talk about how she finally, at the age of forty, had the luck of meeting Frank. Of course, Chris O'Hara had given her a hard time about the divorce, but in December 1941, after returning from Daniella's wedding, he finally caved in.

"And how is your daughter?" Kathryn finally got a chance to ask.

"Well, she met a nice young Irishman who left ten days after their short civil ceremony as a Navy Lieutenant, and is stationed in San Francisco on a submarine going to a little island in Manila Bay called Corregidor. There he got captured by the Japs. By the time MacArthur left the Philippines and promised 'I shall return', which was to my knowledge March 11 of last year, Lt. Thomas Buchanan was already a P.O.W."

"Oh, no! Poor Daniella."

"That's not all," she tried to catch her breath. "Nine months later she gave birth to a boy."

"How wonderful."

"Although I was not ready to be a 'granny', I love that darling child with all my heart. To be quite honest with you, I am a better grandmother than I was a mother."

"Happens quite frequently as we get older."

"But here is the funny part … Thomas calls his wife 'Dany'. I don't like it but what can I do about it? But the baby was called Christopher George after Chris O'Hara."

"It shows how much she thinks of her fine stepfather. Anne, we all still love Chris."

"I know, but you will love Frank Leitner even more."

"I hope so. Where is your Daniella living now?"

"Still on the corner of Park Avenue and 79th Street, where she always lived. Remember?"

Kathryn gave a happy nod as it was a beautiful place with a short walk to Central Park. "But Chris bought them— for a wedding gift, mind you— a place in Scarsdale."

"No!"

"It was quite a surprise for her too. But he really got a bargain with so many houses for sale. Don't forget the men are in the service, receiving only a trifle of their former pay."

"And how often can you see your grandchild?"

"Anytime I want. Chris and I are now best friends."

"That's wonderful!"

"Believe it or not, he even likes my new husband."

"Great!" Kathryn replied in surprise. "What do they have in common?"

"Money and the war."

"Well, then my husband will fit in perfectly," she smiled, ordering more wine.

"How about your family, Kathryn? So far I've done all the talking."

"Well, where should I begin? Don Reed is a bomber pilot stationed in England like most of them are. He bombs Germany quite frequently, claiming that sooner or later, the population will live in ruins. And William Grant, after graduating from Harvard and two years in England on a Rhodes scholarship," she said very proudly. "he worked for his father for a while, but seeing all his friends joining the service, he got the urge to do the same. He entered last year on his thirtieth birthday. What a surprise!"

"Poor Kathryn, thank God for your daughter Barbara."

"You can say that again, but her husband is, like William, in the Army Air Corp and I had a hard time talking her out of becoming a WAC. Imagine every one of my children gone."

"Where did Don Reed graduate? I thought he was a Harvard man like your husband."

"No. He had his eyes on Princeton like his uncle since he already had a girlfriend."

"Now I remember. Anything ever become of it?"

"No. He and William change girls like shirts. It's downright disgusting."

"Someone will come along."

"I hope so. I would love to be a 'granny', as at my age everyone else is."

"Fifty-five is not *that* old, Kathryn."

"Old enough."

They talked more about insignificant things, but set a date for Anne's new place in New York so their husbands could meet, and also spend a day in Scarsdale to see Daniella, Chris and the baby. When each one arrived home, they felt so happy about their get-together and Frank and Donald agreed with their wives on a day to meet. After all, it was late October, Indian summer in New York, and both families would leave for winter; Frank for two weeks in Palm Beach, his wife staying until March, and Kathryn McAllister to Sedona, Arizona, doing the same thing. Their husbands didn't mind the cold in New York. In fact, it was welcomed after their hot summers.

~

Don Reed McAllister was flying the B17 over Germany, and William Grant was now in Sicily. The U.S. 7th Army invaded Italy on July 10, and while his parents enjoyed the Indian summer, he fought Germany's fierce resistance. But then again, both of the McAllister's sons didn't want it any other way.

1944

28

This was supposed to be the year which by all accounts would end the war. Rumors followed rumors about an American invasion somewhere in France. But where it would take place was Hitler's and his staff's greatest worry and they only guessed. Russia was pressing forward still with the same determination since regaining Stalingrad, and so far, they had greatly succeeded. There was no turning back, but the Germans kept on fighting with all they had in men and artillery. By now, the air raids were so frequent and taken so much for granted that the people wondered what it would be like if they had a night without bombers roaring and the noise of their anti-aircraft in full force.

But on March 6th, there was round-the-clock bombing against Berlin with about 800 bombers and mustang fighter escorts. SS Major Rupert Foster and his family were, like the other Berliners, at the air raid shelters near their villa, and as always, endured the many heavy bombers pounding the city. But this time it seemed to be extra loud and the anti-aircraft heavy. So far, the Fosters had been spared until today, when a direct hit killed hundreds of people instantly, Gisela, Rupert and the children among them. Yet it was one of the most secure shelters in Berlin. Not good enough for thousands of other ones either.

~

Don Reed McAllister returned safely to England but wrote to his parents that many of his good buddies didn't make it back. His family was a bundle of nerves by the time his letters arrived. William was in Italy, promoted the previous day to Major, and on the General's staff working on logistics. He was gifted with a quick and photographic memory, having no problem taking care of ten things at once. And the fact that the General's name was Ian McCain didn't hurt. Two Scotsmen would do just fine in a staff of many unpronounceable names. Both were quite somber, although they had a very dry sense of humor and a high level of tolerance.

By May, about one-and-a-half million U.S. soldiers were brought to England for the invasion. Those 'damn Yankees' caused at times some tension, especially when it came to women. One English paper wrote they were 'overpaid, oversexed, and over here'. The following month, it was an entirely different situation. It was June 6, D-Day, and thousands of the accused 'Yanks' were gone forever.

William was still in Italy, awaiting orders to be moved somewhere else, along with many other GIs. So far, he had enjoyed the beautiful parts of Italy, their works of art being exquisite. Italy was now on America's side, as once the Germans started to lose, they knew it was hopeless.

If June 6 was the official 'D-Day' and the McAllisters still had two letters arriving dated on the tenth and eighteenth of June, the twentieth would be for them their very own D-Day, standing for 'Don Reed'. He was bombing Berlin and continued on with other U.S. planes and fighters to Poltava, Russia, where the Germans still had an airstrip to defend with anti-aircraft guns. He was one of many to be shot down.

The McAllisters, upon hearing about it, were devastated. Kathryn took to her bed and had a nurse attending her day and night, as her husband and brother-in-law, who had lived with the family all of his adult life, were in no position to help. Kathryn McAllister would never admit it to anyone, but Don Reed, the younger of their two sons, was her favorite. William was born barely a year after their marriage and Kathryn, who put him in the care of a nanny, felt he had marred her six-month honeymoon around the world, as she was sick most of the time. Don Reed, on the other hand, was born five years later. By then, Kathryn and Donald were longing for another child. Two years later, Barbara came along and their family was complete.

William Grant was a very difficult boy, changing nurses and governesses frequently, as his parents were gone for many weeks. They whispered that the 'G' in Grant stood for 'God'. He always got what he wanted, especially later in life as he was the more handsome and smarter of the two sons. And Barbara was nothing but vain.

Although having entirely different interests and never being particularly close as brothers, the news about Don Reed hit hard. His Uncle William, called Bill by everyone, was very saddened, but his favorite nephew was always William Grant, and not for his name's sake either. Tall, good-looking with blond wavy hair, which on any sunny day had a reddish tint to it, along with bright blue eyes, he looked every bit like his uncle looked at thirty. Bill McAllister fell one time deeply in love, but the girl was of the Jewish faith and neither family permitted such a marriage. Both were still single, as neither had fallen in love again.

Kathryn McAllister recuperated very slowly and gave orders to leave Don Reed's rooms untouched, and she never entered again. It was too painful. Her busy husband barely had a chance to mourn, spending every free moment consoling his grieving wife. The fact that many of their friends had lost a son too never occurred to her, and her brother-in-law Bill was irate about it, but knew better than to give his opinion. Barbara came to stay, with her own husband somewhere in Europe. However, mail from him still arrived though sometimes two months apart. But so far, he was well.

~

Hitler retaliated for D-Day with his 'V-one' rockets, bombing England day and night. The English population suffered, at times, as much as Germany's. Their city became a pile of rubble with the hungry survivors not knowing where to turn. The German radio still blasted its march music, 'Today we own Germany and tomorrow the whole wide world'. Most Germans wondered, however, now fearing the worst. But then again, there was Joseph Goebbles, who came up with new propaganda daily to convince the downtrodden Germans that in the end, they would win, as their newly invented wonder rockets were not the only surprise for the enemy of the great Aryan race. They would crush the Jewish country of America with V2.

Vienna was, by now, bombed too. However, it was light compared to the industrial towns of Germany, as well as beautiful, little quaint towns whose bombings made no sense at all. On July 20, some of Hitler's own officers tried to assassinate him without success. Hitler retaliated by putting tens of thousands of Jews or other innocent victims in concentration camps to death. Himmler, whose motto was that 'a Jew is not a human being' was only too happy to oblige the Führer.

~

The Reinhardts and Fosters were in no way different than any other family who lost their loved ones. In their case, there were six. After hearing via the radio and reading in the newspapers about those severe air attacks over Berlin and receiving no letters the past ten weeks, they had little choice but to assume the worst. Their own letters were returned without any explanation except 'Return to Vienna'. Even the stoic Victoria took it extremely hard, just walking from room to room, nervously hoping for a miracle. The two Fosters were even worse off, as they lost everything they lived for. Although Victoria's sons and their wives came for visits, they left even sadder. When a few officers and industrialists pleaded to a high Nazi official to declare Vienna an open city, the Führer replied that it must be defended like any other German city, which meant defend it to the last man. With the Americans and Russians pressing forward, encircling Germany from both sides, the soldiers still fought ferociously as if a win were possible.

Paul felt he had to make a decision with the weather still passable. He sat down and explained to his family in a calm manner that his wife, son, and mother had to leave as soon as possible. Since it was a family meeting, Peter suggested Erika and their two little ones would go along, as well as many of their servants. Peter and Paul knew that once those hordes of Russians set foot on enemy soil, nothing would be sacred. And no one blamed them either, especially the Reinhardts, who had seen how the prisoners were treated in Austria. Gaby knew how badly Paul must have felt, as they had never been separated since their marriage. Peter, too, seemed to agree, as he was spending every day and some nights at the hospital.

It was quite common that they barely saw one another. Like everyone else, Peter and Paul always looked overly tired. Paul was afraid of an uprising leading to a civil war. There was not one of his engineers or old recalled workers who believed this war could be won. They were, through the underground radio broadcasts, very well-informed that by August there was a new, third army making its way towards the west. They were also told that the new Commander, General Patton, was quite a man to be reckoned with. However, one was always better off to have a western enemy. After all, Russia's people went several times to hell and back.

By the end of October, the Reinhardt women and children had left, except for Isabella, who like all those connected with the hospital, stayed. So did the von Waldens. Andreas was, after all, a doctor, his wife Theresa, like Isabella, a nurse in surgery, and Astrid had to think it over. Though no one knew why, their gut feeling was that America or England might take Salzburg. Lillian and little Karl stayed too, along with the servants, to look after everything. Every Reinhardt place had a few secret passageways in which to hide. There were beautifully painted doors, like many other ornate panels, which had an entrance only a Reinhardt knew. It was the late architect Otto Reinhardt's idea after the uprising of 1848, where many mansions lost priceless items by the out-of-control mobs.

Paul also showed the Wilands those special hiding places, should it ever come to that. It was Karl's dream house which had on each floor two beautifully painted panels which were entrances or exits, any way one wanted to use it. The men were equally grateful and told Paul they thought of leaving Vienna too. *"Well, a lawyer can afford to leave,"* he thought. But the owner of three factories along with a few hundred employees, most of them prisoners, cannot.

~

The winter of 1944 would be in the memories of any survivor of this war. What was foreseen as the end was, for many, the beginning of an even fiercer campaign. A few years before, it was Stalingrad, which after two years of siege was finally free, although with uncountable deaths through starvation. Now it was the Battle of the Bulge in Luxemburg. Every soldier fought for his life with the same determination he fought for his country. And as far as Christmas went, it was the most somber and cheerless one anyone could remember.

The Reinhardts put up a tree in Salzburg strictly for the sake of their children. Otherwise, there were only tears connected with memories of all previous Christmases. The Reinhardts in Vienna were not much different. Little Karl got a tree and was permitted to hang a few cookies himself. The servants looked sorrowful, having by now lost a loved one or hoping for one's return. There were still those many missing. France was now completely liberated, exchanging their Germans for Americans. However, they too were thinking how their sons or husbands were doing as P.O.W.s . If they had the luck to be at the Reinhardts' place, they did quite well. Also, other Austrians treated them well. With every able man in the war, many love affairs were the norm. Isabella volunteered her Christmas Eve for nurses who were mothers and were needed at home this evening. Everyone hoped 1945 would be the year that would bring peace.

1945

29

As far as New Year's Day went, it was for every Viennese, and for that matter every other human-being, as uneventful as it could possibly get, providing he was lucky enough to be a civilian. While Isabella and Theresa slept soundly after a seventeen-hour day of uninterrupted work, Peter, Paul, and Andreas listened to the "Enemy Broadcasting", and had the great luck not to encounter the usual noisy interception. Their greatest concern was still all the fighting at the Battle of the Bulge, as Hitler put every able soldier in Belgium to take revenge against the loss of France.

Most Americans were stunned, with many being called back from their furlough in Paris. Hitler also found solace at the results of his rockets, which not only bombarded London but now even Antwerp, Belgium with what he considered great successes. But it was the only one, as by now the Americans, thanks to the lifting of the heavy fog and General Patton's arriving tanks, gained the upper hand. Until that time, there were heavy casualties on both sides. Now everything seemed to be going well again and the listeners who were cheering for the opposition of Hitler were greatly relieved. But the fast advancing Russian troops were another story. They created a problem, as no one looked forward to encountering any of them, even if it meant shortening the war. The German soldiers were retreating, blowing up every available bridge and whatever other damage could be done to avoid being taken as prisoners of the Russians.

It was no different for the many thousands of fleeing refugees, be it by horse or cattle wagon. They all were entering Vienna to rest up a bit. It became a city of mass transit, with the sick ones looking for a doctor or a hospital. No one had any plans to stay longer than absolutely necessary, as by now most of the Viennese had themselves left to be as far west as possible. The winter of 1944-1945 was extremely harsh, and it was again a case of the survival of the fittest.

This grave situation gave Paul and Peter a great idea. They would open Lindenfels castle along with their Viennese mansion as a Red Cross station, hang a sizeable large flag out, and help everyone possible. Andreas von Walden was overjoyed. Their patients were scattered all over the hospital, mostly in hallways, where it was often very difficult to get a patient on a stretcher to the operating room in a hurry.

Instead of getting their needed rest and sleep, that trio of Peter, Paul, and Andreas made lists and plans for the most urgently needed items with beds and blankets topping the list. They would ask all their friends and acquaintances for help, and knew that each and every one would be happy to supply. There were also the Fosters. All their time was spent looking out of the window for a sign of their loved ones. Since no one lived in Rupert Jr.'s house, there were many empty beds, plenty of linens and pillows, nevermind all those many badly needed blankets. The distraught Fosters also begged the Reinhardts to take all of Gisela's good furniture, as some of their neighbors were now making red armbands and had prepared themselves for a takeover by the Russians, belonging to an underground Communist Party. Knowing

Rupert, Jr. belonged to the infamous SS, they would strip the house of everything, including the doorknobs. The Reinhardts agreed. The Fosters had closed their grocery store to customers, but had plenty of food hidden in their cellar. And what better place than to transport them legally via a sled and ambulance to the new hospitals.

There were occasionally air raids by the Russians to let Austria know they were coming nearer and were very close to Vienna. After two heavy air raids on January 15 and February 7, most of the citizens spent their days and night in their shelters awaiting their fate. But on March 12, the British-American air attack was the heaviest so far and most Viennese left their shelters afterwards.

Their beloved opera house took a direct hit beyond help, and one could only watch day and night as it burned to the ground. Also, the famous Burgtheater was severely damaged and the roof from St. Stephans dome was burning. Those were some of Vienna's beloved landmarks and one cried regardless of the many other houses and buildings that were destroyed. The sky was, by late evening, bright red from east to west and the many onlookers were too stunned and too numb to move.

The Reinhardts rushed to the late Karl and Louise's dream house and couldn't believe that it was still standing untouched in a row of bombed-out and burning buildings. Doubtless, the servants were killed, as their masters were all somewhere west. "Maybe Karl and Louise are still watching out for their place," Paul remarked sadly.

"Ask them to watch for all our hospitals. We need them now, and in the future even more. The drama and destruction has just begun. Only God knows where and when it will end," Peter responded dejectedly.

They decided to see the opera house, where they encountered some of their friends, who were visibly disturbed and who remarked that it was exactly seven years to the day that the Germans marched into Austria. It all seemed like yesterday, and yet somehow it had been an eternity.

~

On March 30, 1945, Russia's third Ukrainian front crossed into Austria from liberated Hungary.

Once more, the Reinhardts, whose places were now hospitals and full to the last bed, including sleeping on stretchers or blankets on the floor, had a private meeting in their beloved breakfast room.

"If only those walls could talk," Peter said, still in good humor as he felt the end was near. "It will not be a good end, but Vienna will make the best of the worst in order to survive."

"Yes, if they only could," Paul replied. "they would possibly use Prince Talleyrand's wise prediction that 'to destroy Austria would replace order with chaos'. But we came together to finally plan for ourselves, as there is not much time to lose before the fighting in the city starts. All transportation has come to a halt and no one is permitted to leave Vienna, be it by horse, car, truck, or train. I have been told that quite a few soldiers hang on a tree for treason."

He aimed his carefully pre-written notes especially to Theresa von Walden. "Your family is also ours and very welcome to hide in our place." Andreas and his wife gave a grateful sigh of relief. "As I am sure, with the exception of Peter of course, no one knows that our wise ancestors deepened all existing cellars in their different homes after Napoleon decided to bombard Vienna in 1809. The same goes for our wine and food cellars which can be reached via a staircase," he smiled. "Fortunately, as I met my lovely wife that way." Isabella applauded loudly, causing sincere laughter. "However, others can only be reached by lifting certain floor panels which are hidden under heavy rugs. The reason no one is ever told about it is simple. I was never sure who would be questioned by an enemy, as right now the

Germans would be sure to do, and you could never be trapped while questioned if you don't know it," he smiled.

"Then, in 1848, with revolution spreading all over Europe, Otto Reinhardt lost no time in disguising storerooms and oversized closets, for whatever purpose, by having panels made and painted by artists who a few years earlier did the hallways. It matched the walls perfectly and no one would ever suspect any hiding place, as the gilded frames had a certain place that would open the entrance."

No one looked more surprised than Theresa and Isabella. One thought of her family, the other of her horse Lillian. She was extremely relieved that all was on the fourth floor, as her Russian ballet teacher Mme. Platikova told her Russians hate to climb stairs. Lillian would just have to learn in a hurry, which shouldn't be any problem. The late Empress Elisabeth, a known horse-lover and equestrian, taught her horses to climb stairs at their residences, including the Castle of Schönbrunn.

"As of today, I will have to teach my Lillian to walk up and down stairs. They would surely take that beautiful creature as soon as they saw her," Isabella spoke up almost shaking all over her body.

"It will take very little effort, Isabella, and I will show you the room best suited for her. She needs one with open windows and a large enough space to be comfortable."

Lillian was now known more as Isabella's 'demi-god' than as a horse. With a hug and an almost teary 'thank you', she appeared more relaxed and listened to Paul's lifesaving ideas. Of course, she would stay in Lillian's hiding place.

Theresa and Andreas drove to her parents. Doctors still had the luxury of getting enough gasoline, though strictly rationed for emergency visits. He considered this one of them. The Bauers were relieved and would send her sisters the following weekend. As for Theresa's mother, their family lived in a large, four-story apartment house, having the fourth floor to themselves, with six other families occupying the third and second floor. Their leather goods store was closed, and their valuable items hidden in the attic, hoping no direct hit would get them. But her jewelry would be sent via Theresa to the Reinhardts' place to be put in a cellar. Peter went to the Fosters to offer them refuge but to no avail. Since their valuables were already safe at the Reinhardts', they felt they had nothing to lose. When Peter told them that Russian soldiers were known to rape women, he showed him proudly his hidden gun. All advice, that they would arrive in groups and behave like savages, was only shrugged off.

"I tried my very best," Peter told Paul, who was very worried.

"Those are the kindest human beings we know," he said, teary-eyed.

A few more of their close friends were visited by Peter or Paul, as they both felt there was no time to lose. But all women were gone, with the men and their servants guarding their homes. Most of their help was from Czechoslovakia and was hired many, many years ago, so they were also familiar with the Russian language. They, too, were all indifferent to the Reinhardts' suggestions. They both felt they did their duty and let it go at that.

The first district looked like an over-crowded camp. However, after the severe winter, spring was exceptionally warm. The people were only in need of food. Some primitive portable sanitary equipment was installed and emptied by the poorly fed Russian prisoners. Otherwise, there were more of Hitler's teenagers with their swastika armbands and old men over sixty years old carrying hand grenades, expecting to defend the city of Vienna from the Russian onslaught.

On April 2, Vienna heard Minister Joseph Goebbels' short broadcast via a radio station called 'Werewolf' for the last time. He expected suicidal resistance and repeated several times that it is better to be dead than red. Some comfort!

The first Russian tanks appeared three days later on the outskirts of Vienna with the Nazi demolition force again blowing up every bridge save for one to halt the very fast approaching enemies. Fierce street fighting followed, as the Germans were still holding a large area between the Danube River and the canal. They found themselves in the famous district of Leopoldstadt, which had been the mainstay for thousands of Jews since the first World War. Also, another famous Vienna landmark became its new victim by the now desperate SS. Their artillery shelled the giant ferris wheel, the roller coasters, and the merry-go-rounds in the beloved amusement park, opened in 1896. For the poor or even middle-class Viennese who had a few schillings to spare and a happy time in mind for his family, regardless of age, it was just as important as operas or concerts for the well-to-do.

No one dared leave their shelters and witness the burning gondolas falling to the ground, as the brutal SS was going from desperate to insane, but with an unbelievable determination to hold the city, never mind the aftermath or their personal dislike for the lazy Viennese. It was still their Germany and their Führer. But then again, many Austrians deserved no better. After all, they screamed themselves hoarse with 'Sieg Heils' as they met the first crossing German army in their splendid uniforms, smiling from their tanks while taking flowers and embraces in stride. They were positively seen as liberators who would turn their misery caused by the unemployment around. They found fast work alright, but it was for Hitler's well-calculated war machine. September 1, 1939, came the payday. World War II had begun, and Germany wanted to have it all.

Now some of the SS troops had reached a Jewish hospital in the second district. They killed those poor, skinny old men and women while shouting, "I thought Vienna was free of every dirty Jew by now! How has this been overlooked?"

"Easy," his friend retorted. "Vienna was always a Jew-loving city. I bet some are still hidden."

"Then let's find out while we are still here."

They left the hospital laughing while some Jews were still alive, lying in blood. But upon leaving the Jewish district they found themselves listening to the shouts of the pursuing Russians, trying to encircle the German army or what was left of it. Street fighting and house-to-house searching, with one looking for the other enemy became routine. The main difference was that some Russians were sure the war was won; they had nothing to fear and started to rape the still naïve and unsuspecting women.

Paul Reinhardt's factories were located in the northern part of the outskirts of Vienna. It had a very wide road needed for transportation, with housing for his workers on the other side. With very few exceptions, like the engineers, they only had to cross the street. The factories had their own railroad tracks leading to the north train station. Somehow the Russians knew about his three adjoining places. It was not only a foundry and two ball bearing factories, but also produced many parts to supply the war machine. To them, it was of great importance, and their soldiers did their utmost to beat the Germans to it by rerouting their carefully planned strategy.

It was April 8, and the last heavy air raid took place by the Russian aircrafts to let the shivering and frightened citizens know who was in charge. They were already entering the Ringstraße with a house-to-house search and fighting was unavoidable. Some SS men managed somehow to climb the stairs of St. Stephan's Cathedral and set the wooden roof, which was previously damaged, on fire; sort of a 'goodbye' to their lost war in the most cruel way.

The Reinhardt factories had stopped all their work, knowing it was just a question of hours until either the Germans or Russians made their appearance. The long, wide road leading from Vienna to the countryside had been almost eerie with stillness since the morning. Paul slept now at the factory office and put during the nighttime all his Russian,

Polish, and Yugoslavian prisoners in his well-concealed cellar, knowing they would be the first ones shot. With the few remaining French and Belgian, as well as his old Austrian workers, they took the same chance as himself. They all knew he could have fled a long time ago.

While pacing rather uneasily back and forth, he kept hearing the roars of the first tanks and reached for his binoculars. Somehow, he was relieved to encounter the unmistakable Russian tanks with their foot soldiers beside them, carrying their rifles over their shoulders. They were doubtlessly assured the enemy was nowhere in sight.

Paul lost no time in hurrying to open his floor panels, shouting delightedly. "Come up in a hurry. Your soldiers are finally here!" They were running like wild animals that had been caged for years. He, along with his workers, had the door wide open watching their joyful embraces while all the tanks rolled forward with the drivers standing up and waving. In no time, white flags could be seen from the worker district across the street. Both prison guards had put on civilian clothes and hid in one of the many widows' apartments. This particular brave woman was a staunch Catholic who lost her husband in a concentration camp and hated the Germans, risking her own life too. Now the tanks had stopped. A Brigadier General with several officers descended their tanks.

So far, Paul counted fourteen of those powerful vehicles with other large cannons following. It was quite an unusual and confusing scene, Russian prisoner women crying and embracing the foot soldiers then walking back to the factory. Now they pleaded with the officers not to harm their Master in any way, as he was the best man they had ever known. He, too, risked his life for all of them and bribed their guards to look the other way. By now, some women were on their knees, crying hysterically.

"Get up!" the General commanded firmly. "You are not dealing with the former Czar."

"Keep quiet. We are just as glad to be here as you are," interrupted a tall, blonde Colonel in black uniform. With his short cropped hair and handsome features, he reminded Paul and his prisoners of a German in an elite SS unit, remembering how much one hated them.

The General introduced himself as Boris Gromov and was in looks and behavior the opposite of the Colonel. Heavy, bushy hair and eyebrows with deep-set eyes, a wide large nose, and heavy lips, he was about fifty years of age and looked like many of his fellow prisoners, with the exception of his weight. Paul asked all to come into his two large offices and take a seat, while offering food. All smiled, pleased. They were hungry. Bread, sausage, butter, cheese, and tea were served. He would never serve alcohol, knowing their fast change in personality. He also noticed how blasé they were to each other's rank. A Captain or Major interrupted their General with great ease, if they had in any way a better idea, like the main engineer who had the rank of a Major.

Paul expected, sooner or later, that something was up once the food was gone. Presently, a French prisoner spoke up for all non-Russians. "Your people are now liberated," he said in broken Russian. "but what about us? Is it safe to leave and look for our Red Cross to get transportation home?"

"No, it's positively not safe. The fighting is now mostly towards the inner districts where Germans can still be found hiding. So far, we took thousands of prisoners and put them in a place the SS destroyed without any reason of military value." Paul thought immediately of the Prater, the people's amusement park, which was on the way to him, but kept quiet. His thoughts were with his own family in the first district.

"I converted my place to a hospital in the first district," Paul said as calmly as possible. "I know you don't belong to the Red Cross, but I hope you respect the flag as all inside the place are sick women and children."

"I only can imagine your *place*," the General retorted. "You are one of many capitalists while we are communists."

The blonde Colonel introduced himself as Yuri Niemev and asked for the address. He agreed to talk to anyone and explain the present situation. "I give you my word of your safe future."

"That is a relief." Paul smiled, but thought they had a plan for him, nevertheless.

Now the General assured Paul that his factory would be guarded as long as Vienna was not free of all Germans. "According to my reports, which I received a few hours ago, it will be several days."

The General thanked Paul in the name of everyone for his food and hospitality and promised to return 'once the enemy is completely defeated'.

~

They left several tanks, heavy artillery, and about a hundred soldiers with six high-ranking officers to guard their unscathed prized possessions, Reinhardt's factories. Now, Major Leonid Metelev, who was the engineer in charge of it all, said to Paul matter-of-factly that he would travel with him, possibly by ship, to Russia because all railway bridges were destroyed except for one called the *Reichsbrücke*. Paul turned white and sat down.

"You will have to teach my colleagues the precision of your perfectly made ball bearings, as the Germans destroyed every known factory in my country. Of course, your machines will go with us as we have none where we will be going. They will be disassembled right away, shipped with us, and re-assembled at our beautiful destination. You will love it there as it is one of the best places south of Russia."

Paul regained his color and only stammered slowly, "I care little about those factories. You can take every brick and door along. I care only about my family."

"Colonel Niemev will eventually reach the hospital and give a full explanation to them. He speaks fluent German but so does General Gromov. Both are highly educated in several languages."

"So is my family."

"I never doubted that," he said kindly. "I don't want you to be afraid. You will be like me, a civil engineer in civilian clothes and treated with all the respect you deserve. Many of your former prisoners will work with you again, as they should be very skilled by now. We need them desperately." He smiled looking in their direction, and they all applauded. But they also knew better than to disobey any order, although it may have sounded like a plea.

"You speak Russian well. That will help you with our other engineers."

"I had plenty of training," Paul replied. "My daughter, who is a nurse in our hospital, reads and writes Russian also. One of her tutors, Miss Platikova, lived for many years with us."

"She probably left with her family after the revolution," the Colonel said with finality.

~

By April 13 in the early afternoon, the fighting in Vienna was over. The tide had turned. Now Paul and his former prisoners were free and standing on the street watching the tired and haggard Germans walking by, who with their once splendid looking uniforms, each one different in their conquered country, lost the promise of their Führer for a thousand year 'Reich'.

Three days earlier, General Gromov and Colonel Niemev reached Reinhardts' hospital. The Germans entered one day before but asked only for food. The kitchen help gave them bread with margarine and a few slices of salami. They devoured it as fast as they could and were on their way.

As the two Russian officers entered and asked for any "Reinhardt" to speak to, Peter appeared in a bloody-looking white coat, not knowing what to expect. After a short introduction, the General explained the present circumstances and Paul's travel for several months or up to a year at the most. Somehow Peter believed them. They still had some rounding up to do, especially the slick and brutal SS who burned the amusement park down, which astonished and saddened Peter.

They would be back, Colonel Yuri Niemev promised. "But as there are so many wounded Russians awaiting care and are presently in empty houses left by the fleeing Germans, they expected his hospital to be emptied and ready for Russian soldiers." Peter had no time to answer as both left in a hurry.

Now, on April 18, they all, including the Russians, sat in Reinhardt's kitchen eating anything served. They had opened many warehouses full of food and brought large bags of flour, sugar, and beans, along with large containers of margarine, oil, and anything for their own soldiers to use. Peter was as happy as the cooks and helpers. A few heavily wounded German soldiers were still in beds when a Russian General arrived, but they were quickly put on stretchers and laid on the street.

"Of course, we could shoot them," Colonel Niemev suggested with a smirk. "That's what they would have done to any of us."

Peter gave a nod and ordered his servants to do as told. Taking a look out on the street, he saw that it was the greatest mess he ever encountered. The war in Vienna was over but the troubles were just beginning.

~

Four female Russian doctors made their entrance, none of them speaking a word of German, but glad to be in the most beautiful hospital they had ever seen. The general set them straight on this matter and they walked up to the second floor. It was Gaby, Paul, Isabella, and little Robert's bedrooms, along with their salons and dressing rooms. They would sleep here from now on, with four more female doctors on the way.

Peter was extremely relieved, as it meant the hidden women, including Lillian, were free to appear. He talked with the General, Colonel, and doctors in his broken Russian, with the two officers replying to him in German while translating to the doctors.

"We also hid many prisoners and wanted to make sure no Germans would ever be back to harm any of them."

"We can guarantee you that much, as the first district is surrounded by our tanks and troops. Every German is either rebuilding their blown-up bridges so we can transport our troops back, or they are on the march to a designated camp," he smiled, for the first time satisfied.

Now it was up to Peter to re-open the floor doors with the help of his servant to pull the rugs back. Up came an onslaught of smiling faces from several nationalities who had been hidden for the last several days. It was a joyous moment for all of them to see the descending women from their paneled hiding places. Isabella, on the arm of the old Mme. Platikova, was looking at the Russian officers. She addressed them in their language, watching their pleased faces.

Then came the question of her horse, Lillian, with large tears flowing down her face about her final safety and well-being. Colonel Niemev was a great lover of horses and a very good rider.

"Bring your horse down. We all will take care of her. You can keep her inside, as one cannot be sure. People fight over any horse for meat."

She ran up the steps and walked her Lillian down, taking their compliments, feeling they were very justified. For Isabella, the war was momentarily over. She took her father's future better than anticipated, feeling he would be back. She was more worried about being found by the SS troops than by the Russians, for whom her father risked his life. The place was in disorder, with many new wounded brought in who desperately needed care. The Reinhardts and the newly arriving doctors worked quickly to ease the pain for everyone as well and as fast as possible.

The mansion was now in good hands and so was the castle in Lindenfels. The hiding of mostly Russian prisoners was solely responsible for the good treatment they received in return. They, too, brought plenty of food for their wounded ones who fought in Vienna, and their new Major General Dimitrov Piotrev made sure that everyone not only respected him, but also feared him. He was an avowed Communist who fought in the revolution, and lost almost all his family save for one brother who lost both legs. Among the officers, he was called 'Commisar' and was proud of it, as after his return to Russia, he would be in politics. His wife Yelena was one of the first female pilots in Russia and was somewhere in liberated Poland.

~

While these two Reinhardt "hospitals" were lucky, their main Marie-Louise Reinhardt hospital was not.

Most of the Lieutenants and Sergeants arrived drunk, having raided several empty villas in Lindenfels. While they were looking for some hidden Germans, they found instead wine cellars filled to the brim with bottles. Vienna's wine was famous like Rhine wine and the soldiers made the best of it. Of course, nobody should underestimate a drunken

Russian. For them it is perfectly all right to get drunk until they are unconscious. It's like a sickness which cannot be helped. In general, the Europeans get weak and, in the end, pass out. Not the Russians. They get stronger and are still able to wrestle three men at a time or overturn the heaviest pieces of furniture. And he is always excused, including of committing murder. Although he may be like an angel when sober, he turns beast-like when drunk. The strange thing about them is no one is ashamed afterwards. It's like a fit of epilepsy which cannot be stopped.

When they came to Lindenfels hospital, they were far from the point of oblivion but drunk nevertheless. They raped everyone in sight, including nuns they had to chase, which many times resulted in broken bones or bleeding noses trying to defend themselves. The doctors could only stand by helpless.

By now, all Vienna was informed about or had experienced the liberating rapists, who mostly took watches and women. Screams could be heard in every district they entered. And every hospital was willing to perform what was referred to as a 'therapeutic abortion'. One was only left to wonder what those poor nuns were thinking, as Vienna's hospitals were mostly cared for by those noble, selfless women.

The Russians' loud improvised radios created another problem as they played all during the night. Hunger and the lack of sleep, aside from the fear of getting raped all over again with new soldiers arriving daily, was not Austria's only tragedy. They felt they deserved better, conveniently forgetting that their defeated army did worse... much, much worse for that matter. But to be a Communist or on the side of the Red Army was, as of now, the new thing in Vienna. The chaotic conditions had to be once more learned the hard way, like a few years earlier when the Germans got a proud Nazi salute followed by an even prouder 'Heil Hitler'. Like after the First World War, they were left to fend for themselves without a leader. But at least they were free and somehow, they would make it.

30

Old printed leaflets were seen on billboards telling Vienna that America's President Franklin Roosevelt had died, and his Vice President Harry Truman had taken over. It meant less to them than the following lines, which let them know that on April 17, the Americans were closing in on Nuremberg and on April 25, the U.S. 69th Division and Russia's 59th guards met at Torgan in a celebrating mood. Two days later, some of the Americans reached Munich and the Austrian border. Now *there* was a reason to get in a happy mood.

"The war will be ending soon," was the only thing which could be heard all over Vienna, everyone wishing sincerely that they were in the hands of the Americans.

Between 1943 and 1945, Vienna had fifty-two bombing attacks, which was considerably less than most German cities that were now in rubble. About 40,000 homes were totally destroyed, thousands damaged, and some guessed that about 8,000 or more lost their lives, never mind their soldiers, the wounded and still missing for several years. One would always remember the long lines of prisoners, heavily guarded and marching towards Russia.

~

On May 7, Germany's high command surrendered unconditionally. The fighting ended officially on May 9, 1945. America's new President gave a short speech while his people were dancing in the streets. And why not? Their sons, husbands, and fathers fought gallantly in a war far away from their shores. Their losses, too, would be in the tens of thousands, not counting the wounded and captured ones. And for them, Japan was still to be fought.

While the Reinhardts in Salzburg celebrated with a small circle of friends, Paul Reinhardt was already on a large ship on the way to Russia. So far, he had nothing to complain about except being away from his family. From time to time, he reminded himself how lucky he was. The Germans could have come first, and no telling what the result would have been. On the ship in the evenings, the three engineers had a glass of fine wine together. Everything was from Hungary, including the well-equipped ship. They would be near Odessa, he emphasized one day before the landing. "Paul Reinhardt will like it so much he may never want to leave." Paul wondered if this was a hint. He only replied, "I hope so," but thought, *"God forbid!"* Once more, he felt under a dictatorship; say one thing while thinking and wishing another.

The day they arrived in Odessa, where the Danube flowed into the Black Sea, Austria was an established Republic. It was May 14 and the new government was formed under Russian sponsorship. Austria's Marshal was Fyodor Tolbukhin and he asked a former concentration camp inmate from Austria's former government to help him with Vienna's hungry population. Both liked each other somehow, possibly having hunger pangs in common. Austria also had a new President, Karl Renner, who had his own bad experience with the Nazis.

Thanks to the new liberators in uniform, regardless of how hard they fought and how much they suffered, their communist party never gained any strength in Austria. The voters gave them only 0.6 percent. No one wondered why.

~

It didn't take all of Austria's liberators very long to partition Austria. The very east was Burgenland and lower Austria belonged to the Russians, who stole and shipped everything back to their homeland. Upper Austria and Salzburg were occupied by Americans. Carinthia and Styria belonged to the English, and somehow the French got Tyrol and Vorarlberg, the most western parts. But the rumor persisted that Vienna, too, would be divided. At least every Viennese hoped for the best. They were amazed at their own efficiency and capability to have, just two weeks after the battle of Vienna, some trolley cars clatter down the Ringstraβe again, with many returning soldiers feverishly working on transportation. And very typical of the Viennese, while they looked for any kind of food scraps, their small undamaged theaters opened, bringing first class performances, even funny musicals! Some coffee houses opened again, dealing more in the black market than their own substitute coffee, which left a lot to be desired. The two hospitals worked as well as the Russians permitted Reinhardt places to do. Somehow, they managed to bring a large supply of food, having, by now, doubtlessly opened every warehouse in Vienna. Not that anyone minded. The citizens helped to plunder too. Their children were crying from hunger. The food stores, like many others which slowly opened, only bartered. Money had lost its value again, with the dollar once more the only good currency.

Colonel Yuri Niemev was now in possession of Paul Reinhardt's car, as there was no one else who cared to have it at that time. General Gromov liked only military vehicles and had his own chauffeur. Aside from that, Niemev's car was a German-made Mercedes. Peter, as a doctor, had permission to drive his own.

His first visit after the fall of Vienna was to the Fosters, accompanied by a Russian. He found the house empty and stripped of everything. He went to their former Communist neighbors who told him that his own wife and three daughters were raped while he and his sons had to watch at gunpoint. The girls screamed for help, possibly warning indirectly the Fosters. "The man had his gun in his hand," the former communist was saying and burned his red arm bands afterwards. "Some other neighbors buried the Fosters a few days later behind their property," was all he could stammer, starting to cry. He told him their name and repeated in parting, "Give me a Nazi any day." Peter was too upset to respond.

Vienna had a lot of lowly people, he thought, and planned to get the Fosters dug up and buried in the Reinhardts' grave site. After all, their son was married to his sister.

By summer, the situation in regard to rape and plundering had slowed down. Most of the trolleys and railways worked, and the Viennese went further into the countryside trying to find food for their freezing winter ahead. Mail had begun to arrive. It took two to three weeks from Salzburg to Vienna, but that was to be expected. Gaby had received the news about Paul's departure to Russia. And although she felt saddened, it could have been much worse. Deep in their hearts, all the Reinhardters in Salzburg felt he would be back.

~

So far, no letter had arrived from him, and when Peter asked the General, he only replied that his work was 'Top Secret', but he could assure him that Paul was fine. Peter was relieved and wrote to Salzburg about it. The Russian doctors who worked with Isabella in the mansion's hospital proved to be great treasures. Isabella could sleep wherever she liked without any worry of harassment. Everything was well organized, and nothing escaped General Gromov's or

Colonel Niemev's eyes, who were permanently stationed in Paul's office with a staff of sixteen officers and five enlisted men. There was plenty of food and the kitchen help was constantly busy, between the wounded soldiers and the staff. For some reason, those female doctors made very sure every dismissed soldier was in the best of shape, as he had weeks to travel on a slow train.

Isabella decided to sleep in the mansion's huge food storage room, which had to be emptied with bags of food, even to be put in the music room and library, so her own bed could be brought down and her Lillian could stay and sleep right next to her. She would ride her everyday under the watchful eye of Colonel Niemev and some enlisted men on the balcony overlooking their garden. Life had become tolerable again, though not normal. That would take quite a long, long time.

~

The rumors of the city being partitioned into four parts had finally come to pass. It took many months of negotiations with all parties involved until an agreement was reached that the first district would also be occupied by the four winners of the war. The Russians didn't like it. They fought so hard to free the city from more damage as far as destruction was concerned. And General Gromov and Colonel Niemev didn't like it, as they loved the setup in the Reinhardts' mansion. It meant not only moving his staff, but some heavily wounded ones as well. Most had an arm or leg still infected and needed more operations, or they had two arms or two legs missing. Peter suggested Lindenfels' two hospitals for personal reasons.

He got to know the strict General well and knew he would keep his discipline up, saving the castle from damage. He drank very little and only with his meals. By now, the General and Colonel's wives had arrived. Both were still in their Captains' uniforms, working in a different office from their husbands. They, too, were educated and kind, living in

Peter's large villa, which was only occupied by two servants. In the evenings, they played cards or listened to their wives playing the piano. Whenever possible, Isabella joined them, and Peter counted his blessings.

~

By now, it was an open secret that September 1 was the official day to bring a big change to the Viennese. Many Russians had left by now, either to be back in Russia or more spread out among their own territory in Austria.

The American 7th Army Corps had arrived a few weeks earlier from Salzburg via Bavaria. They linked up with the 5th Army the day the fighting stopped. It was May 5th, three days before peace was signed with Europe, but many Americans were shipped right to the Pacific. As they had the best villas and apartments in Salzburg, they planned to have the same in Vienna by arriving earlier than the English or French. Since their sections were designated, it didn't really matter to the average Americans, but General McCain needed a headquarters and wanted a beautiful, large, and convenient one at that. Otherwise, there were many sumptuous villas left from former Nazis. Now those monsters, Gestapo or any other sadistic leaders, were either in hiding or in many cases took their own life. Vienna became known to be the city with the most suicides in Europe.

When General McCain got his new orders pertaining to Vienna's first district, he read them to Major William McAllister. "We got the nicest streets and location. There is no shortage of beautiful villas."

"That sounds great," he replied equally happy. "Now find us one headquarters suited for kings!"

"I'll do my best," he said, still very elated. The McAllisters visited Europe on a yearly basis until 1938. His late brother and he were always included. At times, when they were in their teens, they would have loved to be away from their parents and the ever-present unattached Uncle Bill, but it was to no avail and never open for discussion. William knew Salzburg by heart, to the General and his staff's delight, as his family loved the yearly music festivals and their plays. Also, the beautiful little villages with their mountains and crystal-clear lakes were to their liking.

Austria's last Emperor had his own hunting lodge in the health spa of Ischl and considered the quaint town the most magnificent place on earth. The result was that Major McAllister was now the perfect tour guide. He now saw Salzburg from a different perspective than as a teen.

The same happened with the city of Vienna. His family stayed year after year at the Hotel Imperial, as it sounded more noble than the equally elegant and famous Hotel Bristol. General McCain was not only happy in choosing his personal aide McAllister for his commanding presence, or for being a great organizer to get things done in a hurry, but his former travels and knowledge about their cities was extremely valuable.

Each WAC, single or married, found him strikingly handsome and many waited in vain to get a date, let alone to start a lasting relationship. He was exactly like his father, a Harvard man who also obtained a Rhodes scholarship. If that was not enough, everyone knew that his father was in the banking business, aside from real estate, lived in New York during the week, and spent his weekends at their estate in Scarsdale, Long Island. His favorite relative, however, was his Uncle Bill, after whom he was named. But William Grant McAllister was nobody's 'Bill'. He was known to be courteous but also demanded respect.

"Now dear William," the General ordered kindly as usual. "Find us the very best place in Vienna. Never mind that you are leaving us next year. Think of us as 'leftovers'," he laughed. "and take the two spaghetti clowns with you. Also, ask Captain Sheila Brown. It may get her in a better mood."

He only smiled and had them brought to his temporary office. WAC Captain Sheila Brown was overjoyed as always when she could be near William. They had a short-lived affair in Salzburg, strictly reserved for the bedroom in his confiscated villa. She wondered ever since those times how a man is capable of making perfect love without being in love. But she was too eager to get him, and with the slightest remark about what the future would hold for her, he told her very bluntly that he would have to be very much in love to make a commitment. He omitted that an easy woman was the furthest thing from his mind. Sheila Brown was a beautiful natural redhead with a great body and was a lot of fun to be with. But she was also twice divorced.

Those two so-called 'spaghetti clowns' didn't mind their title at all. They were always the life of the party and somehow had the talent to arrange one, no matter how low the company's morale got. One had to like them. Captain Bradford Torelli and Joseph Respini were from New York. It was always 'Brad' and 'Joel', even for William McAllister, who at the present asked them and Sheila to help him find the proper headquarters.

They walked for about two hours in the warm sun during the last days of August and decided to take a rest at one of the re-opened coffee houses near St. Stephan's Cathedral. "What better man to ask than a waiter," Brad suggested. "Major McAllister, use your 'Harvard-German' again," he laughed.

William did just that and was told that there was a place only two blocks from there, a large Baroque palace with a Red Cross flag hanging out. Two Russian soldiers were patrolling the place.

"I know exactly the place."

Sheila replied again happily, "I admired the building for the grandiose staircase." William only smirked, as he had pointed out many grand places in Salzburg to which she showed very little interest.

"If you admired the outside, you will be astonished by the inside much more," the waiter remarked, thanking them for their generous tip. They only ordered hot water and brought their own instant coffee, sugar, and cream all in paper wraps. Viennese coffee was like dishwater and they learned very fast to bring their own.

They encountered immediately two Russians in their high buttoned tunics, blue breeches with thin red stripes, and riding boots. Approaching them together, they got the nicest smile from those look-a-like Privates. The difference was that one had a mouthful of golden teeth. It was a first for all of them.

William motioned to go upstairs, and they happily obliged, taking them to the beautiful grilled iron door with a copper 'R' on it. They rang the bell and when two uniformed soldiers answered, both Russians said in unison, "Amerikansky". The servant asked them to come in the hall, which was over-crowded with hospital beds. "They are all leaving tomorrow," he said, before looking for Peter Reinhardt.

All wounded soldiers smiled in their friendliest way, with some waving and calling out cheerfully, "Amerikansky!" William suggested they shake each hand. They were possibly former mistreated prisoners seeing Americans for the first time. Some even took both their hands, getting quite emotional repeating 'Mir'.

"That means peace," the nearby doctor said. When Peter Reinhardt appeared, she introduced him as 'Doctor' before going back to her still flabbergasted patients.

William excused himself for his unannounced entering and explained the circumstances. William spoke in

German and was answered in English again. Peter asked all of them to come in his dining room, offered a seat, and explained that he had lived two years in New York City, taking his internship at the Angel of Mercy hospital.

"I am so happy to practice my English after many years, if that is what one still can call it."

"Better than mine," Brad responded. "Except for Captain Brown, we are all New Yorkers, though from different neighborhoods."

"And your city?" came from Peter with interest.

"Sacramento, California," she smiled.

"I was in San Francisco. I actually toured your vast country for two months before returning home." He rang for a servant who came in a great hurry. "Please bring us some wine glasses, and do we still have sandwiches?"

"Yes, Doctor."

"Thank you, Sophie. These people look hungry for good Austrian food," he smiled.

"You are a mind reader, Doctor Reinhardt," Sheila said gratefully. "We only had coffee at a nearby café, whose waiter gave us your address."

"Coffee?" he laughed, leaning back. "And you drank it?"

"No... we brought our own."

"That sounds better. Even I buy America's instant on the black market."

"You won't have to anymore," Joel assured him with a grin.

"The poor doctor has worked sixteen hours straight and now he entertains Americans. Very good-looking ones too. All officers in their splendid looking uniforms. I hope they will be the ones moving in. I like them already," one servant said elatedly.

"As long as we don't get any French men," another servant replied in disgust, having spent some time in their prison.

Peter was more than happy to let them have the place as their headquarters. He invited their General and staff for the next morning's breakfast, and to get to know the Russian General and his staff. "Those doors slide open to make five large rooms," he explained. "And thanks to the Russians, there is plenty of food."

"We are in supply and will bring some more," William assured him. "especially once we are in this place."

Peter ordered a servant to give them a closer look at the place so they could get some idea. But he had to leave, as he had sixteen hours of surgery behind him in his own hospital, as his two converted places lacked the proper equipment. With a friendly handshake and an "Until tomorrow at 7 AM," he departed.

The headmistress, Fanny Hirt, was now in charge to show the place she was born in fifty-six years ago. She was one of the most devoted servants of Czech descent, like her parents, and stayed purposely in Vienna to act as interpreter in Russian. She was determined that no harm would come to any Reinhardter in her presence, but Peter never took a chance.

She started at the fourth floor, explaining the many hidden antiques, also emphasizing the panels which served as doors which only a very few people knew how to open. She was, of course, one of them. Also, the Baroness and her horse's hideaway was pointed out among many young girls' and women's' too from Reinhardt's large circle of friends.

"I stood my ground," she added in pride, but no one could imagine that anyone had a desire to get her in a bedroom except to put it in order. But then again, the Americans were frequently told that all Russians loved those big women, never mind their age or shape.

The third floor was for the servants who lived in Salzburg with the Reinhardts who had fled last October. "My poor master was taken to Russia because he owns factories and is an engineer. We are told he will be back, but we pray, doubting their promise," she said quivering, wiping her tears, taking the Americans to the second floor. "Those rooms are my master's and the family bedrooms and their salons and dressing rooms." She even opened one of the large bathrooms. "The place is now in a mess, but will be put in order very soon. All paintings and portraits will be back. We were afraid they may have used them for target practice when drunk, but we were lucky with the rigid General and his obedient staff."

Now they descended to the converted entrance hall again and she mentioned that about fifty patients on the average were to be taken care of. There were four nice Russian doctors and about eight to ten male nurses. She gave a fast glance and pointed at the grand parlor, music room, library, and five adjoining dining rooms which could be made into one.

William had the joyful task of translating until they reached the downstairs kitchen. Captain Brad Torreli gulped. "We own a restaurant in New York and our kitchen is half this size!"

"The Reinhardts have belonged for centuries to Vienna's great society," Fanny Hirt said extremely proudly. "They entertained several hundred guests depending on the occasion. But the two wars changed everything."

They stood in the hallway now, outside the kitchen near their pantry when William uttered, "I smell a horse. Is there one in the room to be possibly slaughtered for a meal? I heard and know the Viennese eat horse meat."

"Not in this place! Reinhardts would rather starve. Their many thoroughbreds are in Salzburg. This one you smell is the Baroness' horse and she sleeps next to it for fear of being stolen."

"We have to see the pantry too," William demanded kindly.

"It's almost the same size as the kitchen and you will see it tomorrow when the Baroness is gone. She is asleep and may be in a short slip, being too tired to fetch a nightgown."

William, Brad, and Joel only smirked. "We've seen women in slips before and lived in Salzburg in villas of old baronesses. They remind me mostly of old relics who belong in the Austria's past."

William laughed. "I'd rather take a look at the horse any day. But we *have* to see the pantry to give us an idea how much food we can store, as we plan to be in this place for quite a while."

Sheila paid no attention to William's insistence. She knew only too well that he hated to be refused by anyone, let alone a servant. She gave Brad a wink and said, "Come on. Let's take a look at the ceilings, which were doubtless done by Italian painters." They also admired the intricate wrought iron staircases, having never seen such beauty in every corner.

"Must be nice to be rich," she lamented with a sigh.

"Not according to McAllister. He always envied me for my good-hearted parents."

"How does he know them?"

"Went on a visit to our restaurant on his last furlough. They never thought of him as rich, but rather plain and friendly, never mentioning his family."

"That's him all right. And yet they are arriving tomorrow afternoon."

"I know, and he is not even looking forward to it, except for his Uncle Bill."

Sheila was amazed that he would visit anyone below his own status. The devoted headmistress was quite disturbed about William's assumption that her Baroness was an 'old relic'. *"I'll show that handsome devil,"* she thought to herself, admiring his imposing figure, bright blue eyes, and pearl white teeth. He put those two dark, hairy, comely Italian-looking officers in a shadow any day, as she always preferred blonde men in general. Possibly because she herself was headmistress of many servants who still belonged to families of Italian background when Austria owned a big part of their country. But at present, she was one of the cunning employees her country was famous for. She would teach him a lesson of utter embarrassment while taking proper revenge. "Alright Major, you win. If you promise to be quiet, I'll open the door," she whispered. "But I have to go in first and cover the Baroness properly." William and Joel smirked again. "It's alright now," she smiled sheepishly. "She is still in her uniform. Poor thing was too tired to get out of it. Don't touch the horse. It neighs very loud." Both gave a nod as Fanny opened the door while watching William, whose face changed colors.

Captain Joel Respini took a fast look too and, thinking of William's remark whispered wistfully, "Some old relic! This is a sleeping beauty if I have ever seen one. It's the first time I ever wished I was a prince!"

Isabella laid sideways with her hands folded like in a prayer, her long black hair falling over her shoulder. Her cap with a red cross was laying on the floor. William was taking a look at the horse, as well as a basket of kittens with their watchful mama giving a quiet "meow."

Fanny closed the door, convinced he never noticed the size of the pantry. He only looked very confused. "Are you satisfied Major? You could see for yourself I was speaking the truth!" said Fanny with a sly look.

"Very," he answered curtly, biting his lips. "Now you all can have a good laugh about us crazy Americans," he smiled.

"We are not permitted to gossip, and I never know where it begins or where it ends. Among the servants we talk; we trust each other. Aside from that, we never repeat a thing we heard or saw. It's an old rule in the Reinhardt household." She smiled proudly.

"I will apologize personally," William replied with a mysterious wink. Somehow those two understood each other quite well.

Returning to the main entrance hall, Sheila and Brad were in the process of giving their cigarettes away to the extremely grateful Russians, who were grinning from ear to ear and repeating, "thank you."

"Brother, this palace is really something else," Sheila uttered, still taken aback. Just take a look at the chandeliers."

Joel looked up and replied, "So is the lady ... she is something else too. She slept in the pantry with her horse and a basket full of kittens."

"It's a Palomino," William replied. "We have several of them in Virginia."

"I love cats and dogs more," Joel replied. "And I may ask for a kitten for company."

"Then you never had a horse," said William again.

"Who has one in New York City?"

"William does," Sheila whispered, with a tinge of sarcasm.

"It's near New York and is called Westchester County," he replied mater-of-factly.

"You got some cigarettes left, William?"

"Why?"

"We gave ours to those poor souls. They nearly cried for joy."

He reached in his pocket and found an unopened pack. So did Joel, who had about half a pack left. "Here, Sheila," he said, throwing Joe's and his in her direction. "It will make your day. I already had mine."

She replied only, "thanks a lot," with a smile, not knowing what he was talking about. Since they were ready to leave, she handed them to the doctor, who slightly bowed and thanked her in perfect English.

"Don't let me forget to send some cigarettes too, when we get some food ready as soon as we reach home," William said determined.

"Today?"

"That's what I said, Sheila," he snapped, thinking of his sleeping beauty.

31

They arrived at their temporary headquarters, which was an oversized villa from a former Nazi official. Sheila did all the talking, including the invitation for breakfast with some Russian staff who were residing there. The General was impressed that they came up with the ideal place and location in just a few hours' time. William, Brad, and Joel went right to work looking in their reserved boxes for needed goods. "Any one of you can take the jeep and be back and forth in no time. I have to talk to the General, as my furlough starts officially in two days."

"I honestly forgot all about it, William," General McCain replied in surprise.

"I miss you already," William smiled. "but I'll be back in two weeks, eliminating Scotland. One week with my family in Vienna and another one in Salzburg is all I can take anyhow."

"I thought of soap and bandages," Sheila interrupted. "They may all be leaving by tomorrow and God knows they need them badly. It seems they had torn pieces of linen wrapped around."

"Good idea," said Brad, who carried with Joel all the jeep would hold to the mansion. The servants seemed to be assembled in the hallway and overjoyed by what they saw.

"At seven sharp," Fanny Hirt repeated after each servant shook their hands, being extremely thankful for the valuable cartons of food and cigarettes.

~

The following morning, General McCain and his staff of five came, as he felt six were enough, having no idea how many Russians he would be facing. Aside from Sheila, he took William, Brad, Joel, and Captain Philip Feingold, known as 'Phil the Jew'. Other than William, he was not only the smartest in his staff of thirty, but felt overlooked, by being a German Jew with a heavy accent. His family left Stuttgart for New York very soon after Hitler's arrival in 1933. They had money and opened a jewelry store on Madison Avenue, similar to the one they left behind. While he loved America, he was spoiled in a peculiar way and complained a lot. He went to Cornell University, claiming it was superior to all others. It didn't go over too well with the rest of his buddies.

As all six walked up the steps, General Gromov walked down to greet them halfway. One would have thought he welcomed these officers to his own home. His English sounded perfect in comparison to Phil's and he claimed to be a self-taught man in French and German too. "I am a determined man," he told them before the door was opened.

Arriving in the main hall was another story. Except in a field hospital they had never encountered more activity and noise. Ian McCain asked the overly bemedaled Russian General if they shouldn't wait outside.

"It's this way every morning," he assured them. "and the table is already set. They will close the dining door if the noise bothers us."

"No, no," General McCain said truthfully. "We only thought we might be in the way."

"So good to see you again," interjected a refreshed Peter Reinhardt. "Make yourselves comfortable. You will have your breakfast in a few minutes."

"Nothing bothers those men," Sheila thought, finding the Doctor extremely sexy.

Now William got the first good look at the Baroness, who was in a blue and white striped uniform, white apron, and an unstarched cap, bandaging the lined-up Russians, either on crutches or in a wheelchair. *"Even more beautiful,"* he thought. They were still in the hallway and each American was introduced by Peter as he read their nametags. Isabella gave each a smiling nod and continued with her duty.

"Thanks a million for those new bandages," she said cheerfully to General McCain, who humbly replied that it was his staff who visited the hospital the day before.

Since Peter introduced his niece as "My assistant, Miss Reinhardt," Sheila lost no time in asking if she was his daughter. "Unfortunately, only my niece. The family lives in Salzburg."

"They fled from us Russians!" General Gromov replied smiling, showing them the way toward the dining room. As soon as they were seated, five servants appeared with huge silver trays filled to the rim with delicious-looking food.

"It even smells good," said Brad, who was a connoisseur of fine food.

While they all took their seats, Peter gave a short speech about the situation, which had somewhat changed since the previous day. General Gromov went right to the phone, demanding all available transportation to have his wounded taken to the Reinhardts' two other hospitals.

"German prisoners will arrive whenever the doctors are ready. They will fold the beds to bring them to our other places."

"We have also beautiful writing tables and chairs at your disposal."

"Sounds great," Ian McCain replied, turning to Sheila. "Have you seen their office?"

"She couldn't have, as I have the key," replied Peter

"What did the Russians use?"

"Our dining rooms, believe it or not." General Gromov entered with Colonel Niemev who smiled and greeted each American.

"We were starved!" McAllister replied, smiling.

"I had to make sure that we got the P.O.W.s on time and the right ones for the job." Then both Russians helped themselves to breakfast.

The Americans were surprised at their good English, but didn't know these two officers were the exception. Captain Torreli and Respini prided themselves on the fact that their Major McAllister spoke French and German. He was their 'Harvard man' and Phil Feingold's English was considered his second language.

General Gromov looked now at Peter and demanded in his forceful voice, "Where are our nurses?"

"Working very hard to get the patients ready."

"They've got to eat, especially 'Stringbean' Isabella."

"I'll get them."

"No, Doctor. I will. You worked since three in the morning. I have more energy."

"All right," he smiled, when the General got up and screamed, "Dr. Leonova, Selinova and Miss Reinhardt! Come here and I mean now!"

All three grinned at his daily repeated outburst, linked their arms in each other's, and entered smiling.

"You sit next to me," he demanded from Isabella, "so I can see how much you eat. It's the last day I can control you, my little stringbean." She only pinched his cheek lightly, completely undisturbed, sat down, and let Peter make the proper introduction.

"You may say we were all wrapped up," she smiled. "Thanks again for the bandages."

Peter smiled again, looking at each American and commenting lightheartedly, "This is, by the way, an everyday occurrence. I hope you didn't take it seriously." They all laughed except the two Russian doctors who never understood a word.

All raved about the great breakfast, with Colonel Niemev commenting, "Although the meals have always been the best, it doesn't seem to show on certain nurses." He smirked, looking straight at Isabella who just wrinkled her nose at him.

"Poor Miss Reinhardt! Being surrounded by men like the Colonel, you sure have to take a lot," said Sheila, who thought Isabella was one of the most beautiful girls she had ever seen.

"I really don't mind, Captain Brown. The General is concerned because his family died of starvation while Leningrad was under siege. And the Colonel loves to tease me because I ride a horse better than he does," she winked, knowing he would now do the pinching.

Peter Reinhardt came right to Yuri Niemev's defense. "Like we men say, let those women have their days of glory, as we know better."

"Amen to that one!" said Ian McCain.

Isabella motioned to her watch and all three women rose with Miss Reinhardt saying sadly that 'good times just don't last' and they have to go back to work.

"Yes," Peter remarked. "You stayed exactly four minutes over your permitted half hour."

"You heard my uncle, General, now we will be four minutes late for lunch."

"That would be nice for our last day together. It's usually twenty to thirty minutes!" He laughed out loud with a loving look at her. It was so obvious that he loved her like a daughter.

~

General Gromov now directed his questions at the Americans, but not before thanking them for the badly needed medical supplies. They only nodded kindly. Isabella made her appearance again, informing the present officers that at 12:30, the German prisoners would arrive to take the first beds away.

"I will tell my troops in the next rooms to help with the wounded and get them on chairs. Excuse me, Officers," Gromov said and, of course, was followed by his aide, Niemev.

"Seem to be nice guys," Ian McCain acknowledged.

"Very well informed too."

"They always surprise you in one way or another. If you go to an opera, it's full of Russians," said Peter, adding that many illiterate Austrian farmers considered them beneath them. "True, they arrived in battle fatigues and acted like savages. But it still amazes me how they can be so forgiving and kind. After all, we know what the Germans did, and the Austrians were by no means better."

That gave Phil Feingold a chance to speak up. He noticed that all three of his buddies were enamored of the doctor's niece, whom he found radiant himself. But then again, it was hopeless as he was a Jew.

"What about us Jews, Doctor? We were persecuted and hurt the most."

"*You* weren't!" replied Sheila in a hurry, with no sign of regret.

"Captain Feingold, I know of hardly a single family who has not lost a loved one or suffered in other ways. I always asked myself, for what?" Peter acknowledged.

"I, too, lost my only brother. He was a bomber pilot and was shot down," McAllister said somberly, but Feingold was irritated knowing this 'rich Christian' never gave a thought about any Jew.

"In our house," Doctor Reinhardt continued after telling the Major how sorry he was. "we had a rule never to discuss politics or religion until Hitler's troops made their entrance. But let me put your mind at ease, since you doubtlessly believe our lives were spared any grief. The first day the Nazis took over, I was taken to Gestapo headquarters, not for long mind you, but I still could hear the screams of many innocent men. Then my niece Isabella's fiancé was shot down over England in his Messerschmitt. First, he was a wounded prisoner, then killed by German bombs. My sister, her husband, and children were killed in an air attack over Berlin." Captain Feingold swallowed, visibly moved, while Ian McCain and McAllister looked sad.

"In the meantime, my brother had to convert his factories from peace to war machinery, risking his life by giving his arriving prisoners extra rations. The Russians were especially mistreated, aside from never receiving a package."

"Except us Jews," Phil Feingold interrupted and was, as always, ignored.

"By the way, that little boy you see running around trying to help everybody is a Jewish child." Now Phil's eyes bulged. "My niece heard whining noises late at night at our other place in Lindenfels. She helped his mother giving birth, came out of breath for my help, and when we returned, found the mother dead. Then we were forced to get rid of the blouse with the Star of David on it. The Catholic nuns in our own hospital helped me with deceiving the doctors and saving the boy. We brought him to my brother's place, as his servants were more trustworthy, which is the place right where we are all sitting." Again, faces of dismay, with Sheila wiping tears. "We raised him as our own and baptized him Karl Otto, after two of our finest family members. Soon we found out he was born a deaf-mute, and do you know, Captain Feingold, what we Reinhardts did? We learned their language to communicate and loved this child like our very own." The two Italian officers applauded, quite moved by now.

"Is he circumcised?" Captain Feingold asked.

"What kind of a question is that?" asked Peter, indignant.

"Because that would make him a Jew. Right now, he is a baptized Christian."

"So what?" replied Major McAllister, annoyed.

"I thought you had more common sense, like your parents had when they left Germany for America in time," Peter said. His face reddened. "Vienna had fifty-two air attacks, which is very little in comparison to Germany's cities, but nevertheless, this house could have been bombed like our Opera. If we were dead, but the little boy somehow lived and the Nazis, in trying to help children, may have seen he was a Jew. How long would it have taken them to either kill him or let him die, possibly of starvation? If you are so desperate to find Jews, why don't you talk to some wounded Russians?" Peter answered finally.

"You think there are some?" he asked, still embarrassed and perplexed.

"Ask my niece. She will tell you."

Captain Feingold had no choice but to get up and talk to Isabella. Not knowing the answer, she asked a Russian medic who went with him, pointing them out, not speaking a word of English.

McAllister thought of brave Isabella, hoping she was still available and somehow capable of loving him.

Fanny Hirt entered with General Gromov and Colonel Niemev. "I will get you more coffee and homemade rolls."

"They all said yes," Peter replied, opening the backlash of her apron. "It's a bad habit of mine," he said fondly after receiving a tap on his shoulder. "Fanny was born here. We were so lucky with our servants. Some are in Salzburg with my larger family, but I told you that already."

"And why did you stay in Vienna?" asked McAllister.

"To hide and watch after my countrymen," Colonel Niemiev said grandly. "That's why! They had many Russians P.O.W.s in their cellars, which I will show you in time."

"We feel really honored to have been here," General Gromov said, obviously moved. "And I would shoot everyone myself if the Reinhardts would be harmed."

"We will do the same, General," Ian McCain assured him, with the rest of them replying, "You bet."

After their second breakfast was gone, both generals left, with Gromov showing them around. Niemiev went from soldier to soldier explaining several things, seeing some for the first time in a clean uniform. Fanny Hirt entered with two huge German shepherds, handing them to 'her Doctor'.

"The German P.O.W.s are already waiting outside," Fanny uttered uneasily. "Colonel Niemev is in charge, but the Germans may ignore his commands."

"You can say that again. I better get the Baroness. She needs to sit down, for one thing, and the dogs will make her happy for another," she smiled.

"Should we leave?" asked Sheila, looking upset.

"Oh, no, Miss Brown. The moment the dogs come in, all the Russians come out from other rooms and watch them at gunpoint."

"What are they usually up to?" William asked with great interest, while looking at the entering Isabella.

"Right now, we don't know, but they know they will be leaving for Russia once their work is finished, so won't take any chances. Isabella responded very calmly and somehow found herself looking at the 'handsome devil' Fanny pointed out, never revealing a word about the pantry. The dogs greeted Isabella by licking her cheeks. "Alright girls, settle down. I love you both. Now lay down," she commanded and down they went.

"Those dogs are the most beautiful creatures I have ever seen," McAllister remarked honestly. Sheila Brown stated that she was always scared of those types of dogs, including Dobermans.

"Both dogs are highly trained and don't even hurt our cat."

"With so many strangers coming in day and night we would be in lots of trouble," Peter replied.

"Isabella, why don't you go to each one and let them smell their hands."

"Good idea. By the way, these dogs play ball with the wounded Russians every evening. That should tell you something."

"What are their names?" asked Brad Torreli.

"Ella and Bella."

"Why not males?" Joel Respini joined in.

"Because females don't fight," Isabella laughed.

"Over me they do," Brad said, returning her laugh.

"For cigarettes or chewing gum?" Isabella bit her lips, teasing him.

"Over my body," he smiled proudly.

"Give me a break!" Sheila replied quickly. "She's seen better ones."

"Not like mine," he said triumphantly.

"Dear Captain Torreli, I assist my uncle on the operating table, and for us it's only a matter of how much we can help. The bodies never matter. It's almost like on an assembly line." Peter Reinhardt had an amusing grin on his face, knowing Isabella would get the best of him in the long run.

"Maybe for you, Miss Reinhardt, but let me tell you, when we slept temporarily in trains until we found quarters, those women crawled through our windows! Right Joel?"

"So what?" he replied.

"Those women are the same ones who crawled in anyone's bed or, as in your case, wagons. We have a name for them, but I refrain from saying it. Just watch out for syphilis, Captain Torreli. We are swamped with cases in many hospitals." He just looked at her and spoke to Joel in Italian.

"English, please, you two spaghetti clowns," an irritated Sheila Brown scolded. "And you are ever so right, Miss Reinhardt. But Brad is highly exaggerating."

"Possibly." Then she turned to both Captains and responded in Italian, once more surprising them.

Now Peter Reinhardt laughed heartily, joined by the rest while watching their astonished faces.

"My niece was born and raised in Switzerland, the first fifteen years in the Italian part on top of that. Her late father was a Swiss pathologist and died the day she was born."

"How?" asked Sheila.

"By racing home with a big bouquet of flowers and hitting a lamppost."

"So sorry to hear that," said Brad and Joel.

"Isabella's mother was a widow for fifteen years before she married my brother in 1938. Until then, her name was Isabella Rosatti. Very Italian I would say," Peter finalized.

"Then why do all the servants call her 'Baroness'?" Sheila had to know at the moment.

"Her mother came from a long line of nobility dating back to the sixteenth century. As for the servants? They love titles no matter how poor their master might be."

Now Colonel Niemev and the Germans came in the hallway. Isabella got up, holding each dog by their chains, and gave the P.O.W.s orders on what had to be done. They only gave her a look of indifference without saying a word. Dr. Leonova came in and told Isabella about all the papers that needed the Doctor's signature, otherwise everyone was ready.

Sheila, hearing her talking in Russian, asked eagerly, "How many languages do you speak?"

"One or two," she smiled, when both Generals returned from their excursion of Reinhardt's place.

I thought the Germans came later?" Ian McCain asked, also noticing the loose running shepherds. "Any reasons or troubles?"

"No," Peter replied in honesty.

~

I called on our six reliable Scotsmen to be here at 1:30 to give those poor departing souls a nice send off," Peter addressed the Americans and two Russians. Then, looking at the pleased Americans he continued. "They came almost weekly to entertain the wounded Russians."

"Bagpipes?" Ian McCain asked, looking at McAllister.

"Bagpipes, harmonicas, and singing. What good times we had!"

Now they saw the Russian guards pointing their rifles at each P.O.W. The Germans worked fast and hard, never giving a glance at anyone except their own Sergeant. And he gave the appearance that they had won the war, still being arrogant to the boot.

"Strange how they all had almost the same facial features. It's their inbreeding," William thought while watching the Russians, as they reacted with a sort of cow or sheep-like obedience. He also watched the dressed up, wounded soldiers who had their crutches leaning on the antique French chairs. The Reinhardts had given them those while their beds were disappearing fast in front of them. Not one Russian had a hateful look on their war-ravaged faces, and many were toothless when they smiled. Yet those Germans burned their villages without giving reasons except 'Adolf Hitler's command'. He had heard about the many sides of them while in Vienna. From a mean Rottweiler when drunk, to a little

kitten when sober. Now the Americans watched the dividing painted panel being folded to several large pieces, carried upstairs by two tall, skinny, but still handsome P.O.W.s. They saw that there was another row of beds which now became visible. Isabella remarked, in her calm manner, that it was at the suggestion of the Russian medics to divide them. One side could walk on crutches, the back side was worse off. They had either no legs or no arms.

"And possibly no families," Peter added, sadly.

"What are you going to do with them?" Ian McCain wanted to know.

"They will be carried to our own Reinhardt hospital and wait for their artificial limbs to be made. Then they have to be taught to walk," he answered grimly.

There were now five Americans with their backs towards two large windows with General Gromov at the end facing Ian McCain. On Gromov's lap sat the deaf-mute, little Karl, which was also a daily occurrence. Then came Colonel Niemev, both Russian doctors, Peter, and Isabella next to the General, across from Sheila Brown and McAllister, who was by now so much in love that nothing else around him mattered, not even the arrival of his family that very evening.

"Apple strudel coming up," Fanny announced cheerfully.

McAllister's face lit up. Somehow, he felt she made it for him as they talked about his favorite dessert. "You know how to make people feel good," he replied while giving her a wink.

Isabella, sitting almost across from him facing Sheila, wondered seriously if they had had an affair. She sincerely hoped not, as she was falling in love with him. *But then again, how many girls are waiting at home,"* she thought, and ignored him as always.

With the work almost done by the P.O.W.s, Peter proposed to leave the room and watch the Scotsmen sing and play their music.

"Not only that, but we give those soldiers a well-deserved salute," Ian McCain replied to Peter. "But first, I want those German bastards out. They are still humming their Nazi songs to get the best of us." They marched out smiling and sang, "Today we own Germany, tomorrow the whole wide world."

"The nerve of them!" said a furious Ian McCain.

"They'll pay for it dearly," replied Niemev, and no one doubted him. "We captured them right on St. Stephan's Cathedral, setting it on fire!" Gromov said in disgust. "I don't believe in God ... but in Justice."

"Well that makes two," Ian McCain thought, when Isabella shrieked "OUCH" with the Russians and Peter watching a body falling down.

"One German less," Peter smiled. "I guess he was hiding on the last floor until the rest were gone. In their spiteful mood they forgot all about him." Sheila made a shivering shrug.

"You don't have to turn around," Isabella said kindly. "For us it's nothing new."

"My God, Miss Reinhardt, for someone so young you sure have seen a lot."

"You forgot to say bodies," Isabella laughed, winking at Brad and Joel.

"No, Miss Brown, in comparison to most people we had a very good life. Right, Uncle Peter?"

"Very, very good I would say." He smiled.

Captain Feingold apologized for thinking the Reinhardts never mentioned their own family, but heard from a Russian how much risk they took in saving many lives. Both only smiled, as it was the most normal thing to do.

"You speak Russian?" asked Colonel Niemev.

"No, Hebrew, Colonel, and I was surprised that barely anyone spoke it."

"It's a religion and we stated previously we don't believe in God."

There was a stillness in the room and the loud and happy arriving Scotsmen saved the somber situation. No one wanted to deny being a religious person, but no one wanted to hurt those two good officers either. Gromov and Niemev fought in Stalingrad, the General told Ian McCain while getting the tour of the house. Why condemn the Russian who suffered so much and fought in a revolution on top of it? He also lost all of his family. Why should he have faith?

"Give us two minutes," Isabella said as all rose from their chairs.

"Two minutes means twenty in Austria," Gromov laughed.

"For a lass like this one, I'll wait two days."

"What is a 'lass'?"

"To us Scots, a beautiful lady in this case." General Gromov gave a deep sigh, possibly thinking the Scots are crazy too.

The six Americans lined up next to the Scotsmen, whose bagpipes already started 'Going Home'. They stood in front of the dining room door which was closed by Gromov. Then he walked on the other side to join Niemev, their two doctors, Peter, and Isabella who held little Karl's hand. Next to her stood Reinhardt's servants in black dresses and snow-white aprons, holding baskets. Each wounded soldier on crutches had a healthy one next to him, saluting the Americans and Scotsmen, who sang their favorite song, 'Come along, Come along'. The healthy guards marched to this tune with a shy smile, hoping they could stay in Vienna and hear those many songs again. Even the hardcore Russians showed their emotions, never expecting such a sendoff. Isabella ran from one stretcher to the next with big tears rolling down her cheeks, shaking hands and telling them they would be in their other hospital.

Little Karl had a paper-made military cap, saluting and making his heart signs simultaneously. He was everyone's friend. Isabella was now stroking the hands of soldiers who lost their legs and the medics gave her their nicest smile with their warmest thanks, unable to shake her hands. The last were the blind ones who had lost some limbs on top of it. She cried openly, "Shalom, aleichem," and this time it was up to a teary-eyed Phil Feingold to translate, as a sobbing Sheila wanted to know the meaning of it.

"Peace be with you," he replied, looking at all the other Westerners. Since everyone was somber too, he felt maybe there was hope in this pitiless world after all.

Major McAllister was no different. He followed Isabella's every move and admired her bravery, emotions, and tears even more if it was possible. He was totally in love.

~

Ian McCain's personal driver gave Major McAllister a ride to Vienna's airport. They exchanged a few kind words, especially about their new beautiful location in the city's First District. William was glad to have arrived quite early and walked around the rather small airport while waiting for the plane, which was one hour late. It didn't matter to him, but it did, of course, to his mother. She now descended the plane slowly on the hand of a stewardess with his father and Uncle Bill behind them.

"I'll never fly again," she greeted him without an embrace.

"No one told you to fly. The weather is perfect for crossing the ocean," William replied tartly.

His father came next with the usual embrace. "How are you doing, son?"

"Fine," he replied, and turned to Uncle Bill, who was always in a jovial mood regardless of the situation. He explained their bumpy ride, exchanging planes in London for Paris, where they decided to stay for a night in Orly's Airfield Hotel, but the food and service were dreadful, and the plane arrived late for Vienna. His mother sounded worse than a soldier after a heavy battle and was in need of a glass of gin.

"Naturally," William thought, and told her he brought a small bottle in case the hotel didn't have some in reserve. "It's crowded with Americans who like to drink a lot," he commented when they entered a taxi. They only made small talk, and someone would have thought they had seen each other yesterday and lived around the corner.

Hotel Imperial was, to her great pleasure, the same as always. Nothing had changed. Even the owner, Mr. Raymond Klein, and his handsome son, Toni, were waiting to greet them, with every porter ready to take their suitcases. The old-timers remembered these generous tippers. Now a dollar or a few cigarettes meant much, much more.

William was now alone in the taxi and it felt good. This day was something else altogether. He never expected anything like it, and he let the morning until the departure of the Russians run like a film in front of him. Of course, the main role went to Isabella. He never came close to meeting a woman like her, so beautiful and her demeanor topped it by far. Aside from her perfect mannerism and control of every given situation, her outlook on morals was also to his liking. But how to get a lady like this to date him was another story.

~

His parents called after breakfast and told William they were all well fed, rested, and ready. His mother apologized for her poor conduct.

"It's quite all right," he said comfortingly, looking forward to seeing Isabella, who promised to be there. It was her day off, but she was in charge of rearranging the room to the General's and his staff's convenience. Also, she wanted the tapestry, paintings, and portraits hung back to give the entrance hall the old look again.

Peter was in his brother's office to get some of his paperwork and Isabella went with little Karl in the garden to cut some late blooming roses. The two Russians were having their second breakfast when all six Americans from the previous day, and William's parents and Uncle, appeared.

Fanny smiled at them with a slight bow and went for the Doctor in a hurry. All the newly arrived McAllisters were in awe of William's new headquarters. Kathryn McAllister didn't know where to look first when Doctor Reinhardt entered, dressed in the customary Austrian gray suit with green lapels and trimming. All three McAllisters liked his secure and authoritative appearance without giving the slightest hint of being a snob. He offered the upstairs balcony for the view, away from the noise.

The Reinhardts had many of their Lindenfels servants there to get the work done as quickly as possible. Arriving on the large balcony with the usual iron work to match the staircase, they sat down with Peter, who had ordered refreshments. They were completely at ease discussing many subjects and Peter was surprised to learn how well they knew Vienna and Salzburg. It gave him an opportunity to ask if they would take a letter to his family, as mail took a long time and was unreliable.

They were only too happy to do it. All four McAllisters smiled, almost in unison. They planned to see Scotland after a two-week stay in Austria. Peter noticed how proud they were being of Scottish descent. Peter, having been more than two years in America, knew all about the 'right people', who were not much different from anywhere else. 'Old family', 'Old money' had always played a great role in any society. Kathryn now spotted Isabella and Karl with their rose baskets and pruning shears. William sat sideways, listening intently to their conversation, never glancing anywhere.

"Excuse me, gentlemen. I noticed a young lady and a boy with roses. I just *have* to see them."

"By all means," Peter replied, rather surprised.

She left the balcony on the arm of Peter, who introduced her to his niece and little Karl. He returned quickly to the balcony for a discussion about William's times during the war after arriving in Sicily. It was 'men's talk', and for Kathryn the war meant only the loss of Don Reed.

Isabella saw in her a pretty woman in her middle fifties, rather tall, dyed light brown hair, big busted, and shapely. But her dark navy dress was only adorned by an expensive brooch of pearls in the setting of a rose. Isabella wore a navy blue dress too, but with large white lapels and a small strand of pearls. They started with their variety of roses and Isabella gave some history of the beautiful garden which was, in 1940, turned into a field of potatoes, cabbage, and carrots. "But it will change again as soon as food is available," she sighed.

"Glad you left those English boxwoods standing. They are so impressive."

"Yes, and here are our flowering trees, more roses, and wisteria, which form the entrance to our next garden with a small lake of swans. Would you like to see it, Madame?"

"I'd love to!"

She explained Karl's deaf-mute condition and the way the Reinhardts got him. They took a seat in front of the pond when Lillian came galloping their way. "My prized possession," she said proudly. "I always forsook my vacation for her."

"We have many horses in Virginia." They talked like two women who had a lot of catching up to do and Lillian stood next to them like an invited guest. Reinhardt's goat, Nelli, made her presence known nearby, bleating very loudly.

"You have quite a collection of animals here," Kathryn acknowledged, laughing. "She also looks like she is ready to give birth."

"Oh, yes, and she may do it right in front of us," Isabella laughed. "She is of a good Saanen breed, and has never disappointed us with her steady milk supply."

They now heard men's voices and Kathryn remarked, "My husband and Bill probably thought I got lost or I am boring you to death with my talk about roses."

"It just so happens that we like the same things," Isabella responded seriously. Kathryn McAllister found her not only charming and beautiful, but knowledgeable as well.

Sheila, after hearing the goat's bleating noise, ran the last few steps. "What on earth happened?"

"Good morning, Miss Brown."

"Oh, good morning, Miss Reinhardt."

They all entered the second garden with Peter introducing William's father and Uncle. "We had a great war talk when my wife spotted you with flowers, which are more to her liking," Don McAllister said kindly.

William saw Isabella out of uniform with her French chignon hairstyle and thought, *"How could God make such a beautiful creature?"*

Since everyone's attention was turned to the goat, he had little choice but to do the same. *"Talk about romance,"* he smiled to himself.

Now Peter stated with a smirk that with a surgeon, an RN, and so many Americans ready to assist, there should be no problem for Nelli to give birth.

"We should call her something else; she never is birthing on time," Isabella smiled, trying to get the attention to her horse, who stood hidden behind large evergreens.

Ian McCain laughed. "I may take her home with me, Miss Reinhardt, as I was raised on a farm."

"With horses too?"

"Of course! It was our only transportation when I grew up."

"Then take a look at my beauty. Come on, Lillian." She took a big jump with a turnaround, acting again like a circus horse.

"What a beauty," Ian McCain remarked sincerely, patting her neck. Joel looked slyly at William, having been the first one to see her.

"Boy she is something else," Sheila said awestruck, looking at William, knowing his love for horses.

"I would say Lillian is exactly befitting her owner in every way."

"How kind of you, Madame," she replied, looking mischievously at Brad and Joel. "What a beautiful body." With the exception of Ian McCain, they roared with laughter.

William got almost a jolt in his back at his mother's compliment, as for some reason she never found anyone worthy of one. Isabella looked around, wondering about the Russians. To them she was always a string bean who would never be able to get a man. But then again, they always had a Russian on their minds. "Where is Gromov and Niemev?" she asked, overlooking their titles.

"They just left our table happily to get some of their own work done," Peter replied.

"I can honestly say I like them," Uncle Bill said truthfully. "Although the relationship between our two countries has changed."

"They may be like us Reinhardts," Peter challenged. "We are above caring unless caring is connected with helping someone, and I mean anyone whose heart is beating."

"Great speech for a surgeon," Don McAllister said approvingly. Once more, William was surprised.

~

As the time came for Nelli to give birth, Isabella went on her knees, stroking Nelli's forehead gently while Peter pushed on her belly. The Americans formed a semi-circle with their arms crossed and stared in amazement at the actions of the other two. Sheila held Karl's hand, but looking at her expression of anxiety, one would think the little boy held hers. After a loud outcry, the little legs showed up and with the next push, the rest followed. All applauded spontaneously.

"It's one more thing we can add to our war stories," William said, keeping his eyes on his future wife, to whom he had yet to utter his first sentence.

"Yeah, and without any help from the Russians," Brad said in jest.

"Or Americans for that matter, Brad."

"What are you talking about Sheila? We were all standing here."

"What a day," Kathryn said fondly, looking at Isabella.

"Yes, Madame. I only wish you were here yesterday."

"It was an event not one of us will likely forget," Ian McCain muttered, reflecting. "Somehow it will always stay with me for as long as I live."

"Same here," agreed Phil Feingold who, as always, was overlooked.

"Where are you from?" Uncle Bill asked.

"New York City, formerly Stuttgart until Hitler arrived," he replied rather arrogantly.

"And you had to fight your own people?" Kathryn frowned.

"I wish I was in a position to shoot each one, but being in logistics meant we got shot at and many of our men got killed, but our job was to supply the troops so they could go on shooting, eating, and keeping warm. We all marched together, forward or retreating, depending on the strength of the Krauts."

"What a waste. What a terrible waste," Don McAllister replied with his voice cracking. They all walked back in silence.

"Do I hear a piano playing?" Kathryn McAllister inquired as they came nearer to the mansion.

"You do, Madame. The wives of our two Russians are here. They probably feel hard work is made easier with music," Isabella replied cheerfully. "And our servants are very grateful since our radios were confiscated."

"Strange people. We only heard they liked watches and wore, at times, five or six on one arm," Uncle Bill joined in, but kept quiet as they re-entered the place with Lillian right behind them.

"Is she permitted to come in?" Don McAllister asked, surprised.

"Lately, yes. Many of our wounded Russians were at one time or another in the cavalry, so we brought Lillian in as she loves to be petted," Isabella replied.

"And for us, it was good to know she was well taken care of, as my niece and I spend most of our time working or sleeping. She is my assistant on the operating table, which is quite a chore."

"I'll say," grimaced Kathryn McAllister.

"Now she stays for a while here with us as an interpreter," Ian McCain said with relish. "We have to find someone who translates in Russian, English, French, and German.

"You know all those languages?" asked Kathryn in shock, who seemed to have taken to Isabella, practically monopolizing her.

"Yes," she replied, very humbly.

Uncle Bill looked at his watch and decided that it was time to go. "We kept you quite long enough and enjoyed every minute of it." All four McAllisters started to depart.

"Until tomorrow in Lindenfels," Peter reminded them.

"What is there?" Kathryn had to ask.

"Our other place," Peter smiled.

~

The two women, Mrs. Gromov and Mrs. Niemev, were told the 'Amerikansky' were in a hurry to return to their hotel and they would meet them tomorrow. They were looking forward to it, although no one spoke a word of English.

The mansion was getting back to its good old days and Ian McCain had Phil Feingold drawing the layout, as McAllister had his first official furlough day. They took a taxi to the hotel for their lunch and William would have given anything to be with his crew. However, he was very pleased about the way his mother acted towards the Reinhardts, as she once wrote in a letter that Austrians were like Germans during wars. And the Germans killed her Don Reed. So far, not a word was mentioned in that regard, and William was not about to bring it up.

William and Uncle Bill were finally alone in the Hotel Imperial's garden while his brother and Kathryn took their naps. Both had to recuperate from the time change of six hours, as well as that horribly bumpy ride. Now they could talk confidentially.

"Are you planning to return next year, William?"

"It all depends."

"Depends on what?"

"On that beautiful young lady you couldn't have helped notice like every other man does."

"Glad to hear it, William. I was sort of afraid that the female Captain Brown was on your mind. She kept so close to you with her eyes fluttering each time you spoke. I assumed she was 'the one'."

"God, no! What made you come to that conclusion?"

"She is very pretty, for one thing, and you always went for red heads." Now William began to tell the Reinhardts' story and Bill was quite impressed. "You need someone like her, very special, and a debutante from Vassar may not be enough. As in some ways, our household is not much different from theirs. I don't mean the mansion or their country place, but all our many holdings put together may equal theirs and will be yours someday."

"Don't I know it. I had my share of it already years ago. But it's still for love only, providing everything else fits too."

"Then try your darnest to bring her back."

"Dear God... I am trying my darnest to get her to look at me," he laughed. "You are way ahead of me. She may not even want to come to the states. That's why I said, 'It all depends.' I can re-enlist and would if that's the only way to be near her."

"That bad, William?"

"Yep. That bad. And believe me, I wish there was an easier way."

"You wouldn't want an easier way, William. A man always likes to be the hunter. So far, you have always been the hunted one. Like we old-timers say, if it's meant to be, it will be."

"With my luck, she will be gone when I return."

"Gone where?"

"Out of the office, when they find an interpreter."

"Well, then Ian McCain will have to keep her just a little longer."

"I cannot tell him that."

"But he would be the first to understand. We met his lovely wife in New York and from what I understand, they are, after almost thirty years of marriage, still as much in love as the day they met."

"She will be here by the beginning of October," William hastened to add. "And believe me, he is marking his calendar every single day."

"One more reason to talk to him about it."

"Well, I will see after my return from Salzburg," he sighed.

"We may just personally deliver the Doctor's and the young lady's letter to her mother. And speaking of mothers, yours seems to be quite taken with Miss Reinhardt."

"So I noticed. But then, the Reinhardts make everyone feel at ease."

32

Gromov and Niemev had barely set foot in the castle and were now completely in charge. The routine began to change. Their wives would move to the upper floor and run their own households like in Peter's place. Not even moved out by now, only just hearing about it, Peter missed them already. They had been excellent company after a hard day's work.

Now he had to make plans to bring his wife and children back. Vienna, of course, was not the town they had left. What a difference a year made. It became a town of spying, prostitutes, pimps, and the black market. A shoddy town to say the least. His family would be shocked upon their return home, but Gaby, Victoria, and the children had no intention of coming back until Paul's return. With Astrid von Walden, no one was ever quite sure. Her house had English soldiers as occupants.

The McAllisters finally got a rental car. "Taxis are for New York," they claimed, forgetting that the war had barely ended. Thank God for their dollars. One could have almost anything one wished, although the soldiers had occupation versions called 'scrips', but those were dollars nevertheless. Peter told the McAllisters to follow his car to Lindenfels to show them around. They happily agreed, although they had a map at their disposal.

~

"There is the General and Colonel again," Peter laughed. "First he had the mansion, now he got upgraded to the master of a castle. God bless him until he and his wife see Russia again."

The McAllisters were again in wonderment after descending the car and seeing that beautiful baroque structure. Once more, Gromov met them halfway with a very warm welcome.

"Lillian is right behind you."

"We noticed she is so happy to be back in her old stomping ground," Isabella replied, giving the happy horse a kiss. Lillian jumped for joy to be in her old environment and Kathryn remarked, "Don't tell me horses are dumb." Then the General offered her his arm, ascending to the castle.

"I have another great surprise waiting," he said in Russian, and Peter replied, "After the last few days, there shouldn't be any more left."

"You will be happy."

Now Peter smiled, looking at Kathryn McAllister. "Sorry, you will see why I cannot talk in English."

"I had no idea you spoke Russian too."

"Just a little. My niece speaks and writes it fluently."

"So my son told me."

When they all reached the top of the stairs, the door opened from inside and all six mammoth mustached Scotsmen stood in their gala uniforms playing and singing

'Scotland the Brave'. It was Gromov and his wounded comrades' favorite.

While on the previous Friday nothing was prearranged and it all fell perfectly in order, the Russians didn't take any chances. They were out to impress the visiting Americans. They formed a large semi-circle behind the musicians with Ian McCain in the middle, surrounded by bemedalled Russian heroes, male or female, the four doctors, and Gromov and Niemev's wives. One surprise was that the General got four ballet dancers from a theater in Vienna who performed a perfect Scottish jig – with McAllister and the rest of the attendees clapping, while many had tears running down their cheeks. Of course, Kathryn and Isabella, who squeezed each other's hands, were the most obvious ones. William, trying to get a glimpse of his mother's reaction, couldn't help but notice their intertwined hands. He was thrilled, to say the least, as his mother was a woman who only did what she felt like doing.

"All seems well with the world," Colonel Niemev said cheerfully, but Gromov and his wife had lost their children and just for a day, they put it in the background.

The McAllisters were now introduced by the General to everyone and felt it would take them until their arrival home to digest everything going on around them. My Lord, what would their friends say seeing them among so many foreigners? Gromov never overlooked any detail and had English-speaking interpreters next to anyone not speaking Russian. William talked to Dr. Andreas Walden and offered to take a letter to his mother in Salzburg.

He loved every one of Isabella's family that he had met, which created a problem to his way of thinking. How would she ever leave them? Of course, her Lillian would be on the boat, but… There were so many 'ifs', 'ands', and 'buts' that his back started to hurt again.

While Isabella was in the process of hugging and kissing everyone, starting with the Russian doctors and ending with their former servants, Peter and Andreas wondered if they should offer their guests a tour of the castle. But everyone was so busy talking that they decided to wait until after dinner. Most of the interpreters were busy introducing the highly decorated female Russians to the McAllisters and Reinhardts. They were cheerful First Lieutenants. One was a pilot who explained how she avoided the pursuing German planes and their 'flak'; the other one shook hands with the first American soldiers in Torgau on the Elbe River. "We all drank and danced and were so very happy," she laughed, while the McAllisters took an interest in their medals, asking the meaning of each one.

They were all in awe of their bravery and with their courage. Of course, General Gromov had to have the last word, taking over the conversation with great pride. "And while the girls were dancing, we had to do all the fighting," he laughed mischievously.

"The only way to go!" Uncle Bill interjected, enjoying himself to the hilt. "If you wouldn't have fought, they couldn't have kept on dancing. Right?"

"Right," Gromov laughed aloud. "That's one way to see it."

McAllister didn't have a chance to see the portraits, as dinner was announced by a uniformed servant. To Kathryn's great astonishment, William offered her his arm.

"How nice and kind of you, son," she exclaimed, never expecting this courteous gesture. Somehow, she felt guilty thinking, *"If only Don Reed were here."*

The Reinhardts' great dining room was incredible and the McAllisters couldn't think of a place back home which compared to it. "Gosh… I am ready to faint," Kathryn whispered.

There was the impressive Chinese silk tapestry, huge crystal chandeliers with small matching wall sconces, and the colossal banquet table. The finest china, crystal, and silverware were a sight to behold. Old liveried male servants were ready to make the guests comfortable on gilded Louis XVI chairs. The Reinhardts had had this finery for as long as the castle had been standing, so Peter only smiled, watching General Gromov and Ian McCain at the head of the table.

There were thirty-two guests, Isabella counted, and Uncle Peter, Andreas, Theresa, and she were four of the original and indirectly related Reinhardters.

"If only my ancestors could see it now," Peter thought.

Gromov raised his glass of vodka. "Let's drink to a long-lasting peace and everyone will be our brother and sister." The Americans and Scots were now convinced he spoke as a Communist and took a sip of that strong alcohol, and let it go at that.

It was now Ian McCain's turn and he only replied, "Let's drink to friendship and your wonderful hospitality." Gromov translated the compliment and all turned to the General with their heartiest smiles.

As always, the food was praised with Gromov's thunderous voice giving the history of 'his' castle in English and Russian. The translators had barely an opportunity to get a word in edgewise. But to the McAllisters' and the Scotsmen's surprise, he gave the servants credit for all the hard work. Peter and his family were not mentioned at all, possibly because they were, in the present Russians' eyes, 'Capitalists' whose lifestyle was, however, enormously enjoyed.

Her took it on himself to show the men his smoking room, where brandy would be served, and Isabella lost no time in showing the ladies their parlor with coffee being served.

"And you also can have tea," she smiled.

General Gromov didn't know this European custom. After noticing his mistake, he entered and apologized. "This is my little stringbean. I love her like a daughter," he uttered with quivering lips.

Kathryn was happy to notice that this big authoritative man, who represented, in her eyes, the average Russian officer, had a soft spot after all. His wife, Svetlana, said, "Outside he is steel, but his heart is as soft as cotton." Well, of anyone, she should know.

Kathryn reminded herself about the similarities among the Russian women. Not only because all wore a uniform, but not one hairstyle was different from the other. However, she admired their respect towards each other, their kind expressions, and a certain envy when looking at western clothes. Now they felt free to ask about many things and Isabella's work of translating was considerable. However, she enjoyed it and Kathryn thought again, *"What a lovely pair she and Don Reed would have made."*

Finally, it was time to show and expound on the Reinhardt's portraits. Gromov and Niemev paid very close attention. Maybe at their next gathering, which would be all Russian, they could joke about all those skinny Capitalists whose castle they now occupy, or praise them as down to earth, hard-working Austrians who risked their lives in order to save many of their people. In time, the Reinhardts would hear about it. After all, their former servants were still and always would be devoted Reinhardters.

~

Peter and Isabella arrived at their own villa in Lindenfels.

"What a day! Gromov really worked hard and even went personally to the 'People's Theater' to find four dancers who knew the Scottish jig," Isabella remarked happily.

"He pulled a good day off, but so did our servants. Fanny got some liveried men from our neighbors. What a dear."

"They all ate well for the first time, I was told by many in the kitchen." She also added, "And Mrs. McAllister goes out of her way to be nice to me. Have you noticed?"

"Society knows society. But speaking of the McAllisters, their son looked at your portrait like a Catholic at the Virgin Mary."

"You may just as well know, we kept looking at each other across the table. It was almost unavoidable. However, I tried to be as discreet as possible and hoped it worked."

"Any reason why it should or should not, Isabella?"

"Because I am sure I have been in love with him since the moment I saw him."

"Well, well, well. That is a surprise after telling me that good girls never date any occupation forces."

"I was told by you that there are always those exceptions. I like to believe he is one of them."

"Isabella, I cannot say I blame you. He is very good looking and comes from a fine family. I looked at the distinguished faces of his father and uncle, never mind his good-looking mother, and I thought to myself that he got the best of both parents."

"Of course, there are so many beautiful American girls too, but maybe the war has taught him to look for more than beauty." Isabella sighed.

"There were many handsome officers and doctors at the hospital who didn't suit you either. Just think about it."

"True, but most were just ready to take me to bed."

"I thought so." He smiled. "I am happy to hear you feel so secure and have so much self-respect that you enter unblemished into a marriage."

"You can be sure of that."

"I thought so." Peter repeated and smiled.

~

Kathryn and Don decided on a long nap, which was to William and Bill's liking. Both went in the lobby to talk about the party and Isabella in their own way and without interference or unsolicited advice.

"At least she looked at me several times today. That is progress already," William smiled, starting the conversation.

"Of course, you sat across from her; it was unavoidable." Uncle Bill returned his smile, but it was his usual sly look.

"Quite a coincidence if someone considers it was the headmistress, Fanny, who put the cards in place. No Russian woman was able to do it."

"Oh, yes." William tapped on his head. "Languages can be such a barrier in life." He smiled, thinking of Fanny's trick. "Mother is amazed at Miss Reinhardt's knowledge. She told Ian McCain that the girl knows even the Latin names of all flowers."

"How old do you think she is?" Uncle Bill asked, curious.

"Born in 1923. November."

"How do you know?"

"That was the day her father died. Doctor Reinhardt told the Italians."

"American Officers," Uncle Bill corrected. "You may not know it, William, but the Russians also stripped her father's... I mean Reinhardt's factories of everything, including the doorknobs. Imagine that."

William was flabbergasted. "Who told you?"

"A servant after a good tip and a few questions."

"Well, I tipped Fanny as she is now the main housekeeper. But she promised to share the money with her help. Wait until I get a hold of Feingold after my furlough is over," William said, furious about hearing that the Reinhardt factories were lost too. They finished their whisky, greeted a few of his friends from his quarters, who had nothing better to do than to drink either, and went upstairs.

"Well, you two?" Kathryn smiled.

"We went to the lobby and William ran into a few of his buddies."

"My God, don't tell me you had to shake more hands. Mine still hurt, but I don't regret it as everyone was very nice. Or at least they tried to be."

"Same with our friends in New York, Mother. They don't love or even like each other but they try to be civil. That's all one can ask," William finalized. Kathryn laughed out loud and she didn't even pay any attention to William's remark.

"And what is so funny?" Don asked.

"That sweet Miss Reinhardt. After some Scotsmen kept winking their eyes at her, she whispered to ask how any girl can kiss such a mammoth mustached fellow. I thought it was so cute of her to tell me that, but it shows how close we have become the last two days."

"What roses and horses won't do for some women," Don smirked.

~

They traveled, of course, in the well-reserved First Class compartment and, before the McAllisters even had a chance to show their tickets on the usually over-crowded sleeper night train, William looked at his parents and admitted that he was hopelessly in love with Isabella Reinhardt and would only return to New York if she would be his wife. Otherwise, he would re-enlist and stay in Vienna. End of conversation.

Kathryn and Don were too stunned to answer, but Bill was prepared. "Congratulations, William. For the first time in your life you made an excellent choice."

"Thank you, Uncle Bill and I won't make the mistake of listening to anyone but myself," he added very sternly, not leaving any doubt where his parents stood.

"You got the wrong impression if you think we don't love that fine young lady," his father challenged. "But frankly I think she is too good for a man like you."

"Well, thanks a lot. However, I am very glad you approve of her."

"To me," Kathryn added solemnly. "she is like a beautiful rosebud, happy and blooming in her own garden, or shall I say environment. If you cut her off the branch or bush, she will wilt in no time."

"Well, you didn't when arriving from Scotland," William replied firmly.

"Times were quite different."

"They are here, too, or have you forgotten about the war already, Mother?"

"That's true," she conceded. "But she lives quite well. You don't have the slightest indication of whether she would even consider a man like you."

"Then I will just have to find out, won't I?"

"Good luck son," she replied in all honesty. "as I love her."

"So I noticed, Mother. It's possible that for the first time we agree on something."

"Count me in too," his father said seriously. "And don't tell me it's the first time *we* agreed on anything."

"I wouldn't, and you know what I am talking about."

Before the late Don Reed became the focus of a lengthy debate again, Uncle Bill, the permanent peacekeeper, suggested they all turn in to get a good night's rest to be ready for Salzburg. They went to their beds and it was almost time to get up before anyone fell asleep.

~

Isabella arrived at her temporary office again, greeted heartily by everyone, as she was considered not only beautiful but humble and smart as well. All portraits were hung, furniture put in place without any interference in how the new occupants placed them to their own comfort. So far, she interviewed about two dozen male and female applicants, but either they had Nazi pasts or, as in most cases, their accents in either Russian or English were hard to understand, let alone Russian writing.

"We may just have to keep you," Ian McCain laughed. "Are they treating you okay?"

"Very much okay." She smiled as she had acquired and also used 'okay' quite frequently.

"I wish you would eat with us," he stated frankly.

"I thought you might have many things to discuss among yourselves. After all, it is a headquarters," she replied simply.

"Our serious conversations take place during office hours. The lunch and coffee breaks are to relax."

"Well then, thank you, General. You are very kind," Miss Reinhardt said modestly.

~

The McAllisters, after their early morning arrival and taxi to the Hotel Elisabeth, needed to take a long nap. William slept even longer than his tired family. His starving parents went into the dining room for something to eat and then for a walk. Afterwards, they encountered William in his room wearing pajamas and a housecoat.

"Don't tell me you are not hungry?" his father inquired.

"No. I live on love," he jested.

"That far already!"

"Yep!"

"I think we should give the Reinhardts here a call and see what is up," his father suggested. "Maybe we should put our letters in the mailbox."

"I will call and take the letters there as promised," William replied.

"When? Today is already shot."

"All you do is try to get out of taking them to her family, especially since I told you about my feelings for Isabella."

"That is one way to see it," said Kathryn.

"Well, Mother, you know little about my determination," he tossed back at her as he left the room. He went to the lobby to use the phone as the one in his room was out of order.

Erika Reinhardt answered with a friendly hello, and William lost no time in telling her who he was and why he was calling. Elated, she gave the phone to Gaby, who seemed beside herself.

"Why not this evening? We have no plans at all and we would love to talk about our family."

William returned his room and informed his family. "It was as I expected it to be. I see them tonight at my convenience. So there!" he said self-assuredly.

"Will you have to take a taxi?"

"No. I love to walk through the park."

"You know where they live?"

"I was stationed here for four months and if you people would have bothered to look at the return address on my letters you would know it too."

~

He arrived at the arranged time and Gaby and Erika greeted him fondly. Taking a fast glance at those two smiling and excited women, he felt Gaby was positively the better looking one, with Erika being more lively and outgoing. To him, Gaby was Isabella only as a blonde with blue eyes, otherwise they had the same features and smile. But he was astonished how, having a daughter aged twenty-two, she could look not much over thirty.

He noticed children playing and running, along with Irish setters, a pony behind a carriage, and a few elderly people watching him from a distance. Once more, he entered a beautiful entrance hall, with hand-carved and painted furniture befitting the spacious 'Villa Karl'. Of course, the servants brought wine and fruit juice. They would read the letters later, but had a thousand questions. Would he mind staying for a while, or better yet come again?

He told them his circumstances, their arrival and departure, but made up his mind that his parents and uncle could do very well without him for a day or two.

"I'll be happy to come anytime."

The next day was Sunday and he just had to tell them about his experience of last Sunday with the Russians in the castle.

Their own Sunday was always spent in Ischl because the chalet was in the hills and Erika's, along with their friends' children had a better time there and schools were re-opening the following Monday. Why did his family cut their trip so short? Scotland was the reason. The Reinhardts understood as they had not seen their homeland for years. William related to his family the invitation, and being curious and having nothing better planned for Thursday, they agreed to a little 'Kaffeeklatsch'. That much German all the McAllisters knew from their years back in Austria. Once more, the handshaking began, not only with Reinhardts' relatives, but all other refugees who refused to return until the following spring. Erika and her two children were the exception, departing the following month. And Gaby would wait until her husband came back. Somehow, William was glad that his mother had ample opportunity to hear that there was not one family who had not lost anyone, aside from many houses either bombed or occupied by one of the four liberators.

~

Once again, they had no choice but to take a flight to London over the many bombed towns of Germany, which appeared like heaps of rubble, without a word of sympathy from Kathryn or Don. Only Uncle Bill remarked that he wondered how many cities Don Reed helped to flatten.

Kathryn replied only that her son did his duty like millions of others and Don added that the Nazis asked for it by being blind, deaf, arrogant, and merciless. "Just remember the Cathedral of St. Stephan in Vienna."

They saw London from the air and, of course, had tears of compassion. They changed to a smaller plane for Edinburgh. It was the same all over again, tired, sleepy, and hungry. Only the Scotsmen with their bagpipes greeting every plane in their customary kilts gave the McAllisters the lift they desperately needed.

After a few days, William returned to Salzburg as he had promised Gaby Reinhardt. There were many letters waiting for William to take back, and he was happy to oblige since he wanted to talk to Gaby alone. They met in the health spa of Ischl at the famous Café Zauner, also one of his family's 'must visits' before the war. No fine pastry on display, but with dollars, those assortments of delicious pieces arrived like magic.

"I am in possession of dollars too," Gaby smiled after William gave his order.

"Glad to hear it," he smiled and paid.

His mother told him to take a look at her diamond, as she had never seen anything like it. Last time he had other things on his mind, like the large family and the cozy surroundings. Even his father and uncle were chastised for overlooking this huge ring.

It didn't take William long to come right to the reason for their meeting, which had to take place away from her large family and friends. But it also didn't take Gaby Reinhardt very long to figure out why. Somehow, she even expected it. In many ways, he reminded her of Paul. Aside from being tall, he had a strong build which left no doubt he was also a sportsman. And while he was blond-haired and blue-eyed like herself, he had in every other way the same striking handsome features of Paul's face. Even the deep commanding voice, and the way he lit and held his pipe awakened her memories. He also came from an old and proud cultured family and Gaby couldn't help but overhear Kathryn's explanation of how much emphasis she put on manners, education, and breeding. Just like a Reinhardt! For her daughter, she couldn't think of a better choice.

The moment he started to tell her that the very day he saw Isabella sleeping in the pantry he fell in love with her right then and there, loving her everyday more if such a thing was possible, she pursed her lips, took his hand across the small table and started with her own story about her Paul. After a long stroll on the esplanade of the River Traun, and across from the famous composer, Franc Lehar's, house, they found a bench to sit on and conclude their conversation.

"So, you see Major McAllister, if you wanted anyone to understand about 'love at first sight', you have just spoken to an expert."

"Now all I need is to get the lady in question, which will take quite some effort. However, I will never give up."

Would she be willing to leave her family? Again the option of re-enlistment was brought up. And religion? He was a devout Protestant and she possibly a devout Catholic.

"I would have changed my religion to Jewish if it was my husband who asked me," she smiled calmly. "Since there is only one God and you are an Episcopalian which, as I recall, is the Church of England, well, who am I to say anything? After all, you are going to marry my daughter, not me."

"Good Lord… if she only will have me."

"I hope so. You will have to ask her for a date. That should tell you more."

"I thank you with all my heart, Mrs. Reinhardt. If Isabella says yes, we will marry in Salzburg. I am so happy she has dual citizenship. With Switzerland we never were at war," he said excitedly, and both parted as good friends already.

Gaby didn't find it necessary to tell her family about William's proposal until she heard it officially from Isabella. She could already hear Victoria's opposition, although she liked him and the McAllisters. She would be very upset about the persistence and haste, comparing it to her own husband. However, neither Isabella nor she herself would have stayed married to a man like Philip.

Paul's last letter, which was always addressed from some Russian engineer to General Boris Gromov to guarantee speedy delivery, much less not tossed in the garbage right in their Post Office, which happened whenever a very abused or former POW sorted the letters, had given her not much hope, as he said that it might take until 1947, but he was very well treated, as always, and there was nothing to worry about.

~

The sleeper train became rather a joke now, as William was once more unable to sleep. So he decided to sort the last two weeks out. Since the arrival of his parents, it had been nothing short of a whirlwind that stopped just a few hours ago. Now he started to wonder if Sheila Brown got a hold of Isabella and told her about their bedroom affairs. He wouldn't put it past her, but she knew he never loved her to begin with. But how will he be judged by Isabella? Maybe she would even refuse a date with him.

It was barely seven in the morning when he arrived. Vienna looked gloomy with a gray sky and possible rain on the way. Since it was Saturday, he expected his roommates to still be asleep as it was an 'off duty' day. However, Ian McCain was a different story. He woke up with the roosters. But then again, according to his own calculation, his wife Betty might be here today. William decided to go to sleep, as he was awfully tired.

When he awoke, several of his comrades had returned from their day's work. It was three in the afternoon and he was told that at the new Colonel Gardener's insistence, Saturday was like any other working day until the office was in ship-shape.

"It's only until Ian McCain is back and he wants to impress him," said one of his roommates. The other news was that Sheila Brown was dating a divorced Lieutenant Colonel she had known in Italy.

"Good for her!" William smiled, feeling quite good about it. "Is there still someone in the office?"

"Sure. Only we got finished early with our assignment."

"Well then, I shall go in and take a look." He also wondered if he was still the General's aide.

He was surprised at his warm welcome from Phil Feingold. Never mind those two Italian spaghetti clowns. They were overjoyed, claiming it was just not the same without the whole clique being together. William was somehow glad to belong to a clique. Now he was ready for Lindenfels.

~

A servant greeted him and Peter, nearby, recognized William's voice at once. "How nice of you to pay us a visit," he said, and showed him the way to his study. "All the Russians are in the castle and seem to be quite happy."

"One would hope so," William smirked rather cynically.

"Isabella is sleeping," Peter said after noticing the stack of letters with hers on the top. "Good God, my family made a mail carrier out of you!"

"I offered, Doctor," he smiled. "May I ask if Miss Reinhardt is still working in the office?"

"Oh, yes. So far, she, or let's say the Americans, had not much luck. If once in a while someone appears qualified, then they belonged at one time or another to the Nazi party and General McCain won't stand for it."

William looked relieved. "Quite different from General Patton who rides horseback and fences with them. And he is forgiven for it because he considers the Germans excellent soldiers. To him, that means everything." Peter only nodded.

William talked about his family in Salzburg and how much he enjoyed the time with them. Also, his wife, Erika, and the children could not wait to be a whole family again.

"I plan to get my wife and children in about two to three weeks."

"Wonderful! I have to tell you in all honesty, you have a very loving and out-of-the-ordinary family." Now that he had all the family in Salzburg behind him, he may just as well ask if he could take Isabella to a play, concert, or any other event that would please her.

"She is old enough, for one thing, and I doubt if she would listen to any of my objections, providing there were any."

"Well that's what her mother told me. I might just go a step further and tell you all of it," he stammered.

"I am listening, Major."

"I asked for her hand in marriage and Mrs. Reinhardt smiled, telling me about her and her husband, which was also a 'love at first sight' love story."

"There is no one in town who doesn't know about it, as it involved two feuding families."

"So she told me."

"Well, if your intentions are this serious, who am I to object?"

"Dead serious, Doctor Reinhardt, and I have thought about it day and night since the first time I saw her. But I feel I am asking too much to ask her to let go of her family. Her horse, Lillian, of course would be on the ship with us."

"Now you are talking. You can come for a visit on a yearly basis. It's peacetime, so no one has to worry about being shot at. Like I said, it's up to both of you.

William thanked him by shaking both hands wordlessly. He was too moved to talk.

~

Entering his house, which was referred to as 'quarters', an officer said, "So good to see you. The General asked that you get in touch with him immediately. He is at home." William was jubilant. Now he could talk with the General about his private affair. His wife Betty greeted him, with Ian McCain standing behind her grinning happily.

"Good God," William thought instantly. *"The photo Ian McCain carries around in his wallet must be twenty years old. Maybe to him she hasn't changed."*

"I met your wonderful parents in New York and we had the best time," she said fondly in her soft voice and southern accent.

"I hear about you daily, Mrs. McCain," William replied truthfully and could see why the General was crazy about his 'Honey'.

"Listen, William, we have a lot to discuss as many things have changed. But before I get into any details, I invite you to join a few of us for a musical evening in Vienna. We took the liberty and got an extra ticket, knowing how much you like Strauss, Lehar, and Lanner."

"That's great, General. I had no other plans and frankly, I need something like that. I have seen it advertised but just having arrived I didn't know what plans anyone had."

"It starts at eight and my wife and I plan to take you to Kreindl's pastry shop'."

"No way! I'll take both of you to the Hotel Imperial and that's an order!" an elated William jested, as always, when both were alone. Both agreed happily, as his 'Honey' had never seen the Hotel Imperial.

～

With make-up and a beautiful dress, she was an entirely different Betty, McAllister thought, thinking of Isabella who looked beautiful no matter what she wore. She was in awe of the beautiful entrance hall and William told them about his parents taking the Reinhardts for dinner. However, having been raised to never be a name dropper, he never mentioned that he knew the owners.

"I hear your parents used to come here before the war," and dozens of other questions had to be answered until they finally departed. They were now at the *Volkstheater,* which William referred to in English as the 'People's Theater', one of the largest and undamaged ones in Vienna. Again, she liked it and William had little choice but to compare the General's marriage to his parents. What 'his Honey' liked, he loved and glowed about happily, just as his father did with Kathryn.

William encountered Captains Torelli and Respini standing next to Phil Feingold. Things had changed. The General, now with his new Colonels, with whom he had little in common, and the three laughing Captains were now separated. Playing it safe, he joined the three laughing buddies ... or his clique, as they called it. They talked about his trip to Salzburg, sharing many memories in different places, bars, and Sheila's new love when Joel muttered awestruck, "Don't turn around too obviously, William, but look who is walking up the stairs with her entourage of doctors."

It was Isabella, Peter, Andreas, and Theresa, who got four tickets from the Russians, who had decided not to attend. However, the Reinhardts and von Waldens were overjoyed at the opportunity. But no one was more delighted than the Major, who had just seen Peter. There came the happy family with their arms linked together and William only heard Betty McCain exclaim, "Aren't those the people we met yesterday at your office?"

"Two of them are," Ian McCain replied, equally surprised, and the introductions started all over again as Dr. Andreas von Walden and his wife, Theresa, were introduced. The two Colonels knew Isabella, of course, and tried to smile amicably.

Betty couldn't help but admire her royal blue velvet suit with an off-white lace blouse and a perfectly matching headband with a tiny veil covering her forehead. Her pumps and handbag were black patent leather, giving her the appearance of a model ready to show a new design.

"You look stunning, Miss Reinhardt," Betty McCain complimented sincerely. "We have to get together as I need help with my wardrobe. You know I plan to stay for at least a year and visit every place possible." Isabella was pleased at her offer and told her she felt honored.

"No German General's wife would be that kind to a former enemy," Isabella thought when she encountered William's stare.

Oh, Major McAllister. Thank you so much for bringing the letters to my uncle. I am so sorry I was sleeping, but I had a change from the night shift."

"Well, until two hours ago we had no idea we would be here," Peter interrupted. "Gromov sent a messenger and asked us if we could use the tickets."

"Major McAllister," Isabella said as formally as possible. "I am so sorry I missed you this afternoon. I would like to ask you a few questions about my family too. Uncle Peter, of course, was mostly interested about his wife and children, which is only natural," she emphasized strongly. "but I'd like to hear about my mother, little brothers, and the grandmothers of course."

It sounded almost like a plea. "Gladly, Miss Reinhardt, anytime at your convenience." There was this jolt in his back again each time he saw her.

"Well, we'll talk about it Monday in the office and set a date," she replied nonchalantly.

"My God," he thought. *"Since I first laid eyes on her I have worried about a date, and now she asks me for one. How lucky can a man get?"* Peter, doubtlessly reading his thoughts, looked at him and tried to suppress a smile.

The fast thinker he was known for came through in him and he asked without any hesitation, "Miss Reinhardt, the café houses are open Sundays too. Let's say about four at Sachers?"

Now Isabella was taken aback and responded almost without knowing why. "Alright, Major. Four is fine with me too."

Peter could only imagine what went through William's mind, but he had to say a word too before the bells rung in the theater and the door opened to their loges. "Major, how about a small evening meal afterwards. Let's say I'd like to show my gratitude."

"That's not necessary, Doctor. Like I told you, I was more than happy to do it."

"At seven," he ordered. "Make sure, Isabella, that he comes."

"Oh, I will," she stammered, knowing he was doing her a favor. After all, she had confided to Peter, who saw an opportunity to get to know him better.

When the doors opened, she linked her arm in Peter's, who got a wink from William. It was a very special wink with a gleam. The loges were far apart and on the same side, so William couldn't look at her. The concert received many standing ovations, and although he enjoyed the evening the same as the other theater attendees, his own thoughts were with Isabella, who looked breathtakingly beautiful. During the intermission he hardly had a chance to get a glance at her, as the Reinhardts and von Waldens were encircled by their friends. But there was tomorrow. And he would make the best of this God-given opportunity.

33

Peter and Isabella had to skip church as an emergency came up and both were needed. Some Russians were in a big fight with each other and, as always, arrived in the emergency room dead drunk. They fought with wine bottles after Gromov and Niemev went to bed and, being used to those events, they did not stop it. Besides, it would not have done any good at all. A drunken Russian knows no rank.

Isabella was told to get ready by two in the afternoon and instruct the servants what to put on the table by seven. "Thanks a million," she said, and departed to get ready. Uncle Andreas offered a ride before he started his own shift.

"Isabella, we all like this American fellow. Even Theresa said what a fine family the McAllisters were. If I were in your shoes, I'd hold on. His gentle, loving looks at you can only come from a man who is sincerely in love."

"It just so happens that I am in love too."

"That is good to hear," he said, stopping in front of Café Sacher.

"Be calm, dear niece," he advised before he drove off.

William McAllister, hungry as he had not had lunch, was in the process of eating when Isabella arrived. He got up and both shook hands.

"What may I order? I have tickets and dollars."

"Coffee, and only if they have real American coffee."

"They do, but just in case, I always carry my own."

He noticed that even in a plain gray dress with white collar and a reddish coral necklace, she looked 'like a million'.

"So what would you like to hear, Miss Reinhardt?" he said anxiously.

"Hmm... well, let's start with when you first met my mother, brother, etc. Everything, Major."

"Then we may have to meet again tomorrow," he laughed. "as I saw them more than my own parents."

"You are joking, of course."

"No, but they have seen them too." he replied.

Both talked endlessly about everything possible until it was time to leave for Peter's place, where dinner was awaiting them. William was still awestruck, not only about her appearance, but honesty and openness on any subject as well. Also, that she felt better about staying in Vienna, and taking care of the many wounded than worrying about her own safety by going to Salzburg.

"But Father insisted in no uncertain terms that the rest of the family had to leave, no matter how much he missed them."

He noticed in all their conversations that her father could never be wrong about anything. William found the courage to ask her for another date the following day.

"I thought we covered everything," she replied teasingly.

"We haven't even begun, Miss Reinhardt."

"Alright, you win. But when we see each other in the office, we act very regular," Isabella urged and smiled.

"We cannot talk about anything private. Besides, I have lots of work to catch up on. Also, the many new changes will keep me busy. So how about six at the Hotel Imperial?"

"All right, six it is."

Peter was happy to see both arriving joyously. "You should have been at the hospital, Isabella."

"No, she shouldn't," William protested in jest.

~

The following day, Isabella and William barely saw each other at the office except for an exchange of a happy wink. Sheila Brown never even addressed William with a 'Welcome Back', which suited him perfectly. There were meetings after meetings, each Colonel trying to be more important than the other. William couldn't have cared less what was said, as his thoughts were, as always, with Isabella. However, he was glad to hear that General Ian McCain insisted that he stayed on as his aide until his departure the following year.

As luck would have it, a man in his middle thirties was finally qualified to replace Isabella. She always wondered why someone was needed to begin with, as she herself was mostly utterly bored. She missed the fast pace in the hospital, and was glad to return. The Colonel took it on himself to interview him, with Miss Reinhardt questioning his French, English, and Russian. He and his mother fled Russia in 1917 to France after his father got shot, and he enrolled in a good school in Paris where he was taught English. His mother met and married a Swiss school teacher, who died after ten years of marriage and left little money. That's when Austria came in handy. She took a course as a seamstress, always having the talent and desire to be one. But at the present neither a seamstress nor a teacher for languages was needed. Being of noble birth, they refused to work for black marketers and took any job until they read in the paper about the Americans.

Colonel Hamilton hired him, as he had the proper papers which stated that neither he nor his mother ever belonged to the Nazi party. Isabella thought that Russian immigrants with the names of Olga and Leonid Arbatov were just as lucky to be alive as her old former teacher, Ballerina Madame Platikova. Leonid Arbatov was hired to start the following day with some translations. Isabella was surprised, as she hardly had any to do. That evening, before her departure, she shook hands with every American she had grown fond of. Of course, she would check in from time to time.

When she finally came to Major McAllister, both only smiled, knowing Captain Sheila Brown was watching them closely. *"Wrong again,"* she thought to herself. *"I could have sworn this woman with her aristocratic look and social grace might have been just what he was looking for."*

~

It was the end of October and Erika returned with her two children, Hannes and Gretl. Peter was ecstatic to have a family again. They had no trouble entering the Russian zone, as hardly anyone did. Only the Americans asked the reason for leaving. William and Isabella dated every day, with the exception of Erika's arrival one evening. That's when he went to Ian McCain's and told them of his plans, and also that he was looking for his own little place. They couldn't have been nicer and happier about it. "Congratulations on your perfect choice," Betty said sincerely. "but when are you going to tell her?"

"At the first chance presenting itself."

"Good," Ian McCain laughed. "William, now that I am back at the office, there is rarely a guy who doesn't still talk about her, and Brad told me that many would give their right arm to have a lady like her."

"I always knew that and at times had nightmares about it. But when she told me that she dated most guys only three to four times… and she didn't have to tell me why either … I feel I have a good chance, as so far we are still only holding hands."

"After more than two weeks? That's something, William! Betty and I were married a month after we met."

"And I would have married my 'Honey Ian' the first day," Betty exclaimed joyfully. William understood after several visits why Ian McCain loved and needed a wife life Betty.

"General, will you help me with the necessary paperwork? She has a dual citizenship from Switzerland and was born there of a Swiss father."

"There won't be any problems. We still go by the place of birth."

"Great!"

"Why aren't you with her today, if I may be so frank?" asked Betty, very curious.

"Her aunt and niece and nephew arrived this evening from Salzburg. So I took this opportunity to drop in. I hope you don't mind," William apologized.

"Now, we know each other well and long enough. Once you are married, Betty and I will do the same."

"I hope so, General."

"I wonder if they'll get married in Vienna or Salzburg?" Betty questioned her husband.

"We will be there no matter where," he replied, very self-assured.

~

Although they had only been apart for one evening, Isabella and William had missed each other terribly and William lost no time in telling her about it. "I went to the McCain's," he said.

They decided to sit on a bench overlooking the city. So far, they had seen either a movie, plays, operas, or musicals. There was never a boring evening. She didn't know why, but she started to talk about Erika's happy marriage, and her father's strong opposition, including Uncle Peter's arrest in retaliation. William was stunned. That led to Rupert Foster. She gave a full truthful account including his early involvement with the SS, and a 'no way out' situation of leaving that outfit unless one likes to be hung or shot.

"Do the Russians know?" William asked immediately.

"Absolutely. Uncle Peter lost not a moment of time to tell them about it. You must understand, at that time there were many underground Communists waiting for us so-called Nazis."

"And how did a man like General Gromov react?"

"Uncle Peter opened our secret floor panels and when he saw his own countrymen appearing with a smile on their faces kissing my uncle's hand, some crying and embracing him, Gromov only smiled and said, "You must have had good connections in order to pull that one off." William smiled, saddened, knowing what it meant to hide an enemy under 'Hitler's time'. "That's when my Uncle told him everything about Rupert Foster the SS man, his wife Gisela and their children. They were transferred to Berlin and died during an air raid. His poor devastated parents killed themselves shortly before the Russians entered their house."

"SS or no SS, if it's any consolation to you, I would still be dating you even if you were Himmler's daughter," William replied seriously, taking her face in both hands and kissing her forehead. "You have no idea how much I love you."

"Thank you," she answered.

"Now here is my opportunity," he thought quickly and sighed deeply. "Well, Miss Reinhardt, by now we seem to know each other's family history, but on the other hand, we seem to get nowhere," he emphasized, still looking at her.

She removed herself instinctively and obviously from his position. "Where would you like to go? Or should I rephrase the question with how *far*?"

He started to relax and smile, being elated at her reaction. He finally found a virgin! He thought and replied, "To our Officer's club as to your question of where, and it's very near your mansion as to how far. Walking distance, I would say. We tried to get the Kinsky palace, but the English beat us to it."

She appeared now so embarrassed that he could hear her heart beat. "Oh, well if that's what you meant," she stammered. "I don't see why we cannot go. We have even been in your American movie house strictly reserved for soldiers. Are there or are there not Austrian guests allowed? Because in Kinsky's palace they are not."

"If I couldn't take you with me why do you think I brought it up?"

"Then what is your problem Major McAllister? Just a few minutes ago I was moved to tears because you would have dated me as the Henchman's daughter and now?"

He didn't let her finish the sentence, noticing how upset she was, which was a first for him since he had known her. "You got it all wrong, Miss Reinhardt. I am trying to tell you that I don't like to introduce you as my 'girlfriend'. Ever since we have gone out together it's on every occasion, 'my friend the Major'. I appreciate friendship enormously, but it got to me lately, especially when it concerns you.

"Then what do you suggest?" she asked seriously.

"I'd like to introduce you as my fiancée," he said proudly, looking straight in her eyes.

"Excuse me, Major. I don't know about your country's customs or rules, but in Austria it means that one is sooner or later getting married," she replied with a serious look in return.

"Now you excuse me, Miss Reinhardt, but that is what it means in my country too."

She looked more confused than ever, doubtlessly searching for the perfect words to save her from another embarrassment in assuming wrongly. "Are you... I mean... are you..." she stammered, almost in a trance. "Are you trying to tell me... that you ask me to marry you?" she finally finished the sentence, shaking.

"No, Miss Reinhardt. It means that I am *begging* you to be my wife as soon as possible. And believe you me, I never begged for anything in my life before."

She never doubted that, but what to answer a man like him was the question racing through her mind. She could have screamed "Yes!" for the whole world to hear. However, with a handsome and rich man who doubtlessly bedded dozens of beautiful women, one had to be very careful. "When did you reach that decision? It's so serious for me and comes so unexpectedly," she asked.

"When? The very moment I found you sleeping in your mansion's pantry."

"And our Fanny let you see me? She will have a lot of explaining to do," she sighed, astonished.

"No, I have. Aside from an apology which is long overdue."

"You lost me completely. As a matter of fact, I have been lost ever since we sat down."

He related the story between Fanny and him, asserting in detail the challenge after he referred to her Baroness as 'an old relic'. "You should have seen the look on her face when she finally opened the door. Then she asked very slyly while watching me closely, 'Are you now satisfied, Major?' I could have died in shame and she knew it. I only replied, "Very" and Joel and I left. But somehow, we liked each other because she baked me an Apfelstrudel and winked at me. Maybe she felt... never mind. I talk too much."

"And how did you feel about the 'old relic' when you saw her?"

"Madly in love." He turned very serious and took her arms to bring them around his neck. She made no move of any objection.

"Isabella, I swear to you I will do my utmost to make you as happy as possible. And by the way, Lillian will be with us."

"She will?" she replied, elated and stunned. "I also found a cute little villa until we go back. And if for some reason you object, I can re-enlist for four more years. I also talked to your mother in Salzburg about my plans."

"You did?"

"She gave us her blessing, knowing love conquers all." Isabella was again in awe. "Uncle Peter knows about it too."

"I am not surprised at anything," she smiled. "Only that I was the last to know."

"Well, I wanted to be proper," he smiled sheepishly.

"The way it looks right now, William, I have little choice but to say yes, which I will with one condition."

"Name it," he said overjoyed.

"I am not like my step-grandmother, Victoria, of whom I told you about her marriage to Philip, the philanderer. William Grant McAllister," she emphasized extremely sternly. "One … and I mean one affair and I am gone. I will not live in that humiliation. I can accept a divorce, no matter how hurtful it would be, but a so-called 'little fling', no matter how hard you try to justify it, will never do."

He held her tightly and only replied solemnly, "You just spoke for both of us. I, too, could never forgive you." He took a big oval-shaped diamond from a small velvet bag, and took her hand. "Please accept this engagement ring. Just never ask me how I got it, or where or from whom, Isabella. And if you'd like to know about its quality or anything else, just ask Phil Feingold. He knows all about the four Cs."

She took a look at the beautiful marquise-cut ring and started to cry while trembling for joy. "Will you please pinch me so I know I am alive?" she pleaded.

"Why not seal it with a kiss, Isabella? I think we are long overdue."

"I think so too," she muttered, wetting his cheeks with her tears as he kissed her ever so gently. It felt incomparably better than sharing a bedroom with any of his former flames, having casual sex without ever being in love. *"How could I have ever stooped so low,"* he thought, while still holding her very tight with her not wanting to let go either.

~

Peter and Erika were relaxing in front of the fire with their usual glass of wine. They expected William to propose tonight and were not surprised when Isabella entered the room with a huge grin.

"Look!" she shouted. "I am engaged, and William wants to set a date to get married! He said the sooner the better!"

They admired her ring and her choice of husband. "You know, this fine man asked me upon his return from Salzburg if I minded if he took you some places. But I knew from the very beginning he was in love with you," Peter acknowledged.

"I have to admit, everyone thought the world of him and his family. Consider yourself lucky as usually one doesn't like the other," Erika said, holding Isabella's hand and turning it. "That is quite some diamond!"

"I think so too. But I had to promise him never to question him where and how he got it. Between us, that wheeler-dealer Phil Feingold probably got it somehow. But since the black market is punishable in a military court, neither I or any of you can ever let on."

"As far as we are concerned, he got it from America," Peter answered.

"God, what will his parents say?"

"William told me that his father thought you were too good for him and his mother compared you to a blooming rosebud, who would wilt from being homesick. I told him there are ships and planes to visit us.

"The main thing is you love each other," Erika voiced. "Look what Peter and I went through … and we are still together."

"And in love," Peter replied quickly.

"It all came so fast to me, though he told me he planned it from the day he first saw me."

"Isabella, we are all taking a week of well-deserved vacation. Andreas will take over for that time."

"Me too?"

"I said all of us, which means you too."

"Thanks a lot Uncle Peter. It gives me the needed time to think about our future."

"Don't change your mind," Erika and Peter laughed.

"Why would I do such a foolish thing?" she replied, amused. "I know a good man when I see one, and he is the first."

34

Kathryn McAllister was in bed with a severe migraine. Even pain pills and an assortment of tranquilizers had no effect. She was in a state of depression, her husband told his brother Bill, who only shrugged it off. "What else is new? She will get over it." As they stayed during the week in New York in their own brownstone house between Madison and Park Avenue, they hoped by their return Friday evening it would have somewhat subsided. The reason for all the excitement was William's telegram stating not only his engagement to Isabella, but a forthcoming marriage in the very near future.

"Without his parents," she sobbed uncontrollably. "Don Reed, God bless his soul, would have never done that to his family."

"You can say that again," her daughter Barbara fumed. She was supposed to calm her distraught mother, but poured gasoline on the burning fire. Having never met William's chosen one, but hearing a few words about her, mostly via Uncle Bill, she hated her already. "It messes our family tree up. Just take a look at it, Mother," she insisted, propping a third pillow under her head. "Our ancestors would turn in their graves with a name like Reinhardt. How much more German can a name sound?"

"Austrian, Barbara."

"They are all Krauts, if you ask me. I read they were not an iota better than any other German. They just try to wiggle themselves out of it, that's all." Kathryn had to agree, but explained the Reinhardts' situation.

"So what if they hid some prisoners? There were no Americans among them. Just think about it."

"Barbara, they never cared for nationality. Anyone who needed help got it."

She didn't have a good retort but brought her mother something to drink. "Mother, I have given up alcohol completely."

"I am so proud of you, dear. I wish I could."

"Mother, I have a great idea. We won't tell anyone about it. Maybe they will break up. You know William. He has had women by the dozen, and I mean *had* them, if you know what I mean."

"I do, Barbara, but somehow I always blamed those easy and willing girls."

"Don't forget, William is a hell of a good-looking guy, if I do say so myself. And with our money on top of it … they all had their hopes up," Barbara snarled again.

"That is so very sad. In my time, it was quite different. If I had had a lover prior to my marriage, your father would have had it annulled or divorced me. One waited for the wedding night."

"So did I, Mother," Barbara lied, but Kathryn never doubted her daughter for a moment. But since the return of her husband from the war, Steve McBride was a changed man.

She blamed the French girls for it, as he was stationed in Paris after the city's liberation. Now her once decent husband wanted all kinds of kinky sex, and she gave him an unmistakable 'no' to his perverted advances, as she confided to her friend Beverly. Her parents were, of course, kept in the dark, as she took it as a passing fancy, still holding the war and France responsible for it.

"Some of those tramps even date colored soldiers, I was told by Beverly. But to me, all of those European women are on the low side. Even being rich doesn't mean one thing."

"I never heard of a colored man dating a white woman, but being rich doesn't mean much in our country either. If it did, how come William had so many women? I am sure he never went on the wrong side of the tracks."

Barbara had to agree, and as always, went to another subject, this one concerning their family album. "Look, Mother. Every name starts with a 'Mc' with the exception of Huntington, Lanceworth, and Wingfields - all fine Englishmen."

"Well, some may have had mistresses. It was quite fashionable when one was rich," Kathryn replied harshly.

"Well, it's October now and until May lots of changes may occur."

"Possibly, Barbara, but I have seen the young lady. Dear Lord, if she were only English."

~

Over the weekend, with Don and Uncle Bill arriving, Barbara was still there and both men wondered why. "Don't neglect Steve. He is your husband and should always come first," her father admonished firmly.

"Right now, Mother needs me more and Steve said he understands."

"Now that we are here, why don't you come back Monday? That is, if she still needs you," Uncle Bill added.

"If you say so. And there is another thing, Uncle Bill. Get William out of your will. That woman may be a gold digger, divorce him and take the money with her."

He was so furious at her statement that he decided right then and there to write a new will and leave *her* out of it. "The way I see it, Barbara, they have a hell of a lot more than we do, and that includes their character," Bill fumed while pouring himself some scotch.

After she left to go home to Steve, who was nowhere to be found, Kathryn lamented about the cheap ring 'the Baroness' may have gotten from William. "Don, I'll bet you anything he got it through the black market. He probably took that Jewish fellow from Stuttgart with him. He is a jeweler, you know."

"Most Jews are, and quite good at it too."

"You don't understand, Don. A ring for this lady has to come from Tiffany in a little blue box or it won't be right," she urged grandly. "All of our jewelry is bought there. You and Bill should know that much by now."

Don only shook his head and joined his brother for a drink. When he told him about his wife's great worry about a diamond which had to come from Tiffany in a blue box, Bill smiled and said, "Come with me, brother."

Kathryn was still turning the pages of her socially correct family album. "Don said you were worried about the proper ring for William's fiancée."

"That's only one of the things."

"Let me tell you, Kathryn, right after he took us to the airport, he returned to Salzburg and asked her mother for her hand in marriage."

"But he barely knew her."

"You surely remember when he told us of his intentions."

"Frankly, Bill, I did not take him seriously," she admitted.

"You should have because William never told us anything like it previously. Isn't that right Kathryn? Or I would have heard about it too."

"Well… the way things stood in our household, you may have been the first one he talked to about it."

"And he did," he replied proud and promptly.

"So what about the ring? Or are you just assuming, Bill?"

"I never assume anything, but her mother dealt with one of the best jewelers in Salzburg and he got Isabella Reinhardt … are you ready?" he stalled to keep her for a moment in suspense.

"Ready as I will ever be. Come on, Bill."

"He got her a twenty-six carat diamond. How about it Kathryn? You think he could have done better at Tiffany's? I received a letter from William via an officer who flew to New York and mailed it to me," he replied smugly.

"And we two were kept in the dark," she pouted like a child.

"You two got a telegram. I didn't."

"So how could he have possibly paid for that kind of ring?"

"I gave him several thousand dollars, sort of a pre-inheritance. After all, it's now when he needed it," Bill said very modestly. "We talked frequently in the hotel while you both were napping," he grinned. "And I always preferred William to your Don Reed. I liked the one, but loved the other and never took to Barbara. Now you can tell me to move out of your premises," he said nonchalantly and walked away.

There was a long silence until Kathryn said, "I am getting out of bed and fixing myself a drink."

"Make that two, Kathryn. No, three. I'll call Bill back and we'll have a toast to William and his wife to be."

"Barbara and I decided not to talk to anyone about it until he returns with her."

"Great idea."

35

Captain Sheila Brown took the day off work and her new date felt something was very wrong.

"You had an affair with him," he confronted her firmly a few hours later.

"So what?"

"It's alright, but are you still in love with him?"

"No, just mad because he dumped me for someone with money."

"That's all I wanted to know, Sheila. Now let's set our own wedding date."

"You mean it?"

"Would I ask you otherwise?"

"I hope not, Allen. We both were married before and know what's it all about."

"Sheila, you make me feel like a man again. You are the best piece I ever had."

She turned red and showed him the door. "Get out, you filthy bastard. You are just like the rest of them. Once you have a woman in the sack, somehow she loses her value."

"What else is there?" he smirked, and left without a good-bye.

Sheila went to the Officer's Club, spread the news about McAllister's nuptials to a few colleagues she had known previously in Italy, and kept on drinking until someone walked her home, put her to bed and left. The next day, she called the General for a transfer.

"Take a few days off, Captain Brown," he advised kindly. "until I get something for you." A week later, she went to Wels-Upper Austria.

~

After a short ceremony in Vienna's civil court, Isabella Reinhardt, formerly Rosatti, became Mrs. William Grant McAllister. Two witnesses were required by law and Dr. Andreas von Walden and his wife, Theresa, were unanimously chosen. Peter would represent his brother in Salzburg and give the bride away.

Although William suspected Isabella to be a virgin, somehow he was overjoyed that she was. Her engagement to that very handsome pilot, Nico Wiland, made him at times think about it. Usually, before a departure for a long tour during the war, a woman would give in. He had, of course, his own experience in mind. But not Isabella. The wedding night for him was the closest thing to heaven, but he was afraid to ask her about it. He assured her that as time went on, she would feel better about it. She only smiled. "I know that much, William," she said like a pro, but he knew she had only heard or read about it.

The honeymoon week went by fast. They invited Peter and Erika to see Puccini's, *La Boheme*, and Andreas and Theresa to see Verdi's *Aida*, and went for long walks in the Viennese woods with exceptional fall weather. They also went to dinner at the McCains', with 'Honey' doing her own cooking, so the new Mrs. McAllister would know what 'Southern Style' was all about. They loved the whole menu.

Both women cleaned the table, washed the dishes, and chatted non-stop about Isabella's new country. "God knows when Ian will retire, but I am ready to stay in one place. We always rented or were given places to live, but could never call anything our own."

Alone with the General, William admitted his short affair with Sheila, saying that she had wanted to get serious too fast. "I never even once told her I loved her. I would be glad to repeat it in front of her."

"That will be impossible. I got her transferred in a hurry to Wels–Upper Austria."

"Good," he said with a sigh of relief. On the way home he told Isabella about Sheila.

"I figured that one out the first time I saw you together. She was always trying to be so near you that in my mind, I compared her to the leaning tower of Pisa," she laughed, but was somehow glad she was gone. Former lovers were not to her taste, though she knew he had had many affairs before. She was looking forward to being with him in America, as Vienna had changed drastically for the worse.

"Are you sure about it, Isabella?" he asked after their arrival home.

"I took your name and will take your country and religion the same way. It's all so simple, William, because I love you very much."

"Not as much as I love you," he said quickly in response.

"As long as you think so."

"Not because I think so, but I know so," he replied convincingly.

～

General Ian McCain was extremely upset, as he got word that a Major General and his staff were on a fact-finding mission and would arrive the day before the wedding on November 6th. Of course, William and Isabella would have to be there a few days before for the blood test, and whatever else the Americans required. But Ian was afraid the mission would be a drawn-out affair and the wedding in Salzburg would take place without him and Betty.

"We'll give a big party here after their return," Betty soothed, but she knew it would not satisfy Ian.

"The Reinhardts will go out of their way to make it an event, as she is the former Baroness von Walden's only daughter. And besides, you've never seen Salzburg."

"We will be there during spring and summer, darling. November is always a dreary time."

"Not for the newlyweds," he replied, displeased, but there was nothing he could do about it. Duty was duty, that's all. Betty, however, planned an elaborate party, Southern style, for all her husband's staff.

Isabella and William, with all the requirements for a civil wedding behind them, were now told by Gaby and Astrid that they decided to have the wedding ceremony at the castle Mirabell, which had one of the most grandiose staircases with red carpet, and on the upper floor a marble hall strictly reserved for weddings and small concerts. The American chaplain gladly agreed, as it would be his first wedding since the end of the war. Isabella and William were ecstatic.

"I thought if we were forced to vacate our own castle, we may just as well use someone else's. It's public property,"

Victoria stated to William, to whom she took very slowly and watched his behavior towards Isabella very closely. After all, she had married a handsome and rich man exactly fifty years ago.

Isabella was overjoyed with her mother's idea to take Verena's exquisite wedding gown out of a silk-lined trunk. She had it altered to fit Isabella, whose measurements around the bust and waistline she knew by heart. Her daughter was barely an inch smaller than Gaby herself, who was a few pounds heavier since she left Vienna. But no one would have ever noticed, only she herself. After Isabella tried it on, she decided not to wear the long veil, just the rose wreath all by itself. "I'll keep my hair long and we'll pin some little roses in my plait." All the women agreed happily. After all, she was legally married three weeks ago, and they doubtless lost no time to use the bedroom. However, her wedding gown had to be white at the insistence of all her family.

"Why did you hurry with your wedding so much? I am sure your parents would have been here by spring," Gaby questioned again, though Paul was not any different from William's insistence.

"Three reasons. First, I couldn't wait to be with her day and night. Second, someone else may have beat me to it. And third, Mrs. Reinhardt, all sensible men are selfish."

"I guess that sums it up," she smiled, giving him a kiss on each cheek. "Just take good care of her, William."

"Just like your husband did. And I know all about him."

"I am sure you do. Isabella adores that man and vice versa. And before I forget, William, when you gave me the money for the ring, I also got the matching necklace with it. We Reinhardts always like that at least one thing matches the other so here it is," she said handing him a black velvet box. William couldn't believe his eyes when he opened it. A scalloped necklace of marquise round and oval shaped diamonds with a ruby drop was in front of him.

"Mrs. Reinhardt, I know I owe you plenty. My mother lives for diamonds and I know what my father pays for them, and she doesn't have anything near this exquisite," he stammered almost in shock.

"Don't forget, one dollar is seventy schillings, William. Everyone is looking desperately for American currency to survive. Did I get a bargain? Yes. Did the jeweler make out all right too? Yes," she smiled, satisfied. "She will get more of the Reinhardts' diamonds before she leaves. They don't like to be outdone when it comes to giving."

"I can just see the stares of Mother and her friends."

"I like your family, William, and I know they like her too. Everything else is up to both of you."

The Reinhardts had the traditional white horses and carriages for friends and family, telling the bridal couple at the last minute that the wedding would not be family only, as too many of the long-time friends of Victoria and Astrid wanted to be there. Then the chaplain, who knew William since the war days, knew he had friends in Salzburg too. So as to keep a fair balance and not leave him the only American among the wedding guests, they were invited also. William, too, had no idea. Every American knew about the Mirabell castle, its famous staircase and marble room; but to be seated there among wedding guests was something else. Since it was for concerts or weddings, one had the choice of a permanent stationed organ or a movable piano.

William, only expecting Reinhardts' friends, was beside himself when he entered with the chaplain to encounter his own friends.

"You didn't think we would forget our boys," he whispered to the surprised and happy William. Both sides of the aisle were now filled, when the organist, who happened to be a WAC played the wedding march from Wagner's *Lohengrin*, making it a traditional American wedding.

Isabella, on the arm of Peter, was equally astonished about the many officers, as at the rehearsal nothing was ever mentioned. But all eyes were on the strikingly beautiful bride followed by two little flower girls, one of them being her niece Gretl, and the ring bearer none other than half-brother Robert.

Like Verena eighty years before, she caused the same sensation with the wedding dress, which still looked new, like it was sewn yesterday in Victorian style. It was a breathtaking sight, even for Salzburg and Ischl's spoiled society. But then again, they were the Reinhardts of Vienna as much as Salzburg.

The chaplain spoke briefly and was inspirational in both languages. William, although listening, had his eyes constantly on his ravishing bride. Both their hands shook just the same as at their civil ceremony in Vienna. Congratulations and photo taking followed, with everyone trying to get a word in edgewise. Many barely remembered Isabella, as she never visited Salzburg for very long unless it was with a horse trailer, which was prohibited the last few years, gasoline rationing being the reason. But all were afraid of mentioning Paul's name, as he was imprisoned in Russia.

"And you are all are invited to an American-style buffet dinner, with champagne," Peter announced with enthusiasm and was relieved that everything went so well.

"Even us?" a friend of William wanted to know.

"I said all of you. Why would I leave you brave soldiers out?" He omitted that most of the food was from William's friends to begin with.

"You have to follow the horses to our house," Gaby yelled, amused. "This time it's our animals against your jeeps." All applauded.

"By the way, William, your radiant and charming wife doesn't happen to have a sister?" his friend asked in jest, while meaning it sincerely.

"No, Bob. Women like her come only in ones," William replied, ecstatic, putting his arm around her. "When I saw her, I knew she was mine forever."

Little brother Robert, who played soldier in his backyard, even when alone, admired his newly acquired brother-in-law. And Isabella made sure that those well-behaved children were in no way overlooked. Robert pulled William's sleeve and said sincerely that he might come visit him and Isabella once his father's work is finished in Russia.

"I hope you will, Robert, as we have lots of horses too and you can ride them all."

"Will I ever get to see any Indians?"

"If you want to. I can take you to some towns where only Indians live."

"Great! Just us two men alone," he whispered, with the happiest smile of a seven-year-old who had just been told a secret.

All had a great time and by eleven, only the family was left. "We are all tired but so very happy. The chaplain's toast with his few words of wisdom will always be with William and me."

"Sorry, we didn't hear it," said Victoria, who was ready to go to her bedroom.

"Well, he said, 'Those who love deeply never grow old. They may die of old age, but they still die young.'"

"How beautiful. So far, it has worked for all my children. I hope it works for you and your husband too," she said, embracing each one of them and wishing all a good night.

～

Isabella decided to take lessons in cooking, after having selected Fanny Hirt as housekeeper until her departure. William was overjoyed.

Between her lessons, family visits, and time spent with her husband, time just flew. Also, letters arrived to her personally from Kathryn, Don and Bill. Kathryn mailed Christmas gifts hoping they would arrive in time. William sent some wedding photos which were not only welcomed, but greatly admired. Barbara was never mentioned. Neither was the fact that no one in New York knew about William's recent marriage.

But Barbara lost no time in writing to William's APO number that he might have conveniently forgotten that there are much better looking girls back home. He was furious about her jealous assessment and told her so in no uncertain terms. He was looking for high virtues, brains, and great kindness. His wife had all of those qualities, and how fortunate he was to have found her. No answer was ever received, as always when his sister felt defeated. Uncle Bill wrote at least once weekly, mentioned the good bargains in houses, as America was presently in a period of transition. Of course, it never mattered to the McAllisters, and his job was still waiting for him. They would stay in their spacious guest room until they found something suitable.

Then came the news about Barbara's rocky marriage, with her husband dating a beautiful young girl. Uncle Bill had no idea if her parents knew, as such private matters were never discussed in front of him. "Now she's turned from a well-known bitch to a witch," he remarked casually, not blaming Steve McBride at all.

By now, William felt he should inform Isabella about his family's dilemma. "Every family we know has problems," she shrugged. "When I became a Reinhardt, I read all their diaries, starting with book one. And there were plenty of problems too."

"You don't know my sister."

"Not yet, but people who feel they got a raw deal are always very bitter, taking it out on everyone who comes along. You know, William, I feel sorry for her already."

"Well don't. She always was a spoiled brat. However, one wrong look at you and I'll let her have it."

Isabella only smiled, thinking of Stephany's diary and Otto's promise. She wished William and she could be just as happy until death takes them apart.

~

Christmas was almost here, and William had a few packages in his jeep, but his face looked gloomy.

"What happened, William?" was his concerned wife's first question.

"General Patton died after his accident on December 9th. Damn! After all he did on the battle fields ... never being afraid to take any risks. There is also another thing, Isabella, which pains me to tell you."

"Which is?"

"General Patton tried to help to get Lillian to America without the quarantine in England. It's a law and Ian McCain and I felt she would never make it. Patton saved the Lippizaners before the Russians got them. He had a lot of connections in Washington and would have somehow pulled it off. Now that had to happen," he said, waiting for Isabella's reaction.

"Then we just leave her with Peter and Erika. That's all there is to it. You don't know how bad I often felt to take Lillian away from those kids when they ride her daily and pamper her like a child. Anytime it's cold, she sleeps with them."

"Where?"

"Living room. They even have their mattresses on the floor. Of course, Lillian was trained by me and so far, she has never had an accident."

"I still don't believe it," he stammered slowly.

"Remember, we let her come in the mansion so the Russians could pet her."

"Oh God, yes."

"Well, Hannes and Gretl will be happy, and so will Lillian."

"And you, Isabella? You are my main concern."

"We'll see about it in the United States."

"I can only imagine how hurt you must be," he said, saddened.

"Not more than thinking about Lillian in quarantine. I'd rather have her shot than die a slow, painful way. She would never understand. It's also still very hard to feed an animal. For England, only the bombing is over, not the shortage of food. That goes for animals too."

He embraced her strongly, feeling very relieved, with the promise that she would have a chance to pick up a foal to her liking and train it.

"William, I feel so lucky to have such a sweet husband."

~

Ian and Betty McCain gave a big Christmas party, American style, as the 25th of December was their big day. Every officer was invited and some WACs who worked for Ian McCain's office.

"They all were pretty," Isabella thought, never a hair out of place among other things she liked about them.

William showed his watch off and Isabella her pearls, as she wore a beautiful oyster-colored dress to give the pearls the perfect color for Christmas.

"So, you have your Santa Claus coming the twenty-fourth," one friend of the former Sheila Brown wanted to know.

"We really don't have a Santa Claus at all. I imagine it's an English custom adopted in America," Isabella replied.

"I guess so. We are a very generous nation. We just adopt everything and everyone," she smiled rather cynically.

"Everyone comes from somewhere, unless one is an Indian," Isabella voiced impulsively, looking at her nametag which read, 'Kokovsky'.

"You are right, Mrs. McAllister. My family is American-Polish. But I was born in Chicago, she replied proudly.

"Yea, we still call you a Polak … unless you marry me," Brad jested as usual.

"And become a spaghetti Italian? You must be crazy. We have too many of your guys in our town already."

Brad and Joel, although Majors by now, were still the same. William was convinced that even the rank of a four-star general would not change either one of them unless threatened with a court martial. Isabella was surrounded by many WACs who doubtlessly wanted to assess why the Major left Sheila for her. It didn't take them long either. She was not only beautiful and rich but everything else a McAllister was looking for in a wife. He never would need money, but all that goes with it to make it worthwhile.

~

Since Peter and Erika's children got so many gifts for Christmas, Isabella waited for New Year's Eve to tell them about Lillian. Both turned white in shock.

"I will be such a good rider with my new jacket on," Hannes shouted. They embraced her so hard and kissed her so much in joy that the nearby standing grown-ups were sincerely moved.

"See, William, it all worked out for the best. Everyone is happy and Lillian will be too." They decided to have a 'family only' New Year's party, knowing it would be their last one for a long time. They reminisced about all past parties, except the war years.

"As soon as the 'Salzburg Reinhardts' are back, and Paul of course, we will start all over again," Erika promised, and William had his eyes as always on Isabella, wondering how his wife would like the McAllisters' American parties. So far, she had adapted quite well.

1946

36

Once leaving Vienna, Ian McCain and his wife would travel with them to Salzburg. He would show his 'Hon' all the beautiful locations he had visited while being stationed there. Betty McCain and Isabella had grown very close, despite the difference in age. Both knew about grace, charm, manners, and kindness. Somehow, they also felt they would meet again after the General's retirement, possibly living close by, as Virginia and Westchester were frequently mentioned. It would be no trouble to find, through the McAllisters' many friends and acquaintances, a nice piece of land, and have a house built.

May 2, 1946, was the departure date from Calais, France, for New York, which was supposed to take six days, but the long train ride from Salzburg to Calais was an experience in itself. She was constantly nauseated, keeping the secret that she was pregnant to herself. No telling what William would have done! There was always the possibility he would have asked for an extension to stay in Vienna, but she was ready to leave.

Once they were on the boat, she started to relax. It was a beautiful French liner called *Liberty* – what better word to flee Europe. She was not the only 'war bride' that was seasick, and was rather glad about it, promenading hand in hand with William across the deck in the afternoons.

"Don't worry, Darling. Everyone I encounter tells me about their wives' seasickness. It's only normal for the weaker sex," he jested and couldn't wait to arrive at Pier Nine in New York, knowing his parents and uncle would be there. He never wasted a thought on Barbara, who was warned well beforehand not to appear ill-tempered.

Isabella took several suitcases and a trunk of beautiful clothes with her, causing an inconvenience on trains, but with the valuable dollars in tips, many porters were more than eager to help. She carefully studied her mother-in-law's fashion magazines to make sure she would be well-dressed no matter what the occasion. However, her former wardrobe from Coco Chanel was timeless and elegant, and she had no intention of leaving them behind. Aside from that, William loved her clothes, and to her it was the only thing that mattered.

She was lounging on the ship's recliner as it was a very quiet day as far as the sea was concerned. William conversed with anyone who wore a uniform, but checked regularly on Isabella's well-being. She was looking through different kinds of magazines which were referring to American homes, with some of them for 'sale'. She was astonished at the 'cottages' in Newport or Hyannis Port, among many other places which were not only larger, but more elaborate than some European castles. Of course, she was taught very early in life that a castle, no matter how neglected, had for generations owners who, even if they had not a penny to their name, still had background and breeding. That is something "new money" owners could not achieve, unless with time it became 'old money'.

The *Liberty* arrived at five in the morning and one had to wait for the customs authority to arrive. What a good feeling when those loud engines stopped their noise. The passengers took their last showers, got dressed, ate some breakfast while daylight sat in, and the Statue of Liberty became visible. William took her hand and said, "Welcome to America, Isabella."

While the customs men checked their luggage and their passports, there were his happy parents, Uncle Bill, and, lo and behold, his sister, Barbara, waiting. William wondered if his parents made her come, but changed his mind abruptly, knowing a McAllister cannot be made to do anything. Hearty embraces came from Kathryn, Don, and Uncle Bill, who insisted on being referred to by William's new wife the same way. Barbara and Isabella shook hands cordially, but no one could think of a word to say, even when properly introduced.

"Like it or not, Barbara, you are now sisters-in-law," said Uncle Bill while William watched her with his eyes narrowed.

"Did you have a pleasant trip?" Barbara finally asked.

"Thank you for asking. At times it was quite stormy, and I think all of us women were seasick."

"Well, a few days of rest will do just fine," Barbara replied smiling, and all present wondered if it was just one of her acts, or if she had taken tranquilizers.

The men talked about their trunks still being off-loaded, and they would stay together until everything was accounted for. Nothing was left to chance.

"Why don't you three ladies drive home and we'll see you later?" Don suggested and Isabella exchanged glances with both of them. Now she was at their mercy.

"Good idea, Don, since you have your own car aside from the truck," Kathryn said and agreed happily, whispering to both girls, "Let's get out of here." Kathryn drove a beautiful 1931 Ford Model A Deluxe Roadster which was called 'Tin Lizzie' with a combination of black outside and a beige leather interior.

"I'll sit in the rumble seat," Barbara declared, somehow cheerful. "The weather is so beautiful. God made it especially for your arrival, Mrs. McAllister."

Barbara smiled and Isabella replied, "Since we are relatives, even in my old-fashioned, formal country, we call each other by first names."

"Suits me fine, Isabell. I leave the 'A' out to make it more American."

"Thank you, Barbara. I like that very much. I, on the other hand, have to keep the 'A' on yours."

"Now that you mention it…". All three laughed and Kathryn relaxed for the first time in weeks.

"We do have a house in New York City for the two men to save them travel time during the week since we live in Scarsdale, but we also spend many weekends on our horse farm… the one I told you about. So sorry to hear about your Lillian, but we cannot be selfish and have to do what is best for our animals."

"You are right, Mrs. McAllister, but not a day goes by without thinking of her."

"If you love an animal, you will always find another one," Barbara, who leaned forward so as not to miss out on anything, replied very encouragingly.

"You will have your choice of many horses very soon. But first you must rest in our guest house. Then I'll give a party to introduce you to our friends, and after that William and you make your own decisions," Kathryn said cheerfully, turning in the McAllister's long driveway.

"I live in Bronxville," Barbara replied and wondered for how much longer.

"It's all so new to me. I have a lot to learn."

"William will be glad to help you," Kathryn replied, having finally stopped the car.

The lawn and garden were manicured to perfection, with an array of flowers already in bloom. There was also an enormous red tiled driveway heading towards the back and to the two guest houses. An Italian fountain with spouting cupids gave the spacious house a very dignified look as it was white brick with black shutters on the huge windows. It looked positively like a mixture of French and English estate, two stories high with three wrought iron balconies in front of French doors. Ivy was on both ends of what seemed to be brick with wide large doors, possibly their garages. Isabella noticed several Negro servants who smiled in their direction.

"Ours go home at night," Kathryn explained, knowing Isabella's unfamiliarity with their help.

"But we treat them so much better than those awful southerners," Barbara joined in, with a certain satisfaction.

Isabell knew all about it from Betty McCain, who gave her many lessons about America's Civil War, the end of slavery, and the animosity which still existed between North and South. Isabella remembered that as she replied. "Take a look at Europe, every country hates every other one." She put their conversation behind her and started to talk about the skyscrapers, while walking slowly towards the main entrance as a Negro held the door wide open.

"Hello, George," both women greeted in unison. "This is William's wife from Switzerland who lived in Germany during the war," Kathryn explained.

George gave a slight nod. "How do you do, Ma'am."

"Now welcome to our house, Isabella," Kathryn said, cheerfully embracing her.

"Thank you, and it's so beautiful!"

The furniture was English Victorian, which was exactly to Kathryn's taste, as roses were visible from the drapes to their carpet motifs without being in any way overdone. Plants were everywhere and the main colors were, of course, in all shades of red. She also loved their paintings, which consisted of a mixture of flowers, dogs, and horses depending on the rooms, which also were plentiful. The house, although appearing long outside, was even larger after one entered. She explained that the house had on the right side four garages which were previously horse stables and, after the death of her parents in the thirties, Don and Bill decided to keep the place because of the beautiful location. There was much acreage and gardens, but it had to be remodeled. Therefore, the garages looked rather like an extension of the house.

"When was it built?" Isabella wanted to know, as it looked positively 'lived in'.

"1870. A few years after the Civil War was over. My family was one of the fortunate who profited by it."

"And in this case, stone by stone came via boat from Scotland and the furniture, of course, from England," Barbara stated matter-of-factly while switching to another subject. "By the way Isabell, I never told you how stunning you look in that suit. I love plaids myself and almost wore one quite similar."

"Wouldn't that have been something?" Kathryn said, before a maid announced that the table was set with little finger sandwiches until lunch is served. They talked about the upcoming party, as it was the custom to introduce the new wife of their son.

"Of course, William cares only about the friends he went to prep school and Harvard with, but it just so happens that we like their parents too. You may say it goes from one generation to the next." No names were mentioned, but they warned Isabella to be cautious about certain people who sting with their tongues, like scorpions.

She became a Reinhardt again and smiled. "I was told a long time ago that when one gets bitten or stung, one has to go for the kill." Both women looked at each other, flabbergasted, not knowing what she had in mind. "We kill them with kindness. They always get so confused, ending up apologizing. So far it has worked every time. But as the Reinhardts always insisted, there are those exceptions."

Kathryn was very relieved, but Barbara wished aloud that either Dani Buchanan or her acid-tongued mother, Ann Leitner, would, for once in their lives, get a good tongue lashing as both families belong to their so-called 'Great Society'. "Well, we'll explain all that to you some other time," Kathryn whispered, now hearing the men enter.

"How can anyone have so many clothes?" Don laughed, followed by Bill and William.

"You are one to ask, Dad," William replied, kissing his wife on the cheek.

"Has he been a good husband, Isabella?"

"The very best any woman could ask for," she replied happily. "Thank you for raising him," she added, squeezing Kathryn's hand who had the least to do with it. But it must have made her feel good and no one objected to the compliment.

"After we have ourselves a little something to eat, we'll get you settled in the guest house, and if you are short on closet space, we have plenty," Don suggested, pulling up a chair. Bill and William did the same, and without any motions two black servants again brought food and drinks.

After the phone rang, another servant came in asking for Barbara to take the call. She went in another room while the family exchanged glances. "I'll bet it's Steve."

"Sorry, I have to go." She returned red-faced. "I'll see you all this evening, if I am still invited."

"Alone," her father said firmly.

"The Customs men take anyone in the military uniform first," Uncle Bill elaborated between sandwiches.

"How nice," said Kathryn, but her thoughts were with Barbara.

"And how did my sister behave?" William looked at Isabella.

"We got along really well, and she had a splendid idea."

"My sister? An idea?" William smiled in jest.

"Yes, she thinks it a good idea if my name is now Isabell. We leave the 'A' out. Of course, it doesn't sound more Anglican or American, but I like it."

"As long as you do," Uncle Bill said amused. "but don't get bullied by her."

"Oh, no, I rather like it myself. Isabell McAllister sounds very nice," she smiled.

"To us too," William replied jubilant. "Welcome home, Darling."

"I was already nicely welcomed by your mother and sister."

"And this evening we'll have a toast," Uncle Bill commanded.

Isabell and William went to their guest house, which was, to her surprise, not very close to the main house. It was spacious, beautifully decorated, and the view of the park was magnificent.

"I love this place, William. I'm glad you brought me here."
They embraced, as always, very heartily.

"It means the world to me, Isabell," he said visibly moved. "I
didn't know what to expect from my sister as she is in the
process of an ugly divorce."

She showed great surprise at his revelation. "Poor thing. She
never let on."

"I think it made her a nicer person. I don't know why, but not
too many people like her."

"Well I do, and it may not be her fault."

"In a way, yes. In another, no. Her husband tried to bring his
girlfriend from France over. Of course, he will leave town.
But she used to treat him like dirt, and now he has someone
whose life revolves around him. I really don't blame the
guy... but keep it to yourself."

"Of course, William. I know nothing, and will act surprised
no matter who tells me."

"Good girl. There may be rough days ahead in the family.
Once the great party is over, we'll look for a house. Needless
to say, I didn't have a chance to talk to Bill alone."

"Well, I brought some dollars too. I will have to talk with
your family about it since they are gold pieces."

"Where did you get them from? Your family in Austria will
need them. We don't need money for the house. Uncle Bill
and I settled many things via mail," he assured her, surprised
that she would even mention it.

"Grandmother Victoria and Astrid gave me gold coins. I also
have a Swiss bank account of my own."

"Well, well, well," William laughed, leaning back filling his
pipe. "Now everyone in Westchester County will think I
married you for your money."

"Everyone will know in no time that we married for love and love only. I just thought I'd mention it for when you look for a house. Remember, I will live there too."

"Gosh, I hope so," he laughed even louder. "Isabell, we have no war and no money problems. Why don't you send it back?" he replied sincerely.

"It would be the greatest insult to each one of them. If they didn't have it, they would have told me so. Grandmother Victoria is even frowning that my mother uses some of her Swiss francs in many stores. But if she didn't, Aunt Ingrid and her own mother would get angry. We always avoid a fight, or for that matter even an argument, as there were so many when mother was still a von Walden."

"Are you trying to tell me you never had an argument?"

"Why should I? I have my own way to respond. Remember the two 'Bodies' Brad and Joel?"

"Oh, yes. How can I possibly forget?

"And I was starting to get quite jealous watching Sheila leaning on you." She smiled. "Wonder how she is doing?"

"Dating someone else… that's all," he shrugged. "Before I forget to tell you, while dad and Uncle Bill were waiting for the luggage, I sent some telegrams to Salzburg and Vienna. I know they will be happy to hear we arrived safely."

"You think of everything, William. Thank you so much."

"You're welcome, and if you are not too tired, we'll walk through the garden."

"Great idea. I am not tired at all. I slept the last two days."

They changed clothes and Isabell looked at his stunning appearance in navy blue slacks and white knitted shirt. She had a pleated, plaid skirt in blue and white with a navy blue blouse.

"You look more beautiful as the days go by. Maybe you are happy after all."

"Very," she replied, not telling him the reason why she felt not only happy, but already blessed with a new life in her body. They walked with their arms around each other's waists, and as the older McAllister clan watched from the window, each one was too moved to say a word. Dinner was at seven and Isabell was surprised that all her clothes were hung up. "Your family changes for dinner?"

"Yes, but no gala, just a bit nicer."

She had many dresses in a variation of red, as it was her favorite color. She took a classic red linen dress with white trim and Kathryn's pearl necklace with her earrings.

"Look," she said to Barbara embracing her lightly. "This is from your mother, and the bracelet is from your brother."

"Gorgeous," she smiled. "And I have something for you too, Isabell."

"So have I. We'll wait until after dinner."

Nothing was mentioned about Steve, but they may have talked before their arrival, Isabell thought, enjoying standing rib roast with all the trimmings. Again, she had fruit juice, claiming wine made her sleepy.

"Did you bring a party dress?" Kathryn asked carefully. "We have great boutiques here."

"I brought several, but will wear red. Dark red; long and beautiful, and the right jewelry to go with it."

"May I see it?" Barbara asked, dying to see all of her clothes.

"Of course. I may need your help with certain things."

"The way I see it, Isabell, I may need yours!" They all were extremely relaxed, hoping Barbara would behave that way until the party was over anyway. After that, most of their friends would leave New York in the following weeks to avoid the heat.

They went to a sitting room with a built-in bar, helping themselves to drinks. Isabell had a few little boxes in a large one, and started to give each one their gift.

"Mrs. McAllister, this is for a rose lover like myself. Barbara, I hope you will like this and wear it in good health."

Kathryn shrieked. "I cannot take that! It's a diamond rose!"

"You have a pearl one already," Isabell smiled, while Kathryn got up almost staggering.

"No… I cannot take it."

Isabell smiled again. "You can, and you must. It's from the Reinhardt collection."

"Oh, my God," she stammered again with Don also extremely happy. He of all people knew if she liked something or not. So did Bill, Barbara, and William.

"Isabell!" Barbara screamed. "I don't deserve this bracelet. Look everybody, it's with sapphires and diamonds. It must have cost fortune!" She replied in awe.

Isabell walked, undisturbed, to the men. "I know you have an abundance of paper weights, money clips, cufflinks, and whatever else a man needs through the years. So we thought of something smart and useless," she laughed out loud. "For each of you two, an engraved Swiss Army knife from the 1837 collection. I have no idea what that means, as it comes from the Reinhardts."

"Good Lord, I've never seen anything like it," said Don.

"Solid gold!" Uncle Bill replied in astonishment, looking at his brother.

"And for my husband, a pen and pencil set which can be clipped on, so you won't lose it," she said with a kiss on his cheek.

"I am now too embarrassed to give you my present," Barbara cried, wearing her bracelet, with her mother repeating the sentence.

"Oh, Barbara. It's the thought that counts. That goes for you too, Mrs. McAllister."

Kathryn went in a room and brought her a beautiful black crocodile handbag, something Isabell had never seen as far as the style was concerned.

Barbara took a large box and embraced Isabell. "Wear it in good health too." It was a beautiful beige mink stole which Isabell quickly wrapped around herself. It gave quite an amusing picture with Kathryn showing her rose etoile pin, Barbara her sapphire bracelet, and Isabell walking with an air of hauteur and smiling in front of three happy McAllister men. William had never experienced a more joyful family gathering as far as he could remember. Needless to say, he attributed all their newfound happiness to none other than his wife, Isabell.

37

It was two days before the McAllisters' big party and, as usual, Ann Leitner and Dani Buchanan left a question mark, since they were traveling from California and may be late; but then both would be there, as they always enjoy McAllister's parties.

"It's a lie, Mother," Barbara acknowledged. "They are always the last to make their big entrance for one thing, and for the other, maybe they heard that Steve moved out and don't like to be associated with me. They never cared for me."

"That would be a joke if you think it's because of Steve. Ann Leitner was an O'Hara— sweet kind Chris deserved much better—and before she was an O'Hara, she was Ann Thornberg." Both smiled.

"I forgot," Barbara conceded.

"Well, I didn't. I know they are coming because they want to see what William's 'war bride' looks like."

"So both can take a stab at her."

"I'd like to see them try. William will tell them where to go, and you know what? I won't even interfere."

"Good for you, Mother. I get so upset when they refer to Mrs. Ann Leitner as 'the Grand Dame of Scarsdale'. You, if anyone, should get the title. She is younger on top of it."

"Barbara, it's money and their connections with who is who. They are invited to places we never are."

"Well, Dani is prettier than I am, happier, and has a child. But nothing is my fault. Well, let's say some of it is."

"Barbara, you can only better yourself. That's what Ann Leitner did each time."

"You have a point."

~

The McAllisters hired a band which served many families in Westchester County quite well. Their spacious place was transformed by professional decorators in no time. The weather played along quite beautifully, so there were many outdoor flowers with intertwined ribbons. Isabell, who was quite used to such parties, was even astonished, and told William she hoped it was not all for her.

"No, Isabell… you have to get used to it, one tries to outdo the other. It's just the name of the game which is played here. As for myself, like many guys, we don't care for it, but what else is one to do?"

"They hired caterers. It's not a habit in our place, but then we have an oversupply of servants the whole year round."

"There were some of your servants I liked a lot, Fanny Hirt topping the list," he said, putting his black tie in order.

"So do I, but no one would ever leave Vienna age-wise and otherwise. They would be totally lost without the Reinhardts."

"I am still worried about you, Isabell," he said solemnly, entering her small dressing room. "My Lord, do you look beautiful," he stammered, shaking his head.

"William, my dear, any woman in a gown like this would." She decided on a ruby red silk charmeuse gown with a square neckline, a wide flowing bias-cut skirt with a chiffon skirt draped over and held by a velvet beaded belt. She used only her ruby earrings to give a perfect appearance. Her hair was, as always for a special occasion, worn in a plaited French twist, giving her a festive look.

When Isabell and William entered the crowded room, the McAllisters couldn't help but notice the many astonished and admiring looks of their guests. Kathryn wore navy blue with small diagonal thin white stripes. Next to her stood mousy-blond Barbara with more makeup than usual to hide her pale face from many sleepless nights. Her dress was multi-colored with oriental flowers on black satin. Kathryn told her she looked very good.

"Mother, take a look at Isabell and William. No matter who comes or likes to make a great entrance, those two are hard to beat."

"I agree wholeheartedly."

Dinner was all buffet-style and so beautifully arranged that even Isabell was in awe. She walked on the arm of William to his parents and sister with a big smile, adding that everything looked so beautiful.

"Especially you!" said Barbara without a tinge of jealousy.

"And so do you and your mother. Don't sell yourself short. You don't know how long it took me," she smiled.

William made sure his wife met everybody, and started with his former school friends, be it from prep school to college or Oxford. Each one had a wife on their arm too who raved about her gown but had otherwise very little to say. William couldn't help but think of their utter surprise about his 'war bride'. But he also knew that she would be checked out by watching her every move.

Barbara stayed next to her mother like she needed a security blanket, afraid someone would have the nerve to ask for Steve. Isabell, after having been introduced to everybody, decided to join Barbara, who looked rather forlorn. William could now go to his friends and have their own talk about the war or whatever else was of great interest after all these many years. She told Barbara to get a bite to eat as her mother was engrossed with her own friends.

"Good idea, though I am not hungry," she said, and they crossed the room when both heard a long, drawn-out, "No! It cannot be! Mother, look and tell me I am not going crazy!", causing most of their guests to turn their heads, including Isabell and Barbara. Many started to whisper and comment that only people like Leitner and Buchanan could get away with such an outburst, while Kathryn hinted to her friend that it was their greatest entrance ever. Isabell held Barbara's hand and looked equally stunned, recognizing 'Ella' and Ann Leitner immediately.

"Ella?" cried Isabell. "Is it really you?"

"Bella, it is!" she replied, equally tearfully, as they embraced each other with a few twirls around in front of an assembled crowd who didn't know what had happened. Ann Leitner lost no time in walking quickly towards the podium and as always, in control no matter what the situation, shouted, "Stop the music please!" Then she motioned her daughter and Isabell to join her and proclaimed, "Let me introduce you to everyone. Oh, God, I am shaking like the girls… This is the former Isabella Reinhardt, my daughter's dearest and longtime friend from her schooldays in Switzerland. We lost contact during the war years and it is inexcusable on our part that we never inquired afterwards. I am sure there is some gentleman here to whom she now belongs," she laughed.

William, with his group of friends and their chatting wives, came closer after hearing the great outburst of none other than Ann Leitner, a woman who is famous for her icy stares and small talk, while always feeling superior towards everyone. He hardly remembered her daughter Daniella, as both were always in different schools.

"And I want all of you to know," she continued undisturbed, knowing that all were listening. "that we have in our midst the closest lady to royalty! I visited her family in one of the grandest castles outside of Vienna and their palace in the heart of the city. Never mind the noble family who can trace its ancestry back to 1509!" She held both girls' hands still not believing her luck.

The McAllisters, although equally surprised and elated about the unforeseen incident, felt it was now their turn to say something. Not only because it was their party, but Isabell was now family. Kathryn looked at William with a wink and told him to take over on their behalf. He took a few fast strides and jumped to the podium with a big smile.

"This is my wife Isabell from Switzerland and Austria. I met her in Vienna where she lived during the war years serving the Red Cross as a nurse at their own hospital. More astonishment and whispers were visible. "Well, to make a long story short, that's where I was transferred after war's end and the rest you will hear as time goes on." Turning to Ann Leitner he said, "Thank you for making the introduction so much easier." All applauded spontaneously, and why not? Ann Leitner declared her 'Royal', and if anyone knew about nobility and high society, she was known to be an expert.

Turning to the musicians she asked politely, "Why not play a Viennese waltz in honor of my friend?"

It was, for Kathryn and Barbara McAllister, unmistakably their finest hour. But, as usual, for the men it meant considerably less. With the dance behind them, everyone went outdoors for food, drinks, fresh air, and a seat. The weather was still delightful.

Ann Leitner's husband pulled, with the help of two waiters, two tables together to sit with the McAllisters. They had now so much in common and so much to discuss. 'Dani' Buchanan, after introducing her rather average-looking but snobbish Tom to her group of close girlfriends, made it clear they were in need of plain 'girl talk'. He was rather happy about it. Of course, three tables had to be pushed together, as Barbara had no intention of leaving Isabell.

The band played melodies from Glen Miller and Tommy Dorsey, throwing from time to time a waltz or tango in. The girls sat each dance out while Daniella held court. There were so many stories from their schooldays in Switzerland, and her great times in Vienna, including Lillian. Isabell's face saddened, explaining the circumstances.

"I never saw your daughter more spellbound," one of Dani's friends voiced, not without a certain sense of pride.

Of course, they heard about those terrible Russians, Germans, and all other devils.

"What about those Japs who kept my Tom in prison? He got a beating anytime one of their savages said so." As it stood right now, only America was in every way right and their poor guys sacrificed their lives to make the world a better place to live. Isabell couldn't have agreed more. On the lighter side, she heard where most of the families and friends spend their winters or summers and she heard the names of Arizona, Newport, and Palm Beach for the first time.

It was now an open secret that William and Isabell would be one of the most desired newcomers for Scarsdale and Bronxville. The McAllisters' background was never in question, but Ann Leitner made sure that Isabell's background was spread like wildfire. The way it stood right now, nobody could claim to come from a 140-room castle, never mind a palace in the heart of Vienna, a villa in Salzburg, and a chalet in the health spa of Ischl.

Isabell took, as she spoke, a glance at Dani's friends and found them beautiful, well-groomed and dressed and, of course, properly raised in what would be doubtless the best schools and colleges America had to offer. And as far as Daniella was concerned, she still had the same facial features which made the two of them hard to tell apart in their Swiss school. The difference was always the color of their eyes, with Daniella's having almost a violet look, while Isabell's were always considered the darkest brown possible. Daniella was also two-and-a-half years older and the more stylish even now. Also, her dark hair was still put up like a ballerina before her great entrance.

Isabell had a chance to look around, not that they ran out of subjects, but one felt like dancing and had to look for a husband. Tom Buchanan seemed to be engrossed between a friend from Harvard and William, who doubtlessly had known each other from their schooldays.

"I am so happy those two men get along so well, Isabell. It's so important for me not to have any friction on those many social functions. In two weeks, Mother has a big double birthday party."

"Really?"

"Frank Leitner is fifty and I am twenty-five."

"Great!" she said quite happily.

"But you will soon be alone with me so we can catch up on everything and also surprise my darling dad, Chris O'Hara. I do it very frequently since his mother passed away. She was quite a woman. I wish you would have had the chance to meet her."

"So do I."

By now, some of the elderly couples started to get ready to leave, but everyone stopped by Daniella and Isabell to congratulate them for their good fortune to have met so miraculously at the McAllisters' party.

The McAllisters were now alone in their cozy family room to have their little 'toddies', as they called their daily drinks among themselves. Don was extremely relieved that neither his wife nor daughter drank over their limits.

"Where are William and Isabell?" questioned Kathryn, ready to discuss their most unusual evening.

"Changing their clothes, Mother. Both claimed to be uncomfortable."

"Well, as long as they join us. I am now all perked up," Kathryn claimed, taking another sip. "I'd like to tell Isabell not only how gorgeous she looked, but also how proud she made us by her gracious behavior."

"And I'd like to ask her to help me with a new hair color and possibly style," Barbara sighed. "I felt for the first time so inadequate. And it's not only because I was without Steve."

"Never mind that scoundrel. I noticed a great improvement in your behavior towards us, and also the way you treated our friends. You were previously hard to take, and I for one keep wondering if your upcoming divorce is indirectly a great relief," her father said sincerely.

"I wonder myself," she replied, but thought of Isabell when she advised her to 'kill her enemies with kindness'. She had to confess to herself that she had many socialites very confused.

William and Isabell changed clothes in their separate closets, but not before he gave his wife the usual embrace. "I imagine I was the most envied fellow this evening." She overlooked his compliment, knowing there were quite a few ladies who, in her opinion, looked even better.

"I am still in complete shock over encountering my former friend of many years ago and her mother. It's a miracle. And by the way, the name 'Dani' doesn't become her at all. To me, she will always be Ella. We started in school to give each other 'secret names'," she laughed. "Therefore, our beautiful shepherds' names, Ella and Bella."

"Now that you mention it, I feel rather stupid not to have thought of it the moment you called her that name. However, I have my reservations about all those girls… women… wives… whatever or whoever they are. Like my own mother and sister, they belong to every club or organization there is in this town, one of the reasons Barbara's husband was finding himself very alone," he replied, a little irritated, possibly giving a hint how he would feel about it.

She had no time to reply as she needed his help with her zippers being stuck. "Please, William, come in and help me. I cannot get out of my dress," she pleaded.

"I am more than happy," he replied, entering instantly. Strange as it seemed, so far, he had never even seen her in a slip. But her frilly nightgowns were quite sufficient, the way he saw it. He managed, carefully, to separate the entangled zippers on both sides and noticed the bulges once she was freed.

"My goodness, Isabell! Our American steak becomes you. You seem to have put on some weight. And I don't mean it in a criticizing way, darling, as I was worried how you would take to it after your superb Austrian cuisine."

"Sit down, William," she ordered with a gleam and threw herself on his lap the moment he sat.

"What has happened?" he asked, astonished, having never experienced her spontaneity previously.

"Well, something has happened to both of us, William."

"Like?" he gulped, wondering.

"We are going to be parents," she replied joyfully.

"When?" he asked, overcome with joy and holding her closer.

"By the middle or end of November."

"That makes you three months pregnant already?"

"Yes, William, and the reason I never told anyone was that I didn't want to worry anyone for my long trip. Besides, I promised Uncle Bill a polka as soon as I got my first chance. So today I had it all. God only knows how much special advice I would have gotten."

"For one thing, I would have extended my duty for a year, Isabell. There's no way I would have let you travel."

"Now you see why I kept it to myself? Because I was ready to go," she smiled, elated.

"Change quickly into something comfortable, darling, and we'll tell the family. If you think Ann Leitner and Daniella made their day, watch their faces now!"

She put on a coatdress with buttons from top to bottom in a hurry, and he offered to carry her in and set her down. "If I am not too heavy?" she smiled.

"For a husband a head taller and double your weight, you must be kidding."

"Soon I'll beat you around your waist," she admonished.

"Then you'll look like dad and Uncle Bill," he laughed, picking her up.

"They are tall, or let's say big, men and carry it well."

"I thought you decided not to come," Kathryn said, happy to see them.

"We made your waiting worthwhile," William said in jest but with a special glow.

"I doubt it. We just talked about the best party we ever had."

"Your sister included," Uncle Bill interrupted. "And that's something."

"All right, William. Let's have it," his father joked. "And I for one hope it beats the party, because it will be the topic for the next few months."

"Oh, it beats it all right. Isabell and I are expecting a new addition in November."

Their joy was indescribable. Everyone jumped up, embracing each other, and Kathryn cried. "That beats any party a million times."

"You can say that again," voiced his father grandly.

"Gosh, now that I am on the way to being an ex-wife, I am going to be Aunt Barbara." Isabell was overjoyed at their heartfelt reaction.

"But I am not going to be a grand-uncle," Bill jested. "I was born to be an uncle, only."

"But I will be a better aunt," Barbara teased.

"Don't bet on it, kid."

"I do, because I, for one, have plenty of experience in babysitting."

"Look who's talking. How about a grandmother?"

"Or father," from Don again.

"What a happy day," William said, his arm around Isabell's waist.

"May I say something?" asked the mother-to-be.

"Of course, Isabell! You have brought us nothing but joy," cried Kathryn, and everyone was quiet.

"I know it's going to be a boy and I thought of the name, Scott Gregory."

"What a beautiful name. I mean, how much more Scottish can we get?" Uncle Bill chuckled. "But what about a girl?"

"That will be the McAllister family's problem," Isabell laughed. "But I know it's a boy."

"Sweetheart, we'll take anything," Kathryn said, hoping there would be more than one.

"We have to look for a house, son. Starting tomorrow," his father said seriously. "It may take a while to get what you both like."

"Let's have a toast first," William said, looking at their embarrassed faces for not offering one sooner. They all toasted to the parents-to-be and to the unborn Scott Gregory, since Isabell was always right.

"You have to call me Mama now, Isabell. After all, I have to be one first before I can be called 'Grandma'."

"Of course, I am glad to do it," she smiled, elated.

"Same here," Don smiled.

"All right, 'Mama'," she laughed aloud, with all joining in.

Barbara, still in her stockings as the high heels got the best of her, said to Isabell quite seriously, "Tomorrow we are going to look for baby items."

"Not without me!" Kathryn replied.

"Alright, Mother, it's settled. You women do your things and we'll do ours. As a future grandfather, I should have some say so too." They all had no choice but to laugh at his serious comment and William thought they were finally a family again. Kathryn, of course, thought of something too, but it would not have been the right time to mention that Don

Reed would have loved to be an uncle too. But one cannot have everything, especially when her greatest wish was fulfilled. She was becoming a grandmother at last.

~

Isabell and William were in bed talking about the days ahead of them. Both were too excited to sleep. "We have to send your family a telegram. Or better yet, try to get a call to Austria. It may take a few hours of waiting, but I am sure your mother wouldn't mind being awakened."

"Of course not, her phone is in her bedroom."

"I hope to God she will be just as happy as my mother. Don't forget, your mother is only forty-one, while mine is fifty-eight."

"That shouldn't matter at all. My grandmother, Astrid von Walden, was forty-two when I was born. Age has nothing to do with the love for one's children or grandchildren. Some should have many and some shouldn't have any at all. Believe me, William, I have seen lots of it."

"I know that, and I agree. I'll bet my mother is on the phone talking about it right now," he smiled.

The next day, the three men went house-hunting, but to be on the safe side took a realtor along, telling him what they were looking for. After all, Isabell wanted a French style place and William didn't object. She was the one who would spend most of the days there.

"There is no hurry," Don proclaimed rather solemnly. "We enjoy having our children with us, and after that, a home near to our place."

38

By September, they finally found a place all agreed on. It was only a few minutes' drive and two houses down the street from where Barbara used to live. Her place was sold within two weeks, but it was never to the McAllisters' taste to begin with. It was Steve's house and it still infuriated the family since they paid for it. Now Barbara moved back in her parents' house.

Bronxville was known to be more snobbish and clannish, but Isabell was so sure of herself and in every way her own person that she gave it very little thought. Aside from that, at the McAllisters' and Leitners' big parties, there were quite a few young couples from Bronxville. William was the last one to care about anything other than Isabell and the baby.

The newfound place was well worth waiting for. It looked like a small French castle in a perfect setting of seven acres, with a fishpond and a small lake, which could be easily enlarged since it was man-made. William and Isabell loved it after taking the first look at it, and the realtor was quite relieved. That place had just come on the market a few days earlier and the McAllisters got a call from a friend who knew, like everyone else by now, how hard they were looking. It was light-green stucco with huge white French windows, black shutters, and a gable roof with four smaller windows on the third floor, which were doubtless servants' quarters. Although Isabell was never particularly fond of those tall Greek columns, those were short to keep a half-round balcony up. Also, a large door led to a comfortable setting of tables and chairs on the portico. The unusual entrance door was almost befitting the Reinhardts' villa in Salzburg, and two staircases made it the perfect home. The realtor explained that the owner was an architect who supervised the construction personally.

"I think the house is about forty-years old and only the kitchen needs updating. Ever since his wife's death due to breast cancer two years ago, Mr. Kehler moved to live with his brother in South Hampton until he finds his own place."

The McAllisters insisted on a deal right then and there, for fear it might be gone the next day. The few remaining pieces of furniture would be picked up within the next few days, they were told, which was alright with them.

"William, I will make it a very beautiful home, and at the same time a very comfortable house for all of us," she promised on the way home.

"As long as you are always there to greet me when I open the door," he beamed, delighted.

She placed in her mind all the furniture which had arrived from Vienna in the meantime, some of William's favorites and those from Switzerland, the pieces they had loved and selected together. After all, the house had twenty-five rooms.

Don and Kathryn were in their own car and she commented that she could hear Ann Leitner already saying, "My houses have at least forty rooms each and some of my friends have more than that."

"Isabell with her exquisite taste will make a showcase out of it and be the envy of many," Don retorted.

~

Ann Leitner returned from her four-month stay in Europe and Frank was quite upset about it. She started with Vienna, staying at Hotel Bristol, visited the Reinhardts and von Waldens several times, telling them everything in detail, including how much they love Isabell. Off she went for two months to Switzerland, revisiting her daughter's school and Aunt Ingrid. She had a long list of places she always wanted to see with her ex-husband, Chris O'Hara, who constantly declined. Now, on her own, she did as she pleased.

Finally, she went to Salzburg to see Gaby and Victoria Reinhardt. They insisted she stay with them, as most refugees had returned to Vienna. As always, she felt very jealous of Gaby's beauty, telling her she hadn't changed a bit and she must have a secret she was not willing to share. She only smiled.

Together they visited many places, attended concerts, and talked again about family matters. By the middle of October, she finally left via plane. She only saw Germany from the air and had no feelings of bitterness or love. But during the long flight, she had to admit that something between Frank and her was gone. She didn't miss him even to share some of the beauty and good times she encountered all over.

Now in December, she was ready to go to her large place in Palm Beach and kept pondering if it was a good idea to leave him alone that much. He just turned fifty and looked great. But so far, he didn't mind so she would see about his reaction once she returned.

"Why don't you just move to Europe?" he greeted her in a sour mood.

"For the first time since 1938, I enjoyed myself and you make me feel like I committed a crime."

"What do you mean 'enjoyed yourself'? You do in every place, all year round."

"I cannot help it if you prefer the New York Stock Exchange to family life." They had her suitcases brought to his car and drove wordlessly to Scarsdale.

She called Daniella right away, explaining Frank's behavior at her arrival. Her daughter was not surprised, knowing he had an affair with a young woman whose husband wouldn't give her a divorce. He told Daniella to never mention it, that it was a big secret. He just didn't seem to care anymore. Also, his two sons from his first marriage spent the summer with him and there were many times he regretted he had fallen in love so very frequently. There was also a time when Ann was the one who made his life worth living, but at the moment he felt like she did nothing.

"Mother, you may have to work on your marriage if you'd like to keep him."

"What are you trying to tell me?"

"Nothing that cannot wait. I am glad you are back, but this time you stayed much too long."

"Frank never minded previously."

"Mother, you have been married barely five years and the places you've been to in the past he could always reach you whenever he felt like it. That alone made him feel better. But four months in Europe?"

"I had such a good time it felt like four weeks ... or even less."

"Sleep on it for a night, and tomorrow we are going to see Isabell and William's new house. It's a beauty."

"Glad to hear it. I'll see you for lunch." Both hung up simultaneously.

~

They called William's house and, of course, it was all right to come. His parents and uncle would be there too, and once again, there would be so much to talk about. A very pregnant Isabell greeted Ann and Daniella and her husband first, waiting for the in-laws to arrive shortly. Ann loved their newly purchased 'castle' and was informed that only part of the furniture had been placed.

"Never mind, Isabell. I just love the layout and everything about it. And those huge oak trees will give plenty of needed shade."

"My in-laws had an air-cooling system installed and it helps a great deal. The summer heat was something else," Isabell half lamented when the McAllisters and William arrived. It was the usual 'long time not to see you' greeting, but Ann was not the usual Ann. The McAllisters heard via Daniella about Frank's affair, but as always, they kept quiet. Isabell was dying to hear all about her loved ones, but nothing at all had changed. According to her Papa's letter, he would be home soon.

"Those Russians," Bill said angrily. "have kept him far longer than promised." But he changed his tone quickly, thinking it would upset all of them.

It was now Ann's turn to complain about Frank's unusual behavior. But if she expected any sympathy, she was wrong.

"If my Kathryn were to leave me alone one month just to have a good time by herself, I'd tell her where to go," Don said very seriously.

Kathryn rolled her eyes looking at Ann, who replied, "Don, I asked him frequently on the phone and he never gave any indication. You know our marriage, Don. We always did what we liked."

"Then I would refrain from calling it a marriage, Ann," Don finalized. Everyone knew how he felt about a commitment and no one answered him. Ann gave Isabell a worried look, but she only smiled and said, "My Papa didn't even let mother go shopping by herself. A servant always had to be with her and he always wanted to know for how long."

"And your mother?"

"I have a feeling she liked it because it told her how much he loved her. He was very, very jealous."

"Well, I couldn't live with a man like that. I need my freedom."

"You may just get it Ann," Uncle Bill said smiling. "You cannot always have it your way."

Ann had enough and, promising to see them later, she left to see Frank.

~

Isabell, however, was disappointed, never expecting the conversation to end so abruptly. But it was just Ann, and she looked quite worried. After all, her marriage was at stake.

Frank's mood had not changed when she entered their house. He admitted quite light-heartedly to his affair. Ann was stunned. "Well, Ann, we can continue with each one does as he or she pleases, or we can get a divorce," he smirked. "It's all up to you. While you were gone, I took an apartment around the corner from Wall Street, so I don't have to travel so far."

"Well, since you have a so-called 'seat' on the stock exchange, I often wondered if there was a 'bed' available too."

He laughed out loud. "Got to make money… it's the only thing we both like."

"Alright, if that's the way you feel about it, we may just continue our lifestyle."

"I thought you might like it," he smiled, offering her a drink.

"I, for one, never cheated on you, Frank."

"So what if you did? It wouldn't change a thing as long as we both do as we please."

She unpacked her suitcases with the help of her maid, whom she had well before her marriage to Chris O'Hara. Since Frank left after their drink, she confided in her, knowing it would never be repeated. Esther knew about it all along, but never let on. She only listened and advised her to stick it out.

She returned to Daniella, only to be told she was still at the 'young McAllisters', as they were known by now. She had no choice but to return to them, and since she was always one of Kathryn's best friends, to tell her the truth. And as always, Kathryn only listened and never gave a reply. All of her friends still loved Chris O'Hara.

She finally had a chance to talk with Daniella and Isabell. Barbara was getting the 'baby room' spruced up and one had the feeling that she was happier than anybody in the family. Ann, seeing her only briefly, noticed a big change in her; new hairstyle and lighter color was only one thing. Less makeup and a very elegant appearance may just get her a new and better husband. Ann was one of those women who never could imagine living alone.

"Will you have an open house this year?" she asked Isabell after her stories about her family had ended.

"Of course. We have an open house just before Christmas."

"Baby and all?"

"Scott and the McAllister clan will be here and I hope everyone we invite will be here, too."

"Got a nanny?"

"Barbara," she answered. "And I couldn't ask for a better one."

"I agree. She needs to get over Steve."

"Mother, Barbara didn't grieve very long. We think it's rather a burden off her shoulders," Daniella smiled.

She left again and promised to bring the still unpacked presents from the Reinhardts and Aunt Ingrid the following day.

~

On November 23, which was Isabell's birthday, Scott Gregory gave his first loud scream at five in the morning. William had taken her the previous evening to St. Vincent Hospital the moment she felt the first labor pains. She was barely nine hours in labor, but to the McAllister clan, who had assembled in the meantime, it was an eternity. The baby was healthy, and Isabell, very much to the delight of Kathryn and Barbara, followed all instructions of her gynecologist. Bottle feeding and circumcision were highly recommended. Also, no wrapping in a bunting, and on the third day she was released. She was forced to walk the very next day. Her thoughts were momentarily with Vienna and the Reinhardts. She would refrain from writing any details, especially about the circumcision. Their friends would swear little Scott was a Jew. And yet, they raised little Karl Otto as a Christian.

Once at home, the stream of visitors with gifts was endless. Many hand-crocheted and knitted items had arrived from Austria and Switzerland, keeping Scott warm until he started school. The McAllisters were now settled in their new 'castle', and it was unanimous that it was the most beautifully decorated place by anyone's standard. Isabell and William only cared about the well-being of their son, who became the center of the McAllister clan.

~

The first Christmas in her newly adopted country was beyond Isabell's expectations. It was not only for the abundance of gifts and the festive celebrations, but for the genuine love from all the McAllisters, knowing by now their heartfelt sincerity. The New Year would be celebrated with family only, as the holidays proved to be quite hectic, but very happy. Everyone was delighted, especially William, who could never spend enough time with Isabell and their little son.

Barbara became the sister Isabell never had, and the McAllister family was astonished at Barbara's new attitude towards everyone, including their friends. Somehow, they felt life had come full circle.

As for Kathryn, who still grieved for her late son Don Reed, Isabell tried to convince her that Don was happy for their arrangement in heaven. Peace and love became the order of the day and William felt it was his contribution for choosing a wife he could love until death separated them.

1947

39

For all of Europe it was quite a different story, the exceptions being only a few small neutral countries who had been to Hitler's advantage as Germany stored many valuable treasures and gold bars. Hungry people in cold homes were still the norm, unless they had some goods left for the black market. Ration cards mostly served the purpose of being able to wait in lines, not always getting the items to which one was entitled. Of course, the bombing and plundering had stopped, and rape became a rarity. But quite a few strictly raised Catholic women gave birth to Russian babies, not even remembering the fathers' faces.

The Russian sector was known to be the worst, as there were absolutely no supplies for their troops as well as the Russian people who went back home. German P.O.W.s died by the thousands on a daily basis for the lack of food and shortage of any kind of medical supplies. It was no different from previous wars, where the conqueror lived free off the land, no matter how meager the portions.

The American zone of upper Austria and Salzburg, with its countless refuges, was a different matter. Most East

Germans had not only lost their land, but there were no young males, as they were either dead or missing in action. They all felt lucky to be alive and far away from the Russians. Thanks to their strong constitutions and iron will, they were able to walk with their families for weeks on end, living on handouts from kind peasants, and sleeping in overcrowded barns. The American Red Cross and some religious charities were a welcome sight. They supplied the refugees with necessary items, including clothes, and arranged for shelters and healthcare.

As for the Reinhardts, the family consisted, at present, only of Victoria, Gaby, Robert and little Karl, who were, as always, the exception to the rule. They not only still lived in Salzburg at the late Verena's favorite home, "the Villa Karl", but were fortunate to share the spacious home with an American chaplain and his large family. As usual, children have no language barrier and played very well together.

~

Gaby spent New Year's Day, 1947 reminiscing about her first encounter with Paul, which was exactly ten years before. It seemed like yesterday, yet it was so long ago. She was deep in her thoughts when the phone rang, it was Isabell calling from America.

"Happy New Year, Mother! I hope you know it's been ten years since a very handsome man called me, Miss."

"The same to you, sweetheart, but this call is nothing short of what I would consider mental telepathy! I was sitting here with a cup of coffee thinking about the very same thing."

The phone was handed from one member to the next of Gaby's loving family. Even little Scott was joining in with a loud cry, causing everyone to laugh. Doubtless, he was wet or hungry. No one was in a hurry to hang up, but Kathryn was most anxious to tell Gaby how much they were looking forward to seeing them again. As the baby would only be seven months old, they would not take him on such a long trip. The younger family members would come the following year. Don McAllister took the phone from his wife, inquiring about the flow of mail from Russia. He asked if she had enough connections to get uncensored letters.

She happily replied, "Yes." She couldn't wait for Paul's return.

It was finally William's turn to speak. He assured Gaby that they had had a marvelous Christmas, all due to her daughter and the new baby, Scott, who had brought them nothing but joy.

~

Gaby's high spirits and great joy were somewhat dampened upon entering Victoria's bedroom. Victoria complained about her sleepless night due to the noisy New Year celebration. But then again, she was seventy-seven and usually in a state of depression. Like many of her contemporaries, she had lost many family members and close friends who were very dear to her.

She did not interrupt or contradict her, but let her lament over past times. As usual, it started with her daughter, Gisela, and all the Fosters, who were killed in the war; then came Elizabeth in South Africa, who always ended her letters with the unreasonable accusation that it was the Reinhardts' greed that had made them stay in Nazi Germany and now it was payday for all of them. After that came the discourse about the fact that, with all of their so-called possessions, they had only a few rooms for their own comfort. Most of their property was in the Russian sector, which left only the palace in Vienna's first district for the Americans.

"I wonder how many rooms they will give us. Which brings me to the chalet in Ischl's health spa. Who did you say lives there?" It was a question repeatedly asked.

"The former mayor of the town! You remember him. He lost his sickly wife in the concentration camp and both of his sons are still missing," Gaby sadly replied.

"So he lives there all alone?" Victoria asked with a twinge of envy.

"Heavens no, Mama! He has at least six or more Americans with him. He told me how well he eats thanks to them. He was like all the rest, only skin covering bones, but very glad to be alive coming from the concentration camp."

Victoria gave a deep sigh, stopping to feel sorry for herself.

"Mama, while you were dozing off, Isabell and her family called. The elderly McAllisters promised a visit this year!" Gaby stated elatedly.

"Without Isabell and my first great-grandchild, it's not really a visit." Victoria emphasized, conveniently forgetting that Isabell was her grandchild only through her son's marriage.

Gaby was convinced that only one thing would make her feel better and she was quite sure she could include herself and her son as well. "What do you think of my suggestion to return by early spring to Vienna?"

Victoria's face lit up. "Are you serious, Gaby?"

"Of course, Mama! I realize that all of our friends will call us crazy, to say the least, because we are so fortunate to have a place in one of the most beautiful cities." Gaby smiled.

"We need our family more than a city and friends, as much as I treasure both," Victoria said solemnly. "Besides, Paul may show up one of these days" she said looking heavenwards, knowing how much Gaby missed him. "There is no chance he could come to us. You know how long Peter has been waiting to get a visa."

"True," Gaby acknowledged, "so let's surprise them all, weather permitting that is."

~

When it came to the weather, the Reinhardts lost the status of being the exception. There was no choice but to sit out the harsh winter. But then again, it was a blessing to be in the American sector with heated homes. Peter's long overdue visa was granted and the big surprise the Reinhardts had planned was therefore reversed, but no one cared. He had four working days at his disposal, which gave him time to greet a few of their friends, who could in no way understand their departure to the Russian sector.

"We have Americans in our first district and, of course, our home is used as an office; but we have been promised some kind of space!" he emphasized.

A very nervous Victoria and Gaby approached the border, relying completely on Peter's mediocre Russian and hoping his skills would do the trick. To their great surprise, it did. The Russians welcomed them into their zone, asking Peter why so many Austrians were not returning. It helped that Peter's passport stated his name as Doctor Peter Reinhardt, as no matter how illiterate a Russian, they did admire knowledge. Since the Russians search through the long train would take hours, one poker-faced but ever so kind soldier offered the fragile Victoria a chair. He assured Peter that his malnourished family would fare better in Vienna. Peter had to suppress his smile, wondering if the soldier lived in a dream world. Everything offered to the Reinhardts, be it chewing gum or crackers, came from America and were well known to them. One had the distinct feeling that the border guards were oblivious to the strained relationship as the kind GIs shared their rations.

After more than five hours of waiting, the stationmaster finally gave the signal to move. The occupants were visibly relieved. The Russian guards were looking through the train for former Nazi bosses as they had been tipped off in advance. The seven they had in custody looked stunned, as they were convinced that they had only done their duty as German officers and therefore had done nothing wrong.

~

It was a very festive welcome in their former palace, which was being used as American Headquarters. General McCain and his wife had the table set, not unlike Gromov and Niemec. Of course, every dish and candelabra had belonged to the Reinhardts; but they were pleased to find their belongings still there. Their former servants were overjoyed to see them and embraced them lovingly. The General's "Honey" had found during her stay in Austria that the Austrians were an emotional race. Four large rooms on the third floor were put to the Reinhardts' disposal along with unlimited access to the kitchen. All were overjoyed, but Victoria had her own thoughts regarding the present arrangement which she kept to herself. On one of her bad days, Peter reminded his mother kindly but firmly that she was a German and that it was an Austrian who had started the war with Germany's help. Her feelings regarding their situation were never again mentioned.

~

Thanks to a cheerful letter from Isabell, Victoria had a big job ahead of her and her family couldn't be happier as boredom was always a problem for her. She was asked to rewrite the Reinhardt diaries from the old-style German alphabet to the new, modern one. Isabell, who was educated in Switzerland, was never taught that style.

"Just imagine, Gaby" she said enthusiastically. "The children of my very own daughter, Elizabeth, only know their father's family tree. It's unforgivable!"

Gaby only nodded in agreement, though she wondered how much of the entire truth would be written; the long-standing Reinhardt – von Walden feud, Christina's death at the hand of two homosexual military officers, and never mind Victoria's own womanizing husband's suicide. She would never dare ask. Besides, it was wonderful that Victoria felt needed.

~

Gaby kept very busy visiting her own family and old friends of the Reinhardts, as Victoria could not be persuaded to leave her writing table. Her mother, Astrid, had arrived early just to be with her religious sisters. Somehow, Gaby was relieved, as her mother never made any other demands. Depression was foreign to Astrid and she found solace in her prayers. Her brother, Andreas, and his lovely wife, Theresa, had just welcomed a baby girl named Raphaela. Astrid abhorred the name, but kept mum. She consoled herself that the baby was healthy and brought such happiness to her parents. In time, Gaby began to tire of her visits to former friends as they were quite envious of her going to Salzburg before the onslaught of the detestable Russian hordes. Somehow, they forgot the Germany's occupation of almost all of Europe and their many atrocities, including imprisoning any German who disagreed with Hitler's policies. To avoid disagreements, she would change the subject to the poor refugees.

~

Summer arrived along with the three elderly McAllisters. Ann Leitner would come two weeks later when her divorce from Frank was final. It seemed both enjoyed single life better. The young McAllisters would take a trip to the Adirondack Mountains, which neither Isabell nor Daniella had ever seen. Of course, Barbara came along, ostensibly as company for baby Scott, but then the chalet belonged to her too. Tom would come later if time permitted. Both families had become very close.

Many Americans chose Austria or Germany for vacations if one of their family members were stationed there. Large parts of Europe were still in rubble. However, the American sectors tended to be less damaged. The McAllisters and McCains went to every reopened theater that played their favorite musicals, except the Opera House, which was totally destroyed.

In October, the McAllisters and Ann departed with the promise to come again the following year with the younger family members. They were exhausted from visiting so many countries, including Scotland. They thought of the old Proverb— it's nice to visit, but twice as nice to go home. However, they enjoyed their time with the Reinhardts, Astrid, Andreas, his wife and new baby, but above all with the McCains, who planned to return to America the next year to retire in Scarsdale.

For the Reinhardts, life went on as usual.

40

The Russians were well known to be unpredictable and this time was no exception. An austere looking Commissar entered the room unannounced. The place was strictly reserved for eight Austrian engineers and just as many Russian apprentices, who he considered Russia's future scientists. He declared solemnly how proud his great leader, Joseph Stalin, was with their accomplishments for their great nation Russia, which would one day rule the world.

One could hear the loud heartbeats of every Austrian as they never knew what his next sentence would bring. But this time, he walked calmly to the visibly nervous group and strongly shook each one's hand while remarking in all honesty, "I hope your time has been most pleasant here in our great country, although I assume you missed your families." He was aware how much Russia still suffered. But a Commissar was taught never to complain if he didn't want a transfer to Siberia. It was something to be avoided at any cost. He walked back and forth, protruding his chest which was full of well-deserved medals. He turned abruptly around and requested that all should follow him. *"Now what?"* was the question on everyone's mind as they glanced at one another, but did as they were told. They came to a large room which was badly in need of paint and full of clothes on labeled hangers. Their hearts beat so loudly that even the Commissar could hear them. He turned around and smiled faintly, remembering for a moment his own ordeal of many years ago.

"We kept your clothes in mothballs" he remarked. "You Austrians have possibly never heard of this procedure, but we've used it in our country for quite a while now."

They suppressed their smiles as Paul Reinhardt innocently asked, "What for, Commissar?"

"There you have it," he replied, completely misunderstanding Paul's question. "to keep your suits from any permanent damage!"

Their greatest wish was now confirmed. They would go home! After so many delays on a monthly basis, they would finally be going home. There was nothing else to do but to embrace each other while the smiling Commissar watched with satisfaction.

"Get dressed and leave your working clothes here" he said as he handed them some money. "Take it, you earned it! It's for the long journey home." While looking at a calendar he continued. "It's the 18th of October, and the way I see it, you should be home within the next two to three weeks. My comrades will bring you to Odessa and give you security so no one will mistake you for fleeing P.O.W.s. Also, our rubles will pay for food and drinks. Now it's time to leave."

While each Austrian abstained from an embrace, they all shook the Commissar's hand vigorously while thanking him again and again. He appeared to be quite pleased, knowing each prisoner's background and education status. At his stern command, two elderly truck drivers entered, and the Commissar followed his departing engineers to a freshly painted truck that had the most uncomfortable newly built seats of thick wooden planks. Of course, the Commissar remarked that it showed progress in transportation. To the Austrians, the two-hour drive was just short of torture as they took most turns standing up. The train station in Odessa was a welcome sight. The driver had strict orders to find comfortable accommodations for the long train ride to Romania. Once there, they would have to fend for themselves. Each one spoke Russian, having had the privilege to study with other educated P.O.W.s. The trip had many detours and delays, but it afforded them the opportunity to see the still bombed out bridges and railways which German P.O.W.s were rebuilding. Many of these P.O.W.s would never live to see their homes.

While on the train for sixteen days, Paul Reinhardt, like the rest of the homeward bound crew, had much time to reflect on the past and look with some apprehension to the future. The past, no matter how painful, was behind them. But six out of eight engineers knew their families were in the Russian sector. If anything was worth having, it was the good knowledge of their language.

~

They arrived to a snowy day on November 3rd, having made so many diversions and, at times, waiting for hours in unheated train stations. They encountered hateful stares, and therefore spoke little and only in Russian. With their suits still in good order, they were mistaken for Russian diplomats, but in most places, there was not much love for diplomats either. All were overjoyed to arrive in southern Austria which was occupied by the very aloof English occupation forces. Their passports were quickly perused as the British soldiers could not decipher the Russian paperwork. Besides, the soldiers had no love for former Austrians or Germans, though no one could blame them.

Paul, like all the others, had a beard, a suit that smelled from long days on smoke filled trains, and had not had a bath in weeks. Regardless of their lack of hygiene, they hugged each other, smiling as they exchanged addresses and promises to keep in touch. Russian soldiers were visible everywhere, and it was as if they were still in the Motherland. They crossed the city by way of the old, loud, jingling tram and thought it a welcoming sound. Some could not wait to reach the American sector, but Paul remained in the Russian sector, as he wanted to see his brother, Peter, first to get cleaned up and borrow a suit. Peter stilled lived in the Russian sector.

Their old servant, Selma, opened the door and let out a big scream, "Frau Doctor, look who is here!"

"Paul, oh my God, Paul!" an equally shocked Erika cried loudly. "I don't believe it!"

"You'd better not get too close because I smell like a skunk! I need a bath, a shave and some of my brother's warm clothes. The early snowfall in Austria, while delightful, is rather a surprise. We had none on our long trip home and I was not prepared for the cold with only this suit to wear." Paul laughed as Erika embraced him anyway.

"What does it matter? You made it home and many others will not!" she exclaimed, as she led him to the bathroom.

Forty-five minutes later, he was still shaving his heavy beard when he recognized his brother's hurried footsteps. He smiled as his brother, out of breath, exclaimed, "Paul, there were times when I had little hope of ever seeing your face again!"

"But my letters via our mutual Russian confidants were always quite accurate," Paul replied.

"Sure, especially when you wrote about the many delays due to a shortage of supplies. You should see your factories! Nothing left but the walls," Peter blurted.

"I will rebuild, again, Peter! Many others will be unable to do that," he replied, as he finished shaving and gave his brother a hearty hug. "How about my family? Dear Gaby and the boys? And Mother?"

"All are well, having adapted to living in only a few rooms; but they are most anxious for your return! By the way, Isabell made you not only a grandfather, but a beloved Austrian hero to her new family.

"I know." He smiled as he thought about his connection to Isabell. At times, it took months to get word of her due to dire risks for those involved, but it was always well worth the wait.

They were interrupted with word that dinner was on the table and for the first time in more than two years, Paul ate a hearty Austrian meal. He was surrounded by beloved servants, a teary-eyed Erika, and a cheerful Peter, all awaiting the children's arrival home from school. He questioned them about the best way to surprise Gaby, the boys, and of course, his mother. Victoria would be the most surprised, as she had become quite negative since the loss of her daughter, Gisela, her family, and her husband's parents.

"I can hardly wait to see Gaby and the boys!" he exclaimed as he finally finished his meal.

"So, what keeps you, Paul?" Erika wondered.

"My nerves," Paul replied a bit sheepishly.

"You are kidding," Erika teased.

"Far from it. My stomach is tied in knots," he replied seriously, as he worried whether Gaby still loved him as she had before he was taken away. Although he had had no indication from her letters to think otherwise, a nagging fear was always in the back of his mind.

"Well then, you had better leave soon or she will never forgive you! If Peter had not come straight to me, and I mean beard, clothes, and all, I don't know what I would have done to him," Erika acknowledged as she expressed the woman's viewpoint.

"I will tell Gaby that I was a former arrogant man, who developed an inferiority complex, and I know she will understand," he replied, smiling. Peter gave him a nod, reassuring his brother that he would have done the very same thing.

Paul asked his brother to drop him off. Before entering his former home, now the American Headquarters, he spoke with the American MPs guarding the place. With a sly, "Welcome home, sir" they let him pass and enter the house. A sergeant motioned for one of the maids, who at the first sight of the visitor, was also ready to scream. Paul held his finger in front of his mouth, whispering to her about his planned surprise.

"Your wife just finished lunch and is ready to meet one of your sons, while the other is still with his teacher. You will be so surprised at his sounds!" she said in a hushed voice. She stood outside the dining room hoping to hear Gaby's reaction to the visitor.

Paul smiled a bit nervously as he knocked on the door. "Ready for a snowball fight, Mrs. Rein—" but never finished the sentence.

A shocked Gaby shrieked, "Paul!" as she ran towards him and fell into his arms. They kissed and hugged each other for a long while before he held her away and remarked how she looked as young and beautiful as the first time he saw her in Locarno!

"You are in desperate need of eyeglasses," she teased, but was overjoyed with the compliment. In her eyes, he was still the most handsome man she had ever known, and she lost no time in telling him.

"Good God, we lost so many years of our lives to separation, Gaby. Now let's do our utmost while we grow old together!"

She agreed. Tearfully, she kissed him and remarked "They must have treated you quite well, Paul. You haven't changed a bit since you left."

"They did, but you should have seen me before I went to Peter's house for a bath, shave and a change of clothes. Never mind that I smelled literally like a skunk!"

Gaby laughed. "It wouldn't have mattered to me, Paul. The most important thing is that you are home to stay!" Tears flowed as she held his hand and walked with him to his mother's room. Knocking, they entered without waiting for an answer.

"You know, Gaby, I just gave Elisabeth a piece of my mind! She wrote in her last letter again that Vienna is a murky city full of spies and gangsters!" she muttered, quite disturbed as she turned to face Gaby.

"I hope she excluded me," Paul laughed, as Victoria almost jumped out of her chair.

"I don't believe it! It's you!" she cried joyfully. "You know, I gave up many times, but Gaby kept me going." He embraced her, thinking how fragile her body and looks were, and wondered what had happened to the beautiful woman of only a few years ago.

"We have four rooms to call our own," she said clumsily, sitting down, still in a happy state of shock.

"Which are three more rooms than most families have where I have just come from! Mother, by the time I get through with some of my stories, you will never complain again."

Suddenly, the door flew open as Paul's son, Robert, rushed into the room and yelled, "I heard..." At the sight of his father he hurled himself into his arms and they hugged each other tightly.

"Mother, you forgot to meet me for a snowball fight!"

"Well, you can see why, Robert." She beamed with joy at her family.

"Can you not think of anything else, Mrs. Reinhardt? I thought things would have changed in ten years, eleven months, three days…"

"And six hours," Gaby quickly finished, knowing how each one remembered.

"I got my father home!" Robert yelled, and then remembered, "Where is Karl?"

"With his teacher. Let's wait a bit as he will get very excited and stop his lessons! Paul, you will be so surprised with his progress."

"You told me in every letter" he acknowledged. He kept his arms around his son and elaborated on how tall and grown up he had become. As Paul looked around his mother's room, he noticed the large display of photos, including some of Isabell with her husband and baby. "She is just as beautiful as her mother," he said as he held the photo up. "Except she has black hair."

Robert interrupted as Karl made his entrance. On seeing his father, he mustered the loudest shrill ever, and ran full towards his arms. He stopped abruptly to make his 'I love you' sign.

Paul's family was together again.

EPILOGUE

1948 - 1955

May 15, 1955, dawned as a beautiful Sunday morning. The Reinhardt and von Walden families were among the many thousands of Viennese on the lawn of the city's famous landmark, the Upper Belvedere, awaiting an important announcement from the former Chief of Austria— "Austria is Free!" Astonishing as it seems, it was the first proposal the Soviet Union made – all foreign troops should be withdrawn, providing Austria remains permanently neutral and never joins any military alliance. The Austrian Chief was surrounded by other Austrian dignitaries and the four foreign ministers of Russia, England, France, and America. They stood together on the balcony, waving to a cheering crowd. America sent their highly esteemed Secretary of State, John Foster Dulles, who enjoyed great popularity among the people. The Reinhardts and von Waldens were elated, and Paul solemnly declared that without America's intervention, many Europeans would be forced to speak German. Countless Americans had died to ensure Europe's freedom. All wholeheartedly agreed with him, as they, like many others, had suffered through the long war and its aftermath.

As Paul watched the momentous occasion unfold before him, his thoughts went back over the ensuing years since his return from Russia. His first priority had been his family. He had vowed to spend as much time of the remainder of his life enjoying the love and camaraderie of the people who meant the most to him – family and friends. His second priority had been to rebuild his factories as quickly as possible, as there had been many returning soldiers in dire need of work. By 1948, he was able to hire skilled craftsmen and many of the engineers who had been P.O.W.s with him in Russia.

Paul remembered his and Gaby's last visit with her widowed Aunt Ingrid in Switzerland. Lausanne had been so beautiful, virtually untouched by the ravages of war. For the two of them it was a wonderful reminder that life goes on no matter what evils men may do. The Baroness Astrid von Walden and the sisters of her convent had been kind, and they were a blessing to her as well. She had been strong-willed and died eight months later of ovarian cancer.

He smiled as he thought about the first visit he and Gaby made to America in 1950. The elder McAllisters were able to secure a six weeks travel visa for them. Gaby had not seen Isabell since her departure to America and Paul had never met William, and of course, neither had seen the grandchildren other than in pictures. Scott was born in November, 1946, and Elizabeth in November, 1948. After a pleasant journey from LeHavre by way of a French ocean liner to New York City, they were embraced by William's family and wined and dined for weeks on end. The hospitality of all the McAllisters and their friends was unsurpassed by anyone in Europe. For Gaby, spending time with her beloved Isabell was a dream, with the added treat of watching Paul and William get along so well. There was so much to see and do and they vowed that the next trip would include the boys, Robert and Karl. And then, three days before returning to Europe, Isabell gave a beautiful party and surprised all with a visit from General McCain and his "Honey". The Reinhardts were estactic as they truly missed the McCains and their special friendship. It had truly been the trip of a lifetime.

Fortunately, as the years passed, the world put WWII on the back burner. Air travel became the mode of transportation and afforded the Reinhardts the opportunity to see Isabell more often. Isabell had another son, John-Paul in October, 1952. And then, to the surprise of all, became a U.S. Citizen. Though she missed her parents and Switzerland, she had found a new home with "her William", three children, the McAllisters, and their many friends.

That night, Paul would give a surprise 5oth birthday party for Gaby in Lindenfels castle, inviting not only family and close friends, but everyone noteworthy to celebrate simultaneously Austria's freedom. Paul was lately quite a reader of the Reinhardt's secretly stored true diary, written by none other than the first real lady, Stephany Reinhardt. Her beloved husband Otto had given her a similar party; one that Vienna's and Lindenfel's society would talk about forever. The year was 1840 and more than one hundred years later, that time, so long ago, still seemed like yesterday.

About the Author

Hedy Thalberg James was born in Austria and educated in Switzerland to further her knowledge in languages. Her desire was to become a journalist. When Hitler invaded Austria, she returned home to resume her studies. After World War II broke out, she used her skills as a translator for the Red Cross, traveling extensively in war-torn Europe. In 1945 Austria was liberated and divided into four sections. The Russians occupied her town.

She returned to Switzerland where she was introduced to writer and diplomat, Romain Gary, and his wife, Lesley, an editor at Vogue. Both were currently working on novels. As a result of their common interest, a friendship ensued, and she was employed to conduct research. Romain Gary was called to serve in the UN and obtained a visa for her to assist them in New York. Once there she met her late husband and raised three sons.

Hedy Thalberg James currently resides in Metro Atlanta.

CPSIA information can be obtained
at www.ICGtesting.com
Printed in the USA
FSHW010504231219
65377FS

9 780578 609928